# THE CALL OF PASSION

With a sigh, Katy closed her eyes, remembering how she had lain awake the first few nights, her nerves as taut as a bowstring as she waited for Iron Wing to drag her forcibly to his bed and brutally attack her. But nothing had happened. He had not touched her since that day at the river, or made any comment on the fact that she slept alone. Katy told herself she was glad he did not find her desirable and yet, perversely, she could not help wondering why he did not want to bed her.

She was almost asleep when Iron Wing's voice pierced the stillness, calling her to him.

Katy's heart began to pound like a hammer as she lay still in the darkness, feigning sleep. She knew, beyond a shadow of a doubt, that Iron Wing meant to have his way with her before the night was through. What to do, what to do? Thoughts chased themselves across her mind like mice in a maze, hurrying, scurrying, going nowhere because there was nowhere to go.

# Love in the Wind

## MADELINE BAKER

LEISURE BOOKS    NEW YORK CITY

*To Mary,*
*my best friend, critic, and advisor;*
*and to my mother,*
*because she's always there when I need her.*

A LEISURE BOOK®

Published by
Dorchester Publishing Co., Inc.
276 Fifth Avenue
New York, NY 10001

ISBN 0-8439-4589-3

# 1 SPRING
## 1874

Katy Marie Alvarez wept softly into a small black lace handkerchief as she followed her mother down the hill away from the freshly turned grave. Wracked by grief, Katy was oblivious to the whispered condolences and sympathetic glances bestowed upon her by her friends. Robert was dead, and all Katy's dreams of love and marriage had gone into the cold ground with him.

When she reached the Alvarez carriage, Katy paused and looked back one last time. It was over, all over. Fresh sobs tore at her throat as she stumbled into the coach and huddled against the plush red velvet seat, her head buried in her hands as she gave vent to the anguish in her heart.

Sarah Alvarez frowned as she stepped gracefully into the conveyance and took a place beside her daughter. Sarah Alvarez was a stern-faced, strong-willed woman, and her daughter's flagrant emotional display annoyed her immensely. It was a hard land, and many a woman had lost a husband or a lover. Sarah, herself, had buried three husbands in the last twenty-five years. But then, Sarah mused ruefully, she had a weakness for a man in uniform. And in these times of constant strife and warfare with Indians and gun-runners, soldiers frequently died young. Sarah had lost her first two husbands in battles below the border; Katy's father had been killed by Apaches seven years before when Katy Marie was eleven.

A small smile softened Sarah's stern countenance momentarily, letting her real beauty shine through as she thought of Katy Marie's father. Juan Diego Tomas Alvarez had been a dashing young lieutenant in the Mexican Army when she married him. Juan had been Sarah's favorite husband, and she still burned with anger and hatred when she thought of the murderous savages who had killed him and hacked his handsome body to pieces.

Katy was still weeping copiously when the carriage pulled into the courtyard of the Alvarez hacienda. Sarah Alvarez had married well all her life, though money had never been a factor in her choice of a husband. Her first two husbands had left her money and jewels, but it had been Juan Alvarez who had made her self-sufficient. He had bequeathed her a thousand acres of prime grazing land, twice that many white-faced cattle, and a house worthy of a Spanish grandee. The house and lands had been left to Juan's parents years ago. Under Sarah's capable hands, the Alvarez estate had flourished.

The house was built in the Spanish style, with a courtyard in the middle. Gaily colored pots filled with gardenias and wild roses lined the wide veranda that ran the length of the front of the house. The outbuildings were all neatly painted, the fences and roofs in good repair. The Alvarez cattle were the best in the territory, and her fine thoroughbred horses were coveted by gentlemen as far east as New York and Boston. Katy Marie turned up her nose at the leggy thoroughbred, preferring to ride a little dapple-gray Arabian mare.

"We're home," Sarah Alvarez announced sharply. "Pull yourself together, Katy Marie. A lady does not air her sorrows in front of the servants. A lady always comports herself with dignity and grace."

"Yes, mama," Katy answered sullenly, and dutifully wiped her eyes with her handkerchief.

Sarah Alvarez peered intently at her only child. "Are you still determined to do this thing?"

Katy's small chin went up defiantly. "Yes, mama."

Harsh words rose to Sarah's lips, but before she could voice them a grizzled Mexican hurried out of the house and down the wide stone steps to open the carriage door.

The aged servant bowed his head respectfully as Sarah Alvarez stepped briskly from the coach and swept past him. Inside the house, Sarah removed her hat and gloves and ran a slim white hand through her thick auburn hair, her thoughts turning to the new seed bull that was scheduled to arrive from California early the following morning.

Moving into the small, austerely furnished room she used for an office, Sarah sat behind the polished mahogany desk that dominated the room and riffled through a sheaf of papers. She had never spent much time mourning the deaths of her own husbands, and she saw no need to dwell on the fact that Robert Andrew Wellingham III had passed away, however unfortunate the circumstances. Life went on, and a widow running a large cattle ranch in the wilds of New Mexico had little time to waste lamenting the deceased. How cold-blooded she sounded, Sarah mused wryly. And how hypocritical, when she had never really stopped mourning the loss of Katy Marie's father.

Katy Marie's footsteps were slow and leaden as she crossed the threshold of the hacienda. Burdened with grief and an aching sense of loss, she walked down the short hallway that led to the parlor. Dropping into a corner of a curved, high-backed sofa, she stared, unseeing, at the Oriental rug at her feet. How could her mother act as though nothing terrible had happened, as if today were just like any other day? Did nothing touch the woman?

Frowning, Katy tried to remember the last time her mother had expressed great joy or sorrow, but no instance came to mind. Through drought, through death, through the joy of Christmas, Sarah Alvarez remained cool and reserved, hiding her true feelings behind a mask of crisp confidence. With a start, Katy realized her mother had never displayed any affection or love other than an occasional pat on the shoulder, or a quick hug. Always, it had been her father who had kissed her hurts, who had tucked her into bed and heard her prayers. Her father who had laughed at her childish pranks, or dried her tears.

With a sigh, Katy lifted her head and gazed

out the window into the courtyard beyond. She made a striking picture sitting there with the late afternoon sun dancing in her thick black hair. Her skin was smooth and creamy, her almond-shaped eyes an astonishing shade of deep sky blue fringed by long black lashes. Her figure, hidden now beneath the voluminous folds of her cloak, was near perfect, with full breasts, slim hips, a narrow waist, and long shapely legs. Indeed, it was the kind of figure women envied and men dreamed of.

Robert Wellingham had often admired Katy's voluptuous curves, boldly declaring she had more charms than the law allowed. He had written her numerous love sonnets extolling the color of her eyes and the modest, maidenly blush of her cheeks. He had brought her countless bouquets of flowers, assuring her that her own beauty put the blossoms to shame. He had sent her chocolate bonbons packed in heart-shaped boxes covered with red satin, each offering accompanied by a note expressing his love and admiration. He had courted her as gallantly as any man had ever courted a woman, and Katy had basked in the radiant glow of his affection. There had been many men who had sought to win Katy's hand, for she was not only beautiful, but heir to a large fortune as well. But Katy had coolly rejected every suitor until Robert Wellington entered her circle of acquaintances. He had swept her off her feet with his boyish charm and brash self-confidence.

And now he was dead, killed by the same tribe of savage Indians who had so brutally

11

murdered her father.

Katy pushed the hideous thought from her mind and contemplated the Little Sisters of Mercy convent instead. She had toured it once when she had been a little girl, and its peaceful atmosphere had lingered in the back of her mind. Whenever something unpleasant had intruded in her life, Katy had conjured up a mental image of the convent, and it had brought her peace.

Its magic did not fail her, not even when news of Robert's death turned from horrible nightmare into harsh reality. And when the reality became too painful to bear, Katy summoned the convent to mind, lingering on the memory of the candlelit chapel, and the beautiful face of the Madonna. She could recall every detail of the statue of the Blessed Virgin: the soft blue of her robe, the silver girdle that circled her tiny waist, the dark blue mantle that covered her dark hair, the sandals on her graceful feet.

And later, drowning in a sea of despair, Katy remembered the restful solitude of the convent, and in that instant she knew what she would do. She would enter the community of nuns and spend the rest of her life in the peaceful shelter of cloistered walls, protected from a life that was suddenly too ugly, too empty, to endure.

Sarah Alvarez had tried in every way possible to discourage Katy's decision to become a nun, but to no avail. Katy Marie had stated emphatically that she would not live in a world without Robert.

Sarah had finally given her consent, convinced that after a few weeks of cloistered life, plain food, a hard bed in a tiny cell, and rigid discipline with no thought for comfort or self, that Katy Marie would be more than willing to return home where she belonged.

"Are you packed?" Sarah inquired as she entered the parlor. "Did you remember to take your blue wool cloak? It will be cool crossing the desert this time of year."

"Yes, mama."

Sarah sighed, exasperated by Katy's sullen expression. "Dinner will be ready soon, Katy Marie. Why don't you run upstairs and change your clothes? I'll send Anna up to help you."

With a nod, Katy climbed the winding staircase that led to her bedroom on the second floor. Unfastening her cloak, she let it fall carelessly to the floor. Anna would pick it up later. Kicking off her shoes, she threw herself across the big feather bed and let the tears flow anew.

"Oh, Robert. Robert." She whispered his name like a prayer, longing to see his brown eyes laughing into her own once more, yearning to feel the touch of his lips on her cheek. Robert had never crossed the bounds of propriety, had never done more than kiss her. His touch had never stirrerd her passions, but she had loved to be held in his arms, had loved the feeling of belonging. She had loved him with all her heart. Her Robert, so tall, so blond, and more handsome than any man she had ever known. And now he was dead, his dancing brown eyes forever closed, his hearty laughter forever stilled. How empty her world seemed without him!

Even now it was hard to believe he was

really gone. Her mother had refused to let her see Robert's body when it was brought home.

"It's been mutilated," Sarah had told her matter-of-factly. "It's best you don't look. Best to remember him as he was."

Katy did not stop to think that her mother spoke from experience, did not know her mother often woke in the night haunted by the memory of Juan's cruelly dismembered body. She did not know why her mother adamantly refused to let her see Robert one last time, and in her ignorance, she thought her mother was being cold and indifferent to her grief.

Mutilated. Katy knew what that meant. She had read dozens of newspaper accounts of soldiers and settlers who had been killed by the Indians. The savages frequently scalped their victims, sometimes while the victims were still alive. The Indians cut off arms and legs. Sometimes they stripped the dead of their clothing and left them lying pitifully naked on the plains, prey to scavengers and wildlife. They did other things, too. Unspeakable things that nice people did not discuss openly.

Katy felt the vomit rise hot and bitter in her throat as she imagined Robert stripped naked, his scalp raw and bleeding, his beautiful blond hair hanging from some Indian's belt. In her mind's eye, she saw the feathered arrows striking his flesh, heard his harsh cry of pain.

A light rap on her bedroom door interrupted Katy's grisly fantasy. She swung her legs over the side of the bed and sat up as the serving girl, Anna, entered the room.

"Señorita, what is wrong?" the girl gasped upon seeing Katy's wan expression. "Are you ill? Should I call the Señora?"

"No," Katy rasped, choking back the bile in her throat. "I'm fine. Just get me some hot water and a towel. I'd like to bathe before dinner."

An hour later, clad in a severe black dress trimmed in heavy white lace, Katy joined her mother in the spacious dining room. A dozen long white tapered candles filled the room with a soft light, casting long shadows on the richly paneled walls and heavy oak furniture.

Katy picked at the food on her plate, hardly aware of what she was eating, not caring that the cook, Juanita, had lovingly prepared all her favorites. On any other night, Katy would have cleaned her plate and laughingly called for more. But not tonight, not with Robert fresh in his grave and her mother scowling at her from across the damask-covered table.

Sarah Alvarez regarded her daughter with mixed emotions. She had not approved of the match between young Wellington and Katy, but Katy was eighteen years old, and on occasion she could be as stubborn as an Army mule.

Sarah sighed as she pushed her plate aside. She had hoped Katy would marry into the family of Jose Alvarado. Jose's eldest son, Pablo, was a fine young man, and he was eager to marry Katy, but Katy had eyes for no one but Robert. And now it looked as if Katy would never marry at all. Sarah sighed again. Imagine, her Katy as a bride of Christ! If only Juan were still alive. He would know how to talk Katy out of this foolish notion of becoming a nun.

Katy Marie retired to her bed early that night. Lying there, with the covers pulled up to her chin, she bid a silent farewell to the room where she had spent much of her life. It was a lovely room, elaborately furnished with everything to make her comfortable, from the canopied bed to the thick blue carpet on the floor.

Her eyes lingered on the worn rag doll sitting on the table beside her bed. The doll, Carlotta, had been a gift from her father when she was five years old, and Katy cherished it above all else.

Katy's eyes shifted to the heavy drapes at the open window, and on the gilt-edged mirror where she had often admired a new gown, or a new hair style. There would be no new gowns at the convent, she mused. No shimmering silks and satins, no soft velvets, no rustling crinolines. There would be no soft carpet under her feet, no fine china and crystal on the table, no one to wait upon her.

She ran her fingers through the thick mass of her waist-length hair. It would be a sacrifice, letting the sisters cut off her hair, but even that could not sway her. The convent beckoned, promising peace and forgetfulness.

Katy glanced out the window at the night sky, a small smile of anticipation on her lips. Tomorrow she would board the stage coach that would carry her to the Little Sisters of Mercy convent in Colorado. There were many other convents closer to home, but none possessed the quaint charm that had so

16

captivated her years ago.

Half-asleep, she recalled the nuns of her school days, always so serene, their faces peaceful, their eyes untroubled by wordly cares or sorrows. Nuns and convents, Katy mused sleepily. They had always fascinated her. Perhaps it had always been her destiny to become a nun. Soon she would find shelter in their beautiful cloistered world. She would don the pristine habit of a postulant and enter their sacred community to serve God and mankind. Never again would she suffer the awful pain of losing a beau. Never again would she risk her heart, only to have it broken.

Closing her eyes, Katy saw herself in the years to come, her white habit exchanged for a black one when she took her final vows, her long hair shorn off, all worldly thoughts erased from her mind as she spent her life in humble service to others.

The day of Katy's departure dawned clear and cold. She had thought she would feel some regret at leaving the only home she had ever known, but she felt nothing, only an odd sense of detachment, as if she were looking at everything through the eyes of a stranger.

"I'll be here if you change your mind," Sarah said stiffly. "Don't be ashamed to admit it if you change your mind. Don't be afraid to come back home."

"I won't change my mind," Katy said firmly.

"Write if you need anything."

"I will, mama."

"Are you sure you don't want me to go with

you?"

"I'd rather go alone," Katy answered tactlessly. "Anyway, you're needed at the ranch." The ranch had always come first, Katy thought with a twinge of anger. Sometimes it had seemed as though crops, cattle, and servants were more important to Sarah Alvarez than her own daughter.

"I could leave for a few days," Sarah offered.

Katy shook her head. Her mother didn't really want to leave the ranch. Even now, Katy could see her mother mentally ticking off the things that would go undone in her absence.

"I'd really rather go alone," Katy repeated. "Besides, Mr. Kelly will look after me until we reach Colorado."

Sarah Alvarez grimaced with distaste. Gus Kelly was a scruffy, middle-aged Irishman who rode shotgun for the stage line whenever he was sober enough to sit erect. He was not, by any stretch of the imagination, a suitable chaperone for a young lady of quality.

"Goodbye, mama," Katy said tremulously. "I'll write just as soon as I can."

Sarah felt her heart soften as she impulsively kissed her daughter's cheek. Katy was so young, so vulnerable. She knew nothing about life, nothing at all, and yet she was determined to give up all the beauty and joy the world had to offer for the chaste, regimented life of a nun. Sweet, spoiled Katy, who had never had anything denied her, who had never known hardship or want of any kind.

"Katy . . ."

"I'll be fine, mama. I know what I'm doing."

"Very well," Sarah said wearily. "Be a good nun, Katy Marie."

Katy watched her mother walk toward the Alvarez buggy. Blinking back her tears, she whispered, "I love you, mama," then turned and climbed hurriedly aboard the Concord that would carry her to her new life in Colorada.

Shortly, three men clamored into the coach. They were drummers, by the look of them, smelling of cigar smoke and whiskey. Katy felt a sudden apprehension as one of the men plopped down beside her, forcing her to slide across the seat or risk being crushed by his ponderous bulk, for he was a grossly fat man with a red handlebar moustache, close-set gray eyes, and several flabby chins.

The other two men, one balding and thin, the other a sallow-faced youth in a blue pinstripe suit, both ogled Katy as they sat down on the seat opposite her.

Katy flinched as the fat man's thigh rubbed against hers.

"Sorry, missy," the fat man said, laughing jovially. "I guess this here little seat weren't built for a man my size."

Katy smiled at him uncertainly, then turned to stare out the window. Perhaps she should have let her mother accompany her to the convent after all. No one would dare make improper advances toward her with Sarah Alvarez sitting at her side. But it was too late to think of that now.

Katy took a last look at the town where she had been born and raised. Probably she would never see it again. Her father had loved Mesa Blanca. On the rare occasion when he had been home from the Indian wars, he had taken Katy to town, stopping at Faught's General Store to buy her a bag of rock candy, or a dozen ribbons for her hair, or a length of cloth for a new dress. On her tenth birthday, her father had taken her into the newspaper office and paid the editor five silver dollars to print up a special edition of the paper with Katy's name in boldface type on the front page. Katy still had that copy of the newspaper in the bottom drawer of her dresser back home.

Another time her father had taken her to Mexico to see the bullfights. Katy had loved the noise and the people and the colorful costumes and the matadors and picadors, but she had cried when they killed the bull. She could never abide seeing anything killed or hurt, could not stomach the sight of blood.

Her father . . . he had been a big, handsome man, with a love for life and a way of making even the most ordinary events seem wonderfully special and exciting. He had taught Katy to ride before she could walk, had taught her to fire his pistol, and to rope anything that moved. He had taught her to speak his native tongue, the soft Spanish words sounding pleasing to Katy's ears, so much more romantic and musical than her mother's harsh English.

Katy had cried for days when the news came that her father had been killed by Apaches. But not her mother. Sarah had retired to her bedroom for one brief day to quietly vent her grief, and the next day she had gone about with her head high and her eyes dry, as if nothing had happened. It had never occurred to Katy that her mother's broken heart had never healed, or that her mother frequently cried herself to sleep. Katy saw only the woman who worked tirelessly, who ran the Alvarez ranch as capably as any man.

Katy smiled and waved as Gus Kelly emerged from the stage office. Staggering across the dusty street, Gus took his place on the high front seat. Gus was a short man with a round face, watery brown eyes, and a mane of shaggy white hair that looked as though it had never seen a comb. Katy knew her mother did not approve of Mr. Kelly, but Katy liked the man because he had been her father's friend.

The driver, Dave Tully, shut the coach door with a bang, then poked his head in the window to make sure his passengers were all aboard. He nodded politely to Katy, admonished the men to be careful with their cigars, then hopped up on the high front seat, his agility belying his sixty-odd years.

"All aboard!" Tully hollered. He cracked the whip above the six-horse team, and the horses leaned into the traces.

Katy's melancholy mood passed as the coach lurched forward. With a little thrill of excitement, she realized she was on her own for the first time in her life. On her own and bound for a new beginning in a new world. There would be no memories of Robert behind the high gray walls of the convent, nothing to remind her of a dashing young man with laughing brown eyes.

As Mesa Blanca passed from view, the man beside Katy pulled a flask from his hip pocket. Taking a long swallow, he passed it across the aisle to his traveling companions.

"Want some, little lady?" the balding man asked after taking a long drink. He had close-set green eyes, a crooked nose, and a leering smile that made Katy nervous and ill at ease.

She shook her head vigorously. "No, thank you." With great exaggeration, she drew her cloak around her and pressed closer to her side of the seat, making it clear, she hoped, that she wished to be left alone.

"No call to be unfriendly," the fat man remarked with an injured air. "I'm Jake Cardall, lately of Tucson. This here's Will Thompson, and that young squirt in the fancy suit is Charlie Edmunds."

"Pleased to make your acquaintance, I'm sure," Katy responded dubiously.

The fat man nodded. "And you'd be?"

"Miss Alvarez," Katy answered coolly.

"Well, Miss Alvarez, I'm purely pleased to meet you." Jake Cardall said, giving her a wink. "Could be we'll all be real good friends by the time we reach Colorado Territory."

For some reason, Cardall's comment elicited a burst of laughter from Thompson and Edmunds.

"Real good friends," Will Thompson said with a sly grin in Katy's direction.

"Maybe even intimate friends," Charlie Edmunds mused, nudging Thompson in the side.

Katy huddled deeper into her cloak, suddenly feeling very alone, and very vulnerable. She knew little of the darker side of men, or of their desires, but she recognized the drunken lust sizzling in the fat man's eyes as he leered at her over the whiskey flask.

Moving slowly, her hands shielded by the folds of her cloak, Katy reached into her reticule and withdrew a small pearl-handled over-and-under derringer. The gun was cold in her palm, and its chill seemed to penetrate her spine as the atmosphere in the coach grew suddenly taut, heavy with the smell of whiskey and wanting.

Katy drew herself up, her chin jutting forward, her sapphire eyes flashing like shards of blue glass as she silently dared the men to touch her.

Her abrupt change of mood from shy victim to defiant antagonist amused the men. A deer might foolishly challenge a wolf, but the wolf always won.

Jake Cardall emptied the flask and tossed it aside. Then, grinning crookedly, he laid his hand over Katy's knee.

Katy gasped in shocked outrage as Cardall's freckled hand squeezed her leg. No gentleman ever touched a lady. No man, not even Robert, had ever dared treat her with anything but the utmost courtesy and respect.

Quite unexpectedly, Katy threw her cloak aside and jabbed the muzzle of the derringer into the fat man's gut.

"Remove your hand," Katy demanded quietly, pleased that her voice betrayed none of the anxiety she was feeling inside.

Charlie Edmunds and Will Thompson were momentarily taken aback by the sight of the gun in Katy's delicate hand. Then they began to laugh.

"Looks like she's got the drop on you, Jake," Edmunds said, grinning broadly. "I think you'd best do as she says."

Thompson nodded eagerly. "Yeah," he said. "I think she means it."

"I do mean it," Katy assured them. "Unhand me this instant."

"Yes, ma'am," the fat man said, and jerked his hand from Katy's leg as if her skirt had suddenly grown fangs and a tail. "I'm sorry, ma'am, it won't happen again," he assured her sincerely. "It's just that a woman traveling alone, we thought . . ." Cardall shrugged, clearing his throat to cover his urge to laugh out loud. The little chit has spunk, damn her!

"I know what you thought," Katy retorted coldly. "But you were mistaken. I am on my way to Colorado to enter the convent there."

"Convent! Lord, forgive me," Jake Cardall murmured. "I am sorry, Miss Alvarez. Truly sorry."

An uncomfortable silence fell over the coach as the three men sent covert glances at Katy. A nun! Who would have guessed that such a pretty little filly was bound for a convent?

Katy pretended to be unaware of their curious glances as she looked out the window, the derringer still tightly clutched in her hand. The coach was traveling across barren desert now, and she wondered idly why God had created such an inhospitable land, fit for neither man nor beast; though it was said the Apache roamed the desert at will. But then, she mused contemptuously,

24

the Apache were neither man nor beast but some kind of depraved inhuman monsters that went about preying on innocent women and children, killing brave men like her father, and Robert.

The next three days were the longest and the most tiring that Katy had ever endured. Each night at sundown the coach stopped at some dismal way station to allow them to change horses, eat, and sleep. The food was usually beans and coarse brown bread washed down with water or bitter black coffee; the sleeping accommodations were equally crude, usually consisting of little more than a pallet on the floor and a thin blanket that was like as not infested with fleas, or worse.

With the coming of dawn, the passengers gathered in the main room for a cheerless breakfast, and then they were on the trail again, journeying across seemingly endless miles of dreary, God-forsaken country populated by little more than stunted trees, rocky ground, and fat lizards. A relentless sun scorched the earth.

Katy's traveling companions treated her with the utmost respect and for that, at least, she was grateful. The interior of the coach was hot and uncomfortable, rank with the smell of perspiring bodies and cigar smoke. The Concord's constant bouncing and jarring made Katy's whole body ache so that she longed for a hot bath and a good night's sleep even more than she yearned for some of Marta's mouth-watering meals.

The men treated Katy with deference,

making sure she was the first one served when they stopped for the night, taking care to see that she had the best of the limited sleeping accommodations provided at the various stage stops along the way. Once, when one of the men who worked at one of the way stations made a pass at Katy, Jake Cardall intervened, promising to break the man's arm if he persisted in bothering "the lady."

Katy was consoling herself with the thought that her journey was half over when the nightmare began. A blood-curdling scream rose on the hot desert wind, sending a chill down Katy's spine, and then, before she had time to think, the coach was surrounded by a dozen paint-daubed Indians wielding rifles and feathered lances.

Katy stared at the savages in horrified fascination as images of fleet calico ponies and grotesquely painted faces imprinted themselves on her mind. She shivered as another war cry sounded in her ears, felt her blood run cold as she realized she was going to die. Seeking comfort, she turned frightened eyes toward Will Thompson, only to see her own fears mirrored in the man's eyes. Charlie Edmunds was no better. His face was the color of paper, and he was babbling incoherently. Jake Cardall was pressed back against the seat, his hands tightly clenched over his ample paunch.

With a sinking heart, Katy realized the men were not going to protect her. They were all greenhorns, new to the West, and as helpless and frightened as she was.

The sudden whine of an arrow, or perhaps

the sight of Katy's taut face, spurred Jake Cardell to action. Grabbing Katy's reticule, he fumbled inside for her derringer, blindly fired one barrel into the chest of a screaming Indian who appeared at the window.

Outside, Katy could hear Dave Tully cussing the horses, his voice high-pitched and shaky as he begged the lathered team for more speed. Dust boiled around the coach, clogging Katy's nose and throat, making everything seem hazy and slightly out of focus. There was the soft hum of an arrow slicing through the air, an ugly thwack as the painted shaft pierced Will Thompson's throat. His hands, soft as those of a young girl, clawed at the arrow embedded in his flesh. A wet gurgling sound rattled in his throat, and then he toppled sideways across Charlie Edmund's lap.

Jake Cardall shouted, "Get down!" as he shoved Katy to the floor of the coach, partially shielding her trembling body with his own massive frame as he fired the second barrel of the derringer at a passing Indian and missed. Muttering a vile oath, Cardall rooted around in Katy's bag looking for more shells.

Katy huddled at Cardall's feet, her hands covering her ears in a vain attempt to shut out the awful shrieks of the Indians. Why did they make such hideous sounds? Why didn't they go away? Why didn't Charlie Edmunds stop his useless babbling? She heard Jake Cardall swear as he dropped one of the precious cartridges, and she felt a rush of affection for the fat man who was trying to protect her.

Outside, a horse screamed in pain, and then Katy added her own terrified cry to the din as Jake Cardall fired point-blank into the face of a leering savage. The gunshot hung in the air and time seemed to grind to a halt as the Indian's head slowly dissolved in a sea of bright red blood.

A moment later, or was it an hour, Charlie Edmunds slid to the floor beside her, a great bloody hole where his nose and mouth had been. Nausea rose in Katy's throat as she stared at Edmunds through wide, uncomprehending eyes. Surely she was dreaming. Surely this could not be happening to her. In a moment she would wake up, safe and secure in her own bed back home. Her mother would be chiding her for sleeping so late, and the smell of frying bacon and Marta's heavenly coffee would tickle her nostrils. It had to be a dream.

Jake Cardall grunted softly as a bullet thudded into his chest. He mumbled a quiet, "Scuse me, ma'am," as he slid off the seat, falling sideways across Katy's lower body so that she was trapped beneath his vast bulk.

There was an abrupt change in the sound of the battle as all firing suddenly ceased. Katy began to shiver uncontrollably as she realized the heavy silence meant all the men were dead. There was no one left to help her. Soon the Indians would stop the runaway coach and she would have to face them, alone.

Katy felt a great knot of fear tighten her insides as every unspeakable tale of rape and abuse she had ever heard flashed across her mind, each story of terror and treachery

28

more awful than the last. She recalled stories of men being staked out over anthills, their faces brushed with honey to attract the insects. There were horror stories of men being skinned alive, or burned at the stake. Once she had read a firsthand account of a man who had been scalped and lived to tell the tale.

Fear gave wings to Katy's imagination and she envisioned herself being repeatedly raped by the savages, being attacked again and again until they tired of their sport and slit her throat.

Abruptly, all panic ceased and a cold sense of dread settled over Katy, bringing with it a measure of calm. There were two choices open to her, she mused grimly. Rape and humiliation at the hands of the Indians, or death by her own hand. It took less than a heartbeat to decide.

Mouthing a silent prayer that God would forgive her, she began to pry her derringer from Jake Cardall's lifeless fingers, but before she could wrest the weapon from his grasp, the coach slammed into a boulder and toppled over onto its side.

# 2

"Uncle, look!" The boy pointed toward the west, where four large black vultures hovered in the sky, then slowly dropped lower, lower, until they were out of sight.

"You have sharp eyes, little one," the warrior acknowledged proudly. "Come, let us see what draws the scavenger birds."

Tall Buffalo touched his heels to his horse's flanks, and the buckskin broke into a slow lope. The boy, Bull Calf, fell in beside the warrior, his oval face filled with the eager curiosity of youth. Perhaps they would find a dead enemy on whom he could count coup! Or, better yet, a live one.

The unbridled excitement in the boy's eyes caused the warrior to grin in retrospect as he recalled the days of his own youth. Always, when riding with his elders, he had hoped for the worst: an encounter with enemy warriors or, better still, with the hated soldier coats. The young ones, the warrior mused, their blood always runs hot.

"Do not get your hopes up too high," Tall Buffalo admonished gently. "It is probably just the carcass of a wounded buffalo that draws the birds."

But it was not an animal. Cresting a small rise, the pair spied an overturned stage coach lying on the desert floor like some huge, pre-historic beast.

Tall Buffalo quickly put his horse down the hill, signaling for Bull Calf to follow. There was no sign of life as they approached the coach, but then it was unlikely that there would be any survivors. Of all the tribes that roamed the vast plains and arid deserts, the Apache were the most warlike, the most feared. They rarely took prisoners; they never left survivors behind.

Dismounting, the tall warrior easily read the tracks surrounding the Concord. A small force of Apache warriors, quickly identified by the cut of their mocassins and by the feathered shafts of the arrows embedded in the driver and guard, had attacked the stage. They had not bothered to search the bodies, for white men rarely carried anything of value to an Indian. Likewise, the dead had not been scalped, for most of the Apache tribes did not take scalps. Their interest had been the six coach horses, and the rifles and ammunition carried by the driver and guard.

Tall Buffalo threw a questioning glance at the boy standing beside him. He had brought Bull Calf on this journey far from home to teach him the ways of a Cheyenne warrior, just as his uncle had once taught him more than twenty summers ago. Now Tall Buffalo waited patiently to see how his nephew would interpret the plentiful signs left by the Apache.

"There were ten or twelve warriors," Bull Calf began confidently, then stopped abruptly as a low groan sounded from inside the coach.

31

Tall Buffalo put a finger to his lips, warning the boy to remain silent as he scaled the side of the overturned coach and peered cautiously inside.

At first glance, Tall Buffalo saw only what he had seen before: the tangled bodies of three white men, all long dead. He was turning away when a second groan rose from beneath the pile of bodies, and a slim white hand forced its way into view.

It was a woman's hand, Tall Buffalo realized, amazed. There was no doubt about that. With a wordless grunt of surprise, he opened the coach door and dumped the first two bodies outside. The last corpse, that of an enormously fat man, required the combined efforts of both Indians, but at last they managed to heave the heavy body outside, only to stare in wonder at the sight of a female figure huddled at the bottom of the coach.

Her black hair was a snarled mass, her clothing was rumpled and stained with sweat and dust, and with the dried blood of her traveling companions. But it was her eyes that held their attention. They were the most incredible shade of vibrant blue, wild now with fear.

Bull Calf looked at his uncle. "What will we do with her?"

"Take her home," Tall Buffalo decided, thinking aloud. "Your aunt might enjoy having a slave to help with the work, especially with a new baby due in the summer."

"She has eyes like the sky at midday," the boy remarked, gesturing at Katy.

"Yes." Tall Buffalo's mouth suddenly twitched into a smile. "I have a wonderful idea!" he exclaimed, pleased with what had occurred to him. "We will give the white woman to Iron Wing."

"Iron Wing," the boy muttered, unable to believe his ears. "He has always shunned the women of our village. He has vowed never to marry."

"That is true, but the white woman is not of our village. She will not be his wife, but his slave."

Bull Calf nodded uncertainly. Iron Wing was a strange warrior. Long ago, he had been badly mauled by a grizzly, and as a result, the left side of his face bore a long thin scar. His left arm also carried the jagged marks of the bear's teeth and claws. Shortly after Iron Wing had recovered from his ordeal with the grizzly, he had asked for Quiet Water's hand in marriage, but she had refused him, boldly declaring she would not spend her life with a warrior whose face repelled her. Quiet Water's parents had tried to make her change her mind. Looks were only skin deep. Iron Wing's scars would fade in time, but a man's courage lasted a lifetime. But Quiet Water would not be swayed. Iron Wing had been deeply hurt, for he was a brave man and a fearless hunter. Did he not wear the claws of the bear who had attacked him? Had he not counted coup on many enemy warriors? Nevertheless, Quiet Water married another and Iron Wing withdrew into himself. With time, the scars on his face and arm faded from bright red to the palest of silver streaks that were hardly noticeable, but the memory of Quiet Water's rejection, and the reason for it, remained strong in Iron Wing's memory. Never again did he court the comely maidens of the Cheyenne.

For all his youth and inexperience, Bull Calf had a feeling that Iron Wing would not be pleased with the white woman.

Katy offered little resistance as Tall Buffalo pulled her out of the wrecked coach and lifted her to the back of his horse. Only a small cry of alarm, and then she was silent as she drew great gulps of fresh air into her lungs.

Bull Calf stared at Katy. He had never seen a white woman before, and he was not much impressed with this one. Her skin was almost as white as his grandfather's braids, and she did not seem to have much spirit.

Katy Marie rode in front of the tall warrior, her face and eyes empty of expression. So much had happened in such a short time: Robert's death, the attack on the stage coach, the horses running out of control until the coach turned over, burying her alive beneath the bodies of Jake Cardall and his friends. She had struggled valiantly to free herself of their suffocating weight, then given thanks to God for the concealment they provided when she heard the Apaches prowling about the coach.

Fearful of discovery, she had squeezed her eyes tight shut and held her breath lest some sound betray her presence to the savages. It had taken all the courage she possessed to keep from screaming hysterically when she heard the coach door open. Fortunately, the Indians had assumed all the passengers were dead and not worth mutilating, for they had left the bodies untouched. Cowering on the floor of the coach, crushed by the dead weight of three bodies, Katy had listened to the shouts and war whoops of the Apaches as they unhitched the team and drove the animals away.

Hours passed. Hours that had seemed like years as a new fear entered Katy's mind. She could not extricate herself from the bodies piled atop her, and it was getting harder and harder to draw air into her lungs. She was going to die trapped in the coach, either from starvation or suffocation, whichever came first, but until then she would have to endure the cloying smell of death and decay which grew steadily worse as the day wore on.

She was going to die. Her mind accepted the fact calmly. She was resigned to it, so that she didn't even struggle when an unseen force began lifting the bodies of the men out of the coach. She was almost relieved when she saw the Indian gazing down at her. Soon it would be over. The fear, the waiting, everything would be over. A vague smile flitted over her face. Robert was dead, and soon she would be dead. Perhaps, in death, she would find him again.

But the Indian did not kill her, and now she was riding before him on his horse, lost in a quiet void where nothing could touch her.

Tall Buffalo and Bull Calf rode until nightfall, then sought shelter in a shallow draw out of the rising wind. They did not dare risk a fire with marauding Apaches in the vicinity. Bull Calf looked to Tall Buffalo for guidance when Katy refused to eat the chunk of pemmican he offered her, but Tall Buffalo only shrugged. When the woman was hungry enough, she would eat.

Katy Marie woke early the following morning, her mind clear, though for a befuddled moment she could not remember where she was. Then, in a rush, she recalled the nightmare events of the day before.

Turning her head, she gasped to find herself sharing a blanket with the tall warrior who had rescued her from the coach. For a breathless moment, she stared at him with mingled fear and curiosity. He did not look particularly frightening, and it occurred to her that he had a rather nice face, for a savage. His skin was smooth and unlined, perfect in every detail. A quick glance in the boy's direction showed he was also sleeping, and it occurred to Katy that she might never have a better opportunity to escape.

With that in mind, she carefully slid out from under the buffalo robe. Gathering her torn skirts in one hand to keep from tripping on the hem, she tiptoed toward the horses. But the warrior's mount, which had seemed like such a tractable beast the day before, snorted and rolled its eyes when she tried to grab hold of the bridle.

Katy was trying to calm the skittish buckskin gelding when a big brown hand closed over her arm. Startled, her cheeks flushed with guilt, Katy whirled around to find the tall warrior standing behind her. Surprisingly, he did not seem to be angry, even though he had caught her trying to steal his horse.

With a wordless smile, the warrior handed

Katy a long strip of jerked meat. It looked quite disgusting, Katy thought, but hunger drove her like a cruel master and she gnawed on the tough meat as she followed the warrior back to his blankets. When he gestured for her to sit down, she did so with great reluctance. Now he would molest her, or kill her. She could not decide which fate she dreaded most. But he only handed her a skin bag of water and indicated she should drink her fill and then wash. It had never occurred to Katy that the Indians bathed.

The water was cool on Katy's face, neck and arms, refreshing after the long dusty ride of the day before. Still, it was embarrassing to perform such a personal act with the boy and man watching her. The boy, especially, seemed fascinated with every move she made.

When she was finished, the warrior lifted her to the back of his horse, then agilely swung up behind her. Touching his moccasined heels to the buckskin's flanks, they resumed their journey.

They rode all that day, stopping only once to breathe the horses and replenish their water supply from a brackish waterhole. The man and the boy talked companionably together, their looks and smiles including Katy even though she could not understand their words. They seemed quite friendly, almost like ordinary people, and not at all like ruthless savages.

The warrior smiled at her often, his dark luminous eyes always kind as he wordlessly reassured her he meant her no harm, and it occurred to Katy that, since she had the misfortune to be captured by Indians, she was lucky to have been taken by one who appeared almost civilized. He was quite a handsome man, probably in his early twenties. His forehead was high and unlined, his nose long and straight, his eyes a very dark brown. His shoulder-length black hair was adorned with a single white eagle feather.

The boy was tall and thin, about twelve years old, Katy guessed. He spoke very little, and listened intently to everything the warrior said. He wore his long black hair in braids.

Both the man and the boy wore deerskin breechcloth, leggings, and sleeveless vests. The front of the man's vest was decorated with vivid red suns and a vibrant yellow moon; the back carried the likeness of a buffalo outlined in black. The boy's vest was plain.

Katy soon grew tired of the constant hours in the saddle. Her back and shoulders began to ache and she closed her eyes, wishing she could soak in a hot bubble bath and wash her hair. The rocking motion of the horse lulled her to the brink of sleep and her head lolled back against the warrior's chest, returning her to full awareness with a start. But the warrior did not seem to mind, and he drew her back against him, his arm resting lightly around her waist. With a little sigh, Katy closed her eyes and fell asleep.

They spent that night camped in the shadow of a high plateau. Again there was only jerky and pemmican for dinner. Katy grimaced with distaste as she accepted a strip of dried meat from the warrior, and he shrugged apologetically.

When Katy woke the next morning, the warrior was gone. Katy looked anxiously at the boy, but he seemed unconcerned by the man's absence. With a shrug, Katy combed her fingers through her hair, wincing as her fingers encountered a snarl. Never had she been so dirty! Her hair, her clothing, her skin, all were covered with dust. Her skirt was stained with Jake Cardall's blood.

She was wishing she could ask the boy where the warrior had gone when suddenly he was there, a fat brown rabbit clenched in one hand.

Tall Buffalo handed the rabbit to Katy, then sat cross-legged on the blanket, an expectant smile on his swarthy countenance.

Katy stared at the furry little carcass and then at the warrior, struck by the realization that he expected her to skin the creature and cook it. Katy's shoulders sagged in dismay. She had never so much as boiled water, let alone prepared any kind of a meal. She was, after all, a lady of means. Servants did the work. Servants did the cooking. Servants cleaned the house. They set the table and washed the dishes. They scrubbed the floors and polished the silver. They washed and ironed her clothes and put them in her closet so that she had only to decide which frock to wear.

The boy quickly interpreted the situation. Shaking his head with disgust, he grabbed the rabbit from Katy's hand, skinned the carcass, skewered it on a slender stick, and roasted it over a low fire.

Katy Marie glanced apologetically at the tall warrior, then frowned. Why should she feel embarrassed because she didn't know how to skin and cook a rabbit? She was a white woman, not an Indian squaw.

The meat was good; lightly brown on the outside, pink and tender inside. Katy ravenously ate all the warrior gave her and greedily licked the juice from her fingers.

When Tall Buffalo and Bull Calf finished eating, they left Katy alone to wash up and relieve herself and then they were riding again, always heading northeast toward the territory of Wyoming.

Katy studied the tall warrior from beneath the dark fringe of her lashes as they made their way across the vast wilderness. She had never heard of any nice Indians. Everyone knew they were vicious killers, totally without morals or scruples. Hadn't they proved it time and again by slaughtering innocent pioneers and settlers? She had hated them all ever since the Apaches killed her father. Yet she did not feel hatred for the warrior or the boy. The man continued to treat her with kindness and respect, and the thought crossed Katy's mind more than once that he might return her to her mother if she could only make him understand what she wanted. Again and again she had tried to ask the warrior to take her home, but no matter how she gestured, she could not pantomime the simple question, "Will you take me home?"

Katy soon lost track of the days as they traveled across great stretches of barren wilderness. She was so weary of riding, of sleeping on the hard ground, that she began to think even life in an Indian tepee would look good to her until the day they crested a wooded ridge and she saw what looked like a hundred conical hide lodges spread across an emerald green valley. Horses of every color grazed in the shade of tall pines and firs. Thin columns of blue-gray smoke spiraled skyward from countless cookfires.

The boy whooped with excitement as he raced his fleet-footed paint pony down the hill, weaving in and out of the trees and bushes that grew along the hillside. His noisy approach drew the attention of the entire village and Katy felt her blood run cold as Indians swarmed around the boy and the warrior, all talking a mile a minute and pointing at Katy as if she were some kind of sideshow freak.

Katy's eyes darted nervously from side to side. Tepees surrounded her on every side, looming over her like mountains, their tops blackened from the smoke of many fires. Large animal skins were pegged to the ground. Long strips of red meat hung on drying racks. There were dogs everywhere, and they all seemed to be barking at once.

Katy stared at the Indians. They all had black hair, dark eyes, and copper-hued skin that ranged from light brown to dark bronze. Most were tall. The women wore ankle-length deerskin dresses decorated with beads and quills and fringe, or colorful calico skirts and loose peasant blouses; the men wore clouts and leggings and buckskin shirts. A few of the warriors wore colorful cotton shirts with the tails hanging out. Most wore feathers or

41

bits of fur in their hair. The children gawked at her from the protection of their mothers' skirts.

Tall Buffalo was laughing as he reined his horse to a stop before a medium-sized lodge located in the center of the village.

"Iron Wing," he called as he dismounted. "Come out and see the fine prize I have brought you from the land of the Apache."

Almost immediately, the lodge flap opened and a tall, well-muscled warrior stepped outside. A cold chill, almost like a premonition, slithered down Katy's spine as she looked at him. He was taller than the warrior who had rescued her from the coach, wider through the shoulders and chest. A faint white scar ran from the outer corner of his left eye across his cheek and down the side of his neck. The warrior was naked to the waist, and Katy saw that the crooked scar ran along his left shoulder and ran down the length of his left arm as well.

"Here," Tall Buffalo said, lifting Katy from his horse and pushing her toward Iron Wing. "She is for you."

Iron Wing's black eyes narrowed ominously as he glanced from Katy to his lifelong friend. "Is this a joke?" he asked gruffly.

"No," Tall Buffalo assured his friend as he placed Katy's delicate white hand into Iron Wing's calloused brown one. "She is for you."

Iron Wing stared at the white woman. Her head was bowed and her hair, every bit as long and black as his own, hid most of her face. A heavy blue cloak covered her from neck to heel, making it difficult to determine if she were fat or thin.

Katy stared at the ground, wishing she could understand the harsh guttural words passing between the two men. She shuddered when Tall Buffalo placed her hand in that of the scar-faced warrior. No words were needed to understand that she was being given away, and there was no mistaking the fact that the scar-faced warrior did not want her. She felt her cheeks flame with humiliation.

Lifting her head, Katy threw a pleading glance at the warrior who had rescued her, mutely begging him not to abandon her, but he was smiling fondly at a pretty young Indian woman who was very, very pregnant. His wife, no doubt, Katy thought absently. No wonder he didn't want her. Oh, it wasn't fair! If she had to be a prisoner, why couldn't she stay with the warrior who had brought her here? He seemed a pleasant sort, not at all arrogant and frightening like the warrior who was scowling down at her. Katy tried to pull away, but the warrior's fingers tightened around her wrist in a grip like iron.

Lifting his eyes from the white woman's face, Iron Wing's icy gaze touched the face of each man and woman gathered around his lodge. He did not want a woman, and everyone knew it. But to refuse a gift, any gift, was a grave insult. To refuse a gift given before witnesses could lead to bloodshed, even between very old and very good friends.

So it was that Iron Wing murmured, "Thank you for your generous gift, old friend."

Tall Buffalo smiled broadly as Iron Wing accepted the girl. Giving Iron Wing a woman was a good joke.

Iron Wing's acceptance of the girl, however reluctant it might have been, drew a collective sigh from the Indians, together with a few ribald remarks from some of the young men as the crowd broke up.

Eyes narrowed with impotent anger, Iron Wing watched his people wander back to their own lodges before he pivoted on his heel and ducked inside his dwelling, dragging the white woman behind him.

Inside the dusky lodge, Katy jerked her hand out of the warrior's grasp and retreated to the opposite side of the teepee where she stood watching Iron Wing, her eyes wide with fear. There was no softness in this warrior, she thought frantically, no compassion. He looked as hard as flint, as unyielding as stone. Something that might have been pain flickered in the depths of the warrior's fathomless black eyes, then was quickly gone.

"Sit," he said. He gestured toward a crude willow backrest covered with a thick tawny hide.

Surprise momentarily replaced the fear in Katy's eyes. "You speak English!" she exclaimed.

The warrior nodded curtly. "Sit. I will not hurt you."

Katy tossed her head defiantly, causing her hair to swirl about her shoulders like a thick black cloud. "I'm not afraid of you!" she lied bravely.

"No?" Iron Wing took a tentative step forward, causing a quick shiver of apprehension to skitter along Katy's spine as she sought a way out of the lodge, and found none. There was only one entrance, and the warrior stood before it, his arms folded negligently across his chest.

Iron Wing laughed softly, his hooded eyes mocking the fear in Katy's face. "Sit," he said again.

This time Katy quickly did as bidden. "What are you going to do with me?" she demanded, unconsciously drawing her cloak tighter, as if its heavy folds would somehow protect her.

Iron Wing shrugged. "Tall Buffalo seems to think I need a woman." Iron Wing made a vague gesture that encompassed his lodge and belongings. "Perhaps my friend is right. It is not fitting for a Cheyenne warrior to gather wood for his fire, or cook his own meals."

"Surely you don't expect me to do those things!" Katy exclaimed, aghast at the very idea of acting as the man's servant.

"That is exactly what I expect you to do," Iron Wing replied calmly.

"Well, I won't," Katy retorted indignantly.

"Do not defy me, white woman," Iron Wing warned in a tone suddenly gone hard, "or I shall take you outside and beat you in front of my people to prove to them, and to you, who is the master in this lodge."

"You wouldn't dare!" Katy cried in dismay, but in her heart she knew he would not hesitate to carry out his threat. He looked quite capable of beating her, and enjoying it.

"I would rather beat Tall Buffalo," Iron

45

Wing admitted with a wry grin, "but I will beat you if the need arises."

Iron Wing studied the white woman intently, his black eyes as fathomless as pools of liquid ebony. She was his, to do with as he pleased. He could keep her for a slave, or give her away. He could bed her once, or a thousand times, or not at all. The idea took some getting used to. Despite her disheveled state, he could see that she was an incredibly beautiful woman. Her long black hair framed a face that was perfect in every detail, from the delicately arched brows and small, tip-tilted nose to her pouting pink lips. But it was her eyes that intrigued him, for they were as blue and clear as a high mountain stream. Her creamy skin, so much lighter than his own, looked soft and inviting, but when he reached out to touch her cheek, she drew away with a little cry of alarm.

Iron Wing's hand fell stiffly to his side. It did not occur to him that the woman would have shied away from any Indian, male or female, who endeavored to touch her. He knew only that she looked at him with revulsion, just as Quiet Water had looked at him so long ago. Always it was the same, he thought morosely. Women recoiled in horror from his touch, their eyes reflecting the ugliness they saw whenever they looked upon his scarred face.

Wordlessly, he turned away from her and left the lodge.

Katy sat quietly for a long time, trying to reconcile herself to the cataclysmic changes the last few weeks had wrought in her life. She had lost Robert, whom she had loved above all else. She had lost her chance to live in quiet seclusion behind cloistered walls and now, worst of all, she had lost her freedom. She, Katy Marie Alvarez, the sweetheart of Mesa Blanca, heir to the Alvarez fortune, now belonged to a half-naked heathen savage who did not even want her. She was his property, his slave, and he could do with her as he wished, even beat her if he so desired, and no one would dispute his right to do so.

Katy glanced apprehensively around the lodge. It was sparsely furnished, containing little more than a few clay pots, some tightly woven baskets, the willow backrest she was reclining on. A bow and quiver of feathered arrows hung from one of the lodge poles. There was a shield decorated with an eagle, and a long lance. A thick black scalp dangled from the end of the lance. Fingering a lock of her own hair, Katy wondered, morbidly, if the scalp had come from a woman.

Katy shuddered as her wandering gaze came to rest on several buffalo robes untidily piled in the rear of the lodge. Her cheeks flamed as she realized it was a bed. Iron Wing had made it quite clear that he expected her to cook and clean for him. Would he also expect her to warm his bed?

Revulsion rose swift and hot in Katy's breast. She knew she would simply curl up and die if he so much as touched her. He was so ominous looking. There was no softness in him, no hint of kindness, only a cool arrogance. And his eyes, they were as black as lumps of coal, as depthless as the bowels of hell.

47

A wordless groan escaped Katy's lips as the tension of the past few weeks caught up with her. Quick tears burned her eyes and she began sobbing uncontrollably, rocking back and forth on her heels, her arms clasped around her waist. Why had God spared her life when the Apaches attacked the stage coach? Why hadn't he let her die with the others? What sin had she committed that she should be so cruelly punished?

Katy cried bitter tears, raging at the unkind hand of fate that had snatched her from the safe haven of the convent and abandoned her in an alien world peopled with Godless savages.

She cried until her eyes were red and swollen, her throat raw. Cried until exhausion overcame her fear and she curled up into a tight ball on the hard-packed earthen floor, her head pillowed on her arms, and slipped into the merciful oblivion of sleep.

# 3

Captain Michael Sommers sighed heavily as he rapped lightly on the front door of the Alvarez hacienda. Of all the distasteful duties he had drawn during his twenty-two years with the United States Army, notifying the next of kin was by far the worst. There never seemed to be an easy way to say, "I'm sorry, your daughter, or son, or husband, is missing, presumed dead." And no matter how often you said the words, they never came any easier.

Sommers came to attention as the heavy oak door swung open to reveal an attractive middle-aged woman clad in a dark blue velvet dress.

"Mrs. Alvarez?" Sommers inquired, removing his hat.

"Yes."

"I'm Captain Sommers. May I come in?"

Sarah Alvarez nodded as she stepped back to allow the officer to enter the hacienda. She had a quick eye for detail and she quickly noted that his service stripes denoted at least twenty years in the Army, that he was quite handsome, and that he carried himself with a certain air of pride and self-confidence that was peculiar to Army men.

With a slight gesture of her hand, Sarah

beckoned for Sommers to follow her into the parlor. Taking a seat on the sofa, she indicated he should join her.

"May I offer you a drink, Captain?" Sarah asked. "A glass of lemonade, perhaps, or a cup of tea?"

"No thank you, ma'am."

Sarah smiled up at him. "Won't you please sit down?"

"No, thank you." Sommers swallowed hard as he ran a nervous hand through his wavy blond hair. "I'm afraid I have some bad news for you, Mrs. Alvarez."

Sarah stopped smiling, and the day seemed to grow suddenly dark and cold as the icy hand of fear wrapped itself around her heart.

"Katy?" The word emerged in a choked whisper.

"Yes, ma'am. I'm afraid her coach was attacked by Apaches. We've accounted for all the passengers, except your daughter."

Sarah nodded, unable to speak.

"The men traveling with her were all killed. There was no trace of your daughter's . . . no trace of your daughter. I'm afraid the Indians took her back to their camp."

"No!" Sarah shook her head, not wanting to believe the Captain's words.

"Can I call someone for you, Mrs. Alvarez? Your husband? A friend?"

"No. There's no one. Do you think Katy is . . ." She could not bring herself to say the word 'dead.'

"I don't know, ma'am. Much as I hate to say it, I think she'd be better off."

Sarah stared blankly at the Captain. It was too awful to think about, too horrible to imagine Katy at the mercy of heathen savages. Katy, who had never known a man, who had never known cruelty or deprivation of any kind.

A sudden sob tore at Sarah's throat as she recalled all the times she could have told her only daughter how much she loved her, all the times she might have put her arms around Katy, and had failed to do so. Now, she would never have the chance. Never again would she hear Katy Marie's sweet laughter, or see her lovely face. Katy would never know how much she had been loved. How foolish she had been, Sarah realized, to lock her heart against her only child.

Michael Sommers looked away. It was a terrible thing, to see someone else's grief. Impulsively, he dropped to his knees at Sarah's feet and put his arms around her waist.

At his touch, Sarah's sobs came harder, and she fell into his arms, finding solace in his embrace. It had been so long since she had felt a man's arms around her, so long since she had let herself cry. It was a relief to let the tears flow unchecked, to give in to the pain and grief she had bottled so tightly inside her. Somehow, even knowing Katy was dead was, in a way, a relief from the awful pain of not knowing what had become of her. For weeks, she had waited for some word of Katy's whereabouts, but the convent knew nothing, only that she had never arrived. Perhaps she had changed her mind and was ashamed to go home? But Sarah disregarded that suggestion. Katy was not a coward. If she thought she had made a mistake, she would have come home and said so.

Michael Sommers sat back on his heels, pulling Sarah into his lap. She came willingly, burying her face against his shoulders as her tears came harder and faster. Tenderly, he stroked her hair, feeling as if he had known her all his life instead of mere moments.

Gradually, Sarah's sobs subsided and she was embarrassed to find herself sitting on the floor in the arms of a total stranger. And yet, oddly, he did not seem like a stranger.

Sarah smiled faintly as the captain pulled a red kerchief from his back pocket and wiped the tears from her face. It was nice, knowing someone cared. For a moment, they sat looking at each other.

"I'm sorry," Sarah said after awhile. "I'm afraid I've drenched your shirt front."

"It doesn't matter," Sommers said with a mild grin. "I'm truly sorry about your daughter, ma'am. Sorry I had to be the one to tell you."

"I'm glad it was you," Sarah replied candidly, and felt her cheeks flame scarlet at her bold reply.

Rising, she smoothed her dress and patted her hair. Sommers rose in a fluid movement to stand beside her.

"I wish we had met under more congenial circumstances, Mrs. Alvarez," he said, extending his hand.

"Yes. Captain, I . . . would you think it dreadfully forward of me if I invited you to stay for dinner?"

"No, ma'am. I'd be happy to oblige."

It was the most pleasant evening Sarah had

known since Katy Marie's father had been killed. She discovered, to her delight, that Captain Michael Sommers had read Shakespeare, and that his favorite play was *A Midsummer Night's Dream*, which was also her favorite. She learned that he had been born in Boston, that his parents were recently deceased, and that he had three sisters residing in Boston, all married to prominent businessmen.

"I guess I'm the black sheep in the family," Sommers mused with a boyish grin. "I ran away from home when I was just a kid and joined the Army. My folks never really forgave me for that, but they accepted my decision. My father was disappointed because I didn't want to follow in his footsteps and be a railroad tycoon."

"I'm so glad you decided to come west instead," Sarah murmured.

Michael's bold brown eyes were warm as they rested on her face. "So am I," he said quietly. "May I call on you again?"

"Yes, please."

Later that night, alone in her bed, Sarah wept for hours. How foolish she had been to put the ranch before Katy, to keep her emotions locked tightly inside.

The captain came to call the next night, and every night for the next three weeks. In that time, Sarah Alvarez lost her heart again, and when Michael Sommers proposed, Sarah said yes without hesitation. And when he announced he was retiring from the Army at the end of the year, her joy was complete.

A week later, they were married in a quiet ceremony in Mesa Blanca.

# 4

When Katy woke the next morning, the first thing she saw was Iron Wing squatting on his heels across from her, a thoughtful expression on his face.

Sometime during the night, he had covered her with a soft brown robe and Katy drew it tightly around her as she realized, with alarm, that he had also undressed her, leaving her naked as a newborn babe. The fact that he had touched her while she slept, unaware and defenseless, brought a surge of heat to Katy's cheeks. And the force of his steady gaze now did little to ease her growing discomfort.

"What's the matter?" she asked irritably. "What do you want?"

"Do you always sleep so late?" he inquired sardonically. "The other women have been up since sunrise. Mine is the only lodge with a cold fire and a hungry warrior."

Katy glared at Iron Wing, annoyed by his remarks. "I'm not your slave," she began crossly, then flushed. She was his slave, for as long as he wanted her.

"Where are my clothes?" she demanded petulantly.

Iron Wing gestured to a pile of clothing stacked beside her, and Katy grimaced with

54

disgust. They were not her clothes at all, but a shapeless dress fashioned of crudely tanned animal skins and a pair of worn moccasins.

"I won't wear those awful things," Katy said, her brilliant blue eyes flashing defiance. "I want my own clothes, my own shoes."

"I burned them," Iron Wing remarked calmly.

"Burned them!" Katy sputtered in helpless fury. "How dare you! You had no right!"

"You will wear what I provide," Iron Wing interjected smoothly, "or you will go naked."

His eyes glinted with the threat, causing Katy to recall that he had already seen her naked while she slept. She did not intend to give him a second look.

Katy glowered at Iron Wing. She was accustomed to giving orders, not taking them. Always, she had done as she pleased, when she pleased, within the limits of good taste, of course. But no more, she thought bitterly. She was a slave now, no longer free to make her own decisions.

Iron Wing was still studying Katy intently, and she shivered under the power of his probing gaze. It was like being watched by a snake coiled to strike. Unable to hold his penetrating stare, Katy glanced at the thin white scar along his left cheek, wondering what had caused it.

Iron Wing's eyes narrowed ominously as he misinterpreted her curiosity for repugnance.

"Get dressed," he ordered brusquely.

"Not until you leave," Katy retorted sharply.

"It is my lodge," Iron Wing pointed out. "I do not wish to leave. If you do not wish to dress in my presence, go outside."

Katy glared at Iron Wing. What a perverse wretch he was! She waited a moment, hoping he would relent and grant her a few minutes of privacy, but he remained where he was, his dark eyes hard upon her, his face impassive.

With a sigh of exasperation, Katy grabbed the shapeless dress and pulled it inside the protective folds of the blanket, then sat there, perplexed as to how she could slip the dress over her head and still maintain her grip on the blanket.

Iron Wing solved the problem for her. "You could manage better without this," he remarked, and snatched the blanket from her grasp.

Katy blushed from the roots of her hair to the soles of her feet as the warrior's lusty gaze traveled leisurely over her naked flesh. No man had ever seen her unclothed, or even in her chemise, and now this savage was leering at her as if she were some common harlot!

With a cry of righteous indignation, Katy yanked the dress over her head. Rising, she smoothed the rough material over her sweetly rounded hips, a decidedly feminine gesture that did not go unnoticed, or unappreciated, by Iron Wing.

The warrior let out a long sigh of regret as Katy's delectable body was hidden from his sight beneath the shapeless doeskin dress. With an effort, he turned his thoughts in another direction.

"We need wood," he told her, annoyed by

the husky note of longing that had crept into his voice. "Come, I will show you where to find it."

Katy followed Iron Wing outside, acutely aware of the curious glances she received from the Indians, especially the women. Many of them stared at her openly, their interest making them forget their manners. A few glared at her with undisguised loathing. She was a white woman, a paleface. She was the enemy. There was hardly a family in the village who had not lost a loved one to the whites in battle.

One very old woman who had skin like sunburned leather spat at Katy, reviling her in the Cheyenne tongue, until a harsh word from Iron Wing sent the old crone scurrying for the shelter of her lodge.

Tears pricked Katy's eyes. She had never known derision or rejection. Always, she had been pampered and cherished, her wishes catered to. It would have been so easy to cry, to surrender to the tears welling in her eyes, but a pride Katy did not know she possessed came to her rescue. Head high and defiant, Katy followed Iron Wing to a grove of trees as if she were a queen granting favors.

"You will come here each morning and gather wood," Iron Wing instructed curtly. "Do not go beyond the trees, or try to cross the river. Do you understand?"

"Yes," Katy answered sullenly. "I'm not completely stupid."

"Good," the warrior replied, ignoring her sarcasm. "After you collect the wood, you will go to the river for water." He thrust a large yellow gourd into her hands. "After you have drawn the water, you will return to my lodge and prepare my morning meal."

Katy stared after Iron Wing as he turned and walked back to the lodge. Who did he think he was, anyway, ordering her around like that.

Feeling much put upon, Katy wandered beneath the towering pines and oaks searching for twigs. It was a task that could easily have been accomplished in a matter of minutes, but she dawdled along, enjoying the lovely morning, and the chance to be alone, if only for a little while. She bypassed several good-sized hunks of wood, deciding on a whim to gather only those pieces of a certain size and shape.

She lingered at the river, too, casting unhappy glances at her reflection. Surely that sour-faced girl clad in a tattered buckskin dress could not be Katy Marie Alvarez! Katy always wore the most fashionable gowns, and her hair was always clean and shiny, not snarled and lackluster.

At length, Katy returned to Iron Wing's lodge to find him reclining against the backrest. He did not remark on her prolonged absence, merely gestured toward the back of the lodge where the cooking pots and utensils were piled in a disorderly heap.

After a great deal of trial and error, Katy managed to prepare a thin, strong-smelling soup flavored with chunks of meat (she did not ask what kind of meat for fear of the answer) and a handful of wild onions and sage.

Iron Wing ate the watery soup without comment and when he was finished, he handed his bowl to Katy and indicated she should help herself.

The idea of eating out of Iron Wing's unwashed bowl was repugnant, but Katy's intuition told her it was just another of the warrior's less than subtle ways of exerting his power over her. If she refused to take his bowl, he would likely make her eat her breakfast off the dirt floor.

Inwardly seething, her tidy nature rebelling at the idea of eating out of someone else's dirty dish, Katy ladled a few spoonfuls of soup into the clay bowl and ate under Iron Wing's amused gaze.

When the bowl was empty, Katy sat back, thinking she would like nothing more than to lay down and take a nap. Gathering wood and water and cooking were tiring work when you weren't accustomed to it. Not only that, but she had slept badly the night before, haunted by dreams rife with scar-faced monsters and shadowy figures of death and destruction.

But there was to be no rest for Katy that day. Iron Wing ordered her to air his sleeping robes, to smooth the dirt floor of his lodge, to mend his war shirt and leggings, to empty the water left over from the day before.

Katy obeyed the warrior's commands grudgingly, inwardly raging at him as she saw her pampered white hands growing rough and red before her very eyes. By midafternoon, she had broken two fingernails and burned her thumb trying to light a fire. Her back felt like it was going to break at any minute, while muscles she had never known she possessed began to knot up on her, protesting at the unaccustomed labors she was performing.

And what was Iron Wing doing while she worked like a field hand? Why, he sat in the shade of a tall tree, his hands folded negligently behind his head, observing her efforts through half-closed eyes.

In the midst of her chores, Katy noticed that most of the men appeared to do very little work. Many of them sat cross-legged before their lodges, mending their weapons, or fashioning new bows and arrows. Others wandered from lodge to lodge, chatting with their friends and relatives, while the women tended the children, cooked the meals, gathered nuts and berries, dug roots, made moccasins, or worked on the hides pegged to the ground. Obviously, all the women worked like slaves, Katy mused sourly, regardless of whether they were red or white.

At dusk, Iron Wing rose smoothly to his feet and motioned for Katy to follow him. Without looking back, he walked briskly toward the river, nodding at several warriors as he strode past their lodges.

Katy followed him obediently. "Just like a darn dog!" she fumed irritably.

Iron Wing walked perhaps a quarter of a mile upriver before he came to an abrupt halt.

"We will bathe here," he stated, pulling off his shirt nad leggings.

"Together?"

"Do the whites not bathe?" the warrior asked with some curiosity.

"Of course," Katy replied, feeling her cheeks grow hot. "But not together."

"I am not a white man," Iron Wing growled. "And it is not safe for you to bathe here alone."

Totally unconcerned about his nudity, Iron Wing stepped out of his breechcloth and stood naked on the riverbank. His copper-hued skin was smooth and sleek, like the hide of a panther. Katy could not help noticing that, except for the faint spidery scars on the left side of his face, neck and arm, his skin was firm and unblemished. His chest was broad, his belly flat, his arms and legs were long and corded with muscle.

Katy had never seen a man fully unclothed before, and her eyes were drawn to his shriveled manhood until she felt Iron Wing's amused gaze. With a gasp of dismay, Katy whirled around, wishing the earth would open and swallow her up.

"Undress," Iron Wing commanded. Grabbing Katy's shoulder, he forced her to face him again.

It was in Katy's mind to refuse, but she had been mindlessly obeying him all day and there seemed no point in arguing now.

"How easy I am to train," she thought in disgust. "One day as a slave, and I obey orders like I've been doing it all my life!"

Iron Wing felt his breath catch in his throat as Katy stepped out of her dress, revealing a body that was beautiful and perfectly proportioned. Like some wild woodland nymph, she stood naked before him, her head thrown back, her blue eyes blazing with anger and indignation. She looked incredibly lovely standing there, with the hills and trees behind her and the fading sunlight dancing in her luxurious black hair. Iron Wing's loins throbbed with a sudden pulsing desire, but he made no move toward Katy, unwilling to see her expression turn from anger to loathing.

"Come," he said huskily, and dove smoothly into the clear water.

Katy followed timidly, shrieking as the chilly water closed over her. She had never liked swimming, and she swam clumsily, her fear of the water making her awkward. But Iron Wing swam like a fish, his arms and legs propelling him through the water with long powerful strokes.

He swam briskly for perhaps ten minutes before going ashore to retrieve a chunk of what Katy later learned was soap made from a yucca plant. Iron Wing handed Katy the soft lump, then floated lazily in the water while she washed her hair. It was embarrassing, taking a bath while he watched, but the water felt so good she thought she would have bathed before a dozen men in order to feel clean again.

She was soaping her arms when Iron Wing appeared at her side. "Let me," he said, reaching for the soap.

"No!"

"Let me." It was another command, not a request. Wordlessly, Katy handed him the soap, her whole body tense with dreadful anticipation. Iron Wing's eyes gleamed with a fierce intensity as he lathered Katy's arms and shoulders. Her skin was smooth beneath his hand, soft as the petals of a wild rose.

Without warning, he began to wash her breasts, his hands moving slowly, deliberately, over her naked flesh. Katy cringed at his touch, gasped as she felt his manhood rise against her buttocks.

Wanting to flee and yet afraid to move, Katy stared unblinking into the distance, remembering how she had threatened to shoot Jake Cardall because he had dared to lay his hand upon her knee. If only she had her little pistol now!

Time seemed to stand still as Iron Wing dropped the soap and let his lathered hands roam freely over Katy's body, touching, caressing, intimately exploring the silky hills and hidden valleys of her slender figure. A peculiar singing sensation hummed in Katy's veins and she felt suddenly hot all over, as if her blood had mysteriously turned to fire. There was an odd tingling in the pit of her stomach, and her heart was hammering so loudly she wondered that Iron Wing could not hear it.

As Iron Wing's hands grew more bold, more suggestive, Katy swayed against him, bracing herself against the solid wall of his chest as her knees turned to water. She heard Iron Wing groan low in his throat as her buttocks pressed against his throbbing manhood.

She closed her eyes, giving herself up to the wondrous sensations his hands were evoking. Her whole being was alive, quivering with delight when, abruptly, Iron Wing turned away from her and plunged into the water, leaving Katy feeling strangely empty and unfulfilled.

# 5

Several days passed. Katy obediently followed Iron Wing's commands, secretly dreaming of the day when someone would rescue her from the Indians and she would be allowed to enter the convent. Surely her mother would send someone out to search for her sooner or later; perhaps, even now, there were soldiers scouring the countryside. Soon, they would find her and take her to the Little Sisters of Mercy convent in Colorado.

Katy held fast to the thought of the convent when the Indian women ridiculed her because she was ignorant of their language and customs. She pictured the peaceful walls and candlelit chapel at night when sleep wouldn't come and nameless fears hovered over her like great birds of prey, waiting to devour her in a weak moment. She conjured up a mental image of the nuns, their faces serene and untroubled, whenever Iron Wing scolded her or his dark eyes smoldered with an emotion she could not fathom.

Katy had been Iron Wing's prisoner for almost two weeks the day he gave her a new dress and a pair of handsomely decorated moccasins, offering them to her as if they were of no consequence. Requesting only that she wear them to Short Bear's giveaway feast that night.

The giveaway feast was an odd ritual among the Cheyenne, one Katy did not fully understand. When Red Elk's oldest daughter had her first menstrual period, Red Elk gave away all of his horses and many fine robes and furs, leaving his family practically destitute. But the next day there were numerous blankets, furs, and other goods stacked in front of his lodge as members of the tribe gave him gifts in return.

Tonight, Short Bear was celebrating the birth of his first son. There would be food for all, followed by singing and dancing, and then Short Bear would give gifts: a horse to Tall Buffalo, who had been named as the child's godfather; a fine black buffalo robe to Sun Dreamer; a red clay pipe for his wife's father; a dozen beaver skins for his wife's mother.

Iron Wing had told Katy about the feast earlier in the day and she thought of it now as she held the new dress against her, admiring the softness of the doeskin. It had been tanned until it was as smooth as velvet, and was as white as snow. Long fringe dangled from the sleeves, red and yellow porcupine quills had been fashioned into a pleasing design across the yoke.

A new dress! Katy could hardly wait to try it on, and her hands caressed it lovingly a dozen times as she went about her chores that day. When it finally came time to get ready for the feast, she was as excited as a girl going to her first grown-up ball.

Turning her back to Iron Wing, Katy slipped the dress over her head, wishing for a

65

mirror so she could see how she looked. The dress fit like a dream, outlining her full breasts, flaring softly over her hips. Feeling suddenly shy, she turned to face Iron Wing. The admiration she saw reflected in his dark eyes told her better than any looking glass how beautiful she was.

A short time later, Katy sat beside Iron Wing, listening to the laughter of those about her while Short Bear's wife, sisters, and mother-in-law scurried around the large circle making sure everyone had enough to eat. Katy marveled at the large quantity and variety of food being served. Short Bear's women had obviously spent days just cooking. Little wonder they all looked weary.

When the food was gone, one of the ancient warriors told a story for the children and they laughed and giggled and poked each other in the ribs much as children did the world over.

When the ancient warrior finished his tale, Short Bear asked Iron Wing to recount his battle with the grizzly. At first, Iron Wing declined, but it was a brave story and the people begged to hear it, and finally he relented.

Rising proudly to his feet, he walked to the center of the crowd. With a shrug, he removed the blanket from his broad shoulders, revealing his naked chest, and the jagged white scar that ran along his neck and down his left arm. He looked tall and forbidding standing there with the firelight playing over his bronze torso, and Katy felt a flutter of excitement quicken in her belly as she stared at him. He was arrogant. He was insufferable. And she hated him. But now, for this moment, he was utterly fascinating.

Katy did not understand the Cheyenne tongue and at first she had no idea what was being said, but as the minutes passed, she began to understand. Iron Wing was relating, in word, dance, and pantomime, how he had met and defeated the bear whose claws he wore on a leather thong around his neck.

Katy leaned forward, her whole being focused on the man standing in the middle of the gathering. Everything else faded into the distance as she watched him, mesmerized by the story he was telling, a story told so vividly she felt as if she had been there when it happened.

It was early summer. The sky was blue, the air was warm, the grass green and soft beneath his pony's feet. He had gone hunting alone that day, riding high in the hills west of the village. He had just rounded a bend in the trail when his horse began to prance nervously. Iron Wing glanced around, his eyes searching for the thing that was spooking his mount, when suddenly the horse reared straight up and fell over backward. Iron Wing rolled free and scrambled to his feet, unhurt, as his horse bolted down the side of the mountain. A low growl reached Iron Wing's ears and he whirled around, reaching for his bow, only to find it had been broken in the fall.

Moving slowly so as not to frighten or anger the bear, he drew his knife from the sheath on his belt and began to back away, praying the grizzly would let him go. But the bear followed him, rising on her hind legs to tower over him, her black eyes shining with menace, her yellow teeth bared in an angry snarl. A swipe from one huge claw laid his left arm open to the bone.

Stifling a cry of pain, Iron Wing stabbed at the bear's chest and belly as she grabbed him and drew him close. Her breath was foul, her coat rough against his face. With a herculean effort, he freed his knife hand and jabbed the bear in the snout with the point of the blade.

Roaring with pain, the bear knocked him aside. It was then that the tip of one razor-sharp claw sliced his cheek.

Dropping to all fours again, the bear charged. Man and beast came together in a tangle of flailing arms and paws as Iron Wing plunged his knife into the bear's throat, severing the jugular vein.

Blood gushed from the wound, drenching Iron wing in a warm stickiness as the bear toppled over, trapping the unconscious warrior beneath its hindquarters.

When he regained consciousness, it was dark. Using what little strength he had left, he managed to extricate himself from the bear's weight. Then, too weak to travel down the mountain, he pulled his knife from the bear's flesh and cut his tattered shirt into strips with which he bandaged his arm, counting himself lucky as he did so that no veins or arteries had been damaged. He ate raw bear meat when he hungered and it was only when his thirst became intolerable that he crawled down the mountainside to collapse beside a small stream. It was there that Tall Buffalo found him, half out of his mind with pain and fever. Weeks of sickness followed, but when he finally recovered, he returned to the site of the struggle and claimed the bear's claws and hide.

Katy sighed as Iron Wing finished his story and returned to her side. He was truly a brave man, to have endured so much and lived to tell the tale. But he was still an Indian, and a heathen.

It was very late when the giveaway feast ended and they returned to Iron Wing's lodge. Katy undressed quickly and slipped under the robe she used for a blanket. She could hear Iron Wing moving about in the darkness, the soft whisper of his clothing against his skin as he undressed and crawled under the buffalo robes in the rear of the lodge.

With a sigh, Katy closed her eyes, remembering how she had lain awake the first few nights, her nerves as taut as a bowstring as she waited for Iron Wing to drag her forcibly to his bed and brutally attack her. But nothing had happened. He had not touched her since that day at the river, or made any comment on the fact that she slept alone. Katy told herself she was glad he did not find her desirable and yet, perversely, she could not help wondering why he did not want to bed her.

She was almost asleep when Iron Wing's voice pierced the stillness, calling her to him.

Katy's heart began to pound like a hammer as she lay still in the darkness, feigning sleep. She knew, knew beyond a shadow of a doubt, that Iron Wing meant to have his way with her before the night was through. What to do, what to do? Thoughts chased themselves across her mind like mice in a maze, hurrying, scurrying, going nowhere because there was nowhere to go.

"Woman." His voice beckoned her a second time. "Come to me."

"No."

"You are my woman," he reminded her gently. "You must come when I call you."

"No! I don't belong to you, or to anyone."

"You are mine for as long as it pleases me." There was anger in Iron Wing's voice now. He had been patient with her, giving her time to adjust to her new life, and to him. But he would be patient no more. The memory of her standing naked on the riverbank was vivid in his mind. "You will come when I call you."

"I will not."

The words were barely out of Katy's mouth when he was towering over her, his naked body glistening in the dim light cast by the fire's dying embers, his swarthy face twisted with rage because she continued to defy him.

Reaching down, he snatched the cover from her grasp, Katy shivered with fear, and with the knowledge that she had pushed him too far and would now have to pay the penalty.

"You will obey me," Iron Wing rasped, and lifted her into his arms effortlessly, as though she weighed no more than a child.

Only a few short steps across the floor, and she was lying on his bed. The buffalo robes were soft beneath her naked flesh, still warm from Iron Wing's body. The faint light from the coals cast eerie shadows on the lodge-skins, and it seemed as though she were caught in a strange waking nightmare as Iron Wing slowly sank down beside her, his ebony eyes glittering with the fires of his lust.

"What do you want from me?" Katy asked, swallowing hard.

"What every man wants from a woman," Iron Wing answered huskily. "I have waited long enough."

His reply came as no surprise. It was what Katy had been dreading all along, but the reality of the moment was no less disturbing because it had been anticipated.

Katy gasped, "I can't!" as she put both hands against Iron Wing's chest and tried to push him away. It was like trying to dislodge a mountain. Her heart was hammering wildly, and her mouth was suddenly dry as the desert on a summer day as she sobbed, "I can't, I don't know how. I've never been with a man that way."

The fact that she had never known a man stoked Iron Wing's desire. Katy struggled frantically as he drew her closer, kicking, biting, scratching in an attempt to thwart his assault on her body. But her strength was nothing compared to his. With ease, he threw one long leg over hers, then trapped both of her hands in one of his, leaving her to writhe helplessly beneath him as his free hand boldly explored her flat belly and heaving breasts.

Eventually, Katy ceased her useless struggles and lay passive beneath him, her eyes wide with fear and loathing. Indian! Indian! Her mind screamed the word.

Slowly, Iron Wing rose over her, blocking everything else from her vision. Hating him, she squeezed her eyes tight shut as his manhood violated the most intimate part of her body. And now came the worst indignity of all as her own flesh betrayed her. Unwanted, unexpected, a tiny spark of desire ignited deep in the core of Katy's being as Iron Wing moved slowly inside her. His hands, hands that had killed and scalped innocent men and women, roamed freely over her sweat-sheened flesh, fanning that spark into a roaring blaze.

A low moan filled the lodge, shocking Katy into silence as she realized the muffled cry of pleasure had erupted from her own throat. No lady was supposed to enjoy sexual intercourse. It was undignified. It was unladylike. Her mother had told her, in hushed whispers, that the act itself was something a woman endured for the sake of having children. But Katy was not enduring it. She was reveling in it.

She offered no resistance as Iron Wing drew her closer still. Instead, she ran her fingers along his sun-bronzed arms, glorying in his hard masculine strength, and in the muscles that bulged beneath her hand. Heart pounding like a drum, she opened her eyes and stared into the face of the man who was driving her wild with desire. If only he would stop torturing her with such exquisite pain. Oh, if he would only stop . . . if he would never stop.

She cried his name aloud as their passion rose to a flaming crescendo, climaxing in waves of fulfillment that gradually receded in intensity, leaving them breathlessly content.

A long shuddering sigh escaped Iron Wing as he rolled over onto his side, drawing Katy with him so that she lay locked within the circle of his arms, her face only inches from his own. Now she was truly his woman, and he would kill any man who dared touch he

Smiling drowsily, he fell asleep.

Katy lay stiff in Iron Wing's arms, confused by the conflicting emotions running rampant in her breast. Her mind screamed with outraged innocence. Her virginity, that prize beyond price, had been taken from her by force by a heathen savage. But that was not the worst of it. No, far worse than Iron Wing's violation of her body was the way she had yielded to his touch. Yielded! Hah! She had surrendered with hardly a struggle.

She grimaced with self-disgust. If the truth be known, she had gloried in his possession of her, delighting in the easy masculine strength that had rendered her helpless. Helpless and loving it, her conscience chided reproachfully. Loving it and already hungry for more. No matter that he was a heathen savage. No matter that they had not received the blessing of a Holy Father, or even a Cheyenne medicine man. In the end, she had risen to meet him, crying his name aloud as his arms pulled her closer, until they were no longer two separate entities, but one flesh forged together by the heat of passion. Even now, with her skin still on fire from his touch, she was wanting him again, wanting to experience the never-imagined pleasure he had brought her. And she had wanted to be a nun!

Feeling suddenly dirty and ashamed, Katy

eased out of Iron Wing's embrace and crawled to the opposite side of the lodge where a pot of water stood waiting to be thrown out. It was clean water, but Iron Wing would not use it in the morning because the Indians believed that water left overnight was dead.

Very quietly, Katy dipped a cloth into the water and began to wipe the bright virginal blood from between her thighs. No decent white man would ever want her now, she mused bitterly, forgetting that she had vowed never to love again. No self-respecting white man would want a woman who had been despoiled by a savage.

Katy stared at the red stain on the cloth, and then at Iron Wing sleeping peacefully on the far side of the lodge. Only the sight of his blood on her hands could atone for the loss of her virginity.

Holding her breath, Katy moved stealthily toward the tripod that held Iron Wing's weapons. The rifle would be too noisy, the lance too awkward. She could not draw the bow. That left the knife. She began to shake all over as she slowly but deliberately drew the wicked-looking blade from the beaded buckskin sheath. On silent feet, she crept to Iron Wing's side.

He did not look particularly dangerous in repose. With his features relaxed and the habitual bitterness in his eyes shuttered behind closed lids, he looked peaceful, almost benign.

But he was not kind. He was a savage, a murderer, a molester of virgins! Katy's anger flared hot again and she raised the knife, ready to plunge it to the hilt in Iron Wing's naked chest, when suddenly his dark eyes snapped open. His left hand, moving swifter than a serpent's tongue, struck Katy's wrist as the knife came down, deflecting the blow so that, instead of piercing his heart, the blade sank into his right shoulder.

Katy screamed with fear as her arm went numb from the wrist up to her shoulder. Once he had threatened to beat her publicly if she defied him. What would he do to her now, when she had tried to kill him? Heart pounding with trepidation, she stared in horror at the knife protruding from his shoulder.

Iron Wing sat up slowly, his face taut with pain as he jerked the knife from his flesh. Blood poured from the wound, and he pressed his hand over the gaping hole as his eyes sought her face.

"Why?" he asked softly. "Do I not have scars enough to please you?"

Tears filled Katy's eyes. She had expected anger, retaliation. But he did not seem angry, only puzzled.

"Because I . . . I hate you," Katy murmured, refusing to meet his eyes. "You killed my father and my betrothed. And now you've stolen my virginity, and I . . ." She broke into violent sobs, unable to go on.

There was a sudden pounding on the outside of the lodge cover. Iron Wing rose slowly to his feet, wincing with pain as he opened the lodge flap to admit Tall Buffalo and Sun Dreamer.

"We heard a scream," Tall Buffalo said, glancing from Katy's tear-stained face to the blood dripping from Iron Wing's shoulder. "We thought . . ." He laughed out loud as he gestured at Iron Wing's injury. "We thought the white woman had killed you."

"Not quite," Iron Wing remarked drily.

"I think we should go," Sun Dreamer muttered, and the two warriors left the lodge, grinning foolishly.

Iron Wing sat cross-legged on the floor while Katy clumsily bandaged his wound. His blood was warm and sticky, and she grimaced as it dripped onto her skin.

"Only the sight of his blood on my hand . . ." The words echoed in Katy's mind, but she found no satisfaction in knowing she had shed his blood, only horror that she had tried to take a human life.

Tying off the ends of the bandage, Katy sat back on her heels, looking up at Iron Wing through the dark fringe of her lashes.

"I'm sorry," she murmured.

"What did you mean when you said I had killed your father and your betrothed?" Iron Wing asked quietly.

"They were both killed by Apaches," Katy answered bitterly. "My father was hacked to pieces, and Robert . . ." She choked on the words.

"I am not an Apache," Iron Wing reminded her gruffly, but his eyes were kind.

"Injuns is Injuns," Katy retorted, parroting a phrase she had often heard.

"That may be," Iron Wing allowed, "but *this* Indian is tired." He stretched out on the robes and closed his eyes. "Come to bed."

It was in Katy's mind to refuse, but she too was suddenly overcome with weariness.

Meekly she crawled under the robes, careful not to jar Iron Wing's wounded shoulder.

He was soon asleep, but Katy lay awake for hours, trying to sort out her jumbled emotions. She hated Iron Wing, hated everything he represented. Why then did his touch excite her? She had tried only moments before to kill him, and now she lay beside him, feeling strangely content. It was all so confusing.

She was still trying to understand her confusion when sleep claimed her. There were no bad dreams that night.

# 6

In the days that followed, Iron Wing spent long hours with Katy, teaching her to speak the language of the Cheyenne. It was a harsh, guttural tongue, difficult for her to master. Often, he would not speak to her unless she responded in his native tongue. His stubbornness irritated Katy, but it made her learn faster.

She discovered many things about the Indian people as the days went by. She had been taught from childhood that all Indians were godless savages, having no natural affection or human emotions. To her surprise, Katy learned such notions were very wrong. Indian mothers loved their children and prayed for them when they were ill. Husbands argued with their wives. Wives nagged their husbands, but only in the privacy of their lodge. Little boys played harmless pranks on their siblings. Grandfathers told stories of their youth. Young men bragged of their adventures. Young women spent hours preening for the young men, and then took great pains to pretend to ignore the very men they secretly hoped to impress.

Eventually, most of the people in the village accepted Katy. The men treated her with respect because she was Iron Wing's woman. The women made small overtures of friendship, offering to teach Katy how to dye the porcupine quills that decorated their clothing, showing her how to locate the herbs and vegetables that grew wild on the plains. They taught Katy which plants cured ache in the belly, and which were good for healing headaches and toothaches. She learned which plants were poisonous—and thought, if only half-heartedly, of slipping a few leaves into Iron Wing's food.

Tall Buffalo's wife, Yellow Flower, gave Katy a deerskin dress. Pretty Eyes, daughter of Sun Dreamer, the medicine man, gave her several ribbons for her hair and a comb carved from a piece of pine.

Katy was pleased by their friendship. It was nice to have the women smile at her and nod their heads in greeting, nice to know the children were no longer afraid of her, even though she was a "paleface."

Nicest of all was having Yellow Flower for a friend. Though Katy's mastery of the Cheyenne tongue was far from complete, the two women managed to communicate quite well by using a combination of English, Cheyenne, and sign language. Yellow Flower taught Katy how to make moccasins, and how to tan into fine robes the furs that Iron Wing brought home. Whenever Katy was not with Iron Wing, she could usually be found in Yellow Flower's lodge helping to sew things for the baby that was due any day.

Katy had been Iron Wing's prisoner almost a month to the day the morning she woke with the dull cramping in her belly that signaled the onslaught of her menses. She blushed with embarrassment when Iron Wing noticed the blood on her sleeping robes.

Before she could ask him to please send Yellow Flower to her, Iron Wing hurried her out of their lodge toward a small hut located near the river. It was, Katy soon discovered, the menstrual lodge where women were required to stay until their mensus ceased. There were several women inside the lodge and they willingly made room for Katy, patiently explaining that no woman suffering the curse was ever allowed to associate with the men. They must never touch a warrior's weapons, or prepare his food, lest misfortune befall him. Brave warriors though the Cheyenne were, they still looked upon a menstruating woman with fear and awe, believing her to be possessed of harmful supernatural powers.

At first, Katy was indigant at such treatment, but as time passed, the days in the hut became less of an ordeal. It was a good time to catch up on village gossip, or sew a new dress, or just relax.

A week after Katy returned to Iron Wing's lodge, Yellow Flower went into labor. Tall Buffalo spent the day with Iron Wing, and Katy almost laughed out loud to see Tall Buffalo restlessly pacing the floor just like any other expectant father. Indians were rumored to be a stoic race, immune to pain or sorrow. Once Katy had believed them incapable of emotion, but now she knew that Indians were just people like everybody else, subject to the same joys, the same fears. They might mask their emotions behind a stern facade in public or in front of strangers, but they felt pain and grief, joy and sorrow, just like whites.

Yellow Flower was in labor for twelve hours, and at last she was delivered of a fat baby boy. Katy felt a surge of maternal longing as she held the baby in her arms and it occurred to her that, if she were forced to remain long with Iron Wing, she too might become pregnant.

Katy stared at the baby in sudden confusion. He was a darling thing, with dark eyes and a thatch of thick black hair. He would be so easy to love. Already she felt a warm swell of affection for him, yet the thought of giving birth to an Indian baby filled her with revulsion.

But perhaps she was worrying needlessly. Iron Wing had not touched her since the night she had stabbed him, although he still insisted she share his bed. For Katy, the nights beside him were long and filled with tension. Each time Iron Wing moved beside her, each time his warm flesh touched hers, she felt her nerves sing with anticipation. She reprimanded herself often for wanting him, reminding herself that sexual intercourse outside of marriage was a sin. Not only that, but Iron Wing was a savage, a heathen. But he had awakened a hunger she had not known she possessed; a hunger that cried out to be fed, and all her arguments to the contrary could not make her stop desiring him.

# 7

Day followed day, and spring gave way to summer. Katy returned to Iron Wing's lodge one afternoon in June to find he was preparing to go hunting with a dozen or so of the other warriors. They would be gone for two weeks.

Katy was pleased at the idea of being alone for a while. It would be nice not having Iron Wing underfoot all the time, bossing her around. For once, she would be able to sleep as late as she pleased, or spend the whole day sitting beside the river doing nothing at all.

Iron Wing made love to her that night, callously ignoring her pleas to be left alone.

"Do not fight me, woman," he murmured, his breath tickling her ear. "You are mine, and I will have my way with you whenever it pleases me. Why not relax and enjoy it?"

"Hah! I'll never enjoy it," Katy hissed, raking her nails across his chest. "You're a savage, an animal! I hate it when you touch me!" But as she spoke the words, she knew they were lies. She had been wanting him to hold her and caress her ever since the first time, and had wondered why he had not tried to make love to her again.

"Do you?" His hands, big and brown and strong, were gentle yet deliberate as they

82

began to stroke her thigh, making her quiver with delight. Unable to help herself, Katy moaned with pleasure as his mouth descended on hers.

"I love the way you hate me," Iron Wing whispered as her arms slipped around his neck. "Hate me some more."

When Katy woke the next morning, she was alone. The lodge seemed strangely empty with Iron Wing gone. Forgetting her intention to remain idle in his absence, she threw herself into vigorous house cleaning, shaking out the sleeping robes and hanging them in the fresh air. She washed all the pots and utensils, and swept the floor of the lodge. She washed all of Iron Wing's clothes, and hers, and still the day was only half gone. Funny, how slowly the time passed now that she was alone. She sought out Yellow Flower, but Yellow Flower was busy with her baby. Indeed, all the women were involved in their chores.

At a loss, Katy walked down to the river and washed her hair. Sitting on the riverbank, she watched a group of would-be warriors racing their ponies on the other side of the river. There were a dozen boys, ranging in age from eight to twelve, and she smiled as they whooped and hollered. Once when she had remarked on their carefree behavior, Iron Wing had told her that the young boys of the tribe were permitted a great deal of freedom. Their childish pranks were usually ignored, or viewed with amusement.

"The life of a warrior is often short," Iron Wing had said by way of explanation. "Sometimes a warrior is killed in his first battle. My people understand this, and let the boys run wild until they become novices. Then the time for play is past, and they must learn the ways of a man. It is not easy, being a warrior."

With a last look at the young boys, Katy stood up and began walking along the river-bank. Wandering aimlessly, she wondered if her mother had grieved for her at all, or if Sarah had considered her daughter a burden well rid of. She wondered if anyone had been sent out to search for her when she failed to show up at the convent. Surely the nuns would have sent inquiries regarding their missing postulant!

The possibility put a spring in Katy's step. Perhaps even now the Army was searching for her. She glanced over her shoulder, half expecting to see a rescue party riding toward her. Instead, she realized that the lodges of the Cheyenne were no longer in sight.

"Why, I'm free!" Katy cried aloud, and laughed with the sheer joy of it. Free! Grinning hugely, she began to run, though she had no clear idea where she was running to. Her feet flew as with wings and laughter bubbled in her throat as she put more and more distance between herself and the Cheyenne village.

She ran until her sides ached and her legs were weak, ran until she could not run any more. Breathless, she fell to her knees beneath a leafy cottonwood for a rest.

Twenty minutes later, she was walking briskly toward the setting sun. Her home was there, somewhere in the shadow of the distant mountains.

Fear strangled Katy's exuberance as darkness settled over the plains. Strange noises conjured up visions of wild animals, and she huddled deeper into the meager shelter of a decaying windfall where she had decided to spend the night, a large rock clutched in her hand.

Sleep did not come that night. Katy started at every sound. Every moving shadow loomed as a possible danger, a threat to her safety. Visions of wolves preyed on her mind. She had seen them often during her stay with the Indians, lurking on the outskirts of the camp. From a distance, they looked like large furry dogs. Sometimes, with their tongues lolling out and their tails wagging, they looked almost friendly. But they were not dogs, and they were not friendly. They were wild predatory beasts capable of pulling down full-grown deer and elk. There were coyotes, too, and snakes, and bears, and Heaven only knew what else. Iron Wing's lodge, which she had fled with such joy and relief, suddenly seemed a haven of refuge, and she heartily wished she were there now, safely wrapped in a warm robe beside a cheery fire.

Katy rose with the dawn, glad that the night was behind her, refusing to think ahead to the night that would inevitably come.

A berry bush provided a meager breakfast, and water from a shallow stream quenched her thirst and washed the berry juice from her hands and face.

Drying her hands on her skirt, Katy started again walking westward. The plains stretched before her, seemingly endless and devoid of life. The grass, which had been bright green only a few weeks ago, was already turning yellow.

Nothing moved on the face of the land. Katy had heard stories of pioneer women who had gone mad while crossing the plains, driven to insanity by the never-ending sea of gentle waving grass and the unchanging sky overhead.

Katy put the dismal thought from her, humming to buoy her spirits as she walked toward the mountains barely visible in the distance. But no matter how fast she walked or how far, the mountains never seemed to get any closer. Their colors changed as the hours passed; now purple, now blue, now gray-green, now tinged with gilt and crimson as the sun gradually dipped behind the craggy peaks.

And then it was dark again, so very dark. Katy's stomach was rumbling loudly when she stumbled into a buffalo wallow. Utterly exhausted, she lay where she had fallen, too tired to move. She was hungry and thirsty, and, oh, so tired! And lost. Despair washed over her as she stared up at the myriad stars twinkling in a black velvet sky. Why had she run away? She could not survive in the wilderness alone, and now she would die alone on the plains, a victim of her own foolishness.

The thought made her sad, but she was too bone weary to cry, and sleep claimed her the minute she closed her eyes.

When she woke in the morning, it was to find a trio of bearded faces staring down at her.

# 8

The three white men peered at the young
woman, in Indian garb, crouched against the
side of the buffalo wallow, their eyes expressing varying degrees of shock and surprise at
finding a lone female so many miles from the
nearest settlement.

"Is she a squaw?" the youngest of the men
asked his companions.

"No," declared the young man to his left.
"Look at those eyes. They're bluer than the
Pacific!"

Katy glared up at them as she gained her
feet. Unconsciously, she threw back her
shoulders and lifted her chin, gazing up at
the buckskin-clad men with an air of confidence she was far from feeling.

"I am Katy Marie Alvarez," she announced
haughtily. "And I have only recently escaped
from the Cheyenne."

"When?"

"How?"

"You can ask questions later," the eldest of
the three men admonished as he offered Katy
a calloused hand. "First, let us get this poor
child a bath and a hot meal."

"Thank you," Katy said, dazzling them all
with her smile. "That sounds wonderful."

The older man, obviously the father of the

other two, nodded in agreement. "Forgive my lack of manners," he said, his voice tinged with a faint French accent. "I am Andre Bordeaux, and these are my sons, Claude and Jean-Paul. We are buffalo hunters." He bowed from the waist. "We are at your service, mademoiselle," he said gallantly, and lifted Katy onto the back of his horse.

It was a short ride to the Frenchmen's camp. The eldest boy, Claude, quickly fixed Katy a hot meal of boiled buffalo meat and potatoes while Jean-Paul filled a large cast iron pot with water and placed it over the fire.

Katy ate ravenously and readily accepted seconds, though she could not help blushing self-consciously when Claude remarked that he liked to see a woman with a healthy appetite.

When she finished eating, Katy followed Jean-Paul into the big covered wagon and gave a little wordless cry of joy when she saw a tin tub filled with steaming water. There was even a towel and a bar of real soap.

Jean-Paul backed out of the wagon, his face flushed with embarrassment. Katy was undeniably attractive, and Jean-Paul was at that age when women were entering his thoughts more and more. Just thinking of Mademoiselle Alvarez sitting naked in the tub made the blood pound in his head and his legs go weak, so that he all but fell out of the back of the wagon.

Katy grinned with amusement as she laced the back cover closed. Disrobing, she stepped into the tub, sighing with pleasure as the hot water enveloped her. What luxury, to bathe in a real tub with real soap! How lucky she was that Andre Bordeaux and his sons had found her. But for their kindness, she would surely have perished in the wilderness.

She had been lucky twice, Katy mused drowsily, first with Tall Buffalo, and now with the Bordeaux men. They would not harm her, she was certain of that. They were decent, honorable men, and she knew instinctively that she had nothing to fear.

It was good to be safe at last, back with her own people. She closed her eyes as the warm water drained the last shreds of tension from her weary body.

Katy lingered in the tub until the water grew cool. Then, dressing quickly, she stepped outside. Claude came forward to meet her, his brown eyes as warm and friendly as his boyish smile.

"You look weary, mademoiselle," Claude remarked. "Come, I have prepared a bed for you beside the fire. I think maybe you would like a little nap, no?"

"I would like a little nap, yes," Katy said with a grateful smile. "Thank you."

Katy stretched out on the soft hides, intending to take only a short nap and then help the men with dinner, but when she opened her eyes again, it was morning. Andre and his sons were sitting around the camp fire, eating breakfast.

Andre smiled at Katy as she sat up, yawning. "So, you are finally awake. Twice, Claude checked on you to see if you were still alive."

Claude grinned good-naturedly as he handed Katy a bowl of soup, a thick slice of bread, and a cup of coffee. "Do not listen to Papa. I only checked once to make sure you were warm enough."

"Once every hour," Jean-Paul said, chuckling. "I think my brother is enchanted by your beautiful blue eyes."

"*Oui*," Claude admitted boldly. "Who would not be enchanted by such a one? She has the face of an angel."

"Enough of this foolishness," Andre chided, grinning fondly at his sons. "It is time to make the hunt."

"Will you be all right here by yourself?" Claude asked Katy doubtfully.

"I guess so. But I'd rather go with you, if it's all right."

"Papa?"

Andre nodded. "Perhaps we should not leave her here alone. Jean-Paul, saddle the horses. Claude, help me hitch the team."

While the men were busy with the animals, Katy quickly washed the dishes and packed the bedrolls inside the wagon. Shortly thereafter, they went out in search of buffalo. Andre drove the heavy flatbed wagon which served as hide carrier, while Katy and the two boys rode beside the wagon. Andre and his sons kept Katy laughing as they joked back and forth, teasing Jean-Paul about the way he blushed whenever Katy looked at him, joshing Claude because he couldn't seem to keep his eyes off her.

Katy basked in the warm, friendly atmosphere. The men shared such a relaxed and loving relationship, she could not help feeling a little envious. Her own home had been so cold and unhappy after her father had died.

Surely this was how families should be, close-knit and caring. How wonderful to know you were loved!

It was mid-morning before they spotted a fairly large herd of bulls.

"Sometimes I feel guilty about hunting them," Claude confided to Katy. "They say that, long ago, the herds were so big you could not ride around them in a day. An old hunter in St. Louis told me about a time he and a group of professional skinners brought down one hundred and fifty buffalo in a single day."

Katy's eyes lingered on the herd as she tried to imagine how it must have been before the white men came with their big buffalo guns, killing the immense animals for their shaggy hides and tongues. It was difficult, imagining buffalo as far as the eye could see. They were such intriguing beasts, with their massive humps, gleaming horns, and tiny black eyes, yet they looked so placid from a distance, grazing on the short tufts of hardy yellow grass.

"I think this will be our last year," Claude reflected gravely. "The buffalo are growing scarce, and the Indians . . ." He shrugged. "They are getting more and more angry all the time, and who can blame them? Soon I think it will not be safe to cross the plains except in very large groups."

White buffalo hunters, Katy soon learned, did not hunt the buffalo from horseback as did the Cheyenne. Instead, they found a sheltered stand downwind from the grazing herd and calmly shot the nearest bulls. Strangely, the animals nearby paid little attention as their companions suddenly fell dead in their midst. Nor did they appear to be bothered by the sound of gunfire. It was not until one old bull suddenly pawed the ground and lumbered off in a shambling trot that the herd took flight. Abruptly, amid a cloud of thick yellow dust and a great thunder of churning cloven hooves, the buffalo stampeded across the prairie, their tufted tails flying in the wind.

Andre wiped a sweaty hand through his close-cropped gray hair. "Not bad," he remarked, laying his rifle aside. "Jean-Paul, pick up our brass. Claude, bring the team."

"Come with me," Claude said, taking Katy by the hand.

When they reached the flatbed, Claude lifted Katy onto the seat and nimbly vaulted up beside her. Flashing her a wide grin, he clucked to the horses, starting them towards the dead buffalo.

"That was our last stand of the year," Claude remarked. "After we skin the buffalo and stretch the hides, we will take them to St. Louis. You will like St. Louis," he told her confidently. "After we sell our hides, I will buy you some pretty clothes and show you the sights."

"You're very kind," Katy replied. "But I can't let you buy me clothes. It isn't proper."

"Perhaps not, but you cannot walk around the streets of St. Louis dressed like an Indian squaw."

Katy glanced down at her deerskin dress. It was badly soiled and the hem was torn where she had snagged it on a bush the day before. "I guess you're right," she agreed, pleased at the thought of a new dress. "But I'll pay you back as soon as I get home."

"Home?"

"Yes, I must go home to Mesa Blanca. I have to let my mother know I'm alive and well."

"You can send her a wire from St. Louis," Claude said. "Please do not be in such a hurry to leave me, Katy. Not when I have just found you."

Katy looked at the handsome young man sitting beside her, startled by the fervent intensity of his words. His eyes were a rich warm brown, and they returned her gaze with open adoration, rendering Katy momentarily speechless.

"Please stay with us," Claude implored softly. "You are everything I have ever dreamed of."

"But we've only just met!" Katy exclaimed. "You don't even know me."

"But I *want* to know you. I think I am in love with you already."

"That's impossible," Katy laughed. "You don't know anything about me."

"I know you like to eat," Claude said, grinning impishly. "And that your eyes are as blue as the skies of Paris in the summer."

"Oh, Claude, you're hopeless!"

"Hopelessly in love," he said, and then grinned triumphantly. "By the time we reach St. Louis, it will be too late in the year to cross the plains. You will have to spend the winter with us, and I will take you home in the spring. By then, you will be mad for me, and I shall make you my wife."

Claude's merry laughter was infectious,

and Katy could not help laughing with him. His face was smooth and unlined, his body straight and tall. His skin was deeply tanned from long hours in the sun, his hair blond and curly. Usually she did not care for men with beards, but the Bordeaux men wore them well. Yes, Claude was a fine looking man but, more importantly, he was good for her. He made her feel young and free and innocent again, as if all that had happened in the Cheyenne village had been nothing more than a bad dream. She could almost believe she was the same naive young woman who had left Mesa Blanca so many months before. Perhaps she would marry him, she mused. It would be so nice to be a part of his family . . .

The next few days were busy ones. Katy helped the men clean the hides, glad that she could do something to repay them for their unfailing kindness. She took over the cooking, laughing merrily when all three Frenchmen claimed they would marry her for her cooking alone. Andre and Jean-Paul were teasing, of course, the one being too old for her, and the other too young. But Claude was not joking. He continued to woo her, paying her outrageous compliments, bringing her bouquets of weeds when he could find no wildflowers, talking about their future as if he was certain they would always be together. He told her of his past, how his mother had died several years ago of pneumonia, and how his father's business had failed the following year.

"So we came to America to seek our fortune," Claude said, his voice tinged with

94

amusement. "Papa thought he would become the fur king of St. Louis, but we got here too late for that. Still, it is a wonderful country. It is even better, now that I have found you. Tell me, *cheri*, how did you happen to be captured by the Indians?"

"I was on my way to Colorado to enter a convent there when the stagecoach was attacked." She did not tell him of Iron Wing. The warrior was a part of her past now, and she wanted to forget him.

"A convent!" Claude exclaimed in horror. *"Merde!* What a waste that would have been."

"A waste? Whatever do you mean?"

"A woman as lovely and vital as you should not be locked away behind cold stone walls. No, *cherie*, you were born to be a wife. To mother many strong sons." Claude took Katy's hand in his and raised it to his lips. "I hope they will be my sons."

"Don't you ever think of anything else?" Katy asked. She had meant to keep her tone light and teasing, but the words came out soft and shaky as she read the tender look in Claude's eyes.

"Not when I am with you," he admitted. "I am grateful to the savages since they kept you from shutting yourself up in a convent."

"I would have been happy there," Katy remarked wistfully.

Claude studied her face intently. "Weren't you happy at home? Surely you had many young men to court you. Ah," he said with a knowing look, "that is the reason. A man! You were running away from someone who had hurt you."

Katy shook her head slowly. "No. I was

running away from life."

"I am sorry, *cherie*. Sorry you have been unhappy." Claude smiled optimistically as he squeezed her hand. "But all that is past now. Claude is here, and I will show you how much fun life can be. I will take you to France! Ah, I should like to show you Paris and Marseille. I think you would turn the head of every man in the country!"

"Paris," Katy breathed. "Oh, I would love to see Paris!"

Claude laughed, pleased that he had drawn her thoughts away from unpleasant memories. "It would be a lovely place for a honeymoon," he remarked, throwing her a teasing smile. "But first we must get these smelly hides to St. Louis!"

Days later, the hides were packed on board the wagon and everything was in readiness for their journey across the plains. They would start early in the morning.

That evening, after dinner, Claude and Katy walked a short distance away from the others. Hand in hand, they stood in the gathering darkness. It was a vast place, the West, Katy thought. The land fell away for miles, awe-inspiring and a little frightening. It was a hard land, uncaring and unforgiving, making her feel small and insignificant.

"It is a beautiful country, is it not?" Claude asked, squeezing Katy's hand affectionately.

"Yes, so beautiful. It's no wonder the Indians want to keep it for themselves."

"I am afraid their days are numbered," Claude remarked matter-of-factly. "There are too many people in the East who will be lured West by tales of gold and free land. I think that before long, civilization will crush the Indians beneath its feet."

"The Cheyenne will never stand by and watch their land be plundered," Katy said with conviction. "They'll fight for their land, for their way of life."

*"Oui, cherie.* But they will lose."

Katy knew there was truth in Claude's words. The Indians could not withstand the endless numbers or the awesome firepower of the white man. They would have to bend or break, and Katy felt a twinge of sorrow as she thought of Iron Wing and Tall Buffalo. They would not bend. They would fight.

Katy's face took on a faraway, melancholy expression, and Claude felt his heart pound with love and desire for the woman standing beside him. She was beautiful, so very beautiful. He longed to run his fingers through the silky black cloud of her hair, to draw her close and bury himself in her sweetness. Instead, he lowered his head and kissed her, very gently.

Katy gave a little gasp of surprise, but she did not pull away. Claude had been kind to her, offering her love and acceptance at a time when she needed both. His mouth was warm and firm, but his kiss evoked no ardor in Katy's breast. No wild rush of wings filled her ears, no surge of desire coursed through her veins as it had when Iron Wing touched her.

"Katy," Claude groaned. "I love you so much, need you . . ."

"No . . ."

He released her immediately. "I'm sorry,

*cherie.* Forgive me."

"Of course. Perhaps we'd better go back to the fire."

Later that night, snug in her blankets in the shelter of the wagon, Katy puzzled over her lack of response to Claude's kiss. She was very fond of him, and he was physically attractive, yet his touch left her unmoved. It was most peculiar. She remembered how quickly Iron Wing's kisses had aroused her, how even a mere glance had made her legs go weak with wanting him. Was there something wrong with her, some element of decency lacking in her character so that she could only respond to the caress of a half-naked savage?

Katy firmly put the thought from her mind. Soon she would return to civilization. Thinking of living in a house, of dressing and acting like a white woman again, filled her with restless excitement so that she slept fitfully, tossing and turning far into the night.

It was past midnight when she sat up, suddenly wide awake and filled with a sense of forboding, as if the night were watching her with hostile eyes and bated breath. She sent a quick glance across the fire, relieved to see Andre standing guard near the flatbed wagon, the butt of his rifle resting across his thigh. Claude and Jean-Paul were snoring softly.

With a sigh, Katy snuggled deeper into her blankets, chiding herself for imagining things. It would be good to live in a real town again, she mused, to be able to sleep without fear. Good to sleep in a real bed between clean sheets instead of beneath a buffalo robe. Good to wear silks and satin instead of skins, shoes and stockings instead of moccasins.

She gazed up at the stars wheeling against the indigo sky and listened to the sounds of the night. A coyote yapped in the distance, and Katy shivered. It was such a sad, melancholy sound. It filled her with a vague sense of loneliness.

Closing her eyes, Katy thought about Claude. He was a good man, as full of mischief as a small boy. Perhaps she would marry him after all. He did not seem to mind that she had been forced to live as a squaw.

"It was not your fault," he had told her one night, his brown eyes sympathetic and caring. "No one can blame you for surviving."

Dear Claude! If he asked her to marry him again, she would accept. He was so sweet, his accent charming, his manners impeccable. Smiling sleepily, Katy tried to summon his image to mind. But instead of Claude's bearded visage, the swarthy countenance of Iron Wing broke into her thoughts, his image clear and sharp in every detail, from his high forehead and strong, hawklike nose to his wide sensuous mouth and square, stubborn jaw. For all his rough ways, she had to admit there was something undeniably attractive about Iron Wing. He possessed an air of vitality, of animal maleness, that Claude lacked.

But it was Claude she would marry, Katy decided resolutely. He would propose to her again, of that she was certain, and this time she would accept. He would make a good and loyal husband, a kind and loving father for her children.

Sometime later, she stirred fretfully, aware that something was wrong. Swimming through layers of sleep, she opened her eyes, blinked at the dark form bending over her.

Iron Wing! Recognition hit Katy like a physical blow. She lifted her arms to push him away, uttered a small cry of dismay when she realized her hands were tightly bound together.

Fear of what Iron Wing would do to her for running away boiled up inside Katy and she opened her mouth to scream, only to have Iron Wing stuff a rag between her teeth, stifling her startled cry. With ease, he lifted her onto his shoulder and began to carry her from the Frenchmen's camp.

Katy's fear increased with each step he took. Frantic, she began to thrash about and her foot struck the rifle Claude had propped near her blankets in case of an emergency. Iron Wing froze as the rifle clattered to the ground.

The noise alerted Andre Bordeaux and he whirled around, tracking the sound. He muttered an obsenity as he saw the Indian outlined in the darkness, and Katy slung over his shoulder. Hoping to make the Indian release Katy, Andre fired at the ground at Iron Wing's feet. The gunshot was very loud in the stillness of the night.

Iron Wing moved like lightning. Dropping Katy to the ground, his hand caught up the rifle that had betrayed his presence.

Andre fired again, the bullet whining near Iron Wing's head. Unshaken, the warrior fired a fraction of a second later. His bullet found the Frenchman's heart, killing him instantly.

And now Claude and Jean-Paul were awake. Claude's first thought was of Katy. Seeing her lying at Iron Wing's feet and thinking her dead, he grabbed up his rifle and began firing blindly, his grief making him careless, heedless of his own safety.

Katy huddled on the ground, her heart pounding with fear as the darkness was torn with bright flashes of rifle fire.

Iron Wing quickly moved away from Katy, fearing she would be hit by a stray bullet. He stood outlined in the darkness, unwavering, as he sighted down the rifle, aiming for Claude's heart.

Katy screamed as Claude dropped his rifle and stumbled forward, one hand clutching at the gaping hole in his chest.

Jean-Paul was moving, too, running toward Iron Wing, the moonlight shining on the skinning knife in his hand.

"*No!*" Katy screamed. "Go back, please go back!"

But Jean-Paul came steadily onward, his eyes brimming with tears of rage. With a sob, he launched himself at Iron Wing as Iron Wing squeezed the trigger of his rifle. The bullet slammed into Jean-Paul's belly, throwing him backward as if he had been grabbed from behind by an invisible hand.

Katy stared at Iron Wing, standing firm as the mountains. Andre and his two sons lay unmoving on the ground.

With a sigh, Iron Wing jacked a fresh round into the breech of the rifle, then went to check on the three men he had shot, making sure they were dead. He thought fleetingly of taking their scalps, but, knowing Katy would never forgive him, he thought better of it.

Tears welled in Katy's eyes. Why did everyone she cared for die so horribly? Lost in sorrow for Andre and his sons, she did not stop to think she would have grieved more for Iron Wing, had he been killed.

Grief washed over her like waves upon the sand, and then was swept away as Iron Wing padded toward her. Fear for her own life made Katy's nerves grow taut; when she saw the anger shining in his eyes, she began to tremble.

Roughly, Iron Wing pulled her to her feet. A single stroke of his knife freed her hands.

"Come," Iron Wing said. "It is time to go."

"I'm not going with you," Katy said dully. "I hate you."

"Is there anything you wish to take?" Iron Wing asked, ignoring the silent tears tracking Katy's cheeks.

"I will not go with you!" Katy screamed, pummeling his chest with her fists. "Do you understand what I'm saying? *I will not go!*"

With lazy grace, Iron Wing reached out and took hold of Katy's shoulders, shaking her as a terrier shakes a mouse. The touch of his big brown hands went through her like an electric shock.

"You will come with me, Ka-ty," Iron Wing said gruffly, speaking her name for the first time. "You are my woman. No other man will possess you so long as I live."

"How do you know I didn't let Claude make

102

love to me?" Katy said defiantly. "And his brother, and his father, too?"

She was immediately sorry she had hinted at such an outrageous thing. Iron Wing's eyes grew ominous as his hand closed tightly over her arm.

"Did you?" he asked, his voice raw with jealousy.

Katy swallowed hard. Too frightened to lie, she shook her head vigorously. "No."

Iron Wing's eyes narrowed as he searched Katy's face. "I do not believe you," he said angrily. "I saw the way the tall one kissed you, the way he looked at you, as if you belonged to him."

"He only kissed me," Katy protested. "I swear it!"

Some of the anger went out of Iron Wing's eyes as he released his hold on Katy's arm. She had lied to hurt him, he realized grimly, and it had worked. The thought of another man touching her was like slow poison eating away at his heart. He threw a glance at Claude and knew a deep sense of satisfaction because the man was dead. The buffalo hunter would never touch Katy again.

Drained by the night's events, Katy watched numbly as Iron Wing gathered up her blankets. Then, taking her by the hand, he led her away from the camp. On the far side of a small rise, out of sight of the dead men, he spread Katy's blankets beneath a stunted pine.

"Come, Ka-ty," he invited as he sat down on her blankets.

"No."

"Do not make me come after you," Iron

Wing warned.

Woodenly, Katy sank down beside him. What was the use of fighting, or running away? He would never let her go, not so long as he lived.

She did not protest as his arm went around her shoulders, and suddenly she was crying as if her heart would break.

Iron Wing held Katy while she cried, sorry he had caused her pain. He had not wanted to kill the Frenchmen, knowing that Katy would only hate him the more. He had meant only to sneak into camp and steal her away. Still, he could not grieve because the three men were dead. They were white men, his enemies, as all white men were his enemies.

He held Katy in his arms until she cried herself to sleep.

In the morning, Katy asked Iron Wing to bury Andre and his sons. Already, the vultures were circling overhead, their winged grace belying their awkward clumsiness on the ground. She shuddered to think of her friends being ripped apart by the big scavenger birds, their bodies torn to shreds by wolves and coyotes, until only a few bleached bones remained.

But Iron Wing curtly refused to bury the Frenchmen. Eyes narrowed in jealous anger, he watched Katy grab a shovel from the wagon. Face set in determined lines, she began to dig the graves herself. Iron Wing watched her for several minutes before he grabbed the shovel from her hands and dug a single large shallow hole.

Katy wept softly as Iron Wing dumped the

bodies of the three Frenchmen into the grave and shoveled dirt over them.

Iron Wing left Katy standing beside the grave while he rounded up the horses of the three white men. He quickly saddled one for Katy, dropping lead ropes around the necks of the others. He also took the rifles that had belonged to the Frenchmen, and a couple of warm red blankets.

When he was ready to go, he lifted Katy onto the back of the mare he had saddled for her, then swung aboard his own mount which had been tethered out of sight some yards away. Leading the captured horses, he started for home.

Katy stared after Iron Wing, her mouth set in a grim line. She longed to jab her heels into her horse's sides and make a run for freedom, but she knew it would be futile. Iron Wing would only come after her again and, in truth, she had no desire to try and cross the plains alone again. She lacked both the strength and the knowledge necessary to survive alone in the wilderness. She knew that now.

With a sigh of resignation, she touched her heels to her horse's flanks and set out after Iron Wing. It irritated her that he had not once looked back to see if she was following him.

They traveled in silence for several miles, each lost in thoughts that could not be shared. Katy mourned for Claude and Jean-Paul and Andre, and for the promise of freedom Iron Wing had so rudely snatched from her grasp. Was she never to be free again? Was she forever destined to be his prisoner, a slave to his wants and desires, with no rights or privileges, a chattel with no control over her own fate? The thought weighed heavily on her mind, filling her with despair.

Iron Wing's face was cold and impassive, masking the anger that burned in his soul whenever he recalled the way Katy had willingly gone into the arms of the brown-eyed buffalo hunter. The sight of her tears, shed for the man's death, did little to quench his rage. Jealousy burned hot and bright in Iron Wing's breast as he remembered how willingly Katy had gone into the Frenchman's arms. She had not resisted the white man's touch, or turned away from his kiss. She had not vowed she hated him. Indeed, she had seemed content to stand in his embrace.

It was nearing midday when Iron Wing paused to rest the horses. Dismounting, he handed Katy a strip of jerked venison. Then, turning away from her, he hunkered down on his heels and gazed into the distance, apparently oblivious to her presence.

Katy gnawed at the dried meat absently, perturbed by Iron Wing's silence. He had not spoken to her since early that morning. Damn him! He chased her, killed for her, and then ignored her!

Fired by her anger, she went to stand in front of him, her hands on her hips, her head thrown back. "How did you find me?" she asked, determined to make him speak. "Why did you come home early from the hunt?"

"A snake spooked Yellow Cloud's horse on our third night away from home. The horse pulled free of its tether and ran wild through the camp. In passing, it kicked Crooked Lance and broke his arm. The horse also broke my bow." He shrugged fatalistically. "Since I could not hunt without my bow, I brought Crooked Lance home. Yellow Flower told me you were missing. Your tracks were easy to follow."

Katy and Iron Wing rode in silence the rest of that day and the next. Katy still grieved for Claude and Andre and Jean-Paul, though she knew now that she had not loved Claude, would never have loved him as a woman loved a husband. But he had been a good friend, and she sorely missed his ready smile and his unfailing ability to make her laugh.

Iron Wing remained silent and withdrawn, and his silence weighed heavily on Katy's mind. She knew he was angry with her for running away, and she waited for him to upbraid her, but he remained stubbornly mute, his face impassive.

The afternoon of the third day, they cut the trail of a small party of Indians on the move.

"Crow," Iron Wing remarked, thinking aloud. "They are moving south toward their winter camp."

They saw the smoke early the following morning. Katy looked askance at Iron Wing. Thick black smoke could only mean one of two things: a prairie fire, or a massacre.

Iron Wing drummed his heels against his horse's flanks, putting the stud into a lope. Katy followed reluctantly. Iron Wing would not ride into a prairie fire, and that meant there was likely death and destruction ahead. The thought of viewing any more dead bodies filled Katy with revulsion.

The Crow camp was smoldering when they reached it. Dead Indians, both young and old, lay scattered about like so many broken dolls. Katy could not read trail signs, but she had no trouble figuring out what had transpired. A cavalry patrol had stumbled onto the Indians' overnight camp and had ambushed them at dawn. The soldiers had even killed the dogs. Katy turned away, sickened by the sight and smell of so much death.

Iron Wing's face was grim as they rode out of the Crow camp. "White men!" He spat the words out of his mouth as if they tasted bad. "They have no honor!"

"You're a fine one to talk of honor," Katy retorted sarcastically, "seeing as how you killed three men who had done you no harm."

"I killed them in self-defense, Ka-ty," Iron Wing replied quietly. "And I would kill a dozen more before I let you go."

Katy felt a twinge of guilt. Perhaps, if she had gone quietly away with Iron Wing, Claude and his family would still be alive. It was a thought that haunted her for many days to come.

They were only a mile from the Cheyenne village when Iron Wing reined his horse to a halt and slid to the ground. Lifting Katy from the back of her mount, he pulled a length of rope from his war bag, deftly fashioned a loop in one end, and dropped it around Katy's neck. Using a strip of rawhide, he bound her hands behind her back.

"Why?" Katy asked, bewildered.

"You have shamed me before my people by

running away from my lodge," he answered as he swung aboard his stallion, the loose end of her tether in his hand.

"And now you mean to shame me." Katy's blue eyes flashed defiance. "I shall hate you until the day I die if you drag me into camp like a slave!"

Iron Wing turned the full force of his gaze upon her, causing Katy to quail inwardly, but she kept her head up and forced herself to meet his eyes, unwilling to let him know she was terribly afraid of his anger.

"You already hate me," the warrior reminded her quietly. "You have told me so many times."

"Please don't humiliate me like this," Katy begged, but he turned a deaf ear to her pleas as he urged his mount forward, forcing her to follow along or risk being dragged, choking, over the rough ground.

It was the most humiliating experience of Katy's life. The Indians were too polite to laugh aloud, but their dark eyes danced with amusement when Iron Wing rode into camp with his runaway squaw in tow. Yellow Flower was in the crowd, and Katy's cheeks flamed scarlet as her friend smiled sympathetically then turned away, smothering a grin.

Katy was red-faced with shame when Iron Wing drew rein before his lodge. Dismounting, he threw an arrogant glance at his people, then stalked into the lodge, dragging Katy behind him.

Katy stood meekly inside the doorway, wondering if he would further humiliate her by beating her in public as he had once threatened to do. A part of her longed to strike out at him, to scream her rage and frustration, but the voice of caution warned her to be silent.

After securing the door of the lodge, Iron Wing removed the noose from Katy's neck and tossed the rope aside. He made no move to untie her hands.

"Why, Ka-ty?" he asked gruffly. "Why did you run away?"

"Because I hate you! Because I want to go back to my own people." She spoke slowly and distinctly, and she spoke the truth. Why, then, did the words sound flat in her ears?

Iron Wing sighed. "Have I mistreated you?" he queried. "Have I not given you the freedom to come and go as you please?"

"But I'm still your prisoner. Your slave! I hate it here. And I hate *you!*"

Iron Wing's expression turned from tolerance to anger. Roughly, he grabbed her by the shoulders, his fingers digging painfully into her tender flesh.

"Then I will bear your hatred," he growled. "I will keep you tied inside my lodge night and day if necessary. You are my woman, Ka-ty. You will always be my woman."

Katy winced as Iron Wing's fingers bit deeper into her arms. He had never treated her with anything but tenderness before. No matter how she had reviled him, he had always been patient, gentle. But now he seemed to want to hurt her, to prove, by humbling her with pain, that he was her master.

Lifting her in his arms, Iron Wing carried Katy to his sleeping robes and placed her upon them. Eyes blazing, he stripped off his clout to stand naked before her, his desire evident and throbbing. Katy's bound hands prevented him from removing her dress. Instead, he lifted her skirt, pulling it up over her hips, making Katy feel cheap and degraded, as if she were a whore.

There was no tenderness in him now, no regard for Katy's feelings. She had often accused him of being a savage and that was how he took her—savagely, hurting her so that she cried out with pain and humiliation. His mouth came down hard on hers, bruising her lips as he stifled her cries.

And then it began, the sweet torture that made her body yield to his touch even as her mind screamed her loathing. With malicious delight, Iron Wing aroused Katy until she thought she would go crazy with wanting him. Whispering his name, she begged him to end her torment, but he refused. Again and again, he carried her up, up, only to withdraw his body and lips, until her need for him was more than she could bear.

"Now," she moaned. "Now, now, now!"

But again Iron Wing withdrew. Sitting back on his haunches, his glittering black eyes mocked her need.

"Say it, Ka-ty," he demanded cruelly. "Tell me you want me."

"No! Never!" she gasped, and then sighed as his hands began their sweet torment again. She arched upward as his hands stroked her thighs, her belly, her breasts. Tears of humiliation welled in her eyes as she choked out the words he waited to hear.

"I—want—you."

His eyes never left her face. "Only me?" he demanded.

"Only you."

At last he entered her, his manhood filling her, making her complete as he carried her higher, higher, until fulfillment burst inside her like fourth of July fireworks, drowning her in pleasure beyond description or belief.

# 9

Katy had hoped, from the force of their love-making the night before, that Iron Wing's anger was past. But she was sorely mistaken. He had left her hands tied through the night, and released her bonds only long enough for her to prepare the morning meal, and eat.

In the afternoon, her humiliation continued. Dropping the hated rope around her neck once again, Iron Wing led Katy outside and secured the loose end of the noose around her neck to the punishment post that stood in the center of the camp. Then, taking up his knife and lance, Iron Wing left the village, ostensibly to go hunting.

Katy stared after him in disbelief. Surely he did not mean to leave her tied up? Only enemy prisoners, or seasoned warriors who had violated some serious tribal law, were ever subjected to such treatment.

Knowing it was useless, Katy pulled against the rope binding her wrists together. People passed within inches of her, but they all ignored her, not wanting to add to her disgrace by acknowledging her presence.

An hour passed—two. Katy stared into the distance, her eyes straining for some sign of Iron Wing. Surely he would return soon.

Even he could not be so cruel as to leave her tied up in the hot sun all day!

Another hour passed, each minute seeming even longer than the last. Sweat gathered across Katy's brow and trickled down her neck and face. She fretted over an itch she could not scratch. Another hour crawled by, and she stared longingly at the river, plagued by a thirst such as she had rarely known. But no one offered her a drink of cool water. She was Iron Wing's prisoner, and though she had made friends in the village, they would not interfere between a warrior and his slave.

Katy's arms and legs grew weary; her back began to ache, but she could not sit down. To do so would tighten the noose around her neck.

Tears burned Katy's eyes, but she blinked them back, too proud to let anyone see how truly miserable she was. Had she known the words, she would have cursed Iron Wing soundly, but the few obscenities she knew seemed hopelessly inadequate to express the hatred sizzling in her veins. How she loathed him! She would never forgive him for tormenting her in such a cruel fashion. Never, so long as she lived.

The sun was turning the western sky to flame when Iron Wing rode into the village. Oblivious to the curious eyes of those who gathered around him, he reined his horse to a halt near the punishment post and stepped agilely from his mount. Slipping the noose from Katy's neck, he turned on his heel and walked to his lodge. He did not look back to see if Katy followed him.

Katy stared after Iron Wing, her mind in

114

turmoil. The temptation was strong to run as far away from him as her legs would carry her, but she knew it was useless to try and escape. He would only come after her, and there was no point in making him any madder than he already was. Lifting her chin and squaring her shoulders, she walked to Iron Wing's lodge, her attitude one of proud defiance.

Iron Wing was waiting for her inside his lodge, his arms folded across his chest, his face inscrutable. Katy entered their dwelling with great trepidation, uncertain as to what Iron Wing's mood might be. Was he still angry with her? Did he really intend to keep her hands tied behind her back indefinitely? Already her wrists were sore and swollen from the chafing of the rough hemp. She gazed up at Iron Wing, a mute appeal in her eyes.

"Do you want a drink, Ka-ty?" he asked solicitously, ignoring the question in her eyes.

"No."

One black brow arched inquisitively. She was lying, and they both knew it, but Iron Wing felt a quick admiration for the stubborn pride that kept Katy from admitting it.

"Have you learned anything from this?" Iron Wing queried.

A dozen sarcastic retorts ran through Katy's mind before she replied coldly, "Yes. I've learned to hate you even more than I did before, if that's possible."

An angry fire consumed the admiration in Iron Wing's eyes; a cold black fire that made

115

Katy shiver with apprehension as he slowly pulled his knife from the deerskin sheath on his belt.

"Come to me, Ka-ty."

Katy shook her head, hypnotized by the knife in Iron Wing's hand. Would he use it on her if she continued to defy him?

"Come to me, Ka-ty," he called insistently.

"No," she gasped, hating the way her trembling voice betrayed the fear she was trying so hard to hide. "I will never come to you willingly, or love you."

Iron Wing cocked his head to one side as he threw Katy a mocking grin. "Love?" he muttered sardonically. "Have I ever asked for your love?"

Cheeks flaming, Katy shook her head vigorously, wondering whatever had possessed her to even mention the word. Love was something he could not begin to comprehend.

"I do not need your love," Iron Wing said with a sneer. "I am a warrior."

"Some warrior," Katy scoffed. "Are you as brave with your enemies as you are with one helpless woman?"

Fresh anger narrowed Iron Wing's eyes, making them glitter like chips of polished obsidian. His fingers grew white around the handle of his knife. Forgetting he had drawn it to cut Katy's hands free, he tossed it aside. Her nearness, and the thought that he had almost lost her to another, fired his desire for her. She was like a fever in his blood, a thirst he could not quench. He knew Katy hated him, would always hate him, but he did not care. She was his, and he wanted her more than he had ever wanted anything in his life.

"You are my woman, Ka-ty," he said harshly. "I do not need your love, nor do I need you warm and willing." His mouth descended on hers, blazing a trail of fire as he kissed her cheeks, her eyelids, the soft white curve of her slender neck.

Katy struggled in Iron Wing's grasp, but it was useless with her hands bound behind her back, and his arms strong around her. She uttered a gasp as she felt his manhood rise against her thigh.

Iron Wing laughed triumphantly as Katy's eyes grew dark with hatred. Her hatred never lasted long, and even now the hate was turning to desire, causing her eyes to burn with a soft blue fire as his hands caressed her smooth flesh.

"Hate me all you want, Ka-ty," he taunted softly. "I will be content with that."

In the morning, Iron Wing freed Katy's hands. She moved silently about the lodge, preparing breakfast, resigned to the fact that there was no way to escape from Iron Wing. He had been right all along. She belonged to him, and she would belong to him until the day she died, or until he grew tired of her and traded her away.

Surprisingly, once Katy acknowledged the fact that there was no way to escape from the Indians, life with the Cheyenne grew easier to bear. What could not be changed, must be endured, and Katy decided to stop complaining about her lot in life and make the best of it.

She asked Iron Wing for new hides and

117

refurbished their bedding. She traded some deerskins for a new cook pot and threw away some old utensils that were taking up space in the rear of the lodge.

To pass the time, she made herself a new dress and a pair of moccasions. And then she cut out a new shirt for Iron Wing. She spent long hours painstakingly decorating the back and yoke with dyed porcupine quills, telling herself all the while that she was going to so much trouble simply to have something to do.

She experimented in cooking, and eventually learned to prepare meals that were varied and tasty. She practiced the Cheyenne language, learning all the gestures and nuances so that she could understand what was going on around her and better communicate with the other women.

She took no pride in her accomplishments, experienced no joy in the knowledge she gained, or in the skills she acquired. Cooking, sewing, tidying up the lodge, they were simply tasks to while away the time.

Her relationship with Iron Wing remained unchanged. He was the master, and she was the slave. She obeyed his commands without question, cooked his food, cleaned his lodge, mended his clothes. The one thing she was grateful for was that he no longer seemed to find her desirable. At least he no longer made any attempt to take her to his bed.

Iron Wing spent much of his time with the warriors, leaving Katy to fill her days as best she could. She had said often enough that she hated him, and he believed her. But he could not give her up. Better to have her in his lodge, cold and untouchable, than to set her free and never see her again. There were many men in the tribe who would gladly have bought the captive white woman from Iron Wing and sometimes, when Katy looked at him through eyes which were cold and unforgiving, Iron Wing considered selling her. But the thought of another man bedding Katy was more than Iron Wing could bear. She was his. She would always be his.

Katy spent many hours with Yellow Flower and her son, Laughing Turtle. The boy was four months old now, and growing every day. Brown and chubby as a bear cub, he was a darling child, and Katy loved to hold him and play with him. He was a good-natured baby and rarely cried or fussed except at bath time.

As the days passed, Katy grew increasingly grateful for Yellow Flower's friendship. The Indian woman was unfailingly cheerful, and her buoyant spirits often boosted Katy's sagging morale. Life with the Cheyenne was hard. You could not go to the store in town for cloth when you needed a new dress. Instead, a deer or some other animal had to be killed and skinned. The hair had to be scraped from the hide, and then the hide had to be worked until it was soft and pliable. You couldn't run to the store for a sugar stick when you had a craving for sweets, or for a spool of thread, or a ribbon for your hair. Everything you needed, you made yourself or you did without, unless you were lucky enough to find someone to trade with.

Sometimes, when Katy looked at her hands, hands that had never done anything more difficult then embroider a piece of fancy work until she was taken by the Indians, she wanted to cry. Gone were the smooth white hands she had once been so proud of. Now they were hardened and calloused, the nails broken and uneven. Her creamy complexion was gone, too. Months of living outdoors had darkened her skin to a deep golden brown. When she studied her reflection in the river, she did not notice that her tanned skin and black hair made her eyes glow with a lovely blue fire; she saw only that the fair skin she had once cherished was gone and that, except for the color of her eyes, she looked almost like an Indian herself. And that was frightening.

As time passed, Katy began to miss more and more the small things she had once taken for granted: a glass of cold buttermilk on a hot day, a slice of dark chocolate cake smothered with frosting, a hot bubble bath, sweet-smelling cologne, the touch of silk against her skin, the sound of the mission bell at Mesa Blanca on Sunday morning, Maria singing off-key as she made the beds and dusted the furniture.

"If I ever get home again, I'll never leave," Katy vowed fervently. "And I'll never take anything for granted again. Never!"

The thought of home brought quick tears to Katy's eyes, and she threw herself into the task at hand, determined not to give in to her tears. Crying accomplished nothing, solved nothing. It only made her eyes burn, and her throat ache.

# 10

On a day in early autumn, Katy followed Iron
Wing into the woods. He had decided to go
hunting, and he had decided Katy should go
with him, even though she had no desire to go
along. How long they would be gone would
be up to Iron Wing. If the hunting was good,
they might be gone more than two weeks.

The ground was heavy with gold and red
leaves that rustled loudly as their horses
made their way deeper into the gloomy
forest. Katy spared hardly a glance at her
surroundings as her eyes were drawn again
and again toward the warrior riding ahead of
her. Iron Wing rode straight and tall, his
waist-length black hair hanging loose down
his bronzed back, his long muscular legs
encased in a pair of knee-high moccasins that
Katy had made for him. He carried his
hunting bow in his right hand; a quiver of
arrows was slung over his left shoulder. A
rifle rested in a fringed scabbard under his
right leg. A long-bladed, bone-handled knife
was sheathed in his belt.

Katy grinned as she surveyed his array of
weapons. They were only going hunting, she
thought, amused, not to war.

They rode steadily for several hours,
passing through the forest and climbing high

into the tree-studded hills. Squirrels and jays chattered and scolded them as they passed by. Once a raccoon scurried across their path.

Riding on, Katy was struck anew by the beauty of the land the Cheyenne called home. The sky was a cloudless, vibrant blue, the trees were alive with changing colors of autumn, the air was crisp and cold. The shallow stream they forded was crystal clear, and Katy saw the silver flash of a fish.

Gazing past Iron Wing, she saw a deer outlined between two tall trees. Iron Wing spotted the buck at the same time, and in a single fluid movement he brought his horse to a halt, put an arrow to his bow, and sighted down the shaft.

Katy looked away, not wanting to see the beautiful animal killed. She held her breath, waiting for the hiss of the arrow leaving the bowstring. Instead, she heard Iron Wing gasp. Turning, she saw a red-feathered shaft protruding from the outside of Iron Wing's left thigh. For a moment, Katy thought he had accidentally shot himself and a faint smile played over her lips. How she would love teasing him about his hunting ability, and how the Indians would laugh when they learned of his accident. And she would be sure they learned of it!

She was about to go to his aid when, to her horror, she saw a Crow warrior rise from the brush sixty feet away.

Katy's heart went cold as she saw a second Crow warrior rise to stand beside the first, his bowstring pulled back as he prepared to let an arrow fly.

What happened next seemed to transpire in slow motion. A war cry rose on Iron Wing's lips as he loosed the arrow meant for the deer. The shaft caught the second Crow brave full in the throat, and he died where he stood, a slightly sheepish expression on his paint-streaked face.

The first Crow nocked a second arrow to his bow and let it fly. Within a second of the time the Crow loosed his arrow, Iron Wing's arrow sliced through the air. Katy screamed as the Crow arrow creased Iron Wing's left temple, knocking him from his horse so that he fell heavily on his wounded leg. There was a sharp crack as the arrow already embedded in Iron Wing's thigh broke in half.

Galvanized into action by a sudden fear for her own life, Katy slid from her horse and ran toward Iron Wing. "Get up!" she shrieked, shaking his shoulder. "Iron Wing, please get up!"

When there was no response, she peered anxiously into his face and saw, to her horror, that he was unconscious. Jerking her head up, she saw the Crow moving toward Iron Wing's horse. If only she could reach Iron Wing's rifle before the Crow warrior!

But even as the thought crossed her mind, the Crow brave was pulling the rifle from the scabbard. He threw Katy a knowing grin as he swung the rifle over his shoulder. It was obvious from the glint in his dark eyes that he did not intend to kill Katy, at least not right away.

Katy's eyes darted from the Crow to Iron Wing, who lay unmoving on the ground. Blood seeped from the arrow wound in his thigh, and flowed freely from the gash in his head. He could not help her now.

With a loud cry of anguish, Katy threw herself across Iron Wing's inert body. Shielding her movements with her own form, she pulled Iron Wing's knife from his belt.

She heard the Crow speaking to her as he advanced toward her, and though Katy could not understand his words, there was no mistaking the ribald glitter in his eyes.

Swallowing hard, Katy scrambled to her feet and hurled the knife at the warrior. The weapon, thrown with little skill and not much strength, caught the Crow brave high in the chest near his shoulder. The warrior's expression was more of stunned surprise than alarm as he stared at the blade partially embedded in his chest. The look in his deep-set black eyes quickly changed from lust to anger as he dropped the rifle and yanked the knife from his flesh.

In that instant, Katy dived for the rifle. Scooping it up, she rolled onto her side and fired blindly in the Indian's direction. The bullet caught the startled warrior just under his heart and he fell heavily, his blood soaking into the earth.

The silence following the gunshot seemed very loud. Sobbing, Katy stood up, the rifle clenched tightly in her hands as she looked fearfully from side to side, afraid that more enemy warriors might be lurking in the vicinity. Long minutes passed, and the only sound in the forest was Katy's labored breathing.

When she felt certain there were no more Crow warriors in the area, she went to kneel beside Iron Wing. Dear God, what if he was dead? The thought filled her with pain, but she did not stop to wonder why, she only knew she could not bear the thought of his death. A warm surge of relief washed through her as his eyes fluttered open.

Iron Wing stared up at Katy for a moment, then glanced past her to where the Crow warrior lay sprawled on the ground. A faint smile twitched Iron Wing's lips as his eyes sought Katy's face again.

"You saved my life," he murmured, his voice sounding faintly amused.

"I saved my own life," Katy countered, not wanting to think of the man she had killed. "Keep still."

Rising, she pulled some moss from one of the trees and pressed it over the narrow gash in Iron Wing's forehead to staunch the blood still seeping from the wound. That done, she knelt beside him, contemplating the broken shaft protruding from his thigh. The arrowhead, buried deep in the meaty part of his leg, would have to be removed, and she would have to do it. But knowing what had to be done, even knowing how to go about it, did not mean she was equal to the task. The arrow could not be pulled out. It would have to be driven through Iron Wing's thigh and pulled out the other side. The very thought made her stomach churn. How much easier to hop on her horse and ride away.

Katy glanced at her horse standing passively only a few feet away, and then put the cowardly thought from her mind. Feeling Iron Wing's gaze, she turned to find his dark eyes searching her face.

"Will you leave me now, Ka-ty?" he asked in a voice hoarse and filled with pain. "You have often wished me dead. Here is your chance to see that wish fulfilled."

Katy scowled at Iron Wing, ashamed that he knew exactly what she had been thinking, ashamed that such an uncharitable thought had even crossed her mind. No matter how much she hated him, no matter how she longed to be free of his domination, she could not callously ride off and leave him to die alone.

"I'm not going anywhere," Katy snapped. "And neither are you."

Iron Wing did not answer her, but his dark eyes were filled with doubt.

"That arrow has got to come out," Katy remarked, more to herself than to Iron Wing.

He nodded, his eyes still intent on her face.

"Can you turn on your side so I can get a good hold on the shaft?"

Iron Wing nodded again, grimacing as he shifted his big body onto his right side.

"This is going to hurt," Katy said, stalling for time.

"I have been hurt before," Iron Wing remarked quietly. There was no hint of accusation in his eyes, or in his voice, but Katy flushed guiltily as she vividly recalled the night she had plunged the knife into his shoulder. Looking at Iron Wing, she knew that he, too, was remembering that night.

"Do it, Ka-ty," he said.

With a sigh, Katy took hold of the shaft near the end. One hard push should drive the arrowhead through Iron Wing's thigh and out the other side.

She glanced at Iron Wing once more. His eyes were closed, his hands knotted into tight fists.

Murmuring, "Dear God, please help me," Katy pushed on the shaft as hard as she could, felt the vomit rise in her throat as she felt the slim wooden shaft tear through meat and muscle and flesh.

Iron Wing gasped, shuddering convulsively, as the flint arrowhead tore through his thigh. Sweat broke out across his brow as Katy drew the arrow out of his leg, unleashing a torrent of bright red blood.

Katy let the wound bleed for a moment, hoping the rush of blood would cleanse the wound. Then, using more moss, she packed both holes and bound Iron Wing's leg with the strip of red cloth she wore around her forehead to keep her hair out of her face.

Iron Wing was watching her again, his eyes dark with pain, his face pale. His mouth formed the word "water," but no sound emerged from his throat.

Nodding that she understood, Katy hurried to his horse and removed the waterskin tied around the animal's neck.

Iron Wing drank deeply, and then went limp. Capping the waterskin, Katy removed the blanket from her horse's back and spread it over the unconscious warrior. That done, she gently wiped the sweat from his brow. A sudden rush of tenderness engulfed her as she lifted the blanket and wiped the blood from his leg. Iron Wing moaned softly in his sleep and Katy stood up, blinking rapidly. Why did she suddenly feel like crying?

Gazing up at the sky, she realized it would

soon be dark. Taking up the rifle, she went in search of the Crow ponies. Perhaps the Indians had some food packed on one of their horses. Or more water. From previous experience, she knew that wounded men craved water.

Katy found the Crow horses tethered to a tree some forty feet from where the two warriors had launched their ambush. Apparently they, too, had been hunting, for a freshly killed deer was slung over the withers of one of the horses. A pair of waterskins were draped around the neck of the second horse.

The Crow ponies snorted and shied at Katy's alien scent, but they soon calmed down enough for Katy to lead them to where Iron Wing lay sleeping. Stripping the blankets from the horses, she spread one under Iron Wing. It took all her strength to roll him from side to side, and she was perspiring by the time the blanket was spread beneath him.

The two dead men were next on her list of things to do. Already, flies had swarmed over the corpses. As she was wondering how to dispose of them, she remembered seeing a dry wash a short distance down the hill, and she laboriously dragged the bodies to the wash and pushed them over the side. That done, she covered them with dirt and brush and rocks.

Exhausted, she gathered an armful of wood and carried it back to their campsite. She groaned softly as she dug a shallow pit with Iron Wing's hunting knife and laid a fire, igniting it with a flint she found in Iron

Wing's war bag.

When Iron Wing regained consciousness, it was dark. Katy sat beside him, a blanket draped across her shoulders, his rifle within easy reach. A small fire burned brightly at their feet, its flames dancing over Katy's face and hair.

"Ka-ty."

She turned to face him, her brow furrowed with worry. "Are you hungry?" she asked. "Thirsty?"

Iron Wing nodded, wincing as the slight movement sent a shaft of pain darting through the side of his head.

Katy held the waterskin for him, then handed him a slice of venison she had cooked earlier. Iron Wing chewed the meat slowly, the simple task of eating draining him of what little energy he had.

Katy noticed he ate little of the meat, but he drank a great deal of water. She knew his thirst was caused by the amount of blood he had lost.

"Rest now," she said, laying the waterskin aside.

Iron Wing's eyes searched Katy's face, noting the lines of tension and fatigue around her mouth and eyes, the smudge of dirt on one suntanned cheek.

"Will you be here when I wake up, Ka-ty?"

"Yes."

"Will you?"

"I said yes," Katy snapped. Then, in a softer tone, "I promise."

Satisfied with her reply, he obligingly closed his eyes and was instantly asleep.

Katy remained awake the whole night long,

too uneasy to close her eyes for even a few seconds. Her nerves were drawn tight as a drumhead. Every noise, every drifting shadow, filled her with apprehension as she imagined every wild beast known to man lurking in the dense underbrush, waiting to pounce on her. Visions of Crow warriors skulking nearby, ready to scalp her, or worse, did nothing to put her mind to rest.

Time and again she checked on Iron Wing to make certain he was still breathing. His moans of pain grieved her heart even as they assured her he was still alive. She did not stop to wonder at her concern for his welfare, concern that far surpassed her fear of being alone in the woods late at night.

At last, as dawn began to brighten the sky-line, her eyelids grew unbearably heavy and she closed her eyes and slept.

When Iron Wing awoke an hour later, the first thing he saw was Katy curled up beside him, one slim hand fisted tight around his rifle, the other resting on his arm.

He lay there, watching her, until she woke up several hours later.

Katy blushed self-consciously when she opened her eyes to find Iron Wing staring at her, his expression one of tender affection and admiration.

"You did not leave," he said wonderingly.

"I said I would stay."

A small smile turned up the corners of Iron Wing's mouth. "I did not believe you."

"Are you all right?" Katy stammered, wondering why her stomach was behaving so queerly. "Are you hungry, or anything?" She wished he would stop looking at her like that, as if she had done something wonderful simply by keeping her promise not to leave him.

"I need to relieve myself," Iron Wing answered, trying to rise.

"You shouldn't stand up," Katy admonished.

"I can take care of myself."

"At least let me help you," Katy said, reaching out to take his arm.

"I do not need your help," he retorted, shrugging her hand aside.

"Really?" Katy stood up, her hands fisted on her softly rounded hips as she regarded him through eyes flashing with anger. "Go ahead," she challenged. "Get up so I can laugh when you fall flat on your face."

Iron Wing's eyes narrowed ominously. Mouth set in a determined line, he got to his knees, ignoring the slivers of pain that danced in his head and thigh. Gaining his feet, he stood, swaying slightly, all his weight balanced on his good leg. He knew immediately that Katy had been right. He should not have stood up.

Shaking her head at the ridiculous pride of some men, Katy went to stand beside Iron Wing, her shoulder braced under his left arm, her face turned away as he lifted his breechclout and relieved himself. When he was through, she helped him lie down on the blanket again.

"You might as well face it," Katy said sternly. "You're going to need my help for the next few days, and I intend to give it to you whether you like it or not."

Iron Wing nodded meekly. She was right.

Like it or not, he would have to depend on Katy to take care of him until his strength returned.

The thought of spending another night out in the open made Katy uneasy. After making sure Iron Wing was resting as comfortably as possible, she took up his rifle and scouted the area until she found a small cave near a shallow stream. She spent the next half hour setting up house in the cave. She laid a fire in the back of the cavern where the flames would not be seen. Some green branches tied together with rawhide made a cooking rack. Some venison and herbs added to a pot of water made their dinner. While the soup cooked, she made up a bed for Iron Wing.

When everything was ready, she went back for Iron Wing. He could not mount his horse, and she could not lift him into the saddle and so, step by slow step, they made their way to the cave with Iron Wing leaning heavily on her shoulder for support.

It took thirty minutes to traverse the short distance to the cave, and they were both sweating profusely when they got there. Katy helped Iron Wing into the bed she had prepared for him, then slid to the ground, utterly weary. She felt a fleeting sense of satisfaction as she glanced around. The soup was bubbling, filling the cavern with a delicious aroma. Iron Wing was resting comfortably, the horses were tethered outside.

She longed to close her eyes for just a few minutes but instead she left the cave and returned to the site where the Crow attack had taken place. Carefully, she erased as much of their presence as she could. Then, using a leafy branch, she tried to brush out the tracks that led to the cave. She was sure any warrior worthy of the name would easily be able to follow her sign, but she did the best she could. She wasn't a warrior, after all, just a white woman out of her element.

Back at the cave, she stirred the soup, checked on the horses. Iron Wing was sleeping. Quietly, she touched his forehead. Did it seem hotter than before, or was it her imagination?

When he woke sometime later, she fed him some of the soup. He had little appetite, but he drank deeply from the waterskin, then slept again.

Weary to the bone, Katy went outside to pull some grass for the horses to eat. That done, she returned to the cave, curled up in a blanket, and was asleep as soon as she closed her eyes.


Katy woke with a start. For a moment, she stared at her surroundings, unable to recall where she was, or what had happened to her. Then it came again, a long low wail. Rising quickly, she went to Iron Wing's side. She did not need to touch him to know he was burning with fever. Perspiration dotted his brow, the blanket was tossed aside.

"Iron Wing?"

His eyes fluttered open, but there was no recognition in his dark-eyed stare.

Frightened, Katy covered him again, offered him a drink of water. He gulped the water greedily, then fell back. With a sense of dread, Katy checked the wound in his thigh.

As she had feared, the wound had festered. It was red and swollen, oozing with pus.

She began to shiver convulsively as she picked up Iron Wing's knife and laid it over the fire to heat. The wound would have to be lanced and then cauterized. She moved woodenly, trying not to think of what she had to do.

When the blade was glowing bright red, she took it from the fire. Now that it was sterilized, she waited for it to cool before she inserted the sharp point of the blade into the edge of the wound. Iron Wing groaned softly as a torrent of thick yellow pus drained from the wound. With her fingertips, Katy pressed on the infected area, forcing out more of the thick yellow pus.

When she was certain she had all the pus out of the wound, she washed his thigh with warm water and herbs. Then, drawing a deep breath, she reheated the blade of the knife.

Katy stared at the blade, mesmerized by the white heat. How could she touch that bit of hot metal to Iron Wing's flesh? Taking a deep breath, she glanced at his face. He seemed to be sleeping. She wished he was unconscious so he would not feel the pain.

Abruptly, she sat on his feet, hoping her weight would be enough to hold him down as she laid the glowing blade on the wound. Iron Wing began to thrash about as the heated metal touched his skin. An anguished wail filled the cave and then he fainted. Lifting the blade, Katy turned away, sickened by the odor of singed flesh that rose in her nostrils. It was an awful smell, one she was sure she would never forget.

That night was the longest she had ever known. She bathed Iron Wing's body with cool water as his fever mounted, covered him with the lightest blanket they had so he would not catch a chill, gave him water, and prayed as she had never prayed before. Over and over her heart cried the words. "Please, God, don't let him die. I'll be so good, just don't let him die."

When the chills came, she piled all the blankets on top of him and when he still trembled violently, she slipped under the covers and drew him close. He tossed restlessly until, not knowing what else to do, she began to talk to him. She told him about her childhood in Mesa Blanca, about how her mother had never seemed to love her, about how she had idolized her father. She described the people in the town, smiling as she told him about funny old Mr. Quigly who lived alone in a ramshackle house with thirteen cats and an old red bone hound. She told him about her days in school, and how she had hated having to learn to read and write and cipher. Her tone was soft, soothing, and gradually Iron Wing grew still, calmed by the sound of her voice.

Katy lay beside him until the fever came again and he began to toss wildly, mumbling incoherently. Once she tried to put his arms under the covers, only to have his flailing fist catch her on the side of the jaw. Dazed, she tumbled to the ground. She stayed there for a moment, rubbing her jaw, while stars danced before her eyes. Rising, she covered Iron Wing, careful to stay clear of his flailing arms. His words became clearer and she realized he was reliving his encounter with the grizzly. He cried aloud, and then brought his hand down hard, as if he were driving his knife into the bear. It grieved Katy to see him wracked with pain and fever, lost in a memory that had been hurtful.

Abruptly, he stopped battling the ghost of the bear and his voice grew soft, tender. In spite of herself, Katy leaned forward, her ears straining to hear what he was saying. She heard the name Quiet Water, saw his face twist with rage as the Indian woman scorned his offer of marriage.

Unable to watch the sorrow on his face, Katy called his name. He turned immediately toward her voice, his eyes searching for her. "Ka-ty?"

"I'm here."

He reached for her hand, held it tight as he fell into a deep sleep.

She sat there the whole night long, while her hand grew numb and her body stiff from sitting in the same position. Outside, the night slipped away and morning dawned bright and clear. Unaccountably, she began to weep.

By midmorning, Iron Wing seemed a little improved. His forehead did not seem quite so hot. When he awoke, his eyes were clear. His expression darkened when he saw the purple bruise on the side of her jaw.

"What happened?" he demanded in a raspy voice.

"You hit me."

Iron Wing frowned, not wanting to believe her.

"You didn't mean to," Katy said. "You

were delirious at the time."

"Does it hurt?"

"A little." She waited, but he did not say he was sorry. Perhaps he wasn't, she thought irritably. "Are you hungry?"

Iron Wing nodded, his eyes never leaving her face.

Going to the back of the cave, Katy took a strip of dried venison from the rack and gave it to Iron Wing. He chewed the meat slowly. She was pleased when he ate it all and asked for more. An increased appetite was a good sign, wasn't it? She offered him the waterskin, held his head while he drank.

His dark eyes drew Katy like a magnet. As if she had no will of her own, she laid the waterskin aside and moved into his arms. Gently, he pulled her down beside him, one arm around her shoulders, the other resting lightly across her waist. Once, he touched her bruised jaw with the tips of his fingers and his eyes filled with remorse.

Moments later, they were asleep.

When Katy woke, it was dark. Incredible as it seemed, they had slept through the whole day. Iron Wing was still holding her close. Turning her head, she saw he was watching her. Slowly, he lifted his hand and began to caress the curve of her cheek, her neck, her hair. Gently, so very gently, he kissed her eyes, her nose, her mouth, the bruise on her jaw. He did not speak, and she did not protest when, with slow deliberation, he removed her dress, his eyes adoring her naked body, his mouth paying homage to the silken flesh that invited his touch.

Katy returned his kisses, feeling all her senses come alive as his hands and mouth lingered over her bared skin. She gloried in the smoothness of his taut skin and the play of muscles beneath her hands. His flesh was warm to the touch, whether from fever or passion or both she could not say.

Iron Wing's breath caught in his throat as Katy's hand moved down his chest, lower, lower. He swallowed hard as she boldly removed his clout, groaned with pleasure as her hand closed around his turgid manhood.

Like a drowning man, he clung to her, reveling in her touch. Her hair was soft against his chest, her skin smooth and warm like a sun-ripened peach. Ignoring the pain in his wounded leg, he rose over her, seeking the shelter of her womanhood. Katy received him gladly, and then she was adrift in a sea of passion, drowning in waves of ecstacy.

Katy could not meet his eyes in the morning. How could she ever face him again after last night? She had gone to him willingly, allowing him to make love to her, and felt no regret. What was happening to her? Why did she feel so happy, so elated, when what she should be feeling was disgust and self-contempt.

Murmuring that she had to go out and check the horses, Katy almost ran out of the cave. It was a gorgeous day, bright and clear. Untying the horses, she led them to the stream to drink, then tethered them where they could graze. That done, she went back to the stream to bathe.

The water was cold, yet invigorating, and

138

she swam for a long time. The trees were turning color, the leaves going from dark green to gold and red and orange. It was a beautiful sight to behold.

Sometime later, feeling refreshed, she returned to the cave. She could feel Iron Wing's eyes on her back as she checked his wound. To her untrained eye, it appeared to be better. At least it was no longer angry and red and the swelling had gone down.

Iron Wing slept most of that day.

The next few days were different from anything Katy had ever known. For the first time in her life, she was completely responsible for another human being. And yet she felt equal to the task. She had proved she could do whatever had to be done, no matter how distasteful the task.

Iron Wing slept a good deal, leaving Katy to pass the time as best she could. She noticed that, even asleep and wounded, he exuded an aura of strength and power. His face was strong and handsome, his body lean and well-muscled, as near to perfection as a human male could be. Looking at him, she could find no fault in his appearance. And yet she could not help wondering why, of all the men in the world, it had to be a heathen savage who made her blood run hot and her heart pound like thunder. Why did this particular man have the ability to arouse her simply by taking her hand?

Reaching out to brush his hair from his forehead, she wondered, not for the first time, why he had never married. There were many Cheyenne maidens who found him desirable. Of course, she knew all about

Quiet Water and how she had rejected Iron Wing, but that had been years ago. Surely his pride could not have been so badly damaged that he had never longed for a wife and children. Surely one rejection could not have turned him against all women of his tribe.

The question lurked in the back of Katy's mind all the next day and when Iron Wing woke up, just before dusk, Katy put the question to him.

"Why?" she asked. "Why aren't you married?"

Iron Wing regarded her through eyes gone cold and hard. "You must know why," he said tonelessly. "Surely Yellow Flower or one of the other women told you about Quiet Water."

"Yes, they told me, but that doesn't explain why you never took another woman to your lodge. I know several who would willingly share your life."

Surprise flickered in Iron Wing's eyes, followed by an expression of genuine disbelief.

Watching him, Katy realized he had no idea that the women of the tribe found him attractive. Could it be that he still saw himself as he had been immediately after his encounter with the grizzly, when his scars were fresh and ugly? Head cocked to one side, Katy studied the faint scar that marred his cheek. Didn't he realize the scar was hardly noticeable, that, if anything, it enhanced his rugged good looks? She felt a queer tug at her heart as she looked at him. He was far and away the most handsome of men. Often, at the river, he was the main topic of conversation among the unmarried women. They spoke highly of his ability as a warrior and a hunter, of his wisdom in council, of his achievements in battle. But mainly they discussed the wide span of his shoulders, the powerful muscles that rippled in his bronzed arms and legs. They admired the way he walked, the way he talked, his voice deep and resonant, the way he sat on a horse. A few speculated openly on what it would be like to be his woman and share his bed. Many of the women had tried to attract his interest, but all had failed.

"It's true," Katy said, wanting to convince him that she spoke the truth. "I've heard the young women talking about you. They have only good things to say."

"I do not believe you," Iron Wing muttered, remembering how Katy had gazed at him with revulsion the first time they met. It did not occur to him that what he took for revulsion had actually been fear.

Katy regarded him silently for a moment. Had she detected a note of uncertainty in his voice? Did he want to believe her? Slowly, an idea blossomed in the back of Katy's mind, and she pondered it carefully. Perhaps, if she could convince Iron Wing that the women of his tribe found him attractive, he would let her go home to her own people.

"Well, it's true whether you believe it or not," Katy retorted, unconsciously fidgeting with the folds of her skirt. "Blue Willow Woman and Wildflower and Shy Eyes have all made comments about you, about how they would be honored to share your lodge." Katy paused, bewildered by the sudden sinking sensation in the pit of her stomach when she thought of another woman making her home in Iron Wing's lodge, cooking for him, caring for him. Doggedly, she went on. "Why don't you spend some time with them when we return to the village if you don't believe me?"

Iron Wing gazed steadily at Katy, weighing her words. And then he grinned crookedly. "It will not work, Ka-ty. You will not persuade me to seek a wife among the Cheyenne. And if, by chance, one of the maidens should catch my eye and I decide to marry her, I still would not let you go. You are my woman, Ka-ty. You will always be my woman."

Katy sighed heavily. She would never convince him that she was telling him the truth, and he would never willingly release her. Whether he took one wife or twenty or none, he would not let his captive go free.

"Ka-ty?"

She glanced up slowly, too depressed to argue further, or insist that she was not his woman.

"I am grateful for what you have done. I owe you my life."

"If you're really grateful, you can prove it by letting me go home."

"I cannot," Iron Wing said softly.

He sounded almost sorry, Katy thought, bemused. But that was silly. He had never been sorry for anything.

Katy fell asleep early that night, and sleeping, began to dream that she was alone beside a still pool. Staring into the water, she studied her reflection, pleased with what she saw. Her skin was a soft golden brown, her eyes were as blue as the sky above, her hair as black as the wing of a raven. Gradually, her smile turned to horror as her skin grew stained with black and yellow war paint. Her hair sprouted two eagle feathers, and her eyes grew dim and lifeless . . . as lifeless as the eyes of the Crow warrior she had killed. A sob rose in her throat as the pool at her feet turned to blood, and then the sob became a scream as blood poured out of her mouth in a scarlet torment.

"Ka-ty. Ka-ty!"

The sound of Iron Wing's voice and the touch of his hand shaking her shoulder pulled Katy from her nightmare. Groggy and confused, she sat up, feeling the tears streaming down her cheeks. "Oh, God," she sobbed brokenly, "I killed a man."

With a great effort, Iron Wing sat up and put his arm around Katy's shoulders. Wordlessly, she pressed her face against his chest, seeking the solid strength of his body as she vented her sorrow and remorse. She had killed a man, and his death would haunt her as long as she lived. No matter that it had been self-defense. No matter that the Crow would have killed Iron Wing as well. The fact remained that she had taken a human life.

"Do not weep, Ka-ty," Iron Wing whispered, his lips moving against her hair. "Do not weep, for it was a brave thing you did."

Iron Wing's voice was wonderfully soothing and Katy's sobs gradually subsided as, in a soft tone, he told her of the first time he had killed a man, a Pawnee warrior who had been part of a raiding party. It was no small thing to take a life, Iron Wing remarked sympathetically, for all life was sacred, but there was no shame in defending one's self from injury, no reason for remorse when you killed the enemy in battle.

Katy listened to his words intently. What Iron Wing said did not take the horror from what she had done, but they did take the sting out of the deed. This was a hard land, and only the strong survived. Had she been less brave, the two of them would now be lying dead in place of the two Crow warriors.

With a small sigh, Katy closed her eyes and felt herself begin to relax. It was so comforting, to be held in Iron Wing's strong arms, to know he understood how she felt, to know he was proud of her. Feeling safe and content, she fell asleep in his arms. The dead Crow warrior did not disturb her dreams again.

At the end of two weeks, Iron Wing felt strong enough to make the journey down the mountain.

The two Crow ponies, and the Crow scalps dangling from Iron Wing's belt, caused considerable excitement when they rode into the village. The thought of those two scalps made Katy sick to her stomach. Iron Wing had insisted on taking them even though it meant taking them from men who were dead and buried. Katy knew scalping an enemy was more than just to take a trophy of a kill. It had to do with the Cheyenne religion and their belief that a warrior who was scalped in this life would be forever bald in the afterlife.

The men of the tribe swarmed around Iron Wing as he drew rein before his lodge, eager to hear the story behind the scalps and the wound he had received.

Later that evening there was a celebration to honor Iron Wing's victory over the enemy. Before the dancing began, Iron Wing recounted their adventure in the hills. With pride, he told of how Katy had killed one of the Crow warriors, and how she had cared for him as ably as any Cheyenne woman. He spoke of her courage in removing the arrow from his leg, and how she had stayed by his side to protect him.

When Iron Wing finished his tale, he removed an eagle feather from his hair and handed it to Katy. She had killed a man in battle and was thus entitled to wear the feather in her hair if she so desired. It was a great honor, one few women ever achieved.

Katy never wore the feather; it was such a heathen symbol and commemorated an event she would rather forget, but she was proud of it just the same.

# 11 WINTER
## 1874

Winter came to the Dakotas in a violent
outburst of rain and thunder. Lightning
slashed across the sky in great jagged bolts
that threatened to rip the heavens apart. It
was scary, Katy thought, to lie in bed in the
dark of night while the thunder rumbled
across the sky, and the wind and the rain
hammered against the lodge skins like angry
fists.

It was a little better when the snow came,
although the thick white blanket that covered
the ground made traveling long distances impossible. Still, bundled up in furs against the
frosty cold, it was possible to go outside.
Sometimes, when the sun broke through the
lowering gray clouds, the snow sparkled with
a dazzling brightness that was almost blinding. Iron Wing made Katy a pair of snow-
shoes to make walking easier for her.

Many activities were sharply curtailed in
the winter, but one clear day several of the
older boys made sleds out of buffalo ribs, and
soon the whole camp was engrossed in racing
down the long hill located behind the village.
The sleds provided a welcome diversion for
adults and children alike. Late in the afternoon,
the warriors began challenging each other to
see who could get down the hill the fastest.

146

There was a great deal of gambling, several crashes, and some good-natured grumbling. All in all, it was a pleasant day for everyone.

As the weather grew more severe, there was no time for play. Life became a constant struggle for survival as the people fought against the wildly raging elements. Katy soon tired of jerky and pemmican, but at least they had food and shelter. .

As January passed into February, food began to grow scarce. Katy was horrified when several old men and women bid their families farewell and walked out into the snow-covered hills to die, sacrificing their lives so that their children and grandchildren might have more to eat.

Horses were culled from the herd and killed for meat. When Katy asked why all the horses weren't killed for food, Iron Wing explained that a few of the hardier animals were always spared because they would be needed for the spring buffalo hunt, and for moving the village when the time came. Not only that, but the Crows would be out raiding as soon as the snow melted, and the warriors needed horses to ride in battle.

Katy thought it barbaric to let people starve when there was meat available, but Iron wing assured her that the horses were necessary to ensure the survival of the tribe. It was, he told her dispassionately, the law of the plains that the old and the weak died so that the strong might survive. Dogs, too, found their way into the stew pot, until there were only a handful of scrawny puppies left in camp.

As the days went by, Katy learned that Iron

Wing had spoken the truth. The very old and the very young suffered the most from the cold and the meager rations. Yellow Flower's baby sickened and died. It was a terrible thing to see so many people dying, but what was most disturbing to Katy was the way the Indian women displayed their grief. Katy watched in horror as Yellow Flower hacked off her beautiful hair, and then slashed her arms with a knife.

The baby's funeral took place on a cold and rainy day. Katy wept softly as the baby she had grown to love was wrapped in a deer hide and placed atop a tiny scaffold on a lonely hill. A favorite toy was left beside the child's body. A young horse was killed and left at the foot of the scaffold so the infant warrior might ride in comfort to the place of spirits. A small bundle of precious food was placed beside the child's head to provide nourishment for the long journey.

Katy wept all that day, weeping for Laughing Turtle, who had died too young, for Yellow Flower, who would not be comforted, and for herself. She had never spent much time pondering her own mortality, but now, with so many people dying, Katy was suddenly very much aware that she, too, might die in the wilderness. For weeks, she was tormented by nightmares in which she saw Iron Wing sewing her wasted body into a deer hide and leaving it on a scaffold atop a windblown hill.

More and more scaffolds were raised against the sky as the weeks passed. There were days on end when going outside was virtually impossible. Iron Wing spent his time making arrows, or honing his knife, or simply sitting cross-legged before the fire, his handsome face impassive, his thoughts obviously far away.

Katy often studied the man who had become the ruling influence in her life, wondering what made him so eternally sure of himself, so indomitable. Nothing seemed to bother him. He endured the cold and the hardships of life without complaint. When their food began to run out, he often went hungry so that Katy might have something to eat.

Katy wished fervently that she possessed Iron Wing's inner strength to sustain her, but she did not. She hated being trapped inside the lodge. She hated being cold and hungry all the time. She hated everything about the Cheyenne way of life and longed for the comfort of her mother's house, comfort she had once taken for granted as her due. How grateful she would be now if she could just sleep in her own soft bed for one night. How wonderful to be able to curl up in a big chair by the fireplace in the parlor and sip a cup of hot chocolate. She even missed the sight of her mother's stern countenance.

In the long hours when there was little to do but stare into the leaping flames, Katy longed for a book to read to pass the time, she who had once hated reading more than anything else.

Because she was bored and homesick, she began to nag Iron Wing to take her home, even though she knew travel was impossible.

But Iron Wing turned a deaf ear to her nagging. "You are my woman," he replied time and time again, as if that were the answer to everything.

One cold day in March, Katy turned to Iron Wing and asked, "Where did you learn to speak English so well?"

Iron Wing regarded Katy with some surprise. She had rarely asked him any personal questions. Sometimes he thought she tried to pretend he did not exist.

"In prison." He answered her question sharply, his face empty of expression.

"Prison!" Katy exclaimed. "Where? When?"

"Ten years ago, in one of the white men's forts."

Katy stared at Iron Wing in stunned silence. She didn't know how old he was, but she didn't think he could be much more than twenty-five or twenty-six. Ten years ago he would have been a young boy.

"Why were you in a jail?" she asked when her initial astonishment had passed.

"It is a long story."

"The day is long, too," Katy retorted. "I have plenty of time, and little amusement."

"I am sure this will amuse you," Iron Wing remarked bitterly. Then turning from her, he stared into the fire, his eyes growing dark with the memory. "It was in the spring," he began slowly. "I was fourteen, and eager to count my first coup. Tall Buffalo and I were both novices that year, out on our first war party. We were after some Crow who had raided our pony herd, but when the leader of our war party spotted some soldier coats camped in a coulee, he decided white scalps would be better than red.

150

"It was a foolish decision. We lost many of our young men that day. I was shot off my horse during the battle and knocked unconscious. When I came to, I was tied up in one of the white man's wagons. The soldiers took me to their fort and locked me in the stockade.

"A missionary lady was staying at the fort at the time. The soldiers were going to hang me, but she argued that I was just a child. She persuaded the other women in the fort to go to the commanding officer and plead for my life, and he finally relented and said I should live."

Iron Wing laughed bitterly. "They wouldn't let me out of their jail, though, because I was a savage and even though I was not a proven warrior, they were all afraid of me. All but the missionary lady. She came to see me every day. She cut my hair and dressed me in the clothes of a white man. And she taught me to speak the white man's tongue.

"They kept me in jail for eight months, until the missionary lady convinced the commanding officer that I was civilized enough to live in her house. I ran away the first night."

"It must have been hard for you, being a prisoner for such a long time."

"Yes."

"It's hard for me, too," Katy said, her eyes darkly accusing.

"You are my woman. It is not the same."

"No, it's not the same," Katy snapped. "It's worse!"

Their eyes met and held across the fire, Katy's as blue as a summer sky, Iron Wing's as black as ten feet down.

"I want to go home!" Katy flung the words at him. "I want to see my mother. I want to live with my own people."

"No. You are my woman."

Always the same answer, Katy thought hopelessly. It was futile to argue with him. What did he care if she was homesick? Home . . . She sighed wistfully as she recalled the soft rolling hills, the fat, white-faced cattle, the young vaqueros who had teased her and laughingly called her "the little princess." She thought longingly of her bedroom, all done in soft blue, and of her warm feather bed and crisp linen sheets. Of the dozens of dresses and hats and shoes she had once taken for granted. Now, she would have given anything to sleep in her own bed instead of beneath a furry robe, to bathe in a tub of scented hot water instead of a kettle of melted snow, to wear a velvet gown instead of an ankle-length dress fashioned of animal skins.

Feeling lost and alone, she began to weep softly, the tears rolling down her cheeks like fat raindrops. She made no effort to wipe the tears away, just sat there, crying harder and harder.

Compassion stirred in Iron Wing's breast. She was so young, so beautiful. He would willingly give her anything her heart desired; anything but her freedom.

On silent feet, he skirted the fire and knelt before her. There was no anger in his eyes now, only a smoldering hunger. Reaching out, he wiped away her tears with the tips of his fingers.

"Ka-ty."

His voice was husky with longing and when Katy met his eyes, she felt a shiver of anticipation run through her. She knew what that look meant. She had seen it, and dreaded it, countless times before.

Iron Wing's hand caressed Katy's cheek, moved down the soft curve of her throat. Leaning forward, he kissed her, his mouth gently coaxing.

A thrill of excitement raced down Katy's spine as Iron Wing's arms drew her close. For once, she did not fight him. He had not held her for a long time, and she was surprised to find she had missed having his arms around her. His chest was hard, as unyielding as stone, and yet so very comforting. His mouth was moving across her face and neck, lightly kissing every inch of her flesh, pleasuring her in a way that left her weak with wanting.

But she had fought him too hard and too long to surrender without at least a token show of resistance, and so she murmured, "I hate you," as her arms twined around his neck, the words sounding more like a caress than a curse.

Somehow, she was lying naked beneath him, her arms pulling him down, her thighs parting to receive him. His skin was smooth beneath her hands, his hair soft across her breasts, his mouth like fire against her naked flesh.

"Hate me, Ka-ty," Iron Wing whispered thickly. "Hate me some more."

# 12 *SPRING 1875*

It seemed like the winter would last forever, but eventually the rains stopped and the snow began to melt, revealing tender shoots of grass. The sky turned a brilliant, breathtaking blue, the river ran high between its banks. Almost overnight, the trees were clothed in bright green leaves and wildflowers bloomed on the hillside. The horses that had been spared began to grow fat on the lush grass. Baby birds chirped in the trees, leggy foals ran alongside their mothers, puppies wobbled through camp, always underfoot.

Katy spent long hours outside, reveling in the warmth of the sun on her face and arms. How wonderful to be able to go outside without bundling up in a heavy fur robe and fur leggings just to keep from freezing.

The first day Iron Wing came home with a rabbit, she almost cried for joy. Fresh meat at last! She skinned the buck quickly, expertly, cooked it over a low fire with infinite care, served it with wild onions and squash, and congratulated herself on the best dinner she had ever prepared.

The medicine man, Sun Dreamer, consulted his omens and proclaimed that the next day would be favorable for the move to their summer camp. This announcement occasioned great excitement, as the summer camp in the hills of Montana was a favorite place of the Cheyenne.

Yellow Flower came early the following morning to show Katy how to dismantle the lodge and fold the skins. The covers, along with the lodge poles, were placed on a travois for transport to their new camp.

Katy was amazed that anything could be accomplished in the midst of such chaos, but in a short time all the lodges were down, belongings were packed, and everyone was ready to go.

Now Katy saw the wisdom in sparing some of the horses. They pulled the heavy travois loaded with the lodge and camp possessions. They carried the Indians who were too sick or too old to make the long trek on foot. Everyone else walked, except the warriors. Mounted on their painted and feathered war ponies, they rode beside the caravan, keeping a watchful eye peeled for their longtime enemy, the Crow.

Katy saw Bull Calf walking with a group of young boys. He had grown at least a foot since she had first seen him. Next year he would take his place with the novice warriors. Already, he possessed the arrogant mien of a seasoned brave.

Feeling her gaze, Bull Calf waved at Katy, then went red around the ears when the other boys began to tease him.

Katy looked for Yellow Flower, and saw her friend standing beside Tall Buffalo. Yellow Flower smiled faintly as Katy joined them.

"Are you ready to go?" Yellow Flower asked.

Katy shrugged. "I guess so." She glanced at the Indians moving across the plains, and then at the place where Iron Wing's lodge had stood only an hour ago. Nothing remained now but a pile of cold ashes, and the vague outline of the lodge.

Tall Buffalo gave Yellow Flower's hand a squeeze before he vaulted onto his horse and rode off to join the other warriors. Yellow Flower's eyes followed her husband as she and Katy fell in behind the last of the women and children. The Cheyenne chief, Little Eagles Flying, rode at the head of the caravan.

Laughter filled the air as the Cheyenne left the site of their winter camp behind. Moving to their summer camp was always a time for rejoicing. Soon they would have fresh buffalo meat. The berry bushes would bloom, the wild fruits and vegetables would ripen, and there would be full bellies and good times for everyone.

Children ran back and forth along the line, shouting and giggling as they played tag. Mothers nursed their young as they walked along. The old ones dozed, lulled to sleep by the noise and the rocking motion of the horses.

Katy walked beside Yellow Flower, grumbling to herself because she had to lead a travois pony while Iron Wing rode in comfort. She could see him just ahead, mounted on his big spotted stallion. He rode easily, as if he and the horse were a single being. He was clad only in a brief clout and ankle-high moccasins, and Katy marveled anew at the aura of strength and confidence that surrounded him. More and more she had noticed the other warriors seeking his advice. Even Little Eagles Flying respected Iron Wing's counsel.

Katy felt an odd flutter of excitement in the pit of her stomach as she studied the powerful muscles that rippled across Iron Wing's back and shoulders. She thrilled at the span of his chest, at the muscles corded in the long brown legs that grasped the stud's spotted flanks, and then felt her cheeks grow hot as she recalled the possessive way his arms tightened around her in the middle of the night when the lodge was dark and the touch of his hands worked their magic on her all-too-willing flesh.

Iron Wing turned to speak to Tall Buffalo, and Katy grudgingly admitted that he had a strong, handsome face, and a proud profile. She did not want to admire him, did not want to be aroused by his touch, but she could not help herself.

The first day passed uneventfully. Katy was almost asleep on her feet when they finally halted for the night, and she fell into her sleeping robes, exhausted, immediately after dinner.

The afternoon of the second day, they met a large number of Sioux who were also heading for Montana. The Sioux and the Cheyenne were longtime allies, and they stopped to talk, exchanging news and gossip. There were many white men crossing the plains, the Sioux said. Soldier-coats with big guns mounted on wagons. Several small

157

Arapahoe villages located near the mouth of the Tongue River had been attacked without provocation, the people killed, their lodges burned to the ground.

Katy paid little attention to the Sioux. Instead, she went to sit beside Yellow Flower, who was resting in the shade of a gnarled, fire-blackened pine tree. Yellow Flower was still grieving for her son. She rarely laughed any more, and her dark luminous eyes were always sad.

Katy was wondering what she could say to lift her friend's sagging spirits when she felt someone watching her. Glancing sideways, Katy noticed a Sioux warrior gazing intently at her. He was of medium height, with a barrel chest and sloping shoulders. His skin was dark copper; his black hair was worn in two braids, a single eagle feather his only decoration. Something in the way the warrior looked at her made Katy nervous and she began talking to Yellow Flower about the new dress she was making, but Yellow Flower was not listening.

Katy glanced over her shoulder to see what was holding Yellow Flower's attention, and felt a chill creep along the back of her neck. The Sioux warrior who had been staring at her was arguing with Iron Wing. Katy could not make out their words, but when the Sioux brave gestured in her direction, Katy felt a premonition of danger.

Iron Wing shook his head one last time, and then stalked over to Katy. "What did you say to Lame Calf Running?" he demanded angrily.

"I didn't say anything to him," Katy

retorted, annoyed by his accusing tone. "Why?"

"He wants to buy you. He offered me twenty ponies."

"Buy me?" Katy repeated, baffled. "Why would he want to buy me?"

"He said you smiled at him and indicated you would be willing to share his lodge."

"I never . . . I didn't," Katy sputtered, astonished by his accusation. "Ask Yellow Flower."

"The man is lying," Yellow Flower stated calmly. "Katy never spoke to him. She has been with me the whole time."

"I believe you," Iron Wing said gruffly.

"Oh, so you believe her," Katy exclaimed irritably. "Why didn't you believe me?"

Iron Wing's eyes were cold as ice when he looked at her. "Why should I believe you?" he asked harshly. "You have made it known many times that you are not happy in my lodge. Perhaps you think life in a Lakota lodge would be better than living with me."

"Perhaps it would be!" Katy snapped.

"Perhaps," Iron Wing sneered. "But you will never know."

"I will give you thirty ponies," Lame Calf Running said, coming up behind them.

Iron Wing whirled around, his eyes glittering savagely. "She is *my* woman!" he roared. "Mine! And she is not for sale at any price."

Lame Calf Running drew himself up to his full height. He was a proven warrior, a man accustomed to having his own way, to taking what he wanted. And he wanted the white woman. His eyes went over her in a long lingering glance. Her skin was smooth, unlined by age. Her figure was full and feminine, and his hands itched to stroke the curve of her breasts. He would not rest until she was his.

"I will fight you for her," Lame Calf Running declared. Taking a step back, he reached for the knife sheathed on his belt.

"To the death?" Iron Wing asked, drawing his own blade.

"To the death," the Sioux agreed.

Katy shook her head, stunned by the sudden turn of events. "No!" she cried. "Stop!"

But it was too late. Already, the two warriors were in a crouch, circling each other warily. A crowd gathered quickly around them, the people standing silent as statues. This was no contest of skill, but a fight to the death.

Lame Calf Running was a few years older than Iron Wing, heavier, and very sure of himself. Among his own people, there was no warrior better with a knife. His mouth curved in an arrogant grin as he lashed out at his opponent. His blade, long and thin and made for fighting, sliced a wicked gash across Iron Wing's rib cage. There was a low murmur of approval from the watching Sioux as their warrior drew first blood.

Iron Wing's eyes glittered with a cold fire. Intent on the other man, he did not hear the whisper of the crowd, did not feel the knife pierce his flesh.

Katy watched in growing horror as the two men circled each other like angry dogs.

Knives flashed in the sunlight, and only the harsh scrape of metal against metal and the soft scuffle of mocassined feet broke the heavy stillness. Lame Calf Running hurled himself at Iron Wing, gambling everything on a quick lunge, his blade poised to rip into Iron Wing's taut belly. It was a maneuver that had worked countless times before. But Iron Wing stepped nimbly aside, pivoting on the ball of his foot. His right arm came down in a wide arc as he buried his knife to the hilt in the Sioux warrior's back.

Lame Calf Running grunted heavily as he fell face down in the dirt. He shuddered convulsively, his eyes on Katy's face, and then he lay still.

Katy turned away, sick at heart to think a man had been killed because of her.

Iron Wing jerked his knife from the dead man's flesh. Sweat poured down his face and chest, mingling with his blood. His black eyes were wild as he faced the crowd.

"Are there others among the warriors of the Lakota who would take my woman from me?" he challenged.

A few of the Sioux braves looked away, others shook their heads. No complaints were raised as the body of Lame Calf Running was carried away.

As quickly as the crowd had gathered, it dispersed. Minutes later, the Sioux were gone.

Katy stared at the bright red blood dribbling from Iron Wing's side. It was not a deep cut, but it needed bandaging. She took a step forward, intending to bind the wound with the sash from her dress, but Iron Wing refused her help.

"Are you sorry, Ka-ty?" he asked angrily. "Sorry it is not Lame Calf Running who stands before you?" His eyes were intent upon her face as he waited for her answer.

Confusion filled Katy's mind. Was she sorry Iron Wing was still alive? Could she bear it if it was Iron Wing lying dead in the dirt, his masculine strength forever stilled, his ebony eyes cold and empty of life? In truth, she did not know, and she mumbled, "Yes . . . no, I don't know," and then fell silent.

"I know," Iron Wing said quietly. He looked at Katy for a long moment, his eyes mirroring a deep hurt that had nothing to do with the wound in his side. "I think it would give you much pleasure to see me lying dead at your feet."

Abruptly, he turned and walked away from her, his right hand pressed against the still-bleeding wound in his side.

Speechless, Katy stared after Iron Wing, watching as he mounted his spotted stallion and rode to the head of the caravan. In the back of her mind, she saw him as he had looked while fighting the Sioux, his face twisted savagely, his eyes dark and menacing. Never had he looked more dangerous, more like the savage she so often accused him of being. And then that image was wiped away, replaced by the haunting look in his eyes when he accused her of being sorry he was still alive. Did he care for her after all? Was it affection for her that made him refuse to give her the freedom she desired? The thought filled her with a pleasant warmth.

Moments later, they were on the move again.

# 13

The summer camp of the Cheyenne was truly a beautiful place. Game was plentiful in the wooded hills, wild fruits and vegetables were abundant, a wide clear river provided fresh water. And over all loomed the Big Horn Mountains. Though they had been in their new camp less than a week, it looked as though they had been there forever. Each lodge stood in its accustomed place, with Chief Little Eagles Flying's lodge nearest the center.

And life went on, the same as before. In the morning, Katy gathered wood for the fire, fresh water for cooking and drinking. She shook out their sleeping robes, prepared breakfast, and tidied up the lodge. In the afternoon, she went with the women to gather nuts and berries, and more wood, if necessary. She mended their clothes, tanned the hides Iron Wing brought her. In the evening, she made up the bed, prepared dinner, and accompanied Iron Wing to the river to bathe. Katy would have preferred to bathe in the morning, but Iron Wing enjoyed the river just after dusk, so that was when they bathed. In truth, it was not a bad life, but Katy would not admit it to anyone, not even herself.

She was sitting outside Iron Wing's lodge one bright summer morning when Tall Buffalo, Bull Calf, and a dozen other braves rode into camp leading four captive white men.

Katy watched with interest as the four men, all soldiers, were tied to four of the cottonwood trees that grew along the northern edge of the camp. The men struggled valiantly, but they were out-numbered and quickly subdued.

Katy stared hard at the men. She had not seen another white person for so long that it seemed odd to see hair and eyes that weren't black or dark brown; stranger still to see a man with a beard. One man, a sergeant, had blond hair and a bright red moustache. Another had brown hair and light eyes; the third was bald, but he wore a handlebar moustache and a full beard. The last prisoner was just a boy, no more than sixteen or seventeen.

There was a good deal of excitement as the Indians began to gather around the captives, reviling them in the Cheyenne tongue. Some of the women poked the prisoners with sharp sticks, shouting with glee when they drew blood.

Shocked and disgusted by such unnecessary cruelty, Katy went into Iron Wing's lodge, her mind awhirl. Were those four men all that was left of a larger group? Perhaps there were other soldiers in the area. Perhaps they were searching for her!

Towards evening, Katy left the lodge and strolled casually toward the prisoners. No one paid any attention to her. Iron Wing was visiting Tall Buffalo. Most of the women were busily preparing the evening meal, or tending their children.

The four white men glared at Katy as she approached them, thinking she was just another squaw come to torment them. The bald man spat at Katy, and she drew back, confused, until she realized that, with her black hair, sun-browned skin, and Indian garb, the soldiers had mistaken her for a Cheyenne.

"Listen, please," Katy whispered in English. "I am a captive, as you are."

"My God," breathed the Sergeant. "She's a white woman."

"Yes." Katy glanced nervously over her shoulder. "Are there other soldiers nearby? Will they come looking for you?"

"No. Damned redskins took us by surprise. They killed the others. We're all that's left."

"Lady, cut us free," begged the bald headed man.

"I can't. Not now." Katy smiled as an idea struck her. "If I can free you, will you take me away with you?"

The Sergeant grinned broadly. "Shit, little lady, if you can get us out of here while we've got our hair, we'll take you anywhere you want to go."

Katy smothered the happy laughter bubbling in her breast. Soon she would be free! It was almost more than she could bear.

"I'll be back later, when everyone is asleep," Katy promised, and hurried back to Iron Wing's lodge before she was missed.

Dinner was a tense meal that night. Katy was on edge the whole time, and she ate without tasting anything. So absorbed was she with her thoughts and plans, she did not notice Iron Wing's speculative gaze, and when he sat back to smoke his pipe, she quickly put the dinner things away, then crawled into bed, pleading a headache.

She pretended to be asleep when Iron Wing crawled in beside her. Nerves humming with excitement, she forced herself to lie still until she was certain Iron Wing was asleep. Lying there, she felt a twinge of apprehension as she contemplated freeing the prisoners. It had seemed such an easy task in the light of day. She would cut them free while the village slept unaware. They would steal five horses, sneak out of camp, and ride like hell!

But now, with Iron Wing sleeping close beside her, his arm flung across her breasts, doubts began to creep into Katy's mind. What if she were caught freeing the prisoners? What if, once out of the Cheyenne camp, they were captured by the Utes, or the Crow? What if she freed the captives and then they refused to take her with them? And what of Iron Wing? How far would he pursue her? He had already killed four men because of his desire for her.

Doubts, doubts, nothing but doubts. With an effort, she cast them aside and slipped out from under the buffalo robes. Taking one of the knives she used to slice meat, she crept outside and stood in the shadow of the lodge, listening to the sounds of the night, and the frantic pounding of her own heart. Heaving a sigh, she tiptoed through the sleeping village toward the prisoners.

The men were awake, waiting for her, and

they called out to her in anxious whispers, begging her to hurry.

Cautioning them to be silent, Katy began to saw through the heavy rawhide cords binding the first man's hands. Fear and excitement hummed in her veins. This is it! she thought. Soon I'll be home.

She had almost cut through the rope when one of the white men uttered a vile oath filled with despair.

Katy froze as a shiver of apprehension slithered down her spine. She was suddenly very cold, as if her blood had turned to ice water. Without turning around, she knew Iron Wing was standing behind her. She could feel his dark eyes drilling into her back. A wordless cry of terror erupted in her throat as she dropped the knife and ran back to Iron Wing's lodge.

Ducking inside, she sank down on the sleeping robes, her legs too weak to support her. What would he do? What would he do?

Heart pounding like a wild thing, eyes wide, ears straining, she waited. And then she heard the soft thud of his footsteps. A rush of cool air brushed her cheeks as he opened the lodge flap and stepped inside.

He loomed large and terrible before her, his face a dark mask of anger. Never had he looked so fierce, or so frightening, and Katy knew that the consquences of her act would be far worse than anything she had imagined.

She waited in dreadful anticipation for him to speak, but the force of his anger held him mute, and only the violent pulsing of a muscle in his jaw betrayed the depth of his fury.

The seconds dragged by, each one seeming like an hour. Finally, without a word, Iron Wing tossed a handful of wood on the sputtering coals, then sat cross-legged before the fire, his eyes intent on the rising flames.

Despite her fears, Katy felt her eyelids grow heavy. With a soft sigh of hopelessness, she curled up on the soft robes and fell into a troubled sleep.

Iron Wing watched Katy sleeping, his thoughts in turmoil. He longed to go to her, to take her in his arms, but he knew if he touched her, he could never do what had to be done. Head raised, arms outstretched, he beseeched Man Above for strength and wisdom.

When Katy woke the next morning, Iron Wing was still sitting beside the fire, though only cold ashes remained in the pit. He raised his head when she sat up, and Katy felt a warm surge of relief when she saw that the anger was gone from his eyes. She read pity in his expression now, and what might have been compassion.

"Get ready," Iron Wing said tonelessly. "It is almost time."

It did not seem wise to argue or ask questions, so Katy obediently put on a clean dress and began to brush her long black hair.

Iron Wing rose smoothly to his feet when she laid the brush aside. For the first time, Katy noticed he was wearing his best wolfskin clout. Fringed leggings hugged his powerful legs. The bearclaw necklace circled his throat.

"Come," he said flatly.

Timidly, Katy asked where they were going.

"The prisoners are going to be killed this morning."

"Killed? Why?"

Iron Wing looked at her as if she were a not-too-bright child. "They are our enemies. What else should we do with them?"

"You could let them go."

"No. They must pay for the Cheyenne blood they have shed."

"I don't want to watch."

"It is necessary for you to be there."

"Necessary?" Katy asked, puzzled. "Why?"

"You were caught in a deliberate act of disobedience. You must be punished."

A small knot of fear began to form in Katy's belly. "Punished how?"

"The usual penalty is ten lashes," Iron Wing answered in the same flat tone. "But since you are not Cheyenne, and a woman, it will only be six."

Katy stared at him in disbelief. "You're going to let them whip me?" she asked incredulously. "What kind of a man are you?"

"I am a Cheyenne warrior, and you are my woman. A law must be for everyone, or it is no good."

"But you're the only one who saw me," Katy said, her voice rising in desperation. "Please don't do this. I'll do anything you want, only please don't let them whip me."

"There is nothing I can do to stop it. Sun Dreamer was making water behind his lodge last night. He saw you cutting the white man free."

Katy listened to Iron Wing's words, but she did not hear them. She was too frightened to understand, too hopelessly scared of what was coming to notice the tormented look in Iron Wing's eyes, or to see that he was dying inside. She could not know that he had spent the night haunted by visions of the lash tearing into her tender flesh.

"I'll never forgive you for this," Katy threatened. "Not the longest day I live."

"It is time," Iron Wing stated. "When we get outside, stay beside me. The prisoners will be killed first."

The whole village was assembled around the four white men. Katy's fears for her own punishment were quickly forgotten when she saw the prisoners. They had been stripped naked, and she realized with horror that the Indians were going to torture the men in some way.

Sun Dreamer stepped into the middle of the crowd, and an immediate hush fell over the tribe.

"When the white man first came to our land, we met him in peace," the medicine man began slowly. "But the white eyes do not want peace. They have killed the buffalo and defiled mother earth with their plows. And now they openly make war against us, shedding the blood of our young men, despoiling our women. There will never be peace as long as the white man lives. But now it is our turn to draw blood!"

And that is what the Indians did. One by one, each member of the tribe old enough to hold a knife stepped forward and slashed at the white men, until there was not an inch of any of the prisoners that was not torn and bleeding.

Katy looked away, unable to watch, as some of the older children ran forward and drove their knives into the arms and legs of the captive white men. There would never be peace, she thought sadly, not when such intense hatred was passed from parent to child.

The Indians were careful not to sever any major veins or arteries. Nevertheless, the blood flowed freely, coursing down the bodies of the white men in scarlet rivers, oozing from cuts in their faces and necks, until the dirt at their feet was stained with crimson.

It was a cruel, painful death, Katy thought sympathetically. The slightest of cuts was painful when the air touched it. She could not imagine such pain multiplied a thousand times.

Two of the white men wept helplessly, their tears turning red as they dripped onto their bloodied faces. The bearded man mumbled the Lord's Prayer over and over again, his voice growing weaker each time as more and more of his blood was spilled. The Sergeant bore the Indians' abuse in stoic silence, even when Iron Wing's hunting knife carved a deep slash across his belly.

Katy's eyes burned with accusation and reproach when Iron Wing returned to her side. "How can you attack four helpless men?" she demanded coldly. "How can you condone such treachery? You're nothing but savages, all of you!"

Iron Wing was still holding his knife in his

hand. He stared at it for some time, watching a single drop of blood slip toward the tip of the blade, glistening brightly in the sunlight before it fell to the earth.

He was still staring at his knife when he began to speak, his voice pitched low so that only Katy could hear him.

"Once, long ago, a peaceful band of Cheyenne were camped at Sand Creek. They were there with the permission of the Army, and were supposedly under the protection of the white man's fort. But one cold winter morning the village was attacked by white men. Almost two hundred Indians were slaughtered that day. Most were women and children." Iron Wing lifted his head and gazed deep into Katy's eyes. "Is that not treachery also?"

"Yes," Katy admitted. "But that was a long time ago. You said so yourself. Surely these men were not responsible."

"Yes, a long time ago," Iron Wing repeated softly. "I was a boy of thirteen summers then."

"You were there, at Sand Creek? How awful!"

"Yes, awful. My parents were killed that day, shot down in cold blood. Our chief, Black Kettle, dragged me to safety."

Iron Wing paused for a moment, staring at the prisoners. The bearded man was already dead. Two were whimpering pathetically. The Sergeant remained stolidly silent, though his whole body trembled convulsively.

"Four years passed, and I became a warrior." Iron Wing picked up his story in the same flat tone of voice. "We were camped in the valley of the Washita when Yellow Hair came. It was winter again, and the snow lay thick upon the ground, but that did not stop the soldier coats from attacking our village. They made music while they slaughtered my people."

Another prisoner died with a high-pitched whine that sent shivers skittering down Katy's spine. A look of satisfaction flitted across Iron Wing's face as he went on with his story.

"Black Kettle, that mighty man of peace, was killed that day, shot down with every other warrior found in the village. When the battle was over, Yellow Hair killed the wounded. Women or children, it made no difference to the soldiers. Tall Buffalo and I were out hunting that day, or we would have died with the others."

Iron Wing finished his story and Katy realized the entire village was silent as a tomb. Death was in the air, and all eyes were focused on the last two prisoners. Against her will, Katy found herself staring at the dying white men. Their bodies were splotched with red, as if someone had thrown paint over them. Their faces were pale and waxy looking, and Katy knew they could not last much longer.

The young boy cried out for his mother. It was a pitiful call for help that brought tears to Katy's eyes. It was the boy's last utterance. A heavy sigh escaped his bloodless lips, and then his body sagged against the ropes that held him erect.

The Sergeant turned his eyes toward Katy.

He sent her a brief smile before death took him.

A collective sigh rippled through the crowd as they turned away from the dead men.

"It is time," Iron Wing said, and his words filled Katy with despair. There was a moment of sheer breathtaking panic that threatened to drain the strength from her limbs, and then a peculiar icy calm engulfed her. Whip her, would they? Well, let them! They were nothing but a bunch of damn savages, and Iron Wing was the worst of the lot!

Head high, chin thrust out in defiance, Katy followed Iron Wing to the whipping post. Someone reached out of the crowd to give her an encouraging pat on the shoulder. Someone else, Yellow Flower, perhaps, whispered, "Have courage, little sister."

The post loomed directly ahead, tall and menacing even in the light of day. She was aware of many eyes fastened upon her, of numerous faces turned in her direction. She knew most of the Cheyenne people, but now they all looked like strangers. She saw Bull Calf standing nearby, but he would not meet her eyes. Tall Buffalo stood beside the boy, his handsome face grave and filled with disapproval.

Iron Wing's face remained impassive as he tied Katy's hands to the post, then ripped her dress from neck to waist, exposing the smooth creamy skin of her back and shoulders.

Katy felt a quick flash of anger because he had ruined her best dress, but then she realized that, had he slipped the garment down to her waist, he would have exposed not only her back to the watching tribe, but her breasts as well. Apparently it was all right for everyone to see her humiliated, she mused bitterly, but it was not all right for anyone else to see her naked.

From the corner of her eye, Katy saw Sun Dreamer hand Iron Wing a long black whip, the kind used by muleskinners and stagecoach drivers. Somehow, the fact that Iron Wing was going to beat her made it seem even more terrible, more degrading, though she could not think why.

A wry smile twisted Katy's lips as Iron Wing shook the whip out to its full deadly length. He had always threatened to beat her, and now he was getting the chance. She wondered if he would enjoy it.

"The woman, Ka-ty, was caught in a deliberate act of disobedience," Iron Wing called out for all to hear. "The penalty is ten lashes, but because she is only a white woman, and not a Cheyenne, the penalty will be six lashes."

Only a woman! Katy let out an angry breath. Damn him! Only a woman, was she? She would show him that a white woman was the equal to any Cheyenne. She would show them all!

"I demand the full penalty!" Katy shouted in the Cheyenne tongue.

"Ka-ty . . ." Iron Wing's voice begged her to accept the lesser penalty that he had argued so hard to win for her.

"Don't speak to me, you savage," Katy hissed through clenched teeth. "You have made me a squaw, now I insist that you treat

176

me like one. I want no special favors from you."

Iron Wing's face went white, and then he felt a surge or pride sweep through him. Truly, she was a remarkable woman, the equal of any Cheyenne, male or female.

There was a low-pitched murmur as Iron Wing raised the whip, and Katy sucked in her breath, all her bravado gone now that the time was at hand. Was this why Iron Wing had killed four men, she thought, on the verge of hysteria, so he could whip her to death? Why didn't he do it and get it over with? Glancing over her shoulder, she saw Tall Buffalo standing beside Iron Wing.

"I will do it," Tall Buffalo said, his voice hushed so only Iron Wing could hear his words.

"No. She is my woman. It is for me to punish her."

"You will never forgive yourself for this if she dies at your hand," Tall Buffalo argued. "And she will never forgive you for hurting her."

Iron Wing nodded in agreement, his eyes dark with torment. But he could not let Tall Buffalo whip Katy. He would kill anyone who dared lay a hand on her. In his heart he knew that he would die a little each time the lash cut into her delicate flesh.

"You are my good friend," Iron Wing said quietly, "and you speak the truth. But I must do it. I cannot be less than a man, not even for her."

Tall Buffalo nodded slowly. Iron Wing was a proud man, a leading warrior among their people. He could not sidestep his responsibility because of his affection for a woman, especially a white woman.

With a sigh, Tall Buffalo laid his hand on his friend's shoulder, then stepped back into the crowd.

Katy closed her eyes and pressed her forehead against the post as Iron Wing raised the heavy rawhide whip over his head. Her whole body tensed in dreadful anticipation of what was to come.

Iron Wing took a deep breath. Had it been possible, he would gladly have taken the whipping in Katy's place. But it was not possible. Katy had broken the law of the tribe, and for that she must be punished.

Knowing the waiting must be playing havoc with Katy's nerves, Iron Wing struck the first blow. He felt a sudden sickness in the pit of his stomach as a narrow ribbon of scarlet appeared on the smooth flesh of Katy's back. Hating himself, he raised the whip again.

The second blow, far worse than anything Katy had expected or imagined, brought tears to her eyes and she sank her teeth into her lower lip to keep from crying out loud. The third blow came hard on the heels of the second. The fourth drove the breath from her body, the fifth seared her tender flesh like a liquid flame.

The sixth and seventh melted together. A warmth she dimly realized was blood trickled down her back.

The eighth blow fell like lightning across her shoulders. Bright colors danced inside her head. The ninth blow took the strength from her legs, so that she sagged weakly against the post, held upright only by her bound hands. As from far away, she heard a strangled cry and knew, somehow, that it had come from Iron Wing.

The last blow spread waves of agony through her lacerated flesh, and from there to every part of her body until it seemed like every inch of her skin was on fire. She could not know that Iron Wing had stayed the power of his arm so that the blows did not fall with the full force of his strength; could not know that each blow that sliced into her flesh sliced through his heart as well. She knew only that the pain was worse than anything she had ever known, and she hated him as never before.

Merciful darkness swirled around Katy, but she struggled to remain conscious, determined to walk away from the whipping post under her own power.

Iron Wing was beside her before the last crack of the whip had died away. Drawing his knife, he cut her hands free and caught her to him, careful not to touch her mutilated flesh.

"Let me go," Katy whispered hoarsely. "I want to walk by myself."

Admiration gleamed in Iron Wing's black eyes as he stepped away from Katy.

Lifting her head high, Katy threw a defiant glance at the watching Indians; then, with her shoulders back and her chin up, she walked proudly to Iron Wing's lodge.

He found her there moments later, lying unconscious across the doorway, and a wordless cry of pain rose in his throat. Why did she continue to defy him? Why did she force him to punish her, first by running away, and then by attempting to free the prisoners?

As gently as a mother tending a loved child, Iron Wing carried Katy to his bed and placed her upon the robes. After putting a kettle of water over the fire to warm, he removed her dress and gently washed the blood from her back and shoulders. When the water in the kettle was hot, he dropped a handful of healing herbs into the pot. Soaking a cloth in the medicated water, he laid it carefully over Katy's torn flesh. A pungent odor filled the lodge as Iron Wing replaced the cooling poutice with a warm one.

Katy whimpered piteously as the warm cloth was placed over her back and shoulders. Her cry was like a knife twisting in Iron Wing's heart. If only it was his back that was torn and bleeding. He had so many scars, a few more would hardly be noticed.

Iron Wing stayed by Katy's side all that night, changing the healing poultices, sponging the sweat from her brow when the fever came, replacing the blankets when she pushed them away.

The warrior's dark brooding eyes rarely left Katy's face. Even unconscious and wracked by pain and fever, she was beautiful. Time and again he reached out to caress her cheek, or touch the silken mass of her hair. When had he first started to love her? Never mind that he had vowed long ago never to risk his heart again. Now, kneeling at Katy's side, he admitted for the first time that he loved her deeply. He admired her stubbornness, her valiant fighting spirit, her refusal to be totally humbled by him.

He nursed her day and night, never leaving her side except to relieve himself, or to gather firewood or fresh water. He ate little, and slept even less, afraid she might need him in the middle of the night.

"Never again," he vowed as he sat by her side. Never again would he do anything to hurt Katy. He would leave his people, leave the country he loved, before he would cause her a moment's harm or pain.

Yellow Flower came daily to sit with Katy, but Iron Wing sent the Indian woman away, not wanting anyone else to care for Katy.

The morning of the third day, Katy woke clear-eyed and ravenous, causing Iron Wing's heart to soar with relief.

Helping Katy to sit up, Iron Wing fed her a bowl of clear broth, helped her into a clean dress, gently combed her hair. Katy accepted Iron Wing's help because she was too weak and too sore to care for herself, but she would not meet his eyes, and she would not speak to him. If he had let her go home as she wished, as she had begged so often, she would not now be helpless and wracked with pain. It was all his fault, and she would never forgive him for shaming her before the entire tribe, or for the cruel whipping that would undoubtedly leave her back scarred for life. She had never known such intense pain. Even now, just lifting her arm to wipe a lock of hair from her cheek made her back throb.

Iron Wing endured Katy's stony silence patiently. He continued to care for her, anticipating her wants, attending to her needs. He acquired special herbs and oint-

181

ments from Sun Dreamer and applied them twice daily to Katy's back and shoulders, pleased to see that the medicine man's secret concoction did indeed speed the healing process and reduce scarring.

Gradually, Katy's strength returned until she was able to care for herself without help. The first morning she was able to go to the river for water, she felt all the women's eyes follow her and she lifted her chin a little higher. Let them stare! She had done nothing to be ashamed of. It was the Cheyenne who should be ashamed. They were all godless barbarians.

Katy had been at the river only a few minutes when Yellow Flower took a place beside her.

"I am happy to see you are feeling better," the Cheyenne girl said, smiling fondly at Katy. "Iron Wing was very worried about you."

"Was he?" Katy asked coolly.

"Of course. He would allow no one else to care for your wounds. He would not even permit Sun Dreamer into the lodge to see you."

"I don't wish to speak of Iron Wing," Katy stated flatly. "It's all his fault that I was punished in the first place. He is a cruel man, and I hate him."

Yellow Flower looked askance at her friend. "His fault? It was you who disobeyed the law of our people."

"I am not Cheyenne," Katy argued stubbornly. "It is not my law."

"You are the woman of a warrior. He is bound by the laws of our tribe. It hurt him deeply to whip you."

"It didn't do me any good either," Katy retorted sarcastically.

"Your wounds have nearly healed," Yellow Flower said patiently. "The scars will fade, and you will forget the humiliation. But Iron Wing's pain will always be with him."

"Iron Wing's pain!" Katy snapped. "What are you talking about?"

"Surely you have seen the way his eyes follow you. Can you not see that he cares for you deeply?"

"He has a strange way of showing it," Katy said caustically. "Among my people, a man protects his woman. He does not beat her."

Yellow Flower shook her head sadly, troubled by the unforgiving bitterness in Katy's eyes. Iron Wing believed that, in time, Katy would adjust to the Cheyenne way of life, but Yellow Flower was not so sure. Katy had learned many of the Cheyenne ways. She spoke the language almost as well as Iron Wing, but her heart was still white. For Iron Wing's sake, Yellow Flower hoped Katy would learn to think like a Cheyenne.

"I must go," Yellow Flower said, lifting her waterskin from the river. "Tall Buffalo does not like to wait too long for his breakfast."

Katy watched her friend walk away. She had not meant to hurt Yellow Flower's feelings with her harsh words, but she could find no forgiveness in her heart for the man who had whipped her, or for the people who had stood by, watching.

Another week passed, and still Katy refused to speak to Iron Wing. He had willingly humored her, hoping she would come to realize that he had done what he had to do. Surely she knew he would not deliberately set out to hurt her. Had he not cared for her as tenderly as a man could?

In an effort to please her, he went hunting and brought her back a beautiful, unblemished doeskin. Katy took the hide from him as though it were a loathsome thing and tossed it into the fire.

He traded one of his fine paint mares for a rich red blanket. She cut it into pieces and used it for rags.

He went for a lonely walk and brought her back a bouquet of flowers, ignoring the laughter of the other warriors. She thew them away.

Putting aside his anger, Iron Wing offered her a fine bay mare. Katy gave the animal to Bull Calf. It was the final insult.

Katy was stirring a pot of soup when Iron Wing stormed into the lodge. Grabbing her by the shoulders, he spun her around to face him.

"Why did you give the mare away?" he demanded, shaking Katy much as an angry terrier shakes a mouse.

"I want nothing from you!" Katy lashed out in fury. "Nothing but my freedom!"

"You are my woman . . ."

"I hate those words!" Katy screamed, stamping her foot. "I am *not* your woman. I will *never* be your woman!"

Iron Wing's ebony eyes narrowed ominously as, with one strong hand, he ripped the dress from Katy's body, then stepped purposefully out of his deerskin clout.

"No!" Katy hissed through clenched teeth. "I will not!"

Iron Wing did not waste time arguing with her. Grabbing a handful of her long black hair in one hand, he dragged Katy to his bed. With the ease of a cat, he stretched out on the rich brown robes, forcing Katy down beside him. Flipping her onto her back, he mounted her and took her with a fierce intensity that left Katy weak and trembling and softly moaning his name.

With a shuddering sigh, Iron Wing raised himself on one elbow and gazed down at her.

"I say you are my woman," he whispered, a challenge rising in his fathomless black eyes. "Do you dare deny it?"

Iron Wing watched Katy's face as he waited for her answer. He knew she enjoyed his lovemaking, though she would never admit it. Her body willingly responded to his touch, eagerly giving and receiving. She might shout that she hated him, that she despised his touch, but he knew it was a lie. It took only a few kisses and the touch of his hand to ignite her desire, and then she clung to him, her arms drawing him close, her body arching to meet his while she cried his name. Perhaps now, at last, she would admit that she belonged to him body and soul.

Katy stared up at Iron Wing through the thick fringe of her lashes, her body awash with the sweat of their joining. He was arrogant, he was stubborn, he would never say he was sorry for whipping her publicly, but he did care for her. It was a hard thing to accept. It was harder still to admit she cared for him, that she only felt complete in his arms. But some streak of stubbornness deep in the core of her being refused to let Katy voice the words he waited to hear.

"I do deny it," she answered sharply, trying to push him away. "I'll never belong to you, or to any savage."

With a wordless cry of frustration, Iron Wing began to caress Katy again, his dark eyes burning with mingled anger and desire as his mouth plundered hers. His hands stroked her naked flesh, searing her skin with a white heat, reawakening her spent passion until she cried his name and he claimed her once more.

When Katy woke, it was midmorning and she was alone in the lodge. The place beside her was still warm, mute evidence that Iron Wing had risen only moments before, and she sighed contentedly as she rolled over onto her stomach. It was no wonder they had slept so long, she thought, amused. Incredible as it seemed, Iron Wing had made love to her the whole night long until they had fallen asleep, exhausted, in each other's arms.

Katy grinned happily as she took a deep breath. The whole lodge was filled with the musky odor of their lovemaking. And it had been love. Iron Wing could call it hate, and she could scream that she would forever loathe and despise him, but what they had shared in the night was as far from hate as east is from west.

Laughing aloud, Katy sat up, stretching

luxuriously. She needed a bath badly, but first she would prepare Iron Wing a breakfast fit for a chief. Surely he was as hungry as she. Humming softly, she laid the fire and began to boil water for tea. Never had she felt so blissfully happy and content, so pleased with the whole world.

Katy glanced up eagerly when Iron Wing entered the lodge. She knew her heart was shining in her eyes, but she didn't care. At last, she had come to terms with her true feelings, and she was eager to share them with Iron Wing. But the warm greeting on her lips died as Iron Wing passed her without a word. Sitting cross-legged on the floor, his face closed against her, he began to hone the blade of his hunting knife.

So that was how it was going to be, Katy thought dispiritedly. Nothing had changed. He was still the master, and she was still the slave, good only for cooking and cleaning and satisfying his animalistic lust. She had been a fool to think he cared for her; a fool to think him capable of any emotion as tender and civilized as love. How he would have laughed if she had bared her soul and told him she loved him!

The atmosphere in the lodge fairly crackled with tension. Katy refused to meet Iron Wing's eyes as she busied herself preparing the morning meal. When it was ready, she served Iron Wing, then sat in the rear of the lodge with her back toward him.

Iron Wing ate quickly, tasting nothing. Once he had told Katy he did not need her love. Now, too late, he knew it had been a lie. Slowly, so slowly he had not even been aware

187

of it, she had taken root in his heart. But he could not admit it to her, could not say the words aloud. His pride, the fierce indomitable pride of a warrior, had been badly wounded when Quiet Water rejected his proposal of marriage. He could not risk rejection a second time.

Without a word, he put his bowl aside and walked out of the lodge.

Katy blinked back her tears as she washed the dishes and straightened the bed. Taking a piece of soap, she stepped outside, her eyes darting from side to side, but Iron Wing was nowhere in sight.

Nodding to Tall Buffalo and Yellow Flower, Katy made her way to a secluded spot to relieve herself, then walked upriver, seeking a sheltered place to bathe. For once, she was oblivious to the beauty of her surroundings. The sight of a young fawn failed to bring a smile to her lips, the graceful soaring of a red-tailed hawk gave her no joy.

Finding a suitable spot, she prepared to undress when she heard a splash. Tiptoeing through the tall yellow grass that grew in abundance near the river, she peered over a flat-topped boulder to see Iron Wing swimming smoothly and effortlessly in the middle of the river.

She studied the warrior from her vantage point, wondering if he excelled at everything he did. She knew he rode like a centaur, was one of the best hunters in the tribe, and was held in high esteem as a warrior. She felt her cheeks flush as she admitted he was also a wonderful lover. She continued to watch, unashamed, as he climbed out of the water and stood in the sun, letting the warm air bake him dry. A quick fire sparked in the core of her being as her eyes lovingly wandered over Iron Wing's broad chest and narrow hips. His arms and legs were corded with muscle; his belly was hard and flat. He was quite the most handsome man she had ever seen, she mused, completely forgetting that she had once looked upon him with horror.

Feeling her gaze, Iron Wing glanced up and saw Katy standing behind the rock. His eyes narrowed thoughtfully. Was she running away again, or merely seeking a place to wash away his touch? He wanted to call her, to ask her to join him, but decided against it. Everytime he called to her, she refused him. And he was in no mood to argue.

Katy felt her pulse quicken under Iron Wing's probing gaze. Stifling the urge to run to his arms and declare her love, she walked slowly down the gentle incline that led to the water's edge.

"I came to bathe," she explained coolly. "Is that all right with you?"

Iron Wing nodded curtly, his face closed against her inquiring gaze. His silence irritated Katy. Ignoring him, she stepped out of her dress and plunged into the icy water.

Iron Wing stretched out on the grassy bank, watching Katy through half-closed eyes. Her thick black hair gleamed wetly around her small shoulders, shining blue-black in the late morning sunshine, making a perfect frame for a perfect face. Did she know what she was doing to him, he wondered idly. Had she chosen this place to bathe just to torment him, to flaunt the slim golden body he desired above all others, but could never possess except by force? She was his woman, deny it though she might. He owned her body and soul, but it was her stubborn heart he yearned to conquer. And that he knew he would never do. She hated him. She had told him so again and again. Only in the privacy of his lodge did she accept him as a man, unable to withstand the smoldering desires of her own flesh.

With a sigh, Iron Wing rose to his feet, his eyes still on Katy. Her swimming had improved, and he watched her with a growing sense of pride as she propelled herself smoothly through the clear water. How very beautiful she was, and how he ached to hold her in his arms.

Iron Wing felt his heart beat faster as Katy stepped gracefully from the river, shaking the water from her hair. The sun caressed her damp golden flesh, and he groaned softly, filled with the bittersweet pain of wanting her.

"Ka-ty." Iron Wing whispered her name, his voice husky with longing.

Slowly, Katy turned to face him. The expression on his face, the hunger shining in his dark eyes, started her heart pounding wildly in her breast. For the first time, Iron Wing's eyes were warm with affection, his expression open and adoring.

Somehow, Katy was in his arms, her face raised for his kiss. Iron Wing's mouth was warm and gently coaxing instead of harshly demanding, his arms a welcome support instead of imprisoning flesh holding her against her will. Time seemed to stand still as

Iron Wing carefully lowered Katy to the ground.

Their lovemaking was special that day, almost magical. It was more than a mere joining of their flesh, more than passion. Katy accepted Iron Wing wholeheartedly, with no reservations. She did not think of him as an Indian, but as a strong virile man who had the power to carry her to the doors of heaven. She loved the touch of his skin beneath her hand, the bulging muscles that rippled beneath her fingertips. The sight of his aroused manhood excited her, making her anxious and eager to receive him. She sighed as he drew her close, whispering her name, his voice deep and husky, softly caressing. When had she stopped hating him? When had she ceased to think of him as an Indian, an enemy, and started seeing him as the epitome of what a man should be?

She knew a deep contentment as Iron Wing kissed her again, chasing everything from her mind but the wondrous ecstacy of his nearness.

Iron Wing drew Katy close, feeling his heart soar as every dream he had ever had came true in her arms. She loved him completely, holding nothing back. She was joy and peace and fulfillment embodied in perfect form, and as he buried himself in her womanly sweetness, he felt all his scars fade and disappear.

Later, cradled in Iron Wing's arms, Katy touched his shoulder where she had stabbed him. She was suddenly sorry she had caused him pain, and she kissed the scar the knife had made.

"I'm sorry," she murmured contritely.

"Perhaps I deserved it," Iron Wing replied, tenderly stroking her cheek.

"Oh, you did," Katy agreed, laughing happily. "You did, indeed! But I'm sorry now that I caused you pain."

Iron Wing's dark eyes caressed her face, his expression as tangible as a caress, and Katy felt the warm sweet longing begin to rise again, swelling, growing, radiating its heat from the center of her being.

"Do I still have your hatred?" Iron Wing asked in a voice gone soft as honey.

"Yes," Katy murmured, suddenly shy. "And my love, too. I guess I've loved you for a long time," she confessed, blushing under Iron Wing's inquiring gaze. "I hope you don't mind."

"No," he answered huskily. "I will bear your love as willingly as your hatred, so long as the results are the same."

"Oh, they will be," Katy assured him with a lingering kiss. " They will be."

And it was a long time before they left the shelter of the tall yellow grass.

# 14

The next few weeks were the most wonderful Katy had ever known. Iron Wing was always at her side, showing her the hidden mysteries and beauties of the wooded hills and plains. He took her on long rides across the burgeoning grassland, showing her a pastoral beauty she had never dreamed existed. The buffalo grass, which would be pale gold and as high as a pony's belly by late summer, now covered the earth like a velvet carpet, the color so green it almost hurt your eyes just to look at it. Wildflowers bloomed everywhere, making bright splashes of color against the hillsides and on the prairie floor. Trees that had been brown and barren only weeks before were suddenly bursting with tender green shoots and delicate pink blossoms.

Once, pausing on a high bluff, they watched a buffalo calf come into the world. It was a sight that brought tears to Katy's eyes, a wondrous miracle of nature that was all the more special because she shared it with the man she loved.

"It is always the same," Iron Wing remarked reverently. "No matter how many times you see life renewing itself, there is always the same sense of wonder and awe."

Katy smiled into Iron Wing's eyes. Was this

the man she had labeled a godless savage?
The man she had accused of having no soul?

How different everything was now that she
saw the world through the eyes of love. Even
the endless chores she had once hated took
on a new dimension. She dug roots and
picked berries and hunted for herbs and
seeds and nuts with a light heart, readily
joining in the laughter and conversation of
the women. She took pride in her cooking,
pleased beyond measure whenever Iron Wing
complimented her efforts. She found she
actually enjoying sewing, and she made Iron
Wing four new shirts, a pair of fringed buckskin leggings, and a new pair of moccasins.
Soon, he was the best dressed warrior in the
village, and the other men began grumbling
that Iron Wing was making them all look like
beggars in comparison.

Katy kept his lodge immaculate, and
blushed with pleasure when Sun Dreamer
remarked, only half-kidding, that maybe he
would take a white woman for a wife.

Iron Wing basked in Katy's attention. His
dark eyes followed her as never before, filled
with love and affection. She had always been
beautiful beyond description but now, overnight, she was radiant. Her blue eyes
sparkled like rare jewels, flashing with
vitality and a newfound love for life. She
smiled at him often, the glow in her eyes
filling him with an inner warmth that was
better than the heat from a campfire. His
lodge rang with the merry sound of her
laughter, and he found himself laughing too,
as he had not laughed in years.

He loved her beyond words, and when the

need to express his love grew overpowering, he took her in his arms and made love to her with infinite tenderness, his hands and his lips expressing the feelings he could not voice.

The days flew by on swift wings. They continued to take long rides into the timbered hills, relishing the moments they spent alone. Iron Wing tried to teach Katy to use his bow, but she had no heart for hunting. The buffalo were so magnificent, the deer and elk so graceful and beautiful, she could not bring herself to shoot at them even though Iron Wing assured her she would likely miss, at least in the beginning.

Sometimes, at night, they took a blanket outside and watched the stars wheel across the vast Montana sky. Katy knew a deep sense of contentment as she lay beside Iron Wing, her head pillowed on his shoulder, his arm across her waist. The stars twinkled brightly, and she wondered if anyone else in the world could possibly be as happy as she was.

Early in the summer, Sun Dreamer made medicine and announced that in three days time the signs would be favorable for a tribal buffalo hunt. Any warrior found hunting on his own before the appointed day would be severely punished.

On hearing Sun Dreamer's proclamation, the warriors began to repair their weapons, checking bowstrings and arrowheads, making sure their buffalo ponies were sound of wind and limb.

Iron Wing spent many hours going over his weapons, his hands deft and sure as they fashioned a new arrow, or honed the blade of his knife. Now, sitting beside him outside their lodge, Katy put the finishing touches on a new deerskin shirt she had made for him. Somehow, it made her feel very domestic, and she wondered if that was the way married life was: two people sharing a home, each attending to their own chores and responsibilities. Two people sharing one heart.

Iron Wing glanced at Katy, and her heart swelled with such love that it was almost a physical pain. Tears stung her eyes, and she looked away, but not before Iron Wing saw the moisture glistening in her eyes.

Quickly, he laid his bow aside and took Katy's hand in his. "What is wrong, Ka-ty?" he asked anxiously.

Katy shook her head as the tears came faster and faster.

"Have I done something to displease you?" he asked, frowning.

"No, it's just that . . ." She laughed through her tears, feeling foolish. "It's just that I love you so much."

"Do you, Ka-ty?" Iron Wing asked in a voice filled with wonder.

"Yes," she sniffled. "So much."

Abruptly, Iron Wing's face closed against hers, and he dropped her hand. "And loving me makes you weep?"

"No! These are tears of joy. Sometimes, when a woman's heart is full, she cries."

"My heart, too, is full," Iron Wing said thickly. "You have made my lodge a happy place."

For a long moment, they smiled at each

other. Then, without saying another word, Katy put her sewing aside and followed Iron Wing into their lodge.

From a distance, Tall Buffalo watched them, a quiet smile playing over his handsome face. Truly, it had been a good day when he brought the white woman home to his friend.

The buffalo hunt proved to be a huge success. Every warrior brought down at least one big bull, and there were no injuries among the Indians. It was hard work, skinning the heavy carcasses, but the women laughed as they worked, anticipating the feast that would come later. Katy skinned the carcass at her feet carefully. It was a fine pelt, thick and soft, and she smiled as she thought of the warm coat she would make for Iron Wing.

That evening, the air was filled with the sweet aroma of roasting buffalo. Adults and children alike gorged themselves on sweet hump meat and fat cow, smacking their lips and laughing as the rich red juices dribbled down their chins. Truly the gods had smiled on the Cheyenne this day.

When everyone had eaten their fill, there was dancing and singing and stories for old and young alike. Most of the stories were of memorable hunts from years gone by, and Katy learned that hunting the great shaggy beasts was much more dangerous than she had imagined. It took a brave man mounted on a brave horse to race alongside a stampeding herd. It took a warrior with a keen eye and a strong arm to drive an arrow or a lance into its heart. It took a pony with speed and sure feet to carry a man in and out of the herd. One slip, one false step, and both man and animal would be pounded into the earth.

During the next few weeks, the women worked from dawn until dark tanning hides, curing meat, making new robes and moccasins and shirts from the skins.

Katy was amazed at the variety of things the buffalo provided. Spoons were fashioned from the horn, thread came from the beard and tail, glue came from the hooves. Summer hides were scraped and sewn together for lodge covers. Skins taken in autumn or winter were thick and warm, and these were used for blankets and robes. The bones of the buffalo were used for saddletrees, or fleshing tools. In the winter, the ribs were lashed together with rawhide and used for sleds.

Yellow Flower taught Katy how to stretch the hides on a willow frame, and how to soften the skin by rubbing them with a mixture of fat and brains, and then pounding them with a rock until they were soft and pliable. It was hard work, but the result was a beautiful robe.

In midsummer, a band of Sioux joined the Cheyenne for the annual Sun Dance festival, and a holiday atmosphere prevailed as the two tribes renewed old acquaintances. There were dances every night, and contests every day.

Katy stood between Yellow Flower and Pretty Eyes to watch the first day's races. Tall Buffalo and Iron Wing were in the contest, and Katy could not help comparing the two men as they waited for the race to start. Tall Buffalo was a little taller, a little younger, his face smooth and unlined, handsome to look upon. But it was Iron Wing who made her heart pound with joy. He was clad in the briefest of wolfkin clouts, and his muscles rippled like silk whenever he moved.

The first contest was a foot race over a mile-long course. There were perhaps thirty warriors at the starting line. The Cheyenne and the Sioux were avid gamblers, and Katy smiled as men and women hurriedly made last minute bets on their favorites. Yellow Flower wagered a thick buffalo robe against a pair of handsomely decorated moccasins that her husband would win the race.

At the signal, all betting ceased and a loud holler went up as the spectators began to cheer the contestants.

Tall Buffalo and Iron Wing surged into the lead and held it all the way, running neck and neck. Then, ever so slowly, Iron Wing pulled ahead, his long powerful legs driving him faster, faster, until he crossed the finish line a good twenty yards ahead of everyone else.

Yellow Flower frowned at her husband as he walked up to her. "You!" she scolded in mock anger. "You just cost me a fine robe. I do not know why I continue to bet on you when Iron Wing wins every time."

As the days passed, Katy assumed the Sun Dance festival was just an excuse for old friends to get together, to hold contests to see who was the strongest, the fastest, the bravest, or who owned the swiftest horse.

But on the ninth day, a marked change came over the camp. A special lodge was erected apart from the others. A warrior was sent out to locate a special cottonwood tree that would become the Sun Dance pole. The warrior came back late that day and announced he had been successful, and that night there was a Buffalo Dance to celebrate the blessings of home and life.

The next day, many women, all renowned for their virtue, went on a ritual hunt for the tree the warrior had "captured" the day before. Four warriors who had been chosen for the task went with the women to count coup on the tree and carry it back to camp.

The next day, the trunk of the tree was painted four different colors representing the four sacred directions. Later, cutouts of a male buffalo and a male human, each with genitals so large they made Katy blush, were placed in the fork of the tree, along with other sacred objects, and then the tree was raised to stand inside a sacred circle where the actual Sun Dance would be performed. When the pole was set in the ground, the men of both tribes joined in a war dance around it, shooting arrows at the cutouts.

At dawn the following morning, the dancers were painted with colors and symbols relating to the degree of pain they had volunteered to suffer. Katy watched in horror as skewers were implanted in the backs of several of the dancers. The skewers were attached, via rawhide thongs, to heavy buffalo skulls. Other participants had the skewers embedded in their chests. Long strips of rawhide were attached to the skewers and fastened to the Sun Dance pole.

Now the real ordeal began. Those warriors

dragging buffalo skulls began to dance around the sacred pole while the heavy skulls bounced behind them. The other warriors, Bull Calf among them, began to pull back on the thongs that held them bound to the Sun Dance pole.

Katy turned to Iron Wing. "Why? Why do they do it?"

"It is our way of giving thanks to Man Above for his blessings. These warriors offer their pain and their blood in behalf of the tribe. Sometimes great visions are bestowed upon those who participate in the Dance."

The drumming went on and on. The warriors continued to dance around the sacred pole, their feet moving to the rhythm of the drums. The sun, object of their adoration, rose hot and relentless in the sky. Sweat poured from the spectators and the participants alike.

Katy watched Bull Calf, his young face bathed in perspiration, his eyes fastened on the sun, the muscles in his body straining against the rawhide. How did he endure the pain without crying out? How could his mother sit and calmly watch while her son suffered?

"How long must they dance?" Katy asked Iron Wing, wondering how much longer she could stand to watch.

"Until they pull free of the skewers in their flesh. Sometimes it takes all night."

Katy looked up at Iron Wing, her eyes intent upon his face. "Have you ever . . .?"

"Yes, when I was a young warrior." Iron Wing fingered the two faint scars on his chest.

"Was it dreadfully painful?" Katy asked, wondering why she had never noticed those two particular scars before.

"At first. But the pain grew less as I stared at the sun."

"Did you have a vision?"

"Yes. A great eagle appeared to me. He told me that if I upheld the ways of the People, I would find that which I had been seeking." Iron Wing smiled into Katy's eyes. "It is you, Ka-ty, who have made my vision come true."

The summer raced by. Katy's fine skin darkened until it was almost as brown as Iron Wing's. Only her brilliant blue eyes distinguished her as a white woman. She spoke the Cheyenne language fluently now, and she had accepted all the tribe's rituals and customs. With her prejudices gone, she saw the Indians as people and discovered that, red or white, male or female, people were pretty much the same wherever you found them.

Iron Wing's pride in Katy knew no bounds. She was warm and gentle, kindhearted to all, and more beautiful than the sacred hills. She cared for his needs, satisfied his wildest desires, and made him feel like the most wonderful man ever created. But it was when she looked at him, her sky-blue eyes warm with love and adoration, that he cherished her most of all.

With the coming of winter, the tribe prepared to move back to the Dakotas. This time Katy needed no help in getting ready. She packed their belongings, dismantled their lodge with ease, and was ready to go at the appointed time.

Iron Wing had given her a horse of her own, and Katy rode beside Iron Wing leading a travois pony, and feeling very proud of herself. She was almost as Indian as he was. Anyone, seeing her from a distance, would have difficulty recognizing her as a white woman. Her hair was as black as an Indian's, her skin deep bronze, her clothing and mannerisms Cheyenne.

Winter was fast upon them when a runner came into their midst with news from the Indian agent at Fort Lincoln. The Grandfather in Washington had ordered all Indians to go to the reservation by January 31 of the new year, or they would be treated as hostiles.

A great murmur rose through the camp. Was the Grandfather crazy in the head? It was the middle of winter. There was no way families could move their lodges through the deep snowdrifts. Children and old ones would sicken and die on the trail. Surely the runner had misunderstood the Grandfather's instructions.

But no, the runner repeated his message. January 31 was the correct day. All Indians must report to the reservation by then, or be considered hostiles and treated accordingly.

"The Grandfather must be mind-gone-far," Iron Wing muttered angrily. "No man travels when the land is white with snow."

Tall Buffalo nodded as he passed the pipe to his friend. "Yes, crazy in the head," he agreed, tapping his temple with one long brown finger. "The Grandfather has wanted war for a long time. The white men have been eager to drive us away from our land. They know we will not drag our people through the snow. They *want* war."

"I think you are right, my brother," Iron Wing remarked thoughtfully. His dark eyes glowed fiercely. "If it is war they want, we will give it to them!"

War! Katy stared at the two men in horror. She had lost her father and Robert because red man and white man could not live together in peace. She could not bear to lose Iron Wing too, not now when he was so precious to her.

Troubled, she knelt beside Iron Wing and laid her hand on his arm. "You will not fight?" she asked anxiously. "You would not leave me?"

"I am a warrior," Iron Wing said firmly. "If my people fight, I fight with them."

Yellow Flower threw a concerned glance at Katy. The white girl had learned much of Indian ways, but she did not yet fully understand the pride of a warrior. It would be hard for Katy to let Iron Wing go, especially when he went to fight the white man. If Katy could not be made to realize why Iron Wing must fight, there would be hard feelings in their lodge.

Yellow Flower sat quietly for a moment, until the two men were deep in a discussion about the many devious ways of the soldier coats. Then, with a loving smile, she moved closer to Katy.

"A Cheyenne warrior is not like other men," Yellow Flower said softy, so the men could not hear her words. "He is a fighter, and he has a strong heart. Iron Wing is a leader among our people. Some say he will be chief one day. If there is war, he must go. Many of our young men look to him for courage. He has counted many coup, more than any other warrior in our village. It would shame him to stay home while others went to defend our people."

Katy stared at Yellow Flower in confusion. What good was honor if your man was dead?

"Don't you care that Tall Buffalo might be killed in battle?" Katy asked. "Aren't you afraid for his life?"

"Of course I am afraid for him," Yellow Flower answered impatiently. "But I would not shame him by asking him to stay home with the women. He must go, just as Iron Wing must go."

"But they cannot win a war against the whites," Katy declared vehemently. "The whites have many more men, and many more guns, than the Cheyenne."

"Our men are worth ten washichu," Yellow Flower retorted arrogantly. "They are not afraid of the white men, or their firesticks."

"Then they are fools," Katy snapped.

There was a sudden silence in the lodge, and Katy realized that Tall Buffalo and Iron Wing had been listening to her conversation with Yellow Flower.

"We are not fools," Iron Wing said stiffly. "We are free men. We were here before the white man crossed the Big Water, and we will fight to stay here."

"But you can't win," Katy argued stubbornly.

"We must fight for what is ours," Tall

Buffalo said. "It is better to die with honor than to live on the white man's reservation; better to die like a man than live with our tails between our legs like dogs."

Katy stared at Iron Wing. His face was closed against her, his eyes dark with anger. She suddenly felt far removed from him, a stranger, and she knew that even though she might master the Cheyenne tongue and wear buckskin dresses and moccasins, she would never fully understand the Indian mind or the Indian heart.

"I'm sorry," she murmured, and left the lodge without a backward glance.

For a moment, she stood outside, undecided, and then she walked swiftly toward the river. How easily they talked of fighting and dying, as if it was of no importance whether a man lived or died, so long as he died with honor. But honor would not comfort her on a cold night.

"Ka-ty?"

"You move as quiet as a shadow," Katy muttered. She stared at the frozen river. It was silver in the moonlight, as cold as the pain in her heart. A wolf howled far off, and she shivered, chilled by the wind blowing through the trees and by the wolf's lonely wail.

"Ka-ty, look at me."

Slowly, she turned to face him. "Do not be angry, Ka-ty. I must do what I must do. I cannot be less than a man, not even for you."

"I thought you cared for me," Katy murmured. "I thought I was as important to you as you are to me."

"You know I care for you," Iron Wing retorted irritably. "Why are you talking nonsense?"

"It isn't nonsense! No woman wants her man to go to war. I don't want to live without you. I could not bear it if you died."

"I will not die."

"Every man I love dies," Katy cried in despair. "First my father and Robert were killed by Indians, and now you'll be killed by white men." She laughed bitterly at the cruel irony of it all. "Oh, Iron Wing!" she sobbed brokenly. "Please don't go to war!"

Tears streaming down her cheeks, she threw herself into his arms, burying her face in the hard wall of his chest.

Iron Wing held her while she cried, one big hand gently stroking the silky mass of her hair. He could understand her fears, but he could not give in to the wishes of a woman. He was a man, a warrior. It was good to die in battle, with a war cry on your lips and a weapon in your hand. No warrior who was worthy of the name could stay behind with his woman and still be a man.

He pressed his lips against Katy's cheek and tasted the salt of her tears. A gust of wind whistled across the icebound river and he felt Katy shiver violently against him. Foolish woman, he thought tenderly, to come outside without the protection of a robe to turn about the cold.

"Come," he said, taking her arm. "We must go back to the lodge."

With a small nod, Katy let Iron Wing lead her back to their lodge. Inside, he removed her wet moccasins and rubbed her feet, his eyes dark with worry. She looked so pale, her skin felt so cold. He offered her a cup of tea, insisted she drink it all, then carried her to their bed and slid in beside her, drawing her close to warm her.

"Iron Wing, please don't go."

Gently, he caressed her cheek, the back of her neck. "We will not speak of it now," he said. "The time of new grass is many days away. Perhaps war will not come. Perhaps the Grandfather in Washington will realize his foolishness and change his mind."

Perhaps, Katy thought doubtfully, and perhaps deer would fly like eagles. She wanted to press Iron Wing further, to make him promise he would not go, but his hands and his lips were working their familiar magic on her quivering flesh, chasing everything from her mind but the swift surge of passion that his touch unfailingly aroused.

# 15 SPRING
## 1876

It was spring once more. The river overran its banks, the trees grew full and green, and the prairie abounded with new life.

Yellow Flower was pregnant again, and she fairly glowed with the prospect of motherhood.

Sun Dreamer, the tribal shaman, was seriously ill. His oldest son, Walks-the-Clouds, stayed close to the old medicine man's side. Walks-the-Clouds had been studying for many years to become the tribe's next healer. He had practiced every cure his father had taught him, but to no avail. The old man was dying.

The first hunt of the year was a big success. That night, when everyone was full and happy, there was a sweetheart dance. All the women and young girls danced in a circle to the soft beat of a single drum. Katy danced with the women for the first time, feeling her heart beat with excitement. It was good to be alive. It had been a mild winter, with few deaths and little sickness. There was fresh meat in the village. Even Sun Dreamer appeared to be feeling better.

Katy's feet moved in time to the music, easily following the simple steps of the dance, so different from the waltzes and polkas she had once known. Soon the music would change, and each woman would leave the circle to tap her husband or sweetheart on the shoulder, and then the man would join the dance.

When the time came, Katy walked toward Iron Wing and lightly touched his shoulder. He rose smoothly to his feet and followed her back to the circle. Joining hands, they continued the dance.

From the shadows, Quiet Water watched Iron Wing and Katy. The white woman gazed into Iron Wing's eyes, her face positively glowing with love and happiness. Quiet Water felt a swift surge of jealousy. She had refused to marry Iron Wing because his looks had repelled her. What good was a brave husband if just looking at his scars made you sick to your stomach? She had wanted a handsome husband, and she had chosen Black Arrow, who was one of the handsomest warriors in the village. Sadly, it had taken only a few weeks to discover that Black Arrow was a lazy hunter, a compulsive gambler, a negligent husband. Reluctantly, Quiet Water admitted her parents had spoken the truth. It took more than just good looks to make a good husband. Ironically, once Iron Wing's scars had healed, they faded until they were scarcely visible.

Quiet Water looked at Iron Wing and felt her pulse quicken with desire. His thick black hair hung loose about his broad shoulders. He was clothed in a sleeveless doeskin vest that emphasized his muscled arms and shoulders. Fringed leggings hugged his strong legs. The bear claw necklace was at his throat, a symbol of his courage.

Quiet Water scowled as Katy and Iron Wing left the dance to walk hand in hand into the shadows.

Several days passed, and Quiet Water grew more and more discontented with her husband. Even his good looks and charming smile failed to cheer her, and she felt her hatred for the white woman grow. Iron Wing was a good husband, obviously a talented lover. One had only to see the way the white woman looked at him to know she was a woman who was satisfied in every way.

Quiet Water was in a foul mood as she walked down the path to the river to bathe. It was unfair for the white woman to have Iron Wing when Quiet Water had wanted him first.

The disgruntled Indian woman came to an abrupt halt as she rounded the bend in the path and saw Iron Wing swimming in the river, alone. Her breath caught in her throat as he stood in the waist-deep water. Ah, but he was magnificent. His skin and hair gleamed wetly in the early morning sun, and she felt a sudden desire erupt in her loins as she imagined his arms around her.

Smiling slyly, Quiet Water shrugged off her dress and walked boldly to the water's edge.

"Oh," she cried in mock alarm. "I did not see you there."

Quiet Water blushed prettily, but she made no move to cover her nakedness, nor did she turn away. She had a body that was slim and

211

softly rounded, breasts that were high and full, legs that were long and shapely. She felt a thrill of pride as Iron Wing's eyes crept over her flesh, his expression showing he clearly liked what he saw.

Iron Wing felt a vague uneasiness as he stepped from the water and picked up his clout. It was not fitting for Quiet Water to remain at the river with him, but she made no move to leave. Turning his back to the woman, he slipped on his clout and reached for his shirt. He gasped with shock when he felt Quiet Water's arms circle his waist. Her breasts, soft and warm, pressed invitingly against his bare back.

And that was how Katy found them.

Iron Wing sucked in a deep breath when he saw the look of horror on Katy's face, but Quiet Water only smiled smugly and held Iron Wing tighter.

"You might as well tell the white woman about us," the Indian girl purred wickedly. "Tell her she is no longer needed in your lodge."

Iron Wing pulled out of Quiet Water's grasp, knowing how guilty he must look. He turned his dark eyes on Quiet Water. "I wanted you once," he admitted in a tight voice. "But you would not have me. Now my heart is cold for you. Go back to your husband, if he will have you."

Red-faced with shame, Quiet Water grabbed her dress and ran along the riverbank, away from the village. She would never go back to Black Arrow. Never! She could not face him after this, nor could she face her friends and family. She had disgraced herself and them, and they would shun her presence. No one would look at her, or speak to her, but they would whisper behind her back, laughing at her because she threw herself at a man who did not want her. She could not bear the humiliation, not even for a short time.

Iron Wing turned pleading eyes on Katy, willing her to understand. "Ka-ty . . ."

A slow smile twitched at the corners of Katy's lips, and she began to laugh. "Oh, Iron Wing, I wish you could have seen the look on your face when I saw the two of you together!"

"You are not angry?"

"No. I know you are too honorable a man to flirt with someone else's wife."

"I have no need of any other woman," Iron Wing said, gently stroking Katy's cheek. "Not when I have you to share my life."

Hand in hand, they walked back to the village. Katy frowned as they drew near their lodge, for the camp was strangely quiet. A crowd had gathered around Sun Dreamer's tepee, their faces grave.

Just then, Walks-the-Clouds stepped out of his father's lodge. "Sun Dreamer has gone to join his ancestors," he announced in a choked voice.

A moment later, a high-pitched wail rose toward the heavens as the shaman's aged wife began to mourn.

That afternoon, the medicine man's body was wrapped in a buffalo robe and carried to the burying ground. His wife burned their lodge and moved in with her sister and brother-in-law.

Later that night, Black Arrow came to Iron Wing's lodge. "I need your help," the warrior said. "Quiet Water has not returned to our lodge. No one has seen her since this morning, when she went to the river."

Katy remained quiet as Iron Wing pulled on a shirt and gathered his weapons. She had no love for the Indian woman who had tried to destroy her life with Iron Wing, but she wished her no harm. Iron Wing was a strong, handsome man. No woman could be blamed for wanting him.

"We may be gone several days," Iron Wing remarked when he was ready to go. "Do not worry."

"Be careful," Katy murmured, lifting her face for his kiss.

Iron Wing's eyes searched Katy's face. "You will be here when I return?"

"Yes. Hurry back. I will miss you."

Katy did not sleep that night. Every night cry seemed as loud as thunder, and she wished Iron Wing were there beside her. The night did not seem long or menacing when he was at her side.

Two days passed. Yellow Flower tried to cheer Katy, assuring her that Iron Wing would return safely, but still Katy could not help worrying. There were so many things that could happen. Iron Wing could be injured by a wild animal; the search party could be attacked by Crow Indians and he might be killed or captured. And deep in the back of her mind lurked the thought that Black Arrow had learned of Quiet Water's duplicity and was plotting some sort of vengeance against Iron Wing, even though Iron Wing had done nothing to encourage the woman.

Doubts and worries plagued Katy day and night and when, at last, the search party returned, Katy flew into Iron Wing's arms, her relief mirrored in her eyes as he drew her close.

It was only when the keening wail of a bereaved woman rose on the wind that Katy noticed the blanket-wrapped body draped over one of the horses.

"We found Quiet Water," Iron Wing said in a subdued tone. "She had been caught by some trappers and badly abused. She was dead when we got there."

"And the white men?"

"They are dead also."

Katy nodded bleakly. "I'm sorry about Quiet Water. I know you once cared for her."

Iron Wing nodded slowly. "I did not think I would ever love a woman again when she turned me away. But then you came into my life, and I knew that my heart was not dead after all."

His words warmed Katy through and through, filling her with joy. "Where is Black Arrow?" she asked. "I don't see him anywhere."

"He has gone into the hills to mourn. He loved her very much."

They buried Quiet Water the next morning. Black Arrow stood beside the scaffold, his handsome face twisted with grief. He remained there at the burial site long after everyone else had gone.

That afternoon, a Sioux warrior rode into camp bearing urgent news. Sitting Bull was calling for all the tribes to unite to fight the white invaders. The Sioux chief had offered one hundred pieces of his flesh to the Great Spirit at the Sun Dance and had been granted a great vision wherein he saw hundreds of white men falling into his camp. Sitting Bull's message was clear.

"It is war," the mighty chief had stated. "Come to the Rosebud."

The days of peace were over.

Runners came and went constantly after that, bringing news of the whereabouts of the Army, carrying the words of Crazy Horse and Sitting Bull.

The Army was preparing to move in force against the Sioux and the Cheyenne. The homeland of the Plains Indians was rumored to be a rich source of gold. Not only that, but greedy white men were turning bright eyes toward the timbered hills and the rich grasslands. The buffalo, once as numerous as the stars in the sky, were being systematically destroyed. The Indians could not live without the buffalo, and the whites were finding it easier to destroy the buffalo than to fight the Indians.

Talk of war spread across the plains like wildfire. The warriors thought of nothing else. Councils were held far into the night. Novice warriors went about the village with a new sense of purpose and dignity. Soon, they would ride into battle. Soon they would prove their bravery and cunning. Their eagerness to fight danced brightly in their black eyes. The old men talked wistfully of days gone by, of great battles fought and won, of coup counted and scalps taken. It was better to die in battle, they assured the young men, than to wind up old and helpless, of use to no one.

Katy felt lost and alone in alien territory. She could not look with favor on the coming battle. War was not noble, it was brutal and ugly. Men might talk of the glory of battle and the thrill of victory, but it meant only pain and heartache to women as they saw their fathers and husbands and sons slain. Repeatedly, she begged Iron Wing not to fight. But he would not be moved. He was a warrior, and he would live and die as a warrior should.

It was mid-May when word came that the Sioux had defeated General George "Three Stars" Crook in battle along the banks of the Rosebud. The Cheyenne crowed in triumph. It was a great coup to defeat Red Beard in battle. Suddenly, those warriors who had been less enthusiastic about the coming battle were fired with energy. Crook had been defeated. Let "Yellow Hair" Custer come! Yes, Custer, who had killed helpless men and women along the banks of the Washita. There were some here who had lost loved ones that bitter cold day when Custer and his men rode through the lodges of the Cheyenne while the Army band played "Garry Owen."

Iron Wing's eyes glittered with the need for vengeance when he heard the name Custer. Too well, he remembered the Washita. He could recall clearly the horror of riding into

217

the ravaged village, of seeing the burnt lodges, the horses that Custer had ordered shot, the dirty brown smudges of dried blood against the white snow. He had lost friends that day long ago. He had vowed to avenge their deaths, and now he was being given the opportunity. It was like a gift from Man Above.

And then the word came from Sitting Bull. "It is war. Come to the Little Big Horn."

No council was needed to determine the will of the tribe. Sitting Bull had called, and they would answer. Preparation for the march to the Greasy Grass would begin the next day.

That night, Iron Wing stared into the fire with a heavy heart. He had made a decision, and it hurt him deeply. But it must be done. When the tribe left to meet Sitting Bull, he would take Katy back to her own people, then circle back and join the Cheyenne.

Katy stared at Iron Wing in stunned disbelief when he told her the news.

"Send me away? Why?"

"You will be safer with your own people. They will send you back to your mother."

"But I don't want to go back," Katy wailed. "I want to stay here with you."

"Ka-ty." Iron Wing murmured her name, his heart aching. "This may be a long fight. I am afraid for you. If we lose the battle, the soldiers will ride through our village, killing everyone. Their bullets will not know that you are not one of us. I cannot take a chance that you might be killed." He grinned ruefully. "You have often said you wanted to go home."

"But not now," Katy pleaded. "Please don't send me away."

"We leave in the morning," Iron Wing said firmly. "There is a washichu settlement ten days ride from here. They will take good care of you."

Katy stared at the face of the man she had grown to love. She forgot all the times she had cried that she hated him, the times she had begged him to send her home, and knew only that she loved him desperately and he was sending her away. Two fat tears rolled down her cheeks.

"Ka-ty."

She went into his arms and buried her face against his shoulder. He smelled of smoke and sage and sweat and she thought how she had grown to love his touch and his scent and the sound of his voice. She lifted her face for his kiss, shivering with delight as his mouth closed on hers and his arms grew tight around her.

They did not bother with dinner that night, but spent the darkening hours locked in each other's arms. Few words were spoken. Katy knew it was useless to argue with Iron Wing once his mind was made up, and she did not want to spend her last hours with him bickering and quarreling. And deep in the back of her mind lingered the hope that, during the ten-day ride to the settlement, he would change his mind.

Iron Wing held Katy close. He could not find words enough to tell her of the love he had for her, or find the right words to express the ache her absence would create in his heart. He thought of Sitting Bull and wished he possessed the eloquence of the Sioux medicine man. Perhaps then he could tell Katy of the love in his heart.

He ran his fingers through her hair, liking the way the silken strands felt against his hand. He buried his face in her neck and breathed deeply, drawing her fresh sweet womanly scent into his nostrils. How empty his lodge would be when she was gone. Never before had he realized how empty his existence had been. Katy had given his life meaning and purpose. She had brought him love and laughter. He had hoped that, one day, she would be the mother of his children. But he could not think of himself now. She would be safer with her own people, away from the violence that was about to explode on the broad grassy plains of Dakota.

And yet he dreaded the thought of living alone again, of eating and sleeping without Katy at his side. There would be no joy in his life when Katy was gone, no love, no laughter.

With a wordless cry, he took her face in his hands and kissed her deeply, passionately. His hands roamed over every inch of her flesh as he poured out his love for her in a torrent of words.

Katy returned his caresses with the same sense of urgent desire. She needed his touch, needed to feel his body pressed against her own, binding them together.

"I will come for you when the war is over," Iron Wing vowed. "Wait for me."

"I will," Katy promised, but in her heart she knew he would never come. The Indians would never defeat the Army. If Iron Wing wasn't killed in battle, he would be sent to live on a reservation and she would never see him again.

As Iron Wing thrust into her, she hoped desperately that he would change his mind about sending her away. She knew she would rather face death than be separated from the man who was even now murmuring that he loved her more than his own life.

But in the morning, nothing had changed. He was still determined to take her back to her own people. With a heavy heart, Katy packed her few belongings, bid a tearful farewell to Yellow Flower, Tall Buffalo and Bull Calf, and followed Iron Wing out of the village.

They rode in silence for several miles. The prairie was in bloom, alive with color, but Katy was oblivious to her surroundings. Her mind was in turmoil as she thought of what was to come. How would the people at the fort accept her? Would they pity her? Shun her? Or mock her? And what would she say to her mother?

For the first time in months, she thought of the Little Sisters of Mercy convent, of peaceful walls, of the statue of the Blessed Virgin. Would the Sisters still accept her? But the convent no longer had the power to soothe her troubled heart. She did not want to spend the rest of her life shut up behind high walls. She wanted to lie safe in Iron Wing's arms, to hear his voice whisper words of love and desire, to share his lodge and bear his children.

They crossed rolling hills and great grassy plains that had once been thick with buffalo.

But now the plains were virtually empty, with only hundreds of the big shaggy-maned beasts where there had once been thousands.

Iron Wing rode in silence. Hard times were coming for the Cheyenne, for all the Plains tribes. He had known it ever since gold was discovered in the Sacred Hill in 1874. The Army had made a vain effort to keep settlers out of the Black Hills, but when the Sioux refused to give up their land, the Army withdrew their efforts. Since then, he had known it was just a matter of time until the white men took the land by force. And now that time was coming. He could not blame the whites for coveting the land, for it was rich with game: antelope, elk, deer, rabbits, beaver. There were forests in the Black Hills heavy with yellow pine, white spruce, poplar, birch, red cedar, aspen, oak. Man Above had blessed the land, and now the whites meant to have it.

Iron Wing felt discouragement settle on his shoulders like a carrion crow. The Indians could not fight the white man forever. There was no end to the constant flood of whites crossing the prairie that had once known only the footprints of the Indian. If a white man was killed, ten others rose to take his place. The Cheyenne and the Sioux did not have ten warriors to take the place of a fallen brave. Nor did they possess the seemingly endless supply of guns and ammunition that was at the Army's disposal. Other tribes had already been defeated by the thunder guns and the soldier coats. A few tribes had vanished from the face of the earth, wiped out by the diseases of the white eyes. Still

other tribes had turned into "friendly"
Indians. The Crow, ancient enemy of the
Sioux and Cheyenne, had befriended the
whites. Crow warriors scouted for the Army.
They sold their women to the soldiers for
whiskey.

It was only a matter of time, Iron Wing
mused bitterly. Sooner or later the Cheyenne
would go down in defeat. He did not intend
for Katy to perish with him.

Katy and Iron Wing exchanged few words
during their journey. Occasionally, as they
rode side by side, Iron Wing reached out to
caress Katy's arm or touch her cheek. His
quiet gestures of affection tugged at Katy's
heart. He had become so dear to her. How
would she endure life without him?

Nights, she lay rigid on her side of the robe
they shared, determined to repulse his
advances. But he had only to lay a hand on
her shoulder and her intentions to rebuff him
melted like snow in the summer sun. Only in
his arms could she ease the pain of their
nearing separation. Her hands touched and
explored every inch of his flesh, memorizing
the way his muscles rippled beneath her
fingertips, the way his hair felt in her hands,
the length and breadth and smell of him. And
nightly, she prayed a child would be born of
their love so that she might have someone to
cherish when he was gone.

The morning of the tenth day, they topped
a rocky hillside. The settlement lay below,
what was left of it. Only the outer walls
remained standing. Everything else had been
burned to the ground, with only blackened

223

foundations to show where buildings had stood. Iron Wing left Katy behind while he rode down the hill to read the sign, though it was clear what had happened. Indians on the move to join Sitting Bull had attacked the settlement, destroying everyone inside and making off with whatever horses and livestock they could find. Bodies littered the ground. Most had been gnawed by wolves, or by the great black birds that took to the air at his approach, circling high overhead while they waited for him to leave.

On foot, he walked through the charred ruins. There was no sign of life. He paused near the back wall of the fort, his face thoughtful. The Indians had suffered much at the hands of the whites. Now, with Sitting Bull and Crazy Horse rallying the tribes together, the white intruders would be made to pay for the many broken treaties, and broken Indian bodies. The Indians might achieve a few victories, he mused, and they would be sweet indeed, but in the end the Indians would lose. He felt it strongly, and it caused him great pain. And yet, he would fight to the end, and fight gladly. Better to die in battle, with a lance in his hand and a war cry on his lips, than to bow in subjection to the white man, or live penned up on a reservation, his freedom gone forever.

His dark thoughts were sharply curtailed by a shrill scream, and he whirled around to see a large group of riders surround Katy. They were a mixed bunch, made up of whites, Mexicans, and a few flat-faced Apaches.

Iron Wing's first impulse was to attack, but he quickly realized that such a course of action would accomplish little but his own death under a fusillade of bullets. Noiseless as a shadow, he melted through a break in the wall and disappeared into the underbrush.

Katy stared at the men surrounding her, mesmerized with fear. They were outlaws, renegades—she was certain of it. They were armed with pistols, rifles, knives, and bandoleros slotted with fat shiny shells. The men leered at her for a long time, all the more frightening because they did not speak. A man on her left slowly reached out and touched her cheek. Another ran a dirty hand through her hair. A third laid a hairy brown paw over her breast and squeezed.

"No, don't!" Katy screamed the words, but only a hoarse whisper emerged from her throat.

Feeling more helpless and afraid than she had ever been in her life, she searched the swarthy faces hovering around her, hoping to find one that showed a spark of pity or compassion, but she saw only lust reflected in their eyes, and in the slack set of their mouths.

No one said a word, but suddenly they were all moving at once, their hands dragging her from her horse, tearing at her clothing, clawing at her exposed flesh.

Sobbing with fear, Katy fought them as one possessed of evil spirits, but they quickly subdued her. Throwing her roughly to the ground, four men grabbed her arms and legs, pinning her down, while a fifth man stripped her naked. An almost reverent hush fell over the outlaws as they stared at the girl writhing on the ground. And then they began to grin.

Crying uncontrollably, Katy craned her neck from side to side, hoping to see Iron Wing, but all she could see was his horse standing hipshot in the shadow of one wall. Despair settled over her like a shroud, and she went suddenly limp. Iron Wing had abandoned her.

One man remained apart from the others. He was short and stocky, with enormous biceps and a barrel chest. His eyes followed Katy's frantic gaze and came to rest on the spotted stallion standing ground-tied near the front wall of the burnt-out settlement.

"*Amigos*," he called quietly, and jerked his head toward Iron Wing's stallion. "She was not alone. Pablo, Vincente, Sam! *Andale!*"

The three designated men mounted their horses and rode into the ruined fort. Guns drawn, they searched through the rubble. Finding no one, they spread out and circled the walls. Again, they found nothing.

The leader turned hard gray eyes on Katy. "Who was with you?" he asked in a voice like steel.

"No one."

The outlaw leader sat on his heels beside Katy, his eyes boring into her own. "Who was with you?" he asked again.

"No one."

His slap made her ears ring. "I will ask you one last time," he warned, "and then I will let Carlito have you. You will not like Carlito."

"But Carlito will like her!" The man called

226

Carlito was the shortest, ugliest man Katy had ever seen. He danced around her, his close-set yellow eyes alive with malice. Saliva dripped from the corner of his mouth. He held a long-bladed dagger in one hand, and he waved it under her nose. "I would like you very much," he cackled.

Katy threw a pleading look at the bandit leader. "There was an Indian with me. He was taking me back to my people. He was . . ." Katy screamed as Carlito ran a hideously deformed hand along the inner part of her thigh. "Don't let him touch me!" she begged. " Please don't let him touch me!"

"Carlito, enough."

The little man scowled at his boss, but he obediently backed away, only to crouch at Katy's feet, an expectant look on his face.

"Where is this Indian now?" the bandit leader demanded.

"I don't know," Katy sobbed hopelessly. "I guess he ran away."

"A wise move," the outlaw remarked. His slate gray eyes studied her as if she were a horse he was thinking of buying. "Tonio, bring the stallion. Pablo, get the lady's horse. Marquett, watch the woman."

"El Lobo," one of the men ventured cautiously. "Surely we are not leaving just yet?" The man inclined his head in Katy's direction. "Surely we must sample the delights of one so fair?"

The leader, El Lobo, shook his head. "I think not, Gaspar. I think we will take her to Herrera's."

Gaspar threw a speculative glance at Katy.

227

"Herrera's?" He whistled under his breath. "I don't know. Herrera likes them skinny and blond."

El Lobo laughed mirthlessly. "Do not be a bigger fool than you are, Gaspar. Look at her! Herrera will want her. And he will pay for her."

"Pay for me!" Katy exclaimed, her curiosity overcoming her fear. "What are you talking about?"

El Lobo grinned at her. It was a decidedly nasty grin. "Herrera is a *compadre* of mine. He runs the biggest brothel in all of Mexico."

"A brothel," Katy gasped in horror. "You aren't going to . . ."

"*Si,*" El Lobo said, pulling Katy to her feet. "I am going to sell you to Herrera. He will pay handsomely for a wench as delectable as you. And if he has suddenly gone blind or impotent, then I will keep you for myself."

"Please let me go," Katy begged, covering her nakedness as best she could with her hands. "If it's money you want, my mother will pay you whatever you wish. She's very rich."

"No, *chiquita*. It is too risky to hold you for ransom. Always, the *rurales* get involved, and someone gets hurt. With Herrera, there is no risk, only profit."

"No!" Katy shrieked hysterically as one of the men slipped a filthy poncho over her nakedness. "You can't sell me. You can't!"

"But I can," El Lobo replied implacably. And turning a deaf ear to her sobs, he lifted her into the saddle of her horse and tied her hands securely to the pommel.

"No, please," Katy sobbed, then whimpered as the outlaw slapped her, twice, reducing her cries to silent tears.

Katy watched dully as El Lobo and his men mounted their horses. One of them took her horse's reins. She looked over her shoulder, hoping to discover some sign of Iron Wing—but what could he do against so many?

There was no sign of him.

Iron Wing watched Katy ride away, surrounded by outlaws. He had heard only bits and pieces of what had been said, but the words were not important. The man, El Lobo, had slapped Katy, and for that he would die.

Iron Wing waited until the outlaws were out of sight before he left his cover and started after them. He had no weapons but the knife in his belt. No horse. No food. His face twisted with anger as he began to run in long easy strides. He had brought Katy to the settlement to protect her, and now she was in greater danger than before.

The tracks of the outlaw band were easy to follow. Iron Wing ran tirelessly, driven by his love for Katy. As the sun went down, he slowed to a walk. The man, El Lobo, was very smart. He had taken precautions in case Katy's unseen companion decided to follow them. Two of the bandits had been sent to get behind Iron Wing and take him unawares. A white man would not have noticed the brushed out hoof prints that veered away from the main body of riders, but in brushing out their tracks, the two outlaws had left another trail, just as easy to follow.

Too easy. The words whispered in the back

of Iron Wing's mind. Feeling suddenly vulnerable as a newborn babe, the warrior went swiftly to ground, his eyes and ears attuned to pick up any unusual sound or movement. The muted vibration of hooves striking the earth warned him. Glancing over his shoulder, Iron Wing saw that the two men following him had separated. The one on his left was closest. The outlaw was leaning over his gelding's neck, checking the ground for signs.

Iron Wing lay motionless, his dark skin and clothing blending in with the shadows. In minutes, he knew he would surely be discovered. He waited until the outlaw was almost on top of him. Then, with a wild cry, he sprang to his feet and dragged the startled outlaw from the saddle. He killed the man quickly with a single stroke of his blade, then whirled around to confront the second man. The outlaw drew rein and brought his rifle up, squeezing the trigger as Iron Wing lunged at him. The outlaw's horse reared as Iron Wing sprinted forward, spoiling the outlaw's aim, so that the bullet meant for Iron Wing's heart went high and creased the fleshy part of his right arm instead.

Iron Wing stumbled, but his momentum kept him moving forward, and he reached out and grasped the horse's bridle. With a twisting motion, he threw the gelding off-balance so that it fell heavily.

The white man rolled free. Scrambling to his feet, he jacked a shell into the breech of his rifle as Iron Wing let his knife fly. The heavy blade penetrated the outlaw's heart before he pulled the trigger, and he died with a garbled cry of pain.

Iron Wing sat down on his heels. Heart hammering, lungs burning, he pressed his hand against his wounded arm to staunch the flow of blood. When his breathing returned to normal, he scooped up a handful of dirt and pressed it over the wound.

When the bleeding stopped, he rose to his feet and walked to where the outlaws' horses were standing head to head. They shied away from him, spooked by the alien Indian smell and the scent of fresh blood. He did not chase them. Instead, he hunkered down on his heels and waited. Horses were naturally curious creatures. Before long, they would come to him.

Iron Wing stared into the darkness, waiting. Twenty minutes later the horses moved slowly toward him, their nostrils flared as they reached out to sniff the strange-smelling man sitting, unmoving, on the ground.

Moving swiftly, Iron Wing grabbed the reins of the nearest horse. Rising, he swung into the saddle and took up the trail once again. The loose horse followed behind, its head lifted to one side to avoid stepping on the dangling reins.

Katy's nerves were drawn tight as a bowstring by the time El Lobo and his men made camp for the night. All day, she had endured the broad leers and lewd comments of the outlaws. None had dared touch her, though they came close, making obscene gestures at her while their ribald laughter grated in her ears.

Now, with her hands and feet tightly bound, she sat beside a small fire, too numb to think of anything but El Lobo's threat to sell her to a brothel. And she had wanted to be a nun! Hysterical laughter bubbled in her throat, but she quickly swallowed it lest El Lobo hear it and slap her again.

Pablo, Carlito, and El Lobo stood a little apart from the others, talking in muted tones. The two men El Lobo had sent to find Iron Wing had not returned. Pablo wanted to go look for his amigos, but the runty Carlito was of the opinion that they were dead.

El Lobo agreed with Carlito. "Maximilliano would be here by now if he were alive," El Lobo reasoned aloud. "Only death would keep him from his dinner."

Katy felt a little thrill of hope rise within her breast. Perhaps Iron Wing had not deserted her in the face of danger after all. Perhaps, even now, he was hidden somewhere in the shadows, waiting to rescue her. The thought made her smile, and then a niggling fear worked its way into her mind. Just because the two outlaws were presumed dead did not mean that Iron Wing was still alive. He, too, might be lying out there in the dirt, dead, or dying.

Three days passed. El Lobo did not send any more of his men to look for Iron Wing. The outlaws rode in a solid front during the day, keeping Katy in their midst. At night half the camp remained awake and on guard while the other half slept. At midnight, they changed shifts.

The constant chafing of the ropes binding her hands and feet made Katy's skin sore and tender. Her thighs were rubbed raw where her bare skin grated against the saddle leather. And she was covered with so much dust she wondered how any of the men could possibly find her desirable.

Carlito, that ugly monkey-like gnome of a man, managed always to be near Katy. He rode by her side, spread his blankets near hers at night. His eyes, close-set and hooded beneath shaggy brows, watched her every move until Katy thought she would scream. There was something eerie about the way Carlito stared at her, his mouth set in a lop-sided grin, his yellow eyes as unblinking as a snake's.

Another six days passed. Katy hoped they would encounter Indians, for life as a slave in an Indian camp was preferable to being a whore. And perhaps, if they were captured by Indians, she could find out if Iron Wing still lived. But they met no one, red or white.

The land was changing a little each day. The flat plains gave way to rolling hills cut by dry sandy washes and slab-sided canyons. Trees and brush grew thick and green, providing shade and shelter from the sun.

El Lobo's men rode with their eyes and ears alert, even though there had been no sign of Iron Wing, or anyone else, for nine days.

The next night, one of the outlaws went out to answer nature's call. He did not come back. El Lobo found the man behind a bush, his throat slashed from ear to ear, his scalp gone.

The man's death, horrible as it was, brightened Katy's flagging spirits. Iron Wing was still alive. And as long as he lived, there was hope.

# 16

Iron Wing followed El Lobo's trail from a safe distance, waiting for the chance to pick off another of the outlaws, but the bandits were chary of him now and they rode warily, ever alert to the threat of an ambush.

When El Lobo's men made camp for the night, Iron Wing holed up in some secluded spot where he could watch the camp without being seen. And while he watched, he fashioned a short stout bow of juniper wood, and made a dozen arrows. The tail feathers from a wild turkey provided the fletching; flat stones, painstakingly shaped and honed, provided arrowheads.

And then the terror began. For six nights, just after sunset, Iron Wing's arrows swished out of the darkness to strike human flesh.

The outlaws spent hours hunting him, but it was like tracking the wind. Arrows left no telltale muzzle flash to follow, no echoing gunshot to indicate from which direction the arrow had come.

El Lobo was seething. Nine of his men had been killed because of the white woman. It was a high price to pay. Too high. It would have to stop.

The night after the sixth arrow had found its mark, the bandit leader built a roaring fire. Then, grabbing Katy by the hair, he jerked her to her feet and held her close to his side, a knife poised at her throat.

"Indian!" El Lobo hollered into the darkness. "You have killed nine of my men. It is enough. If one more of my *compadres* dies, the woman will be killed immediately. Do you hear me, Indian?"

The threat echoed and reechoed in the stillness of the night, but no answer came from the impenetrable darkness.

Katy sighed as El Lobo boosted her into the saddle the following morning. She was weary to the bone. Weary of being constantly tied hand and foot; weary of riding day after endless day, weary of having her every movement watched. She was never left alone, not even to relieve herself, and that was the most humiliating of all. What could be worse than crouching in the dirt while a man stood by, his eyes mocking, his mouth twisted into a leering grin?

Thus far, none of the outlaws had dared touch her, but they continued to stare at her, their lurid thoughts always visible in their swarthy faces and lust-filled eyes.

Riding across the seemingly endless miles of prairie, Katy wondered how much longer El Lobo could keep his men under control, and how she would live with the shame if the outlaws raped her en masse.

She thought constantly of Iron Wing, wondering where he was, and how much longer he would follow El Lobo before he gave up and went back to his own people. Soon the outlaws would arrive at their destination, and El Lobo would sell her to the man, Herrera She would be lost then. Iron Wing would have to turn back, or risk being shot on sight by the first white man who saw him.

Despair perched on Katy's shoulders like a hungry buzzard. Nothing in life had ever turned out the way she planned. She had expected to live out her days in happy contentment as Robert's wife. But Robert had been killed by Apaches. She had yearned to bury her grief in the peace and solitude of the convent. But that had been denied her. She had found true happiness with Iron Wing after months of misery, and now he, too, was lost to her.

Tears welled in Katy's eyes and slid down her cheeks, coming faster and faster, until silent sobs tore at her throat. It was so unfair! Everyone she had loved had been killed or brutally snatched from her grasp.

Katy cried herself to sleep that night. And sleeping, began to dream . . . She was alone on a high plateau when suddenly Iron Wing stood beside her. He smiled at her, his dark eyes glowing with love. Whispering his name, she melted into his arms, her whole body singing with joy at his nearness. His hand touched her cheek, but when she looked up, Iron wing was gone and Carlito stood in his place. Wrenching out of the little man's arms, she ran blindly into a building that loomed out of the darkness. Bright lights turned the night to day, and she gasped as she saw El Lobo standing there, a great sum of money clutched in his hand. A faceless man stepped out from behind El Lobo. It was Herrera,

Katy knew, and she ran screaming out of the room. A door appeared before her and she quickly opened it and ducked inside, to find herself in a small room. There was no furniture in the room except a stained and lumpy mattress that stretched from wall to wall. The door closed, and Carlito was there. His arms grabbed her, crushing the breath from her body, while his mouth found hers. Helpless, she looked over the outlaw's shoulder to see Iron Wing standing beside the door, his expression one of disgust. "Whore," he sneered, and vanished from her sight.

Katy's scream was loud in the stillness of the night and she sat up, shivering violently, to find Carlito staring at her.

Morning came at last. Preoccupied with her own unhappy thoughts, Katy did not notice when the outlaw known as Pablo stayed behind, on foot.

Iron Wing continued to follow El Lobo's trail, his face set in hard lines, his eyes alight with a burning need for vengeance. He had killed nine of the outlaws, but he would not rest until they were all dead and Katy stood by his side again. Never again would he leave her. They would face the future together, no matter what it held in store for them.

Katy . . . the hard lines of his face softened when he thought of her, warm and willing in his arms, her lips parted in a shy smile, her sky-blue eyes shining with affection. She had filled his life with meaning, healed the scars Quiet Water had left on his soul, and his arms ached with the need to hold her close.

It was just before noon when a sudden uneasiness caused the back of Iron Wing's neck to grow taut. Reining his mount to a halt, he turned sideways in the saddle, his narrowed eyes probing every bush and shadow. He caught the faint glint of sunlight reflecting on metal just as the outlaw pulled the trigger.

The heavy .44/.40 slug caught Iron Wing high in the chest, slamming into him with the force of a sledgehammer, so that he toppled over the side of his horse to lie stunned on the ground. Blinding white pain splintered down his right side, rendering him momentarily helpless. Moments later the sound of footsteps penetrated the mists of pain. Glancing sideways, he saw the outlaw walking purposefully toward him.

Pablo smiled smugly. Slowly, deliberately, he pulled his sidearm, cocked the pistol, sighted down the barrel. Abruptly, he eased the hammer down and holstered the Colt.

"No sense wasting another bullet," the outlaw muttered to himself. "You're a dead man already."

Laughing softly, the outlaw walked to Iron Wing's horse and swung into the saddle.

Iron Wing closed his eyes, listening to the sound of hoofbeats recede into the distance as the outlaw rode away. The pain in his chest throbbed monotonously. Clenching his teeth against the pain, he opened his eyes and rolled to his knees, then sprawled face down into the dust as blackness washed over him, carrying him down, down, into nothingness.

El Lobo looked at his right-hand man impatiently. "Well?" he growled. "Is it done?"

"Done!" Pablo said, patting Iron Wing's horse on the neck. "That redskin won't be giving us any more trouble."

Katy stared at the two men, her face paling as Pablo's words sank in. Iron Wing was dead. It wasn't true, she thought dully. It couldn't be true.

But it was. El Lobo was smirking with satisfaction as he congratulated Pablo on a job well done, laughing loudly with the others because Iron Wing's silent arrows of death would kill no more.

With a wordless cry of pain and hopelessness, Katy sank to her knees. She hurt deep inside, hurt as she had never hurt before. A hard lump rose in her throat, aching to be released in a torrent of tears. But the tears would not come. Guilt wrapped around her heart as she remembered all the times she had wished Iron Wing dead, the times she had screamed she hated him, would always hate him. Vividly, she remembered the night she had plunged a knife into his flesh. She had wished him dead a hundred times in a hundred ways, and now her wish had come true.

She stared blankly at the dish of food El Lobo was holding under her nose. "Eat," he commanded gruffly. Spearing a chunk of meat, he raised the fork to her lips, but Katy shook her head and turned away.

El Lobo shrugged indifferently. If the woman did not want to eat, so be it. Herrera liked his women on the skinny side, and if the white girl lost a few pounds, so much the better.

* * *

The moon was high when Iron Wing regained consciousness. He gazed up at the sky, gathering his strength. Then, with teeth gritted, he got to his hands and knees. Head hanging, body sheened with sweat, he fought against the urge to lie down, to close his eyes and slip away into the warm darkness that hovered all around him, waiting to claim him forever.

With an effort, he lurched to his feet. The world spun crazily out of focus, a sharp pain exploded through his chest, spreading waves of agony down his entire right side, but he stood fast until the world stopped spinning.

Lifting his head, he studied the moon and the stars and then he started walking, his slow footsteps carrying him west in the general direction El Lobo had been going.

He had gone less than a mile when he spotted the faint glow of a campfire. Pausing, he sniffed the wind. You could always smell coffee boiling in a white man's camp. But now he smelled only roasting buffalo and he continued forward, hoping he was not walking into a Crow camp.

The warriors sitting around the fire rose to their feet, their eyes showing surprise at seeing a lone man stumble into their camp in the dead of night.

"Ho, brothers," Iron Wing mumbled hoarsely, and collapsed at their feet.

When he woke, he was laying on a buffalo robe near the fire. Three Sioux braves hovered over him. One held a thin-bladed knife in his hand.

"The bullet in your chest will have to come out," the warrior holding the knife said.

Iron Wing nodded. He stared past the warrior's left shoulder, his eyes fastened on a distant star as the knife probed his flesh, penetrating deeper, deeper, until, with a final twist, the warrior extracted the slug from Iron Wing's chest.

They let the wound bleed a minute, until the blood ran bright red and clean. Then one of the warriors withdrew a flaming stick from the fire and laid it over the wound. Iron Wing's body went rigid as the smoking brand touched his flesh. And then merciful darkness closed in on him once more.

When Iron Wing regained consciousness, it was dawn. One of the warriors offered him a cup of weak broth and he drank it slowly, feeling its warmth strengthen him. When the cup was empty, he asked for more.

The warrior who had removed the bullet from his chest hunkered down beside him. "I am Standing Bull of the Lakota," he said politely. Holding to Indian custom, he did not ask for the stranger's name.

"I am Iron Wing, of the Cheyenne."

Standing Bull nodded. The name Iron Wing was known to his people. It was rumored he would be the next chief of the Cheyenne. "Have you been long from the lodges of your people?"

"Many days. I am trailing some white men who took my woman from me."

"Then you do not know of Pahaska, and how he was slain in the valley of the Greasy Grass?"

Iron Wing regarded Standing Bull in awed

silence. So, Custer had been killed at the Little Big Horn.

"The vision of Sitting Bull was a true vision after all," Iron Wing murmured.

"Yes. The Sioux and the Cheyenne, together with our brothers, the Aparaphoe, killed Custer and all his men. It was a great victory for our people. Now we are on our way back home."

Iron Wing grunted softly. General George Amstrong Custer, that pompous, glory-seeking Indian fighter, had been defeated in battle. At last, the spirits of all those who had been killed that cold winter morning at the Washita could rest in peace. Their deaths had been avenged. No more would Yellow Hair bring terror and death to the lodges of the Cheyenne.

Iron Wing sighed heavily. He would have liked to have been there to see Yellow Hair wiped out. It would have been good to go to battle against the Seventh Cavalry, good to see soldiers dead on the field of battle. But there was no time for regret now. There would be other encounters with the whites. There would always be war with the white man so long as one Indian remained alive and free.

Iron Wing rose unsteadily to his feet. "I must go."

"You are in no condition to travel, or to fight," Standing Bull remarked. "Why not come home with us until you are stronger?"

"I cannot," Iron Wing answered. "I cannot take a chance of losing the trail of the white men who took my woman."

"Take my horse, then," Standing Bull offered generously. "He is fast as the wind, as sure-footed as the goats who live in the mountains."

"*Le mita pila, kola,*" Iron Wing said in the Lakota tongue. "Thank you, my friend."

Standing Bull led his horse forward. It was a big blood-bay, with long legs, a deep chest, and large nostrils to drink the wind.

"He is truly a fine horse," Iron Wing acknowledged, taking the reins. But he made no attempt to mount. Standing Bull was right. He was in no condition to travel. He was weak from the blood he had lost. His legs were unsteady, his vision blurred.

He was of no use to anyone just now, Iron Wing admitted sourly. He could not ride. He could not fight. And there was a nagging pain in his chest, a pain that would grow steadily worse, rendering him weaker and weaker each day unless he gave the wound time to heal.

With a wry grin, Iron Wing handed the reins to Standing Bull.

"I think I will rest with you awhile after all."

# 17

Katy dropped heavily onto the blanket that Carlito spread for her. With each passing mile, she knew a greater sense of hopelessness and despair. During the last five days, they had passed through land familiar to Katy, and the pain it caused her was overpowering. To be so close to home! If only she could find a way to escape, she would fly to her mother's arms and never leave. But escape was impossible. Her hands and feet were tied constantly; each day, one of the outlaws checked her bonds to make sure they were secure.

She was weeping softly when the outlaw came up behind her. Startled, Katy whirled around, and then relaxed when she saw it was not Carlito, but the young bandit known as Tom. He was a mild-mannered youth who spoke little, but of late he had taken to looking after her. She had done nothing to encourage him, but she was glad of his presence, because it kept the loathsome Carlito at bay.

"Here, lady," Tom said, handing her a cup of hot coffee. "Drink that, and then get some rest. We'll be heading out early in the morning. Herrera's is only about twenty miles due south."

Twenty miles! Despair rose in Katy's eyes. Desperate for help, she took Tom's hand in hers and pressed it to her breast.

"Can't you do something?" she pleaded. "Please don't let El Lobo sell me to that awful man. For God's sake, I was going to be a nun!"

Tom stared at the woman weeping before him. Her bound hands were so small and helpless, he felt a sudden wave of sympathy for her. He had always taken women as he found them, using them to satisfy the needs of his flesh. He had never known a good girl from a good family. And it was for damn sure he had never known a girl who wanted to be a nun.

"Please help me," Katy begged. She looked up at him through blue eyes bright with tears, making him feel strangely protective toward her. The heat of her breast through her tattered bodice filled his palm with a pulsing heat.

"Lady," he said thickly, "I . . . what do you want me to do?"

"Please help me get away. I'll do whatever you ask. Anything at all, only please don't let El Lobo sell me to a brothel. I'll . . . I'll be your woman if you want me, I promise."

His woman. The thought made him almost lightheaded. Imagine, having this well-bred woman for his own. She didn't look like much now, with her face dirty and stained with tears, but he'd just bet she would be an eyeful when she was cleaned up.

"You mean it?" Tom asked suspiciously.

"Yes."

Roughly, he grabbed Katy by the shoulders

and pulled her close. His mouth was hard, his breath reeked of cigarettes and whiskey, but she did not turn away from his kiss.

"Okay," he said, releasing her. "I'll come for you when it's my turn to keep watch. Be ready."

For the first time, Katy felt a small flicker of hope. If Tom could get her safely away from El Lobo, maybe she could persuade him to take her home.

Katy was wide awake when Tom came for her. He quickly cut her hands and feet free, then they crept quietly out of camp to where Tom had two horses waiting. Cautiously, they led the horses away from the outlaw camp, until they were out of hearing distance. Then they mounted and rode swiftly through the dark night. Since Iron Wing's death, only one man guarded the outlaw camp. With luck, they would be miles away before their absence was discovered.

Katy clutched at her horse's mane as the animal raced over the darkened ground in the wake of Tom's horse. It was frightening, racing madly through the night, unable to see anything but the shadowed outline of trees and shrubs and the man ahead of her. At such speed, a fall could be fatal, and Katy closed her eyes, not wanting to see what was coming. The wind stung her cheeks and once a pebble struck her forehead. And still they rode, the muffled sound of their horses' hooves sounding like thunder in the quiet night.

She was exhausted when, at last, Tom reined his gelding to a halt. Dismounting, he pulled Katy from the saddle and led her into a cave recessed deep in the side of a brush-covered slope. Shoving a blanket into her hands, he left her to tend the horses, tethering them out of sight behind a thick stand of young cottonwood trees.

Katy watched him warily as he entered the cave. She had promised to be his woman, would have promised him anything in the world to save herself from the degrading life of a whore; but now, alone in the cave with him, she knew she could not fulfill that promise. He was a stranger, an outlaw wanted for heinous crimes, and she was terribly afraid of him.

"Get some sleep," Tom said gruffly. "We're gonna be on the trail again before sunup."

Nodding vigorously, Katy rolled into the blanket and closed her eyes. She could feel the bandit watching her and she stirred self-consciously, wishing he would stop staring at her.

"Go to sleep, girl," Tom said, chuckling with wry amusement. "I won't be bothering you tonight, but I can't help lookin'. You're a mighty pretty woman. Mighty pretty."

Cheeks flushing, Katy turned away from him. After a long while, she fell into a deep sleep.

It seemed only moments had passed before Tom was shaking her awake.

"Get up, girl," he said curtly. "We're leaving."

Groaning softy, Katy stood up and rolled her blanket into a tight cylinder, then followed the outlaw outside. The horses were saddled and ready, their breath coming out in great white vapors as they snorted and pawed the earth. Tom secured Katy's bedroll behind her saddle, lifted her onto her horse. She bit her lip as his hand caressed her thigh.

Another day of riding until dark. Another night of seeking shelter in a secluded place, of sleeping on the hard ground.

The afternoon of the fourth day, they arrived at a small ranch. Judging by the look of it, Katy thought the place had been long deserted. The house was badly in need of paint, the windows were broken, there was a hole in the roof. The barn door was hanging by a single hinge. An entire section of fence was missing from the single corral located beside the barn.

"This is home," Tom announced, stepping from the saddle. Removing his hat, he slapped it against his thigh to shake away the dust. "It ain't much now, but it has real possibilities."

Katy nodded as she dismounted. It wasn't really such a bad place. There were some trees and the remains of what had once been a garden. The water Tom drew from the well was cold and clear.

Katy was apprehensive as she followed Tom into the house. Looking around, she saw a large parlor, a sunny kitchen, and a door that lead to a bedroom. What little furniture the house contained was crude and covered with a thick layer of yellow dust.

"It's . . . nice," Katy said lamely.

Tom nodded. "Yeah. Why don't you clean the place up a little while I go hunt us up some meat?" His eyes drilled into hers. "I won't be gone long."

Katy nodded. She understood exactly what he was saying. He was warning her not to try to run away.

A search through some cupboards produced a couple of rags and Katy began to dust the furniture. When that was done, she unpacked Tom's saddlebags, putting what little food they contained in the kitchen. His extra clothing she placed in the scarred oak dresser in the bedroom. She spared a brief glance at the big double bed. How could she let Tom touch her? She would never love him, would never love any man again. How could she after knowing Iron Wing? No man in the world could compare with his muscular perfection. Closing her eyes, she summoned his countenance to mind: the high proud cheekbones, the fine straight nose, the strong square jaw, the wide sensual mouth that had given her hours of pleasure . . .

Abruptly, she opened her eyes. Remembering was a futile, painful endeavor. Returning to the kitchen, she began to wash the few mismatched dishes and utensils stored in the cupboard. She was washing the last of the dented pots and pans when Tom returned with a pair of rabbits and a quail slung over his shoulder.

"Can you cook?" he asked doubtfully.

"Yes."

"Damn!" he exclaimed. "Good-looking and useful to boot." Grinning, he handed her the rabbits and the bird, sat on one of the rickety kitchen chairs while she skinned the rabbits for dinner.

They ate in silence. Katy found it hard to concentrate on her food. Glancing out the kitchen window, she saw that it would soon be dark. Before long, it would be time for bed, and then Tom would claim the reward she had foolishly promised him.

Sliding a covert glance at the outlaw, she saw by his expression that he was thinking along the same lines.

"Tell me about yourself," Katy said, hoping to put off the inevitable. "Where are you from?"

"Texas," Tom replied.

"Oh. Do you have any family?"

"Yeah. Whole passel of kinfolk still living at home."

"Do they know . . . I mean . . ." Katy's voice trailed off. It would not do to ask the wrong questions and offend him.

"You're wondering if they know about me, and how I got to be what I am," he guessed.

"Yes, but I don't mean to pry. It's really none of my business."

Tom laughed. "I guess you got a right to know what kind of a man you've hooked up with," he mused good-naturedly. "I fell in with El Lobo and his bunch because I was tired of working from sunup to sundown with nothing to show for it but callouses. I been riding with El Lobo for nigh onto two years. He's a mean bastard when he's drunk, but otherwise he's okay. But, hell, lately I've had the urge to settle down. I can't go back to Texas, but this place ain't bad."

"Did you ever kill anyone?"

"When I had to. You got any more questions?" he asked gruffly, his good humor gone.

"No."

Tom sat back in his chair, smoking a long black cigar, while Katy cleared the table and did the dishes. Knowing what was to come, Katy dawdled over the dishes, washing each one thoroughly, wiping them past the time when they were dry, stacking them neatly in the cupboard.

Tom watched her with an indulgent grin, well aware of what she was doing. But he was a patient man. She could stall all she wanted. She was his now, and he could wait.

When the last dish had been put away, Tom stood up, stretching. "Been a long day," he drawled. "I'm ready for bed."

Katy swallowed hard as his long arm reached out to circle her waist. She felt her heart began to beat wildly as he drew her close.

"You gonna keep your end of the bargain," he asked, "or shall I take you back to El Lobo?"

"I'll keep it," Katy said tremulously. "But please don't hurt me."

"Now what makes you think I'd wanna hurt a little bitty thing like you?"

"I don't know," she answered quickly. "I'm sorry."

His smile was cruel as he grabbed a handful of her long hair and jerked her head back. For the first time, Katy noticed the cruel slant of his mouth, the sadistic gleam in his light brown eyes.

"We'll get along just fine, so long as you remember I'm the boss. You savvy?"

"Yes."

"Good." He released his hold on her hair and walked into the bedroom. When Katy did not immediately follow, he beckoned to her with his finger, and she stumbled toward him, numb with fear.

"That's a good girl," Tom said. "Now undress."

"I can't."

"Do it." The words were as soft as velvet, as unyielding as steel.

Hands shaking, Katy began to untie the lacings at the neck of her dress. Slowly, she let the garment drop around her feet. She wore no underwear, and Tom sucked in a deep breath as her smooth creamy flesh was revealed. His eyes glowed hotly as he slowly stood up. His steps were unsteady as he roughly pulled her close. A vile obsenity rose in his throat as he began to kiss her face and breasts, unable to believe his good fortune. *Herrera, eat your heart out*, he thought as he nipped at Katy's slender neck.

Katy shuddered with revulsion as Tom's lips and tongue washed over her body, and when he began to fumble with his belt, she ran out of the room, and into El Lobo's arms.

Tom whirled around as Katy screamed, and died as El Lobo shot him in the chest.

"Get dressed, *chiquita*," El Lobo ordered, pushing her away from him. "And then fix us some food. We have been traveling all day to find you."

Katy dressed hurriedly, awkward in her haste. Carlito leered at her all the while, his little pig-eyes bright with desire. He followed her into the kitchen, stood at her elbow while

253

she fried up bacon and beans for El Lobo and his men.

Katy cringed as Pablo gave her a sharp slap on her buttocks. "Welcome home, *puta*," he said with a leer. "Look for me in your bed when Herrera puts you to work."

Katy glared at the outlaw who had killed Iron Wing. She searched her mind for some retort, but there were no words vile enough to convey her hatred or her contempt.

El Lobo's men lounged on the floor, eating and drinking, laughing, as Katy served them. Hands reached out to caress her legs, her buttocks, her breasts. The outlaws talked about her as if she were no more than a piece of property, speculating on how much Herrera would charge for her services, and if she would be worth the price. They tried in vain to convince El Lobo to let them sample her delights, but he adamantly refused.

"What would be left to sell once you were through with her?" El Lobo said, chuckling. "Too many stallions can ruin a mare."

Katy did not sleep that night. Hands tied behind her back, ankles bound and lashed to the bed, she stared up at the sagging ceiling. All was lost, and she was destined to become a whore in a border town brothel. She would never see her mother again, would never associate with decent, god-fearing people. Henceforth, she would be in the company of outlaws, men who earned their living by cruel and devious means. Better she should have stayed with the Cheyenne and perished in one of their fights against the Army than live a life of shame and degradation.

Katy prayed that night as she had not

prayed in months; prayed that she would die in the night and thus be spared the awful life that awaited her. But her frantic petitions were denied, and when dawn came, El Lobo released her bonds and boosted her onto the back of a horse, and once again the outlaws turned south toward Herrera's.

# 18

The town appeared as if my magic. One minute there was nothing in sight but sand and sage, and the next moment the town was there, crouched against the desert floor like some hulking beast ready to pounce on the first unwary traveler.

It was a decidedly ugly place, Katy thought listlessly. The buildings, mostly cribs and cantinas, were crude and unpainted; constructed of wood or adobe or both, they had been erected in haphazard fashion along both sides of the wide dirt road that was the town's only street. A small Catholic church topped by a tall sunbleached wooden cross stood at the far end of the town. Katy wondered if the dregs of humanity that would certainly be found in such a town even knew the church existed. A few ramshackle houses were strung out behind the church.

There was no sign of life on the street other than a lone horse standing hipshot at the rail of the nearest saloon. In the distance, well away from the town, stood a fortress of some kind.

El Lobo reined his horse to a halt before a large, two-story building that was located at the far end of the dusty road. A weather-beaten sign hung over the unpainted door.

The letters, barely visible, made Katy shiver with apprehension.

"HERRERA'S," the sign proclaimed. "BEST WHORES SOUTH OF THE BORDER."

El Lobo dismounted. Stretching hugely, he lifted Katy from her horse and hustled her up the sagging stairs and into the dimly-lit building.

Katy's eyes widened with surprise as she stepped into a spacious room. She had expected to find a dirty, dingy brothel smelling of whiskey and sweat. She could not have been more mistaken. Heavy red velvet draperies covered the tall windows, shutting out the scorching heat of the sun. A thick carpet muffled her footsteps as El Lobo pushed her into the next room. Gilt-edged mirrors hung from every wall, reflecting the shimmering crystal chandeliers that were suspended from the high beamed ceiling. Carved mahogany sofas and high-backed armchairs covered in rich red brocade were arranged in intimate groupings. Shiny brass spittoons were placed at strategic intervals around the room. Several paintings depicting amply endowed women in various stages of undress hung behind a long curved bar.

Katy shook her head in disgust as she took in the gaudy colors and rich appointments. Even without being told, she would have recognized the place for what it was.

There was the sound of footsteps and the jingle of spurs as El Lobo's men crowded around the bar, their voices shattering the heavy stillness.

Shortly, a blowsy, over-painted woman in a

brilliant green silk wrapper appeared at the head of the staircase.

"Quiet, pigs," she ordered brusquely. "Can't you see we're closed? Come back tonight."

"Rosa!" El Lobo exclaimed. "Always the queen of hospitality."

"Lobo, is that you?" the woman squealed, and hurried down the long stairway to throw herself into the outlaw's open arms. "Where have you been, you scoundrel?" she demanded petulantly. "I haven't seen you since last winter."

"Ah, and what a winter it was," El Lobo said, laughing loudly as he pinched the woman's ample rump. "Nothing but food, sex, and whiskey every day. If only I could spend all my winters lying snug in your bed."

"It could be arranged, my pet," Rosa assured the outlaw with a broad grin. "Indeed, it could be arranged."

"We will speak of it later tonight," El Lobo promised. "But now I must see Herrera on a matter of business."

"Business, eh?" the woman murmured with a knowing wink. "Are you buying or selling?"

"Selling," El Lobo answered. He gestured at Katy, who was standing between Pablo and Carlito, a sullen expression on her face. "I have brought Herrera a new *puta.*"

Hands on her hips, her head tilted thoughtfully to one side, Rosa contemplated the white girl. "Her hair is the wrong color, and she is a little too round, but I think maybe . . . yes, I think Frank might like her." The woman shrugged. "And if he does not, Don-

258

nelly will take her off your hands. He will buy anything with breasts."

El Lobo snorted disdainfully. "Donnelly! He does not know quality from trash."

"But you would not bring me trash, eh, *amigo?*"

All heads turned toward a man emerging from a door at the foot of the winding staircase.

"Frank!" El Lobo said jovially. "It is good to see you again, *compadre.*"

"And you," Herrera said amiably.

The two men shook hands like long lost friends. Frank Herrera was tall and slender, with close-cropped black hair and dark brown eyes. He was clean-shaven, impeccably dressed in tight black pants and a bright blue silk shirt. A long white neckerchief was loosely knotted at his throat. His feet were encased in a pair of expensive black leather boots.

Katy blushed furiously as Herrera's attention shifted from El Lobo to herself. Herrera's eyes were intense as they studied her inch by inch, leaving Katy with the feeling that he knew exactly what she looked like inside and out.

"Not bad," Herrera decided. "Yellow hair would be better, but . . ." He shrugged. "You can't have everything. How much do you want for her?"

"Only a thousand dollars," El Lobo said in a voice as soft and smooth as satin. His tone indicated it was not enough for such a prize but, because they were friends, he was willing to be generous.

"Done," Herrera said. Without batting an

eye, he reached into his pocket and withdrew a fat wad of bills. Looking almost bored, he peeled off ten one hundred dollar bills and handed them to El Lobo.

"Rosa!" El Lobo cried, transferring the money to his own pocket. "Drinks all around."

"What's your name, *puta?*" Herrera asked Katy. His voice was deep and rich, like velvet over steel.

"I am not a whore," Katy said indignantly. "Not for you. Not for anyone."

"I like a girl with spirit," Herrera remarked. Lazily, his hand reached out to curl around Katy's slender throat. The gesture was clearly a warning. "But do not push me too far. What is your name?"

"Katy Marie Alvarez."

Herrera dropped his hand from her throat. "You have some Spanish blood, *es verdad?*"

"Yes," Katy answered. "My father was a Spaniard, if that makes any difference."

"No difference at all," Herrera said, grinning arrogantly. "I buy and sell without prejudice."

"How noble of you," Katy retorted caustically. "What are your plans for me?"

Herrera made a broad gesture that encompassed the whole house. "You will work here, for me. I think you will be good for business."

"And I will be her first customer," Carlito announced. "How much for a night with your new whore?"

"More than you can afford, little man," Herrera assured him.

But Carlito was not so easily discouraged. He had been lusting after the white woman since the moment he first saw her. His hands ached to touch her, his dreams were filled with images of her golden body writhing beneath him. He meant to have her, no matter what the cost.

"How much?" Carlito insisted. "I have money."

"For the whole night?" Herrera said. "One hundred American dollars."

Carlito looked stricken. "How much for just one hour?" he asked plaintively.

"Twenty-five dollars, amigo. In advance."

A crooked grin split Carlito's ugly face. "Done!" he cried jubilantly. Delving into his pocket, he withdrew a wad of crumpled bills and thrust the greenbacks into Herrera's hand.

Grabbing Katy's arm, he headed for the stairs, calling over his shoulder, "What room can I use?"

Katy's face went white with fear and revulsion as she realized Herrera had just sold her body to Carlito, and that the ugly little man meant to take advantage of her as soon as he could get her into a bed. With a wordless cry, she tried to twist out of Carlito's grasp. When that failed, she sank her teeth into his wrist.

Carlito howled with pain, but he did not release his hold on Katy's arm. Tears of frustration welled in Katy's eyes as she realized she could not escape the outlaw and that no one in the room was going to help her. Indeed, the other outlaws were laughing uproariously as they shouted words of encouragement to Carlito as he endeavored to drag Katy up the stairs.

"Carlito. Let the woman go."

The ugly little man stopped dead in his tracks. Still holding tightly to Katy, his eyes darted to Herrera. "Do I have to let her go, Frank?" he whined. "Do I? You said I could have her."

Herrera shrugged. "Miguel is my partner. I must listen to him."

Shoulders slumped in defeat, face sullen with disappointment, Carlito dropped Katy's arm. Muttering under his breath, the outlaw went to the bar and poured himself a glass of whiskey.

Katy looked past Herrera to the man who had spoken in her behalf. He was sitting alone in a darkened corner of the room. He bore a striking resemblance to Frank Herrera. The same black hair, the same wide mouth, the same good looks. Only this man's eyes were different. They were of a lighter brown than Herrera's and filled with compassion.

"Well, Miguel?" Herrera asked. "What do you want to do with her?"

"I want her for myself."

"You want her?" Carlito laughed, as if he had just heard a good joke. "Why would you want a woman?"

"Shut your mouth, Carlito!" Frank Herrera snarled, "or I will shut it for you. Permanently!" Frank smiled fondly at the man in the chair. "Very well, *hermano,* she is yours. Alfaro! Take Miguel and the woman to the house."

A huge Mexican appeared out of an adjoining room. Stooping, he lifted Miguel Herrera out of the chair as if he were a child, and it

262

was then that Katy saw that Miguel Herrera's legs were shriveled and useless.

"*Venga*," Alfaro said to Katy, and she quickly followed the big man out of the brothel and into the sunlight, grateful to be spared the humiliation and degradation of life as a prostitute.

Outside, Katy thought fleetingly of trying to run away, but there was really no place to run. Lost and alone, she would be easy prey for man or beast. She saw her thoughts mirrored in Alfaro's eyes as he spared her one brief glance, then led the way toward the fortress Katy had noticed when they first rode into the town.

As they drew near, Katy saw there were armed guards patrolling the high walls. Massive gates swung open to admit them. A house stood in the middle of the fortress. It was an impressive structure. Two stories high, it was built of red brick and adobe. A wide veranda spanned the front of the house. Flowers bloomed in red clay pots. A fountain bubbled in the courtyard. Peacocks strutted in the yard. Peons dressed in stark white were busily engaged in tending sheep and goats and cattle, or working in the vast gardens alongside the house. A little beyond, a huge blacksmith was forging a horseshoe.

Awed by the magnificence of the place, Katy followed Alfaro into the house and down a wide, whitewashed hallway into a spacious sunlit parlor. Gently, the big Mexican placed Miguel in a large armchair and covered his wasted legs with a brightly colored blanket.

"Can I get you anything, senor?" Alfaro queried. "Brandy, perhaps?"

"Not now," Miguel answered, his eyes on Katy's face. "I will send for you if I require anything."

With a bow, Alfaro left the room.

Questions, Katy mused. So many questions tumbling through her mind. Bluntly, she asked the one causing her the most concern, though it brought a bright flush to her cheeks.

"Am I to be your mistress?"

Sadly, Miguel shook his head. "I wish it were to be so, *chiquita*, for you are very beautiful. But I am no better than a gelding. I remember how it was done, but I can no longer perform."

"I'm sorry. How did it happen?"

Miguel shrugged. "A fall from a horse. One day I was a vaquero, the next day I was a useless cripple. I have no feeling below my waist, no movement. Nothing."

"I'm sorry," Katy said again. "Truly sorry."

"It happened a long time ago," Miguel said with a wave of a graceful hand. "Sit down, Katy Marie, and tell me how you came to be in my brother's cantina."

"It's a long story."

"I am not going anywhere," Miguel said with a wistful smile.

"I've been living with the Cheyenne," Katy began. "When the man who owned me learned there was going to be war with the whites, he decided to take me back to my own people where I would be safe."

"He cared for you, this savage?"

264

"Yes."

"And how did you come to be living with the Cheyenne?"

"I was on my way to enter a convent when some Indians attacked the coach. Everyone else was killed. I thought I would also die when the savages left me for dead, but later that day another Indian came along. He took me back to his people and gave me to his friend, to be a slave."

"You were going to be a nun?"

"Yes." Katy stared out the window into the courtyard. How different her life had turned out from what she had expected. For a woman who had been determined to shun men the rest of her life, she had certainly been involved with a variety of them in the past two years. First she had been Tall Buffalo's captive, then she had been Iron Wing's slave and, later, his willing mistress. She had narrowly escaped being a harlot, and now she was to be . . . what? Surely no other woman who had started out to be a nun had taken such a wide detour!

"Would you care for something to drink?" Miguel asked solicitously. "Some lemonade, perhaps, or a glass of wine?"

"No, thank you."

Katy sat on the edge of the sofa, poised like a bird ready to take flight. "If I am not to be your mistress, what do you want with me?"

"I want you to be my companion. I get lonely here, with no one to talk to but Alfaro and the servants. Frank spends most of his time at the cantina."

"That's all?" Katy whispered in disbelief. "Just a companion?"

"Yes. You look like a young woman of some quality and intelligence. You are certainly beautiful. Perhaps you will bring some charm and grace into this old house."

Relief washed over Katy, leaving her suddenly limp and weak. A companion! Unexpectedly, she began to cry. What a blessing when compared to the awful fate she had imagined at Herrera's.

"I'll be happy to be your companion," she said, blinking back her tears. "I'm so grateful to you for saving me from that beast, Carlito, I'll gladly do anything you say."

Miguel smiled as he handed her a crisp linen handkerchief. "I think we will get on well, you and I," he said, beaming at her. "Very well, indeed."

And they did. Katy spent her days at Miguel's side. Together, they read the plays of Shakespeare, sometimes taking parts and acting them out, sometimes switching roles, so that Katy played the male parts and Miguel read the women's lines. Miguel had a wonderful voice, deep and resonant, and Katy thought the stage had missed a great talent, for his voice had the power to evoke deep emotions. They ready poetry by the hour and Katy, who had never had more than a shallow appreciation for poems or verse, gained a rich appreciation for the beauty and versatility of words that could fill a heart with laughter, or bring quick tears to her eyes. Sometimes they discussed politics or religion or the complex nature of humanity.

Miguel was a knowledgeable man. Unable to pursue any other interests, he had spent years reading books, all kinds of books. He had a vast library, the shelves filled to over-flowing with books on every topic one could imagine. There were plays, Bibles, histories, comedies, books on foreign countries and languages, on folklore and witchcraft.

Sometimes Katy felt as though she were a schoolgirl again, and Miguel was her professor. He spoke French and Latin fluently, and Katy began to learn a bit of both languages.

Miguel taught her to play poker, and to play chess, and they whiled away long hours at both.

Except for Alfaro, the cook and the house-keeper, they lived in the fortress alone.

"Why do you stay here?" Katy asked one evening. "It's like being in prison."

"My father built this house for my mother. The high walls were for protection against Indians and Comancheros." Miguel laughed softly. "It protected us from the savages, but not life. My parents both died of pneumonia when Frank and I were children. Anna raised us. As for why I stay . . ." Miguel shrugged. "There are still outlaws and Indians, and I have nowhere else to go."

Katy nodded. Helpless as Miguel was, the high walls of the fortress obviously gave him a sense of security. It was, after all, virtually impregnable. And his brother was here. Though they were vastly different, Katy knew the two men shared a deep bond.

Frank Herrera rarely came to the house. When he did, it was usually for Sunday dinner, or to discuss a problem at the cantina. Time and again, Katy thanked her lucky stars for Miguel, knowing that without his timely intervention in her behalf, she would have been forced to prostitute herself to any man who could meet Herrera's price.

She could see the Herrera cantina from her bedroom window on the second floor, and she daily thanked God that she was not locked in one of the rooms upstairs. As time passed, she learned that Frank took care of running the cantina. He handled the customers, kept the girls in line, and occasionally dealt poker at one of the tables. Miguel, bound to a chair, kept the receipts, balanced the books, ordered supplies, and paid the bills.

Miguel was a kind and generous man. He allowed Katy to use the bedroom that adjoined his so she could have a place to call her own. It was a lovely room. The housekeeper told Katy it had once belonged to Miguel's mother. Frank had a room at the opposite end of the hall, but he rarely spent the night at the fortress, preferring to stay at the cantina. He had a room there, and a variety of girls to warm his bed.

And so the days passed, and they were not unpleasant. The only thing that bothered Katy was that Miguel insisted she share his bed, even though it was impossible for him to possess her. Still, he was a man; a man tormented by desires. A man whose mind longed for the release his body could no longer provide. There were nights when he could not keep from touching Katy, nights when his hands gently caressed her body while his mouth rained kisses on her face and neck and breasts until, torn by a need he could not satisfy, he gruffly sent her to her own room.

Sometimes, in the small hours of the morning, Katy heard him sobbing. It was an awful thing, to hear a man cry. Sometimes Miguel cursed the fate that had made him an impotent cripple. Once, she heard him beg God for death.

That night, Katy tiptoed quietly into Miguel's room and took him in her arms, comforting him as she would a child. She spoke to him in soft whispers, assuring him that it took more than the ability to copulate to make a man a man. She praised him lavishly for his kindness, for his ability to make her appreciate the beauty of Shakespeare and Homer, for the knowledge he had imparted to her, for his ability to make her laugh, for his unselfish concern for others that had saved her from a life of shame.

Miguel had been horribly embarrassed at first, humiliated because a woman had seen his tears. But Katy's quiet words and her obvious affection for him acted like a soothing balm to his troubled spirit. He found comfort in her arms, and the sweet words and gentle tears that were sincere and unfeigned. That night, a warm bond of love was forged between them. Never again did he send her away.

And suddenly life was good again. Miguel needed her. And, in a curious way, she needed him. She did not love Miguel as she had loved Iron Wing. She would never love like that again. But Miguel gave meaning to her life. Often, Katy gave the cook the day off and prepared Miguel's meals herself. She planned indoor picnics, and lavish candlelit dinners. She spent hours in the kitchen, learning to prepare foreign dishes to surprise him. She took care of his personal needs, bathing him, dressing him, until Anna and Alfaro had little to occupy their time.

Katy rarely left the house because it depressed her to go outside and see the high stone walls and the guards who patrolled them. No one was permitted in or out of the gates without first being screened by one of the guards.

But for the most part, Katy was content. The house was beautiful, comfortable. She had everything she could wish for, and if she suddenly had a craving for a particular food or a new dress or a book, she had only to mention it and the item appeared in her room as if by magic. Miguel was very generous, and he plied Katy with gifts of jewelry and costly gowns of silk and satin. Katy had brought joy into his dreary existence and he never tired of buying her presents, of seeing the appreciation in her eyes. She knew he was trying to tell her how much she meant to him, and his gestures of affection were warmly received.

Sometimes Katy thought it a bit foolish to dress in silks and satin when she never left the fortress, but it pleased Miguel to see her adorned like a queen, and she would have done anything to please him.

It was only sometimes, when Alfaro played the guitar and sang the haunting Spanish love songs so dear to the Mexican heart, that Katy felt her loss. Iron Wing. Her heart still ached for his touch, for the sight of his beloved face. If she closed her eyes, she could summon his image, so clear, so vital and alive, it was hard to believe he was really dead. Hard to believe she would never again know the fire of his touch, or hear his voice whisper her name.

Iron Wing. Katy pressed her hands against her belly. He was not really dead, she mused wistfully, not when his child grew beneath her heart. For days, she had refused to accept the possibility that she could be pregnant, but she knew now that it was true. It had been over two months since her last montly flow.

She gazed out the window as a solitary tear welled in the corner of one eye and rolled down her cheek. What was she going to do? How would she explain her pregnancy to Miguel? Would he be repelled because she was carrying another man's child? Would he think she had been unfaithful to him, that she had satisfied her needs at the hands of another? And what of her child?

"Oh, Iron Wing," she sobbed. "What am I to do?"

# 19

It took six weeks for Iron Wing to recover from his wound. When, at last, he could stand on his own two feet, he was thin and terribly weak, but strong in his determination to find Katy.

Standing Bull and his wife were sorry to see him leave their lodge. They gave him a fine black gelding, clothing, moccasins, a rifle and a waterskin, then wished him well.

"There are no words to express my thanks," Iron Wing said humbly. "You have saved my life and treated me as a member of your own family. If I can ever do anything for you, I will do it."

"Go in peace," Standing Bull said, laying his hand on Iron Wing's shoulder. "I hope you find your woman."

"I will find her," Iron Wing declared. "Farewell, my good friend."

It took Iron Wing several days to return to the place where he had been shot. El Lobo's tracks were faint, in places they were very neatly wiped out. But Iron Wing clung tenaciously to the trail. Sometimes he had to get down on his hands and knees to search out a single hoof print, but he persisted. Across barren flats and over rocky slopes, his keen well-trained eyes led him steadily forward until he came to a dirty little town. Here, the tracks of El Lobo's horses were swallowed up in the prints of dozens of other horses.

Bringing his gelding to a halt out of sight behind a stunted cottonwood tree, Iron Wing stared at the town. Was Katy there?

He spent a week watching the people come and go, but there was no sign of Katy or El Lobo or any of his men. Had they rested here and moved on? If so, where would he begin to look? He scouted the trails that branched out from the main road, but could find no trace of El Lobo's horse.

Three days later, he was still undecided about what to do when a lone rider came into view. The man was about Iron Wing's size, and Iron Wing smiled faintly as he drew his knife and crept noiselessly toward the unsuspecting rider.

Twenty minutes later, clad in the dead man's clothes, his long black hair cut short, Iron Wing rode into the town. Leaving his horse hitched to a rail at one end of the street, he went into every cantina, his dark eyes searching for Katy, his ears listening for the sound of her voice, or the mention of her name, but to no avail.

He was on the verge of despair when a chance remark caught his ear.

" . . . pretty little thing she was, too," the vaquero was saying. "Herrera bought her from some outlaws. I was hoping to get my hands on her but Miguel took her home."

The vaquero's companion nodded. "I, too,

have heard of this woman who has captured the heart of the cripple. They say she lives at the fortress . . ."

A short time later, Iron Wing was knocking at the massive wooden gates of the Herrera fortress.

A man guarding the gates frowned at the stranger. Another renegade looking for a handout, he thought contemptuously. Sooner or later, they all came begging to Miguel Herrera.

"Move on," the guard ordered. "We don't give charity here."

"I am looking for work," Iron Wing said with what he hoped was the right degree of servility. "I am good with horses."

The guard stared at the man standing before him, noting the faint scar on his left cheek, the muscles bulging beneath the faded blue chambray shirt, the strong horseman's legs.

"Go to the house and knock at the back door. One of our vaqueros got killed last week. Maybe the boss will put you on. If he says no, you hightail it back here and get going. *Comprende?*"

"I understand," Iron Wing answered tonelessly.

Iron Wing walked swiftly toward the house, noting as he did so that the fortress was as well guarded as the white man's prison. A short Mexican woman with a broad face and lively black eyes came in answer to his knock on the back door. She frowned at Iron Wing. "What do you want?"

"I came to see about a job working with horses."

Anna nodded. "Come, I will take you to Alfaro."

"I am looking for a man, Herrera," Iron Wing said.

"First you must see Alfaro. He is in charge of hiring the vaqueros."

Alfaro was in the parlor, reading, when Anna knocked on the door. In a torrent of quick Spanish, the woman explained what Iron Wing wanted, then left the room.

Iron Wing stared at the big man. Never had he seen anyone so tall and broad as the Mexican standing before him.

"So you think you would like to work here," Alfaro mused. "We have strict rules. You cannot leave the fortress without my permission. You must never enter the house unless you are summoned here. You must not fight with the other vaqueros. You must not drink. You will be paid once each month. Do you still want the job?"

"Yes."

"*Bueno*. You will start tomorrow. Mondo Ortiz is the segundo here. You will find him at the corrals this time of day. He will tell you where to bed down."

With a curt nod, Iron Wing left the room. Anna was waiting outside the door. Wordlessly, she led him through the house to the back door.

Alfaro watched the new man cross the yard toward the horse corrals. He did not doubt that the man could ride, but there was something unusual about him, something Alfaro could not put his finger on.

# 20

It was a beautiful September day, cool and crisp, fragrant with the smell of rich black earth and jasmine. Much too beautiful a day to be cooped up in the house.

Just before noon, Katy slipped out of the back door and walked down the curved dirt path that led to the flower garden. It was one of her favorite places, though she rarely went there. Too often, it reminded her of home. She had asked Miguel time and time again if he would not relent and let her write a letter to her mother, but he always refused, just as he refused to let her have any contact with the outside world, afraid, perhaps, that somehow her mother would learn of her whereabouts and spirit her away from him.

Katy sighed as she strolled leisurely through the garden. There were few flowers still blooming, but the garden was in a lovely setting, surrounded by tall trees and shrubs. She had wound up locked behind high stone walls after all, Katy mused, but they were not convent walls. Still, it was a chaste life, for all that Miguel slept with her in his arms. Sometimes he watched her undress, his luminous brown eyes alight with a desire he could not fulfill. His hands would stroke her breasts, her hips, her arms and legs, but his touch left her cold and unmoved. Despite her fondness for the man, he stirred no passion within her being. Only Iron Wing's touch had been able to arouse her, and she had yielded to him like a wanton—unashamed and unafraid. A mere look had been enough to make her go weak with excitement.

"Iron Wing." She whispered his name as she wandered from the garden down to the horse corrals. He invaded her thoughts, haunted her dreams, so that she woke wanting him. She had been pitying Miguel, she thought, bemused, and yet they were much alike. He yearned for a woman he could not possess, and she hungered for a man who was long dead.

Heaving a great sigh, Katy sat down on an iron bench in the shade of the hacienda, staring at the horses standing head to tail in the nearest corral. It was pleasant, being alone. Usually, Miguel was with her, or Anna, or even Alfaro. Yes, it was nice to be alone; nice to sit in the shade with her own thoughts, even when the thoughts were somewhat melancholy. She wondered if Iron Wing had suffered much, and if he was in the spirit world hunting spirit buffalo. She wondered if Yellow Flower's baby had been a boy or a girl, if Bull Calf had taken the necessary steps to become a full-fledged warrior of the Cheyenne nation.

A faint smile played over Katy's lips as she placed her hand on her belly and said a little prayer that the child she carried would be a strong healthy boy, handsome like his father.

Katy's thoughts came to an abrupt halt as a tall man emerged from the barn and walked toward her, his face shadowed by a floppy brimmed sombrero. Katy stared at the man, her heart catching in her throat. Then she laughed self-consciously. It could not be Iron Wing. He was dead, somewhere out in the wilderness, killed by one of El Lobo's cutthroats. But the man's walk looked so familiar . . .

Katy whispered his name when he raised his head, would have run joyfully into his arms if Alfaro had not chosen that moment to come looking for her.

Dazed, Katy followed Alfaro into the house where Miguel was waiting lunch for her. She ate her food without tasting it. Iron Wing was alive! She could not concentrate on what Miguel was saying and when lunch was over, she pleaded a headache and escaped to her room where she could be alone with her chaotic thoughts. Iron Wing was here, inside the fortress. It was impossible. It was incredible, but it was true nonetheless. She had seen him with her own eyes.

Restless, she paced her room, pausing now and then to stare out the window into the courtyard below, hoping to catch a glimpse of him, but to no avail. Other men came and went by the dozen, but there was no sign of Iron Wing.

Dinnertime came and went and then, too soon, it was time for bed. Miguel regarded Katy through thoughtful eyes, puzzled by her distracted attitude. She looked happy and sad at the same time, and he wondered what had wrought the change in her. Was she upset with him? Was she suddenly unhappy? He questioned Alfaro, hoping to gain a clue as to Katy's erratic behavior, but Alfaro only shrugged and mumbled something about the moodiness of women.

That night, in bed, Miguel held Katy close. Something had come between them, but he was at a loss to know what it was. As if to ward off the unseen intruder, he drew Katy closer, fearing suddenly that she was slipping away from him, and knowing that he was powerless to hold her.

Sleep did not come to Iron Wing that night. Every time he closed his eyes, he saw Katy's face, saw the love and recognition that had kindled a warm light in her sky-blue eyes.

Rising, he slipped out of the bunkhouse and wandered across the darkened yard toward the main house. Somewhere inside the hacienda, Katy was sleeping, perhaps dreaming of him. Thinking of her so close made his whole body tingle with longing. For a moment, he considered breaking into the house and going from room to room until he found her. But such a course was fraught with danger and he dared not risk getting caught inside the main house. He would jeopardize his chances of spiriting Katy away from the man who kept her prisoner.

With a last glance at the hacienda, Iron Wing turned and padded softly back to the bunkhouse.

Katy rose early the next morning, her heart fluttering with excitement. Today she would find Iron Wing. Today she would see for herself that she had not imagined him.

She hummed happily as she prepared a big

breakfast for Miguel and carried it to his room.

Miguel regarded her quizzically as she entered his bedroom bearing a tray. "Good morning," Katy said brightly. "I thought I'd serve you breakfast in bed this morning."

Miguel smiled, charmed as always by her thoughtfulness. Katy sat beside him while he ate, chatting about the new dress she was making, and about the birthday party Herrera was giving for Miguel the following week. Miguel was soon caught up in her excitement, but a small inner voice nagged at him, warning him that something was amiss.

Later, when Miguel was engrossed in his accounts, Katy slipped out of the house and wandered, with studied nonchalance, toward the horse corrals, her heart fluttering with joyous anticipation.

And then she saw Iron Wing perched on the back of a wildly bucking horse. Entranced, she let her eyes roam over him, admiring the way his strong thighs gripped the bronc's sides. There was a broad smile on his face, as if he truly enjoyed pitting his power and strength against that of the pitching, twisting mustang. He seemed bigger than she remembered, stronger, more handsome. His hair had been cut until it barely touched his shoulders, and she mourned the loss of the flowing mass that had once hung to his waist.

At last, the horse surrendered to the will of the man on its back and came to a halt in the center of the corral. With a grin, Iron Wing stepped fluidly to the ground. Giving the lathered gelding a gentle slap on the shoulder, Iron Wing handed the reins to one of the other wranglers and lightly vaulted over the corral fence, coming face to face with Katy.

For a moment, they stared at each other, too overwhelmed to speak.

"That was a fine ride," Katy said, aware of watching eyes.

Iron Wing nodded his thanks. She was so near, so beautiful, it took every ounce of his willpower to keep from sweeping her into his arms.

"There's a garden behind the blacksmith shop," Katy murmured. "Meet me there in ten minutes."

"Yes, ma'am," Iron Wing said in a servile tone. "Thank you, ma'am."

Katy turned away, smothering the urge to laugh. Imagine Iron Wing speaking to her as if she were a grand lady and he nothing but a lowly peon.

Without appearing to hurry, Katy made her way to the garden. It was an Eden-like setting, quiet and green, screened from prying eyes by tall shrubs and bushes.

The minutes dragged by until, at last, he was there. Breathing his name, Katy hurled herself into his arms, lifted her face for his kiss.

At the first touch of his lips, a thrill ran through Katy. Her heart beat rapidly, her skin grew hot, her stomach seemed to be made of jelly. Joy flowed through her veins, making her lightheaded as wave after wave of pleasure engulfed her.

"Oh, Iron Wing," she murmured when they

parted. "El Lobo said you were dead."

"Almost, Ka-ty, but the Great Spirit was kind." His eyes devoured her while his hands caressed her face and arms.

For a timeless moment, they gazed lovingly at each other, their hearts too full for words. Hand in hand, they sank down on the grass, unable to stop staring at each other.

"How did you find me?" Katy asked tremulously. "How did you get here?"

Iron Wing told her, briefly, how Pablo had taken him unawares and left him for dead, and how Standing Bull had nursed him through his illness and convalescence. How he had followed El Lobo's trail to this sleepy little town.

"And you, Ka-ty? Are you well? Has the man, Miguel, mistreated you?"

"No," Katy answered. "Miguel has been very kind to me."

Iron Wing's face grew dark. He did not like the note of affection he detected in Katy's voice when she spoke of Miguel, or the pity that showed in her eyes.

"Do you share his bed?" Iron Wing asked in a hard tone.

"Yes," Katy admitted, blushing furiously. "But he has never had me in the way a man has a woman."

"Why not?" Iron Wing asked skeptically. No man could hold Katy close and not possess her.

"He cannot."

"But he has touched you. Looked upon you." It was not a question, but a statement of fact.

"Iron Wing," Katy said softly. "He has been good to me. He saved me from a terrible life. I cannot help being grateful to him for that."

"Tonight we will go." Iron Wing said. "Meet me behind the barn when he is asleep."

"It will be dangerous," Katy replied. "There are guards everywhere."

"We will go tonight," Iron Wing repeated. "I do not like it here. Nor do I like the thought of your spending another night with that man."

"But . . ."

"You are my woman, Ka-ty. I will not share you with another."

Katy smiled. Once the phrase "my woman" had filled her with rage, but now the words filled her with joy. The smile quickly faded as she recalled what had happened to Claude and his family.

"My woman," Iron Wing said again. "Do not argue with me."

"I won't. Iron Wing, you won't harm Miguel?"

"No. I will let him live because you ask it."

"Thank you," Katy murmured, and went willingly into his arms.

The familiar touch of Iron Wing's mouth on hers, the hard wall of his chest pressed against her breasts, his hands lovingly stroking her back, all made Katy's senses come vibrantly alive, as if every nerve ending in her body had suddenly revived after a long sleep. Her blood seemed hot and sweet, like liquid honey, as she strained toward him, wanting to get closer and closer, until there was nothing in all the world but the touch of his lips on hers.

Somehow, she was lying naked beneath him, her arms around his neck. The grass was warm and soft against her bare flesh, the sky above incredibly blue as Iron Wing drove into her. His face was inches from her own, blotting everything else from her sight, making her forget everything but the need to be possessed by this man that she loved above all others. Slowly, they began the age-old rhythm that forged them into one flesh. Katy threw her head back, caught up in the wonder of his touch, in the swirling ecstacy that carried her higher, higher, until the earth was left far behind and there was nothing left but Iron Wing and the love they shared.

Later, alone in her room, Katy realized she had forgotten to tell Iron Wing about the baby.

She was nervous as a cat at dinner that night, unable to meet Miguel's eyes. Her mouth was still swollen, bruised from the force of Iron Wing's kisses, her flesh still tingled from his touch. Oddly, even though Miguel was not her husband, she felt as if she had betrayed him. It was most peculiar.

"Come, Katy, sit beside me," Miguel requested when they were alone in the parlor after dinner. "You seem preoccupied this evening," he observed. "Is anything wrong?"

"No," Katy answered quickly. "Would you like to play chess? Poker, perhaps?"

"No." Miguel's dark eyes studied her face.

Was her mouth swollen? Certainly her eyes glowed with an inner contentment he had never seen there before. Was it possible she had taken a lover? He dismissed the idea immediately. None of the peons who labored within the walls of the fortress would dare to touch her, and even if they did, surely Katy would not give herself to any of them.

"You were gone a long time after breakfast," Miguel remarked. "Alfaro said he could not find you."

Confusion reined in Katy's mind. What should she say? What could she say? Miguel was a kind and generous man. He was in love with her, would marry her if she but said the word. He would not take kindly to the fact that she had spent the morning in the arms of another man.

"I . . . I went walking," Katy stammered. "I didn't mean to be gone so long, but . . . I'm sorry I wasn't here when you wanted me."

Miguel's eyes probed Katy's. He did not believe her, but he wanted to desperately. And so, rather than risk a confrontation that might reveal what he feared most, he said, "Next time, tell Afaro where you are going."

"Yes," Katy said, not meeting his eyes. "Next time."

Katy lay rigid in Miguel's arms later that night, her thoughts running wild. Iron Wing was here. Tonight, when everyone was asleep, they would leave the fortress together. She could think of nothing else. Soon she would be his woman again. The thought filled her heart until she was sure it would burst. Iron Wing . . . He was so strong, so beautiful, her whole body, her whole soul, longed for his presence beside her.

Turning her head on the pillow, she gazed at Miguel, sleeping peacefully alongside her. He would be hurt when he woke in the morning to find she had left him without a word. He loved her. He had been kind to her. And she would miss him. But Iron Wing was waiting for her outside.

When Katy was certain Miguel was sound asleep, she slid out of bed. Barefooted, she padded noiselessly down the hallway to her own room. Inside, she quickly changed into a dress of dark blue cotton. Slipping a pair of sturdy shoes on, she grabbed a pillowcase she had packed earlier, then tiptoed toward the stairway. Her heart was pounding wildly as she crossed the parlor floor and made her way blindly to the front door. She was fumbling with the lock when she heard the scrape of a bootheel on the hardwood floor.

Startled, Katy dropped the pillowcase behind one of the tall plants that stood beside the door. Eyes wide, she turned toward the light that filled the room as Alfaro touched a match to the candle in his hand.

"Señorita," he breathed, relieved to see Katy instead of a prowler. "What are you doing down here at this time of the night?"

"I . . . I couldn't sleep. I was going outside for some air."

"Senor Herrera would not like you roaming around outside by yourself at this time of night."

"I'll be fine," Katy said quickly. She turned toward the front door, her hand reaching for the knob, as if there was nothing more to be said.

Alfaro watched her silently for a moment, then, with a sigh, his hand closed over hers. "Sorry, senorita," he said, lifting her hand from the latch. "I think I must insist you do not leave the house."

Katy summoned what she hoped was a disarming smile. "Perhaps you're right, Alfaro. Good night."

Defeat sat heavily on Katy's shoulders as she turned and walked up the stairs to her room. Changing into her nightgown once again, she crept quietly back into Miguel's bed. Tears welled in her eyes and fell in salty rivers down her cheeks. Iron Wing was waiting for her. She longed to fly into his arms, to feel the strength of his long lean body pressed close to her own. Instead, she was trapped in the house. She knew Alfaro would be keeping watch now, to make sure she did not try to leave again.

Katy bit down on her lower lip to keep from sobbing aloud as Miguel's arm fell across her waist, its weight as heavy and confining as iron bars.

Miguel eyed Katy sharply the next morning. Her eyes were puffy and red-rimmed, as if she had been crying, her face was drawn and haggard. She remained cool and aloof during breakfast, hardly touching her food. She left the table and went to her room as soon as the meal was over.

Later that afternoon, when everyone was taking a siesta, Katy crept out of the house and made her way toward the garden, hoping Iron Wing would seek her out.

And he did. Katy went swifly into his arms,

sighing as his hands drew her close.

"What happened?" Iron Wing asked, stroking her hair.

"Alfaro caught me trying to sneak out of the house. He sent me back to my room. Oh, Iron Wing, what if he tells Miguel?"

Iron Wing shrugged. "The man knows nothing. What can he say?"

"I don't know."

"We will try again tonight," Iron Wing said resolutely.

"No. I have a better idea. Miguel's birthday party is next week. Herrera is giving him a party. I'll get one of Miguel's suits for you to wear, and we'll take one of the carriages and leave through the gate with some of the other guests."

"It might work," Iron Wing said dubiously.

"It's got to work! I'd better go now, before Alfaro comes looking for me. I love you."

Iron Wing nodded as he drew her close once more. One long kiss, and then he was gone.

Katy walked slowly back to the house. Dressed in one of Miguel's suits, Iron Wing could easily pass for a Spaniard. And if she wore a shawl over her head and kept her face turned away, perhaps no one would recognize her. It would be risky, but it had to work.

Miguel was waiting for Katy in her bedroom when she walked into the room. She knew at once by the grim expression on his face that something was very wrong. His first words confirmed her worst fears.

"Who is the man you were kissing in the garden?" he demanded harshly.

"I don't know what you mean," Katy said, forcing herself to meet his accusing gaze.

"Do not lie to me, Katy. Alfaro saw you kissing one of the peons."

Mute, Katy hung her head, knowing that further lies were useless.

"You have not had your monthly flow since you came here," Miguel mused aloud. His calm words belied the fierce anger building in his eyes.

"Miguel, I . . ."

"Be still, you slut! You are pregnant, are you not? And that man is the father!"

"Miguel . . ."

"Do you deny it?"

"No," Katy admitted miserably.

"How could you betray me, Katy? Have I not been good to you? Have I not given you everything you desired?"

"If you'll just let me explain for a moment, I'll tell you everything."

"Frank was right," Miguel said with a sneer. "You do belong in the cantina, flat on your back like the other whores."

"Won't you please listen to me?" Katy begged.

"Do not speak to me, *puta!*" Miguel admonished in a choked voice. "I will hear no more of your lies. Alfaro!"

Wordlessly, the big man entered the room. He gave Katy a look of contempt as he took Miguel out of the room. A moment later, Katy heard the key turn in the lock of her bedroom door.

With a choked sob, Katy flung herself across the bed and let the tears flow. Everything was lost now. Miguel hated her. Most likely, he would send her back to Herrera's. And what of Iron Wing? What would become of him?

Katy cried until her throat was raw and her eyes were sore and red; cried until she was dry inside, and then she fell asleep, only to be haunted by visions of herself in a bright red dress, forced to please any man who could pay the price.

When she woke, it was dark outside. Shivering, she pulled a blanket around her shoulders and went to stand at the window. The house was still as death. Where was Miguel? What had become of Iron Wing? She heard a clock strike the hour. Moments later, her bedroom door swung open and Alfaro stepped in, a tray balanced in one big hand. His eyes condemned her as he placed the tray on the table beside her bed, then turned to leave the room.

"Alfaro?"

The Mexican hesitated, his hand on the knob, but he did not face her.

"Alfaro, what have they done with Iron Wing?"

"He is in the cellar."

"Is he all right?"

Alfaro shrugged.

"Please take me to see Miguel. I must talk to him."

"He will not see you."

"Please, Alfaro, beg him for me."

"Good night, senorita," the big man said heavily, and left the room. The key turning in the lock was very loud in the stillness.

For two days, Katy paced the floor, her mind in torment. She could not eat, she could not sleep, could only pace hour after hour, or lie unmoving on her bed, staring blankly at the ceiling.

The morning of the third day, Miguel came to her room. He looked gaunt and haggard. There were dark shadows under his eyes, and he had not shaved. His face was sad when he looked at her.

"Frank said he has room for you in the cantina."

"Miguel, please . . ."

"He will come for you in the morning. Be ready."

"And what of Iron Wing?" Katy asked the question with trepidation, fearful of the answer.

"He looks well in the cellar. I shall keep him there so long as it pleases me."

"No."

But Miguel had left the room, leaving her to weep alone.


Frank Herrera grinned as he handed Katy a skimpy red satin dress, a pair of black net stockings, and a pair of red high-heeled slippers.

"I can't wear this," Katy began in a choked voice. The rest of the words died in her throat as Frank Herrera slapped her hard across the face.

"You will wear what I say, when I say, for as long as I say." He looked at her expectantly.

Katy put a hand to her throbbing cheek.

"Yes," she said thinly. "Whatever you say."

Herrera nodded. "You learn fast, little one. You will serve drinks to my customers until your bastard is born. And then you will service my customers."

Herrera placed his finger under Katy's chin and raised her head when she did not reply. "What do you say, *puta?*"

"I'll do whatever you wish."

"I know you will, little flower. Now change your clothes and come downstairs. My customers are eager to see you."

It was too horrible. From noon until midnight, Katy was forced to serve drinks to the rabble that frequented Frank Herrera's cantina. In the days that followed, Katy saw men of the most vile sort, men without conscience, men devoid of compassion, men without morals. They viewed her as nothing more than an object of lust, a vessel to be used and abused and forgotten. Their hands were cruel when they reached out to touch her, pinching her buttocks, pawing her swollen breasts, yanking at her hair.

They called her dirty names, cursed her when she accidentally spilled their drinks, taunted her mercilessly about her thickening waistline. And yet, for all that, they seemed to find her desirable. They acted like they were angry, as if they were mad at her for being pregnant and therefore untouchable. Incredibly, a few of them were counting the days until her baby would be born, so anxious were they to buy her favors.

One night, Frank Herrera lifted Katy onto the bar and then, to her shame, took bets from his customers on when her child would be born, and whether it would be a boy or a girl. He also auctioned off a night of her time. A one-eyed man with greasy blond hair and a full beard came through with the highest bid, offering an unprecedented amount of three hundred dollars to be Katy's first customer after the baby was born.

Another night, Herrera sold Katy's kisses for five dollars each. It was all Katy could do not to vomit as one odious man after another stuffed dirty greenbacks and coins down the bodice of her dress and then claimed a kiss. Katy shuddered as the last man planted a wet kiss on her lips. How could something as wonderful as a kiss be so disgusting, she wondered, wiping her mouth with the back of her hand. Iron Wing's kisses had filled her with a soft sweet yearning even before she realized she loved him. But these kisses filled her with bitter revulsion, making her sick to her stomach, making her feel dirty and defiled.

Rosa and the other whores laughed at Katy's squeamishness. How the mighty have fallen, they crowed, and took great pains to tell her of the sordid life that awaited her in one of the dingy rooms at the top of the stairs.

Katy listened with growing horror as the women spelled out, in lurid detail, the many ways a man sought to find pleasure in a woman's arms. They described acts that filled Katy with disgust. She hoped they were exaggerating, though she could think of nothing worse than being intimate with a man for whom she had no feeling or regard. She looked with loathing on the men who accompanied the other girls upstairs. They were all such mean-spirited men, without warmth or sympathy, and she knew she would rather be dead than let one of them touch her.

One night El Lobo and his men appeared at the cantina. Katy shuddered when she saw that Carlito was among the outlaws. The ugly little man spotted Katy immediately, and a wide grin spread over his face.

"Katy," Herrera ordered, "serve El Lobo and his men."

With a nod of resignation, Katy went to El Lobo's table. The bandit leader grinned at her as he patted her stomach. "You should be more careful, *chiquita*. A swollen belly is not good for business."

Katy flushed at the implication that she was one of the whores, and that she had foolishly failed to take precautions to keep from getting caught.

"Bring us some whiskey," El Lobo said. "And some food. We are hungry!"

"Hungry," Carlito echoed. "But not for food. Tonight I will buy your favors. That fat belly will not stop me." He pulled a wad of paper money from his pocket. "I have been saving my money, and I have enough to buy your time for the whole night."

"No," Katy said hoarsely. "I won't!"

"Rosa!" Carlito hollered shrilly. "This wench has refused me."

Rosa strutted over to the table. Leaning down, she patted Carlito on the thigh. "You will have to choose another," she purred, caressing his leg. "Frank has said she is not

to be touched until after her brat is born."
Rosa put her fingertips over Carlito's mouth
as he began to protest. "Dolores will be down
soon. You remember how much you liked her
before? She has been waiting for your
return."

Carlito smiled crookedly. "Dolores," he
said, licking his lips. "Yes, I remember her."
Mollified, he glanced up at Katy. "I will have
you yet, blue eyes. Only wait and see if I
don't."

Katy almost ran from the table, so anxious
was she to get away from El Lobo and his
men. But for them, she would not be here
now. As she waited for the bartender to fill El
Lobo's order, she felt herself shiver uncontrollably as she thought of Carlito. In time,
her baby would be born, and she would be at
the mercy of men like Carlito. It was too
dreadful to contemplate, like a nightmare
that repeated itself night after night.

Swallowing hard, she carried the whiskey
to El Lobo's table. The outlaw leader ran his
hand over her buttocks and down one leg.
"Nice," he remarked. "Perhaps I, too, will
buy a little of your time one day."

It was too much. With a wordless cry of
dismay, Katy left the table and ran up the
stairs to her room. Throwing herself across
the bed, she began to weep. How ugly her life
had become! If only she could get word to her
mother. If only Iron Wing could help her. If
only she could escape from the awful hell
that surrounded her.

As her sobs subsided, she heard bedsprings
in the next room groan as one of the girls

went to work. There were muffled cries and squeals, and Katy recognized Carlito's voice. Mesmerized, she listened to Dolores pleasure the outlaw. Soon that would be her fate.

The thought was too wretched to bear. Bile rose in her throat, hot and bitter, and she grabbed the bowl beside her bed and vomited until her stomach was empty and her throat was sore.

Katy sat up, her stomach still uneasy, as Rosa swept into the room. "You are wanted downstairs," the blowsy woman said curtly. "Clean yourself up and get back to work."

Katy nodded obediently. She was afraid of Rosa. She knew the woman was as cold as ice, as hard as flint. It was Rosa who punished the girls when they dared disobey. Katy had seen the whip the woman used, a thick rawhide lash with a cruel knot in the end. The sight of that whip was enough to give Katy cold chills, and she thought she would do anything to avoid being whipped. She had not forgotten the pain she had endured when Iron Wing whipped her.

After wiping her face and rinsing her mouth, she returned to the saloon. El Lobo and his men were gone and she knew a moment of relief. Perhaps they had already left town.

Katy had been cooped up in the cantina for eight weeks when Miguel appeared at the door, accompanied, as always, by Alfaro.

Katy watched surreptitiously as the two men took seats at the table near the back of the room. She could feel Miguel's eyes on her back as she moved from table to table, serving drinks, cleaning up spills, and fending off the patron's groping hands.

It was humiliating, having Miguel watch her in such degrading circumstances, to have him sit idly by while murderers and bank robbers and cattle thieves pawed her flesh and made obscene remarks. The skimpy costume Frank made her wear was stretched thin over her expanding belly, and her breasts strained against the low-cut bodice, exposing the tops of her creamy flesh. She had begged Frank for a larger dress, but he had only laughed and said she should be grateful he clothed her at all.

Miguel stayed at the cantina for the better part of the evening, morosely tossing down one glass of whiskey after aother. His eyes never left Katy. He was very drunk when Alfaro finally persuaded him to go home.

"The house is empty," Miguel lamented as Alfaro carried him over the threshold. "So empty."

"Shall I put you to bed?" Alfaro asked. Carefully, he placed Miguel in his chair, and covered his wasted legs with a colorful blanket.

"No. Take me to the cellar."

"Is that wise?" Alfaro questioned. "It is late. You will feel better when you have had some rest."

"Take me down."

Alfaro's face reflected his disapproval as he lifted Miguel, chair and all, and carried him down the short flight of steps that led to the cellar.

The sound of footsteps roused Iron Wing

and he sprang to his feet, the chain that shackled his right leg to the wall clanking noisily in the stillness. He had been imprisoned in the cellar for two months. It had been the longest two months of his life. Every day was the same as the last, nothing but empty hours spent in varying degrees of darkness. Nothing to do but pace the length of his chain and think of Katy, always Katy.

He felt himself grow tense as light flooded the cellar. He felt a shiver of apprehension as he saw Alfaro and Miguel coming toward him.

"Chain his hands," Miguel ordered, his voice slurred and uneven. His hand was unsteady as he placed a candle on a barrel to his right.

Iron Wing backed away as Alfaro lumbered toward him. The Mexican's arms were spread wide, and he reminded Iron Wing of the grizzly he had killed so many years ago. He wished fervently that he had a weapon now.

The sound of a gun being cocked echoed loudly in the stillness of the cavernous room. "Raise your hands," Miguel demanded in a loud voice. "Raise them, or I will shoot you now."

Iron Wing complied. As bad as life was, he had no desire to leave it.

"That is better," Miguel remarked, sounding pleased. "Chain him up tight, Alfaro, my old friend, and we shall have some fun." He giggled drunkenly as he placed the gun beside the candle. "Now the whip, Alfaro. Bring me the whip."

Iron Wing took a deep breath as Alfaro handed Miguel Herrera a long rawhide whip.

He thought briefly of Katy, and of the time he had flogged her before the tribe. Then he blotted everything from his mind save his hatred for the man sitting before him.

Miguel's eyes were dark with jealousy as he raised the whip over his head. "You!" he hissed, striking Iron Wing across his chest and shoulders. "It is you she loves. Damn you!"

Iron Wing glared at Miguel as the whip bit into his flesh. The Spaniard was very drunk and he babbled incoherently as the whip rose and fell. Gradually, the strength went out of Miguel's arms and the blows grew weaker and weaker until, with a strangled sob, he dropped the whip, his head lolled forward on his chest, and he passed out.

Tenderly, Alfaro lifted Miguel from the chair and carried him out of the cellar.

Iron Wing released his pent-up breath in a long sigh. His chest throbbed, but he could endure the pain. What he could not endure was the pain of not knowing what had become of Katy. Was she in this house, or had Miguel Herrera sent her away?

A cry of rage filled the cellar as Iron Wing pulled against the chains that held him. Two months of being locked up like an animal. Two months of wondering where Katy was, if she was well. It was almost more than he could bear. It would be easy to give in to the anger and frustration tearing at him, to yell and scream and beat his head against the wall. Swallowing hard, he took a deep breath, willing himself to be calm, to think of Katy. Katy with eyes like a calm summer sky. Katy, who had made his life worth living. Katy . . .

* * *

Shortly after sunrise the next morning, Alfaro came for Katy.

"Senor Herrera has asked that you return to his house," the big Mexican said politely. "If you are willing, please change into this dress and meet me downstairs."

"Yes," Katy breathed gratefully. "Oh, yes, thank you." She ran her hand over the blue velvet gown Miguel had sent for her to wear. How rich and luxurious it felt beneath her fingertips after weeks of wearing the sleazy red satin costume.

She dressed hurriedly, anxious to be out of the cantina, anxious to find out once and for all if Iron Wing still lived.

She took a deep breath as she followed Alfaro out of the cantina. How good the sunlight felt on her face. How sweet and fresh the outdoors smelled after the days and nights spent in the smoky cantina.

Alfaro had a carriage waiting. He handed her into the conveyance, bowed as he closed the door. How good it was to feel like a lady again.

Her feeling of euphoria faded as they drove through the gates of the Herrera fortress. She was only trading one jail for another, after all.

Miguel was waiting for her in the parlor. He looked thin and tired, as if he had not been sleeping well, or eating very much.

"Hello, Miguel," Katy said tremulously.

"Katy."

"I . . . thank you for getting me out of the cantina. It was horrible there."

"I have decided to keep you here, with me,

after all. The house is lonely without you." Miguel's eyes moved to her belly, then returned to her face. "When your baby is born, I will give it to one of the peons to raise."

Katy looked at him, unable to believe what she had just heard. Miguel had always been so good to her, so kind, surely he would not separate her from her child.

"No," she said, pressing her hands against her swollen belly protectively. Already, she loved the child beyond description.

"You are in no position to argue," Miguel retorted coldly. "Be glad I am letting the child live."

"And Iron Wing? Is he still alive?" Katy forced the words past the hard lump in her throat.

"Yes. But he dies tomorrow."

Katy's insides went cold, as if her blood had turned to ice water. She could not bear to think of Iron Wing being shot down in cold blood, murdered because he had loved her and fathered her child.

"I will never forgive you if you kill him," Katy said. "He has done nothing wrong."

"He dies."

"Miguel, do you remember the first day I came here? I told you then about Iron Wing. I was his woman. You cannot kill a man for trying to claim what is his. Please let him go."

"And will you stay here of your own free will if I set him free?" Miguel asked. "Will you stay with me as long as you live?"

Despair filled Katy's breast. Stay here with Miguel when she yearned to be with Iron Wing. Live in chaste misery when she longed

to share her life and her love with Iron Wing?
It was too awful to even consider and yet,
what choice did she have? If she refused to
stay with Miguel, Iron Wing would die, and
she could not have his death on her
conscience.

"Very well," Katy said dully. "I'll stay."

"I will send Alfaro to free the Indian within
the hour."

"May I see Iron Wing before he goes?"

Miguel hesitated briefly, and then nodded.

"Thank you," Katy whispered.

Miguel watched Katy leave the room. She
was his again. He would see her every day,
hear her voice, touch her hand. The house
would be alive again. And yet it would not be
the same. Her heart would never be his and
yet, he could not let her go. But how would he
learn to live with the unhappiness that lurked
behind her lovely blue eyes?

The cellar was dark and cold. Grotesque
shadows danced on the walls as Katy made
her way down the stairs, her way lit by a
single candle set in a brass holder.

She gasped as a small furry creature scam-
pered across her foot. Lifting her skirts, she
cautiously made her way deeper into the
bowels of the dank cellar that ran the length
of the house. She had never been in the cellar
before, and now she saw several large trunks,
casks of wine, old furniture and paintings,
some carpets rolled into tight cylinders, a
huge chandelier.

Carefully, she picked her way through the
room, her eyes looking ahead, searching for

the man she loved. She found him at the far end of the cellar. He was chained to the west wall, his arms stretched high above his head, his legs spread apart, shackled to the wall by heavy irons. His eyes narrowed against the light as she came to stand beside him.

Love and compassion stirred in Katy's breast as she placed the candle on the floor. "Iron Wing." She whispered his name, and then gasped as she saw the ugly red welts that crisscrossed his bare chest and shoulders. "What happened?"

"Miguel came to pay me a farewell visit late last night."

Last night, Katy mused. Miguel had been very drunk.

"He whipped you?" Katy murmured. "Why?"

Iron Wing shrugged. "Who can say?"

Standing on tiptoe, Katy pressed her mouth to his, felt his quick hungry response before he groaned softly in his throat and drew away.

"Have you been chained up like this the whole time?" Katy asked, wanting to cry.

"No. My arms were free until last night."

"Oh, Iron Wing," she said miserably. "What are we going to do?"

"Leave me, Ka-ty," he said gruffly. "It will only cause more trouble if he finds you have been down here."

"Miguel knows I'm here."

Iron Wing raised a sardonic eyebrow. "It was generous of him to let you come and tell me good-bye before he kills me," he muttered.

"He's going to let you go."

"Why?"

Katy hesitated; then, taking a deep breath, she said, "I've promised to stay with Miguel if he lets you go."

"Do you want to stay with him?"

"No. Oh, God, no! But I can't let him kill you, not when I can prevent it."

Iron Wing scowled darkly. It did not sit well, having his woman offer herself to another man to save his life. Still, Katy could make all the promises she wanted to the man Miguel. None were binding on him. Katy was his woman, and he would not ride away and leave her for another man to possess. Somehow, he would find a way to return to the fortress and take Katy away with him. Somehow, she would be his again.

There were tears in Katy's eyes as she put her arms around Iron Wing's neck. Two months in chains had left him thin, so very thin. She yearned to feel his arms around her, but the chains that shackled him to the wall made that impossible.

She kissed him greedily, knowing it was for the last time. She longed to tell him she was pregnant, but she was afraid that, if he knew of the child, he would not go back to his people. Fortunately, the dress she was wearing was long and flowing, concealing her swollen figure. The dim light helped disguise her condition, and she was careful not to press against him lest he feel the difference in her figure, a figure he knew as well as his own.

"Be happy," Katy said, touching his cheek.

"Give my love to Yellow Flower and the others."

Iron Wing nodded. "I will, when I see them."

Katy smiled faintly. How hard it was to give him up again and yet, it was better that he should return to his people and spend the rest of his life with another woman than die because of her. And die he surely would if he tried to return to the fortress.

She stayed with Iron Wing until Alfaro came for her.

# 21

Alfaro set the candle on the floor of the cellar. Then, mouth set in a grim line, he lined his gunsights on the Indian's chest while one of the peons who had accompanied him unlocked the heavy shackles that secured the Indian to the wall.

Iron Wing grimaced as the blood rushed down into his arms. His shoulders and back ached mightily from being forced to remain in one position for such a long time; his legs were weary from standing for so long, but he allowed no trace of his discomfort to show on his face. A warrior did not show weakness before an enemy.

"Put your hands behind your back," Alfaro instructed curtly, and Iron Wing did as he was told, knowing there was no point in arguing, and little to be gained but his own death if he refused.

His face remained impassive as the peon lashed his hands behind his back. The big Mexican checked the knots, then motioned for him to leave the cellar.

Iron Wing blinked against the harsh sunlight as he stepped into the open. Prodded by the rifle in Alfaro's capable hands, he walked toward the entrance to the fortress, paused briefly while one of the guards opened the gates.

Resisting the urge to look back, Iron Wing stepped outside the fortress walls.

"Indian." Alfaro's voice stopped Iron Wing in his tracks. "Senor Herrera has given you your freedom. Do not come here again. You will be shot on sight if you are found within these walls again. *Comprende?*"

"I understand," Iron Wing answered stiffly.

Alfaro nodded as he drew a knife from his belt and cut the Indian's hands free. Deep inside, he had a premonition that the Indian would return.

From the window of her bedroom, Katy watched Alfaro cut Iron Wing free. Two fat teardrops rolled down her cheeks as Iron Wing strode swiftly away without a backward glance. Then the gates closed, and he was gone. Never before had she felt so utterly alone. How could she face the future without him? Every day she would wonder where he was, if he was well, if he remembered her, or if he had put her out of his mind. Earlier, she thought she would not mind if he took another woman, so long as he were alive and well. Now, the very thought filled her with jealousy. He was her man, the father of her child. She would gladly scratch out the eyes of any woman who dared look at him. But then, she would never know . . .

She turned from the window at the sound of a key turning in the lock, brushed the tears from her eyes as Miguel wheeled into the room.

"He is gone," Miguel said brusquely. "Pray he does not come back."

Katy nodded, unable to speak past the lump in her throat.

"You remember you gave me your word you would stay?" Miguel asked, eyeing her sharply. "Do you mean to keep it, or must I keep you locked in your room?"

"My word is as good as yours," Katy retorted, her anger flaring. "I said I would stay, and I will."

"Good. Lunch is ready. Come, eat with me."

It was in Katy's mind to refuse, to yell that she hated him, that she would never forgive him for separating her from the man she loved. But recriminations were useless, childish. She had made a bargain with Miguel, and she would keep it. And perhaps, if she tried very hard, she could convince Miguel to let her keep her baby.

Forcing herself to smile, she followed Miguel to the dining room.

The days passed slowly. Miguel did not insist that Katy return to his bed, but he demanded most of her waking hours. He wooed Katy tenderly, trying to regain her affection, plying her with gifts and sweet words. He complimented her when she wore her hair in a new style, thanked her when she did him a favor.

Thinking of her child, Katy tried to respond to Miguel with warmth and affection, hoping if she pleased him, he would relent and let her keep the baby. But her efforts were hollow and hardly convincing. She felt empty inside, as if a vital part of her being had withered and died. Her appetite waned, her sunny smile was gone, and her eyes were always sad.

December came, and the main house began to fill with the signs and symbols of Christmas. Wreaths were hung on the doors, a life-size statue of the Virgin holding the Christ Child was displayed in the entry hall, surrounded by winter greenery. Miguel and the servants, even the guards at the walls, seemed more cheerful. But not Katy.

She could not keep her thoughts from straying toward home. Christmas at the Alvarez hacienda had always been a special time of year. Juanita baked sweet bread and angel cookies, Anna and Maria decorated the house with fragrant pine boughs and adorned them with big red bows and silver bells. It had been Katy's privilege to set up the intricately carved oak nativity scene. She had always handled each piece with reverence, remembering that her father had carved each one, his big hands deft and sure as he created Mary and Joseph and the Babe. And there had been presents for everyone on the ranch.

Now, far from home, Katy realized that Christmas was more than presents and decorations. It was the warmth of being surrounded by family and friends, the joy of giving, the satisfaction of sharing the Alvarez bounty with those less fortunate. Each Christmas Eve, they had taken baskets of food and clothing and toys to the orphanage in Mesa Blanca.

Katy sighed heavily as she remembered

how everyone at home had gone to midnight mass together. House servants, vaqueros and their families, the toothless old man who tended the goats, all had attended church with Katy and her mother. It was the best part of Christmas, kneeling at the altar to take communion, singing songs of praise and adoration to the Blessed Virgin Mary and her Holy Child, receiving a blessing at the hand of Father Diaz . . .

Christmas came, but Katy found no joy in the gifts Miguel showered upon her. What good were velvet gowns and satin slippers when her heart was dead? What good were silk stockings and dainty convent-made nightgowns when she could not keep Iron Wing's child? How could she sing of love and peace on earth when she felt so utterly lost and alone?

She went to midnight mass with Miguel and Alfaro, but even that failed to cheer her. Staring at the lovely Madonna and the Christ Child, Katy could think only of her own unborn babe resting beneath her heart. Closing her eyes, she prayed to the sweet-faced Madonna, begging that most perfect mother to take pity on her and find a way for her to keep her baby.

That night, alone in her room, Katy wept bitter tears. Her life was not worth living. Iron Wing was gone, her child would be given to another as soon as it was born, and she was trapped in a relationship with a man she did not love. She did not regret her agreement with Miguel. Gladly would she do it over again to save Iron Wing's life, but, oh, how she longed to feel her beloved's arms around her just once more, to hear him whisper her name, his voice husky with desire, to feel his hands moving in her hair. She ached to be held, to be loved as only Iron Wing could love her. She missed the sight of his face, the sound of his voice, the deep rumble of his laughter, the scent of his flesh, the touch of his skin against her own.

Turning her face into her pillow to muffle her sobs, she cried herself to sleep.

A month passed. Katy's belly swelled as her child grew. Often, it kicked vigorously, but instead of bringing Katy joy, it only made her feel worse. With each passing day, the time drew nearer when the child, too, would be lost to her, given to a stranger. She would never see her child smile, or hear it cry. She would not be there when it learned to sit up, when it took its first precious steps. She would never hear the sound of its laughter, or its first words. She would miss so much, and as she tried to prepare herself for the loss, she grew quieter and thinner.

Miguel watched Katy through eyes dark with worry. She seemed to grow more pale with each passing day, more listless. Her beautiful blue eyes were shadowed and sad. Gone was the cheerful girl who had brought joy and laughter into his life, and in her place stood an unhappy woman whose sorrowful expression haunted his dreams.

Late one night, when he heard her weeping uncontrollably in her room, he called her to him. She came, obedient as always, and sat down on the edge of his bed. She looked like an angel, Miguel thought. A sad-eyed angel.

Her thick black hair fell over her shoulders like a dark nimbus. Her nightgown, made of fine silk, was the same shade of blue as her eyes.

Conscious of the deal she had made, Katy did not protest when Miguel drew her into his arms and kissed her cheek. She belonged to him. He could do with her as he pleased.

"You win, Katy mia," he said quietly. "I will not send the child away if only you will smile at me again."

Katy looked into Miguel's eyes, afraid she was dreaming. "You mean it?" she breathed, afraid to hope. "You truly mean it?"

"I give you my word, Katy mia."

"You won't be sorry," Katy promised, raining kisses of joy and gratitude on his face and hands.

Miguel smiled happily as he accepted her kisses. It would be hard, having another man's child underfoot, but if it would make Katy smile again, it would be worth it."

"Come, lie beside me," Miguel said, and Katy slipped into bed beside him and pillowed her head on his shoulder.

"I have missed having you here, beside me," Miguel said, toying with a lock of her hair. "The nights have been long and lonely without your sweet warmth."

Unable to respond equally, Katy squeezed Miguel's hand, hoping he would understand. She could not deceive him with false words of love, could not pretend she had missed him when it was Iron Wing who held her heart.

Hiding his disappointment, Miguel kissed Katy's hand. She did not love him. Perhaps she never would. But she was here, beside him, and that was all that mattered.

Life took on meaning once again as Katy began to plan for the birth of her child. True, Iron Wing was gone, but she would soon have his child, the child of their love. Where she had once dreaded the passing of each day, she now counted them with impatience as she eagerly anticipated the thrill of holding Iron Wing's child in her arms.

She began to sew clothes for the baby— shirts and saques and a white dress for the christening. She made curtains for the nursery that adjoined her room, ordered paper for the walls, and a thick carpet for the floor. The housekeeper began to knit little pink and blue booties and hats and sweaters. Alfaro built a cradle, intricately carved with delicate animals and flowers.

Even Miguel found himself looking forward to the child's birth. Perhaps it would be good to have a baby in the house. He had always been fond of children; if he could not father a child of his own, Katy's babe would be the next best thing. Perhaps he could even adopt the child. He had plenty of money. He could provide for the infant, perhaps send it off to the east when it was of age. College, the Continent, whatever Katy thought best.

Frank Herrera was the only one who disapproved. "I cannot believe what I am hearing," he muttered one night as they shared a bottle of brandy. "You are actually thinking of adopting that woman's bastard? Have you lost your mind?"

"I love Katy," Miguel said quietly. "I will

313

do anything I can to win her love."

Frank Herrera stared at his brother in astonishment. He had made love to many women, but he had never loved a woman. They were all whores at heart, good for only one thing, and when you tired of one, you found another to assuage your needs. He found it incomprehensible that Miguel could be so completely smitten with a woman, especially a woman carrying another man's child.

With a disgusted shake of his head, Frank Herrera left the fortress.

That same night, Miguel asked Katy to marry him.

"Marry you," Katy echoed. "Are you serious?"

"I love you, Katy mia. I think we can be happy together. I will cherish you always, and treat your child as my own."

"But I don't love you."

"I know, but perhaps you will, in time."

"But . . . I don't know what to say."

"Say yes," Miguel pleaded fervently. "I love you."

"If you truly loved me, you would let me go."

"I cannot," Miguel said miserably. "You are the only good thing in my life."

Katy bowed her head, touched by the pleading look in Miguel's eyes. He had been good to her. Perhaps he did love her. And if she were destined to spend her life with him, why not marry him? At least it would give her child a name, a home, security. Miguel was a wealthy man. Her child would never want for anything—except to know his true father, his true heritage. She put the thought from her. It hurt too much to think of Iron Wing and the life that was forever lost to her.

Lifting her head, she met Miguel's eyes. Perhaps, in time, she would come to love him. If not, she would be no worse off than she was now.

And so she said, bleakly, "Very well, Miguel. I'll marry you."

"Bless you, Katy," he said, kissing her hand. "You will not regret it."

Miguel set the date for February first. Though the wedding would be a private ceremony, with just the two of them, the priest, and Frank, he insisted Katy have a special wedding dress, and he commissioned three of the local women to make it. He gave Katy a beautiful diamond necklace for a wedding present. The necklace had been in the Herrera family for generations.

Katy tried to be enthusiastic about their coming marriage, if only to please Miguel. He was so happy, she sometimes thought he would shout for joy. He fairly beamed at her whenever they were in the same room. Often, he laid his hand over her belly, smiling with delight when he felt the baby move.

The night before the wedding, Katy tossed and turned restlessly in her bed. She was plagued by doubts and indecisions. How could she marry a man she didn't love? How could she spent the rest of her life in chaste misery? Always, in the back of her mind, she had dreamed that, somehow, someway, an avenue of escape would miraculously appear and she would flee the fortress and find her way back to Iron Wing. Once, she had tried to

315

smuggle a letter out to her mother, but Alfaro had intercepted it. Miguel had not been angry. He never got angry. Instead, he had promised her that once they were married, she could write to her mother, even invite her to come and stay with them when the baby was born.

Frank Herrera yawned hugely as he stepped outside to spend a few quiet moments before locking up the cantina for the night. Lighting a thin black cigar, he rested one shoulder against the side of the porch rail. His mouth twitched into a wry grin as he contemplated his brother's forthcoming marriage. Who would have thought that Miguel would become so infatuated with a black-haired *gringa* that he would actually marry her. But even marrying the girl was not so surprising as Miguel talking about adopting the woman's brat.

Muttering an oath, Herrera took a deep drag on his cigar, then jerked upright, every muscle tense, as someone jabbed a gun barrel into his back. A voice sounded in his ear.

"Very slowly," the voice said, "remove your gunbelt and drop it."

Nodding, Frank Herrera did as he was told. "Now what?" he asked, his tone carefully controlled, though his heart was hammering wildly. Murders and robbery were common in such a town, where most of the inhabitants were outlaws on the run. Desperate men did desperate things, and rarely a day went by without one crime or another being committed.

"To the fortress," the gunman directed. "Move."

It was a long walk. Herrera was sweating when they reached the massive gates. The gun pressed against his spine never wavered.

"Tell the guard to open the gate," the gunman ordered.

"Luis! Open up. It's me, Frank."

The man patrolling the catwalk waved at Herrera. Moments later, the gate swung open.

"Go straight to the house," the gunman instructed as the gates closed behind them. "One wrong move, and you are dead."

Herrera nodded. He did not doubt for a minute that the man with the gun meant just what he said.

A light burned in the parlor. Miguel sat at his desk, his brow furrowed as he added a long column of figures. Pausing, he stretched his arms wide, groaning softly as the muscles in his back and shoulders protested.

"Miguel . . ."

"Hello, Frank." Miguel smiled at his brother, surprised to see him at the house at such a late hour. "Profits are up this month," he began, and then frowned as he recognized the dark visage of the man who stepped out of the shadows. "You!" he hissed. Miguel turned his gaze on his brother. "Why did you bring him here?"

"He brought me," Frank said dryly, and stepped aside, revealing the gun aimed at his back.

"What do you want?" Miguel demanded, his whole body coiled like a spring as he waited for the reply.

"I have come for Ka-ty," Iron Wing said stonily.

"You cannot have her," Miguel exclaimed. "She is to be my wife."

"Where is she?"

"Please do not take her from me," Miguel begged. "We are to be married tomorrow." His eyes darted past Iron Wing and then returned to the Indian's face. "Please do not take her," he babbled shrilly. "I love her. I cannot live without her."

Frank Herrera stared at his brother, wondering if he was going mad. Conscious of the gun in his back, he didn't move, but waited patiently for the man behind him to lower his guard.

Iron Wing looked at the crippled man in disgust. Too late, he realized the man was acting in such an odd manner to divert his attention from something taking place behind him. The realization came too late.

Miguel shouted, "Alfaro, take him!" But Iron Wing was already moving. Dropping to the floor, he rolled agilely to one side, firing twice. The first bullet struck Alfaro in the chest, killing the big man instantly. The second slug caught Frank Herrera in the side of the neck. He fell with a strangled sob, his hands clutching at the ragged wound in his throat.

Miguel stared at his brother in horror as Frank writhed on the floor like a spider on a hot stove. A torrent of bright crimson spewed from his mouth.

The sound of footsteps running down the stairs sounded very loud in the silence that

318

trailed in the wake of the gunshots. Iron Wing rolled nimbly to his feet as Katy rushed into the room.

Katy came to an abrupt halt inside the doorway, her expression turning from worry to revulsion as she saw the two men lying on the parlor floor. Alfaro was dead, but Frank was still alive. Blood oozed from an ugly wound in his neck, making a dark stain on the carpet.

"Ka-ty. Change your clothes. We are leaving."

She turned slowly toward the sound of his voice, her eyes wide as she saw him for the first time.

"Katy, do not go with him," Miguel cried in a tortured voice. "You are all I have left in the world."

"Ka-ty."

Katy's gaze moved woodenly from Herrera's writhing form to Miguel's pale face, and then back to Iron Wing's stern countenance. Like a sleepwalker, she crossed the floor to stand beside Iron Wing. Her hand reached out to stroke his cheek. He was not a dream, as she had feared, but warm flesh and blood. A shadow of a smile played over her lips as Iron Wing's dark eyes caressed her face. Abrubtly, he frowned as his eyes came to rest on her distended abdomen. When he met her eyes again, his face was dark with accusation.

"It's yours," Katy said, reading the jealous suspicion in his eyes.

"No!" Miguel shouted. "The baby is mine. That is why we are getting married."

"That's a lie," Katy gasped. What if Iron

Wing did not believe the child was his? She knew how jealous he was. What if he refused to take her with him?

Iron Wing's darkly hooded eyes bored into Katy. She had once told him that the man, Miguel, could not perform the sexual act. Had she lied to him? His fingers grew white around the gun in his fist.

"It is yours," Katy said fervently. "Iron Wing, you must believe me."

"I believe you," he said after a long moment. "Go now, get dressed." Iron Wing threw a sympathetic glance at Miguel. He could not blame the man for wanting to keep Katy for his own. No man, having known her, could bear to lose her.

When Katy returned to the parlor, Iron Wing and Miguel had not moved. Herrera lay still, a thin trickle of blood staining his mouth. His eyes stared, unseeing, at the ceiling.

"I'm ready," Katy said.

"Katy mia, please do not leave me," Miguel cried in anguish. "I need you."

"I'm sorry, Miguel," Katy said tenderly. "You have been very good to me. But I have to go."

"You promised you would stay."

"I did not promise," Iron Wing said. "Be glad I am letting you live."

Katy bit back her tears as Iron Wing tied Miguel's hands behind his back, then stuffed a gag into his mouth. She gave a last glance around the room. It had not been all bad, living with Miguel. But she could not wait to leave.

"How will we get past the guards?" Katy asked Iron Wing.

"I have an idea," he said, grinning at her.

It would never work, Katy mused glumly as they rode toward the gates. Never in a million years. She glanced at Iron Wing. He rode beside her, with Frank Herrera's body in front of the saddle. A long wool scarf covered the ghastly wound in Herrera's throat, but anyone looking at him closely would have known he was dead, not unconscious.

Katy's voice was convincingly concerned as she told Luis that Frank had been taken suddenly ill and had asked to be taken home where Rosa could look after him. Rosa's skills did not lie entirely in the bedroom. She was a noted healer, and the closest thing to a doctor within a hundred miles.

Luis didn't look twice at Iron Wing, who was humbly garbed in the white work clothes of the fortress peons. Without question, the guard opened the heavy gates and wished them well.

Once clear of the fortress wall, Katy wanted to jab her heels into her horse's flanks and ride away as fast as the animal could carry her, but Iron Wing said no. Instead, they walked their horses slowly toward the town. When Iron Wing was certain they were out of sight of the fortress guards, he dumped Herrera's body into a gully.

And then they rode like hell.

Katy was groggy with fatigue when Iron

Wing sought shelter in a ravine. She fell into his arms as he helped her from her horse, asleep before she was out of the saddle.

When she woke, Iron Wing was sitting beside her. He laid a restraining hand on her shoulder when she started to sit up. "Rest, Ka-ty," he said quietly.

"We have to go. Hurry, before they find us."

"They will not find us. They have already passed us by."

"Are you sure?"

"I am sure. Sleep now."

With a little sigh of contentment, Katy reached for Iron Wing's hand. Holding it close against her breast, she fell asleep.

# 22

The next few weeks were hard. Wary of being seen by Indians, outlaws, or Miguel's men, Katy and Iron Wing traveled by night and slept by day in whatever shelter they could find. Each evening, just after dark, Iron Wing went out in search of food, leaving Katy to wait on tenterhooks until he returned. She never asked where he found the food they ate, never asked where he got the knife that he wore inside the waistband of his cotton trousers.

For his part, Iron Wing was relieved when Katy did not question him. She was a tender-hearted woman who abhorred violence and bloodshed. It would have grieved her to know he had killed one man and seriously wounded another. And yet he would cheerfully have killed a dozen men so that Katy might have food and water.

Even though they lived like hunted beasts, afraid to reveal themselves in the light of day, Katy was content. At last, she was with Iron Wing again. He was her strength, her courage, and she feared neither man nor beast nor dark of night so long as he was beside her.

For the first few days, she seemed to be constantly touching him, as if to reassure herself that he was really there. She had dreamed of him so often in days gone by, only to awake and find him gone. But this time he was real. Again and again, she let her fingers slide over his chest, the muscles in his arms, across his thighs, reassured when solid flesh moved beneath her hands.

She gazed at his face lovingly. Was it possible that he had grown more handsome? Had his eyes always been so deeply black, his smile so alluring, his voice so full and resonant? He was unfailingly gentle with her, always aware of her needs, careful not to let her strain herself lest she injure the baby. He was so kind, so concerned, sometimes it brought tears to her eyes. She felt so loved, so cherished. Surely no other man had ever treated a woman with such tender concern. She could endure any hardship as long as he was with her.

The days were hard on Iron Wing, too, but for far different reasons. Indian men did not have intercourse with their wives until the pregnancy was over, and often not until after the child was weaned. The thought was driving him crazy. It had been months since he had buried himself in her sweetness, months since he had possessed her. And the child was not even born yet! Katy was unaware of his torment, and she seemed to be continually touching him, kissing him, holding him close. She slept pressed against him, her head pillowed on his shoulder, as if she could not get close enough. Each time her bare flesh brushed his, his desire flamed. It was the most exquisite kind of torture, seeing her, touching her, and yet not being able to possess her. Surely, if Man Above had any compassion at all, the child would be born soon.

One morning, when Katy was idly running her fingers across his chest and stomach, Iron Wing rolled away from her, a groan on his lips.

"What's the matter?" Katy asked.

"Nothing," Iron Wing replied tersely.

"You're lying," Katy accused softly. "What's the matter?"

Rising, Iron Wing turned to face her. He was naked, and his desire for her was blatantly evident.

Katy's eyes grew wide as she saw his distended manhood and then she began to giggle. "I'm sorry," she said as her giggles exploded into full-fledged laughter. "I thought you were mad about something, or in pain . . ."

"There are all kinds of pain," Iron Wing muttered.

When Katy saw he was serious, the laughter died in her throat. His words explained so many things—why he had kept his distance from her, why he did not respond to her caresses. She had thought him preoccupied with other things.

"I'm sorry," she said contritely. "Forgive me."

"Now you know why so many warriors take a second wife when the first swells with a new life," Iron Wing said wryly.

"Do you want a second wife?" Katy asked, no longer amused.

"No. You are enough woman for me."

"Show me."

"We must wait until the child is born."

"Why?"

"It is the Cheyenne way."

"It is not my way," Katy said, smiling seductively. "I would not be a good wife if I did not try to ease your suffering."

"Is it wise, with the baby to be born so soon?"

"I'm not made of glass. It will be all right."

How could he deny her; how could he deny himself what he had been yearning for? Gently, tenderly, he undressed her, his eyes caressing her flesh. Her breasts were swollen, her belly large with his child, yet she had never looked more beautiful, or more desirable. And still he hesitated to take her, fearful of hurting her.

Katy smiled as she reached out to run her hand over his thigh. With a groan, he sank to his knees beside her and took her in his arms. Her hand was a flame on his flesh, her mouth sweeter than any nectar as she kissed him . . .

Three weeks after leaving the Herrera fortress, they reached Katy's hometown. It was well after midnight when they rode into the Alvarez ranch.

Tears filled Katy's eyes as Iron Wing lifted her from her horse. It was hard to believe she was really home at last. Hard to believe so much time had passed since she had boarded the Mesa Blanca stagecoach bound for the Little Sisters of Mercy convent. So much had happened since then. It was difficult to believe so many things had happened in such a relatively short time.

Iron Wing had not wanted to come here. He

had been reluctant to enter a white settlement, reluctant to meet Katy's mother. But Katy had pleaded to go home, and he could not deny her anything that was in his power to give.

They had to knock on the front door three times before anyone heard them, but finally the heavy oak door swung open.

Sarah Alvarez Sommers stared at her daughter, too stunned to even speak her name. Shaking her head in disbelief, Sarah reached out a hand that was trembling and touched Katy's cheek. Dear God, she was real and not a dream! With an inarticulate cry of joy, she threw her arms around Katy and began to cry. Tears filled Katy's eyes, too, as she held her mother close and for several minutes neither woman could speak.

When, at last, their tears subsided, Sarah noticed the man standing in the shadows on the veranda, and Katy gazed in astonishment at the tall pajama-clad man standing behind her mother. Hatred chased the joy from Sarah's eyes as she realized the man standing behind Katy was not one of the Alvarez peons, as she had first supposed, but an Indian.

"Who is that?" Sarah asked curtly.

Katy stepped away from her mother and reached for Iron Wing's hand. "This is Iron Wing," Katy replied in a cool voice. "He's a Cheyenne warrior." Her chin went up defiantly. "He's the father of my child, and I love him."

There was a taut silence as Sarah's eyes moved from Iron Wing's face to Katy's bulging stomach. An Indian, Sarah thought bleakly. She's gone and fallen in love with a damned Indian! Better she should have become a nun, or died, than give herself to a heathen savage . . . No, she thought, blinking back a wave of fresh tears. Whatever Katy had done, no matter what had happened since she had gone, she was glad to have her home alive and well.

Before either woman could speak again, Michael Sommers stepped forward and took Katy's hand in his.

"I'm Michael Sommers," he said warmly, shaking Katy's hand and then Iron Wing's. "Welcome home, Katy Marie. You too, son."

Katy looked askance at her mother. Who was this stranger who had made himself so at home under their roof? And what was he doing here at this time of night?

Sarah Sommers blushed under her daughter's probing gaze. "It's not what you think, Katy," Sarah explained quickly. "Michael and I were married shortly after you disappeared."

"Congratulations, mama," Katy murmured. She smiled tentatively at Michael Sommers. "Congratulations to you, too, sir."

"Call me Mike," he said, and closed the door as Sarah ushered the two young people into the parlor.

"Are you hungry, Katy?" Sarah asked, ignoring Iron Wing. "Would you like to eat and bathe tonight, or wait until morning? I have dozens of questions to ask."

"I'm really very tired, mama," Katy said. She was not ready to answer the myriad questions she read in her mother's eyes. "We've been riding since sundown."

"Of course. Your . . . friend can sleep in the guest room at the end of the hall. I'll send Anna to make up the bed."

"That won't be necessary," Katy said, blushing from the roots of her hair to the soles of her feet. "Iron Wing will share my room."

Sarah stared at her daughter in shock. No matter that Katy was carrying the man's child and not even ashamed. An unmarried man and woman did not share the same room. It just wasn't done.

Sarah turned to her husband. "Michael?"

"Let it be, Sarah. Don't say anything you'll regret later."

Katy threw Michael Sommers a look of gratitude as she took Iron Wing by the hand and led him up the stairs to her room. Imagine, Katy thought, bemused, my mother asking someone else for advice!

Sarah frowned as the couple disappeared down the hall. It did not sit well, having an Indian in the house. Especially one who was sharing Katy's bed.

"They're in love, Sarah," Michael said softly. "Can't you see that?"

"How can she love him!" Sarah exclaimed. "He's a dirty Indian. A heathen! The thought of that savage touching my daughter makes my skin crawl."

Michael Sommers heaved a sigh as he took his wife into his arms and held her tight. He had lived with the Indians. They were not heathen savages, as most white people believed. Oh, it was true they lived a hard life in a hard land. But they had their own god, and they were kind and generous to their own people, and to those who lived long enough among them to earn their respect and friendship. Still he could understand Sarah's feelings. She had lost much because of the hatred between red man and white. Pain and hatred did not die quickly. Sometimes not at all.

Katy smiled as she closed the bedroom door and lit the lamp beside her bed. Her room was just as she had left it. Yawning, she pulled a clean nightgown from the chest of drawers. Fortunately, it was a flowing gown and readily accommodated her thickened waistline.

Iron Wing stood in the middle of the room, watching with interest as Katy shed her dusty clothes and slipped the silky gown over her head. The color of the nightgown enhanced the pale gold of her skin and made her eyes seem even more blue.

Smothering another yawn, Katy threw back the covers and slid between the sheets. How good it felt, to lie in her own bed again, to be surrounded by things she had known all her life. Lifting her eyes to Iron Wing's face, she patted the bed beside her.

Iron Wing frowned as he sat on the edge of the bed and felt the mattress sag beneath his weight. "Too soft," he said scornfully. "I will sleep on the floor."

"Oh, very well," Katy muttered. Rising, she stripped the blankets from the bed and spread them on the floor.

"Ka-ty . . ."

"If you think I'm going to sleep in that bed alone, you're sadly mistaken," she scolded saucily. "I don't intend for us to ever sleep apart again." Pulling her pillow from the bed, she snuggled under the covers.

With a shrug, Iron Wing crawled in beside her. Katy was asleep instantly, but Iron Wing lay awake for a long time. The sounds of the house were strange, the floor beneath him as hard and unyielding as the earth he was accustomed to sleeping on, and yet so very different. He listened, eyes narrowed, as a clock chimed the hour. He missed the familiar sounds and smells of the village in the Dakotas, missing the furred softness of buffalo robes beneath him, the faint red of glowing coals as the lodge fire hissed and died.

Turning on his side, he stared at the woman sleeping peacefully beside him. How beautiful she was, and how precious. He placed his hand on her rounded belly, smiled as he felt his child's lusty kick. He gazed at Katy until, at long last, sleep claimed him.

He was up before the sun. He smiled at Katy, still sleeping soundly, one hand tucked under her cheek. At last, she was home where she belonged, where she had longed to be.

Quiet as a drifting shadow, he left Katy's bedroom and padded through the sleeping house. It was the largest dwelling he had ever seen, bigger, even, than the Herrera hacienda. There was the parlor, a spacious dining room, a large sunlit kitchen, a room filled with plants and potted flowers, another room filled with books, a smaller room dominated by a mahogany desk.

He was standing in the kitchen when

331

Juanita entered the room to fix breakfast. The woman uttered a shriek of terror when she saw an Indian looking out the window.

Iron Wing whirled around, his hand reaching for the knife at his belt.

Juanita's face turned pale as death. Her mouth moved in prayer, but sheer terror trapped the words in her throat so that no sound emerged.

Michael Sommers, roused by Juanita's scream, flew out of bed and ran down the stairs into the kitchen. He came to an abrupt halt, his lips twitching in soundless mirth, at the sight that met his eyes. Iron Wing stood near the window, his expression one of amused disgust as he stared at the woman kneeling at his feet, her face buried in her hands, her whole body trembling.

Iron Wing looked beseechingly at Mike.

"Juanita," Mike said softly. "It's all right. He won't hurt you."

"Oh, senor!" Juanita wailed. "Save me!"

"Juanita, it's all right." Taking the woman by the shoulders, he lifted her to her feet. "This is Katy Marie's . . . friend. He won't hurt you."

Juanita risked a glance at Iron Wing. Though he was dressed in the baggy white clothes of a peon, there was no mistaking the fact that he was an Indian, and her expression clearly revealed she was in fear for her life.

Sommers grinned wryly. He'd never seen anyone look so scared in his life. "Juanita, fix us some coffee."

"Si, Senor Mike," she said shakily.

"Come on, Iron Wing, let's go into the din-

332

ing room and wait. I think she'll work faster if we leave her alone."

Katy woke slowly, stretching luxuriously. Then, as she recalled where she was, she came fully awake. Home! She was home, in her own room. And Juanita was frying bacon. The rich aroma tickled Katy's nose, reminding her of all the times she had yearned for Juanita's wonderful cooking and marvelous coffee.

Suddenly famished, Katy jumped to her feet, then frowned when she saw that Iron Wing was not in the room. A sudden weight replaced the hunger in her belly. He had not wanted to come here, and only her gentle pleading had persuaded him to enter a white man's dwelling. Surely he wouldn't leave her without a word of farewell!

Going to her closet, she opened the doors, then frowned. None of her dresses would fit her increased girth. Still, she ran her hand over the smooth silks and satins as her eyes roamed over the hats and shoes and petticoats that filled the wardrobe to overflowing. She'd wear them all again soon.

Grabbing her robe, Katy ran down the hall, taking the stairs two at a time.

Relief washed over Katy when she entered the dining room and saw Iron Wing sitting at the table, lazily sipping a cup of Juanita's heavenly coffee. Sarah and Michael sat across the table from Iron Wing. Sarah's face was stern, her eyes faintly red-rimmed, as though she had spent the night crying.

"Good morning, mama," Katy said, dropping a kiss on her mother's cheek. "Mr.

Sommers."

"Mike," he reminded her.

"Mike," Katy said, liking the man for his friendly smile.

Katy sat down beside Iron Wing and reached for his hand. It was obvious her mother and Iron Wing had been having a heated discussion. She could feel the tension in the room, and in the grip of Iron Wing's hand. Katy bit her lower lip. She had forgotten, in the joy of being home and safe, how much her mother hated Indians.

"Good morning, Katy Marie," Sarah said, her tone measured and reserved. "We were just discussing your future."

"Oh?" A million butterflies danced in Katy's stomach. She slid a glance at Iron Wing, but his face was wiped clean of all expression. She looked up at Mike, and he winked at her as if to reassure her that everything would be all right.

Katy sat up a little straighter. "If you want to discuss my future, don't you think you should discuss it with me?"

"Of course," Sarah said. "About the baby . . ."

"What about my baby?"

"Well, I think that, under the circumstances, perhaps you should go away somewhere until the child is born. Perhaps to the convent in Mesa. I'm sure the good sisters there will be able to find a home for the child, perhaps with its own kind."

Katy winced as Iron Wing's grip on her hand grew painful. He stood up, his bearing proud, almost arrogant, his black eyes flashing with anger.

"We will not give our child away," he said, each word cracking across the room like a pistol shot. "If Ka-ty is not welcome here, we will leave."

"Katy, be reasonable," Sarah pleaded. "What will people say?"

"I don't care what people say," Katy retorted. "I love Iron Wing, and I'm proud to be carrying his child. I was foolish enough to think you would be glad to have me home again, pregnant or not. I had forgotten how cold and selfish you always were."

The color drained from Sarah's face. "Katy, I'm sorry. Please don't go. It's only your reputation I was concerned about. Pregnant and not married. It will cause a horrible scandal."

"I don't care," Katy said defiantly. But she did care. She did not want people gossiping about her behind her back, calling her names. But she could endure it if she had to. She could endure anything to be with Iron Wing.

"Perhaps we can make everyone happy," Michael Sommers said. "I'm sure we could find a priest to marry Katy and Iron Wing. Nothing fancy. Just a quiet ceremony here at the house."

Sarah bit back the words of protest that sprang to her lips. Katy, marry a savage! It was unthinkable. Nice girls from good families did not marry Indians. And yet, she dared not voice her objections, for to do so would surely drive Katy out of the house. And that she could not bear.

"I'd like that, Mike," Katy said, loving him the more for his calm manner and good sense. "If it's all right with Iron Wing."

Iron Wing shrugged. If Katy wished to be married by one of the black robes, it was all right with him. In his heart, she was already his wife, even though no formal words had been said.

"Very well," Sarah agreed in a resigned tone. She gestured at the food Juanita had placed on the table. "Sit down and eat, you two. I'll send Juan after Father Diaz. Perhaps he can marry you this morning."

"Your mother does not approve of me, or of this marriage," Iron Wing said when he and Katy were alone at the table.

"I know. But don't take it personally. Indians killed my father, you know. My mother has hated all Indians ever since."

"Are you sure you want to stay here, Ka-ty?"

"Yes."

"Very well, we will stay."

The priest came that afternoon just before lunch. He was cordial and polite, but it was obvious from his expression that he, too, was opposed to such a match. Of course, the Indians were God's children, too, but it was better for all concerned if they remained with their own kind. No good ever came of mixing the races.

Katy did not care a fig whether the good father approved of her marriage or not. She loved Iron Wing and she meant to marry him with or without the church's approval.

Dressed in a high-necked light blue dress that had been altered to accommodate her pregnancy, Katy stood beside Iron Wing and spoke the solemn words that made her his wife. He looked wonderfully handsome, Katy thought, dressed in a pair of tight brown twill pants and a white silk shirt that emphasized his bronze skin and dark eyes.

Iron Wing spoke the vows slowly and distinctly, his eyes never leaving Katy's face. Now she was truly his. No other man could ever dispute his right to have her, no one could take her from him.

Sarah tried not to look displeased as Katy and Iron Wing exchanged the vows that made them husband and wife. But as they knelt before the priest for his blessing on their marriage, a vision of Katy's dead father rose vividly before Sarah's eyes, and she felt her hatred for the whole red race flare anew.

Katy felt her insides melt as Iron Wing helped her to her feet and placed his first husbandly kiss on her eagerly waiting lips. Now, at last, she was really his woman.

There was no celebration following the ceremony, only a quiet lunch shared by Katy, Iron Wing, Sarah and Mike. Father Diaz had declined to stay, saying he had to return to the parish to perform a baptism.

Iron Wing keenly felt the disapproval of his new mother-in-law, but Katy seemed oblivious to everything but the man beside her. Again and again she reached out to touch him, her eyes filled with love and reassurance.

That night, alone in Katy's room, Iron Wing held Katy close.

"I say you are my woman," he murmured, grinning. "What do you say?"

337

"I have always been your woman," Katy answered, nuzzling his neck.

Iron Wing smiled into the darkness as their child moved beneath his hand. Silently, he prayed to Man Above for a strong healthy son. The child would not have an easy life. There were many, both red and white, who would despise the child for its mixed blood. Many half-breeds never found true happiness in either world and so drifted restlessly between the two, never feeling at home, never feeling wanted or accepted. A woman could not live like that and be happy. A woman needed roots, security, a sense of belonging. And so he prayed for a son, knowing such an insecure lifestyle would be easier on a man.

His troubled thoughts were interrupted as Katy kissed him. There was magic in her touch, and he put his dismal musings far from him. The future would take care of itself. It was the here and now that mattered, and Katy was here now . . .

# 23 *SPRING* *1877*

News of Katy's homecoming spread quickly through Mesa Blanca. In less than two days, everyone within a hundred mile radius knew she had returned with an Indian husband, and that she was pregnant. Gossip spread like wildfire in a dry season.

Three days after Katy returned home, her best friend, Riva McIntryre, gave a party in Katy's honor. There were dainty finger sandwiches, pitchers of lemonade and iced tea; there was a cake with "Welcome home, Katy Marie" written in lacy pink icing. And there were questions. And looks that asked questions that nice ladies did not put into words.

"It must have been awful," Daphne Rogers lamented, looking perfectly horrified. "Imagine, living with savages. Weren't you terrified?"

"Yes, at first," Katy said.

"Did they . . . abuse you?" Melanie Grayson asked.

"No," Katy lied, not wishing to discuss the whipping she had received from Iron Wing, or the brutal way he had possessed her in those first months of her captivity.

"I'm surprised you survived," Elaine

Blackwell remarked nastily. "Most women would have killed themselves."

Katy's mind flashed back to the day the Apaches had attacked the stagecoach. She had thought to kill herself then. Now she was glad that fate had intervened.

"Would anyone care for more sandwiches?" Riva said, interrupting before Katy could answer. "More lemonade, perhaps?"

At last, everyone went home. Riva sat down beside Katy and took her hand. "I'm sorry, Katy," she said sincerely. "I had no idea they would behave so abominably. I thought they would be happy to have you home, happy to know you had survived such a terrible ordeal."

"You can't blame them for being curious," Katy said, trying not to let Riva see how hurt she was by the way the women had treated her. "After all, I am something of a freak, you know."

"Katy, that's not true."

"Of course it is. They all think I'm ruined because I lived with the Cheyenne and married Iron Wing."

"Maybe it will pass, in time."

"Yes," Katy murmured. "In time." She rose to her feet and moved across the floor with her head high, fighting back tears. "Thank you for the homecoming party, Riva," she said stiffly, and ran out the door.

As the days passed, Katy's life settled into a pleasant routine. She spent the days decorating the room that had been selected as the nursery, or working on dainty baby things.

Occasionally, one of her girl friends came to call. Not all of them were as judgmental as Daphne and Elaine. Most were happy for her, even if they could not understand how she could love an Indian. A few of the girls, married to men who were as exciting as dirty dishwater, were even a tiny bit jealous because Katy radiated an inner joy and contentment that was obviously caused by the remarkably handsome man she had married. Most of the women deplored her decision to marry Iron Wing. But there wasn't one of them who did not find him terribly attractive.

Katy had taken Iron Wing shopping soon after they arrived in Mesa Blanca. People stared at them openly as they walked through the town, gawking at the sight of an Indian in their midst.

Iron Wing had balked at the idea of wearing the cumbersome clothing of a white man, but Katy coaxed him so prettily, he could not refuse for long. At her insistence, he bought several colorful shirts, a half-dozen pair of trousers, a pair of beautifully crafted boots (that he wore once and put away forever, preferring his soft moccasins), and several sets of underwear, which he adamantly refused to touch. He bought a dark blue suit, a black hat, and a red silk scarf that caught his eye.

Though Iron Wing disliked his new wardrobe, the clothes fit well, and he looked good in them. But then, he was tall, dark and handsome, Katy mused, and would have looked good in rags.

For weeks, he was the main topic of conversation, especially among the good women of the town who wondered, in hushed voices, what it would be like to be married to a savage. Not that they would ever want to share a heathen's bed, mind you, but he was terribly attractive. He fairly exuded an aura of strength and virility, and those dark eyes . . . they made you think he could see into your soul. He didn't say much, was amazingly polite. Maybe being married to a savage wouldn't be so bad after all . . .

Iron Wing spent his days on the range with Pedro Montoya, the aged Alvarez segundo, and Michael Sommers. Iron Wing had no particular interest in cattle, but riding with Sommers and Montoya gave him a good excuse to be out in the open, away from the hacienda's confining walls. It also put a good deal of distance between himself and Sarah Sommers. Katy's mother made an honest effort to mask her dislike, but Iron Wing sensed her hatred, and though he understood the reason for it, he was nonetheless uncomfortable in her presence, and in her house. The Indians had the right idea, he thought. Indian men never spoke to their mothers-in-law. It was forbidden for them to speak, or even to be in the same lodge. More and more, he could appreciate such a law.

Spending the day on the range also spared Iron Wing the curious glances of Katy's friends, many of whom eyed him as though he were a new species of wild animal. A few of her girl friends were attracted to him. He could read the wanting in their eyes when he caught them looking at him. It was flattering, but very disconcerting.

Occasionally, Sarah invited one or more of the neighboring families to dinner. Iron Wing found such gatherings especially distasteful. Dressed in his dark blue suit, he felt ill at ease and completely out of place. Katy had instructed him on the proper use of knife and fork and napkin, but he still felt self-conscious using the gleaming silver utensils. It made little difference that he ate like a civilized man, that he spoke English as well as any of Sarah's guests, or that Katy was his wife. He did not belong, and he felt it keenly.

But Katy basked under all the attention that came their way. Now that her marriage had been accepted, it was nice to be the center of attention, to wear nice clothes. When people pestered her with questions about her life with the Indians, she glossed over the hardships and made light of her fears. Iron Wing was amazed at how easily she parried their questions, many of which were rude. To hear her tell it, her life with the Cheyenne had been a lark instead of an ordeal.

Katy was aware that Iron Wing was not as happy in their new home as she was, but she was too caught up in the joy of being home again, surrounded by familiar faces and lavish possessions, to fret. She had endured so many hardships, surely she deserved a little luxury. Besides, she had adapted to Iron Wing's way of life, surely he could adapt to hers.

It did not occur to Katy that it might be

easier for a tame creature to adjust to a wild life than for a wild thing to adjust to a civilized environment. She knew only that it was wonderful to be spoiled and pampered again. After months of living with the Indians, where every day had been a battle for survival, it was heavenly to be home, to be able to sit back and relax, knowing everyone she loved was safe and secure under one roof. She did not have to fret about Iron Wing's absences, wondering if he would be killed in a raid, or worry that the village might be attacked. She did not have to worry about tanning hides, or hunting for wood, or hauling water. It was good to be waited on and looked after. She had only to mention her desire for a glass of cold lemonade or a bowl of fruit, and it was there. Best of all, her relationship with her mother had changed radically. Sarah, once so cold and aloof, seemed genuinely pleased to have her daughter home again, and she expressed her happiness in countless ways.

And so the days passed. Spring warmed the earth once more. Flowers bloomed, cows dropped fat red and white calves, new foals ran and kicked up their heels in the corrals.

And on a warm night in late March, Katy went into labor.

Iron Wing paced the parlor floor, his eyes darting uptairs time and again as the hours passed. Like most men, he knew little of childbirth. Indian men were never present at the births of their children. It was a thing left to the women. He knew it often took a long time, but was it supposed to take this long?

When he could wait no longer, he ran up the stairs and burst into Katy's bedroom.

Sarah's mouth dropped open as Katy's husband dashed into the room. No decent man ever attended his wife's laying in. It was unheard-of.

But Iron Wing brushed Sarah's objections aside as he knelt beside the bed and took Katy's hand in his. She looked pale and weary. His dark eyes were full of concern as he brushed a strand of damp hair from her forehead.

"You shouldn't be here," Katy said, forcing a weak smile. "But I'm so glad you are."

Her hand clasped his in a grip of iron as a contraction hit her, and Iron Wing groaned low in his throat, as if the pain had knifed through his own flesh.

"Talk to me," Katy begged.

Iron Wing frowned. Then in a soft, soothing voice he said, "Do not be afraid of the pain, Ka-ty. Ride with it. Become a part of it."

"How?" Katy gasped. Her fingernails dug into his forearms as another pain tore through her.

"What cannot be changed must be endured. You know the pain will come. Do not fight it."

"I can't help it," Katy sobbed as her body tensed to meet the next contraction. "I'm afraid."

"No. You must not be afraid. I am here. Hang onto me."

Sarah Sommers changed her opinion of Iron Wing that night as hour after hour he sat beside Katy, tenderly wiping the perspiration from her furrowed brow, murmuring low words of love and encouragement, rubbing Katy's back.

Katy clung to Iron Wing's hands as though they were lifelines, her sky-blue eyes dark with pain as contraction after contraction wracked her body. Soon his hands were red and swollen where her nails raked his flesh.

When ten hours had passed, Sarah sent Anna for the doctor, but Anna returned to say the doctor was out on another call and wasn't expected back for several hours.

Iron Wing saw the panic in Katy's eyes as another three hours crawled by and the pains grew more severe. Outside, the sun was up and the vaqueros were riding the range. He could hear the cows bawling, hear the men shouting back and forth. But in this room there was only Katy's labored breathing.

"Ka-ty," Iron Wing murmured. "Listen to me. Think of the mountains. Think only of the mountains. Picture them in your mind. Can you see them?"

"Yes."

"What color are they?"

"Different colors."

"Yes. In the afternoon, they are green and brown. And in the evening, when the sun is setting, they turn red like blood. Do you remember? Can you see them?"

"Yes."

"Look for me on the mountain, Ka-ty. I am there. Can you see me? I am alone."

"I see you." Her hands tightened on his as another pain knifed through her, but she rode with it, breathing rapidly, until it passed.

"I am a young brave of fourteen summers, Ka-ty. I am seeking my vision. Each morning and each evening I kneel in prayer to Man Above. I have nothing to drink, and nothing to eat. Do you see me?"

"Yes."

"I have been on the mountain for three days. My belly is like a hungry wolf, my throat is as dry as the land of the Comanche. Each day, I beseech the Great Spirit for a vision to guide me, but no answer comes, only silence. It is an awesome stillness, Ka-ty, as if the whole earth had died. Can you hear it?"

"Yes." Another pain tore through her, but her mind was intent on Iron Wing and the soothing sound of his voice. She could see him as a young boy, sitting alone on a mountain top, praying to his god. He was handsome, even then.

"On the fourth day, a great golden eagle appeared to me. He promised that if I walked always in the way of the People, I would find happiness."

"Push, Katy Marie," Sarah said quietly, not wanting to break the spell Iron Wing's words had worked. "Push."

Katy pushed, her hands gripping Iron Wing's, her eyes riveted on his face. "Did you find happiness?"

"Yes, Ka-ty. You are my happiness."

"One more push, Katy Marie," Sarah urged.

"I can't," Katy panted. "I'm too tired."

"Push, Ka-ty," Iron Wing said softly. "Hang onto me. I will be your strength."

With the last of her energy, Katy gave a final push, then fell back, exhausted, as her child made its way into the world, mewling softly.

"It's a boy," Sarah announced, blinking rapidly as tears filled her eyes.

Katy took one look at her son, and then fell into a deep sleep.

"He's beautiful," Sarah murmured as she washed the infant and wrapped it in a warm blanket. "Just beautiful."

"Yes," Iron Wing agreed, taking the child from its grandmother's arms. "As beautiful as his mother."

There was silence in the room for the next few moments as Sarah washed Katy, collected the afterbirth, and dressed Katy in a clean gown. From time to time, she glanced at the man standing by the bedroom window. His eyes were warm with love as he gazed at the infant cradled in his arms.

"You love my daughter very much, don't you?" There was a note of wonder in Sarah's voice, as if she could not quite believe an Indian could be capable of such a civilized emotion.

"More than my own life," Iron Wing answered.

"I'm sorry for the way I've treated you," Sarah murmured. "Indians killed Katy's father. I've hated all Indians ever since that day. Please forgive me."

"There is nothing to forgive," Iron Wing replied. "Old hates die hard."

"Yes. Shall we go downstairs? Juanita will fix us something to eat."

"You go. I want to be here when Ka-ty wakes up."

With a nod, Sarah left the room. For years, she had hated Indians. She had thought them cruel, heartless savages, incapable of love or tenderness. How wrong she had been!

Iron Wing sat beside Katy, occasionally reaching out to stroke her cheek, or touch her arm. Never had she looked more beautiful. Never had he loved her more. He gazed at the tiny infant sleeping peacefully in his arms. The child had thick black hair and tawny skin. A son, Iron Wing thought exultantly. I have a son.

When Katy woke, the first thing she saw was Iron Wing sitting on the edge of the bed, their son cradled in one strong arm. It was a sight to stir any new mother's heart and she smiled happily.

Seeing that she was awake, Iron Wing placed the baby in her arms. Bending, he kissed her cheek. "I love you, Ka-ty," he whispered in a voice thick with emotion.

"And I love you." Her eyes caressed her child as she guided the baby's mouth toward her breast. "Isn't he beautiful? He looks just like you."

"Am I beautiful, Ka-ty?" Iron Wing asked, grinning down at her.

"To me you are."

"Have you a name for our son?"

"I'd like to call him John, after my father, if it's all right with you."

Iron Wing nodded. "Whatever you want, I

want."

Katy smiled drowsily, and then, with a sigh, she fell asleep again.

Two weeks later, they took the child to church to be baptized. Iron Wing had never accompanied Katy to church before, though she went with her mother every week. Now he stared in awe at the elaborate edifice, at the colorful stained glass windows, at the life-sized statues of the Catholic saints, at the figure of a half-naked man hanging from a cross.

Bemused by it all, he stood near the font cradling his son in his arms while a priest dressed in flowing black robes blessed the child and bestowed upon him the name Katy had chosen: John Iron Wing Alvarez.

Katy was positively glowing as they left the church. Never had she been happier than she was now, safe and warm within the circle of those she loved.

A party, Katy thought excitedly as she stepped into her dress and smoothed the ruffled skirt over her hips. Standing before the mirror, she smiled at her reflection. The dress was new, a gift from her mother. China blue in color, the gown made her eyes glow like sapphires, and the thrill of being dressed up made her cheeks flush with color. It was a beautiful dress, Katy thought. The neck was low, but not too low, the skirts so full it made her waist tiny in comparison. The sleeves were full to her elbow, then fitted tight to her wrists. Her hair, black and shiny, was wound in a knot atop her head save for one long curl that fell over her left shoulder. Laughter bubbled in her throat as she twirled before the mirror. Oh, but it was wonderful to be home again, to see old friends, to be spoiled and pampered, to know you were loved . . .

She felt her heart flutter as Iron Wing came up behind her and slipped his arms around her waist. How handsome he was! And how she loved him.

Iron Wing felt his heart swell with emotion as Katy swayed against him, brazenly grinding her softly rounded buttocks against his groin. Bending, he kissed the soft curve of her throat, felt his manhood rise as Katy turned in his arms and pressed her lips to his. Her breasts pushed against his chest provocatively.

"Must we go downstairs, Ka-ty?" he asked, his voice husky with desire.

"I'm afraid so," Katy said, pleased by the love and longing she saw reflected in the depths of his dark eyes. "After all, the party is for us."

With a sigh of resignation, Iron Wing released her, reaching for the black broadcloth jacket he had carelessly tossed on the bed.

He looked so handsome, it fairly took Katy's breath away as she watched him slip into the fashionable jacket. The dark gray pants he wore outlined his muscular legs, and emphasized the slight bulge lingering in his crotch. Katy grinned as her eyes lingered on the sign of his desire. How awful to be a man, unable to hide what you were thinking. A woman could entertain all manner of interesting thoughts and desires, and no one was ever the wiser. She lifted her eyes to her husband's face. His black jacket handsomely accented his thick black hair and fathomless black eyes, and made a perfect foil for his rich, copper-hued skin. He was perfect in every way, she mused proudly, and she could hardly wait to get him downstairs and show him off.

Arm in arm, Katy and Iron Wing left their bedroom and made their way down the stairs.

Entering the ballroom, Katy saw that many of the guests had already arrived. A few couples were dancing, others stood in small groups, laughing and talking over drinks. Katy saw her mother and Michael Sommers waltz by. They made a handsome couple, her mother small and dark, Sommers tall and blond. It was easy to see they were very much in love. Sarah's face was radiant.

Pablo Alvarado watched Katy as she entered the room on the arm of her husband, and he felt his blood flame with jealousy. Katy had been a lovely young girl, and he had always thought that one day she would be his. But then Wellingham had entered her life, and she had ignored every one else. When Wellingham died, Pablo had thought perhaps she would turn to him for comfort. Instead, she had declared her intention to become a nun, of all things. And now, impossible as it seemed, she was back home with an Indian for a husband and a half-breed child. He scowled as Katy laughed at something Iron Wing said. It was incredible, but she was even more beautiful than he remembered. Her hair was piled regally atop her

head, her lovely figure, ripened by motherhood, made his heat rise. He did not stop to
think that Katy's radiance was the result of
her love for her husband, he knew only that
he wanted her more than ever.

Squaring his shoulders, Pablo crossed the
floor to where Katy stood beside Iron Wing.

"Katy, how lovely you look this evening,"
he said with a courtly bow. "May I have this
dance?"

"Of course," Katy replied, smiling up at
her childhood sweetheart as she took his
arm.

Pablo danced excellently, and Katy's
cheeks flushed with pleasure as he twirled
her around the floor.

Pablo beamed down at Katy. They had
always danced well together. One July
Fourth, they had won a dance contest. She
was a part of his childhood, a part of his
memories. Looking at her, he could easily
imagine her as the mistress of his house. She
would add charm and elegance to the
Alvarado estate. He had always insisted on
having the best of everything, and now he
resolved to have Katy for his wife. The fact
that she already had a husband meant
nothing. After all, how binding could
marriage to a savage be?

Iron Wing frowned as Pablo Alvarado
whirled Katy around the dance floor. They
looked well together, he thought irritably.
Too well. He scowled blackly as Pablo whispered something in Katy's ear, causing her to
laugh merrily.

Iron Wing's displeasure grew steadily
worse as one man after another asked Katy

to dance. Among the Cheyenne, a man danced only with his future bride, or his wife. Katy tried repeatedly to coax him out onto the dance floor, but he was ignorant of the dances of the white man and refused to be taught the complicated steps in the presence of others. Surely they would laugh at him, and he would not subject himself to their amusement.

Later in the evening, the guests adjourned to the patio for a buffet dinner. Juanita had done herself proud. There was ham, turkey and beef. Three kinds of potatoes. Five vegetables. Four kinds of bread. And seven desserts.

Iron Wing remained close to Katy, his dark eyes smoldering with suppressed jealousy. The food was excellent, but he ate it without tasting it, wanting to strangle every man present who looked at his wife.

Katy chatted and laughed amiably with her friends, totally unaware of the volcano seething within her husband's breast. It was so good to gossip with the women and laugh with the men she had known all her life.

When the dancing started again, Pablo Alvarez sought her out once more.

"I had forgotten how well you dance, Katy Marie," he said, smiling at her affectionately. "You're like a feather in my arms."

"Thank you, Pablo," Katy said. "Mother tells me you're still not married."

"Not yet."

"Can't you find a girl to please you?"

"I found one," he replied, drawing her closer in his arms, "but she is wed to another."

"Pablo, you mustn't hold me so tight."

"I love you, Katy. I have always loved you."

"Pablo," Katy said, trying to wriggle out of his grasp, "please. You shouldn't say such things. It isn't proper. I'm a married woman."

"You're too good for that savage, Katy. Don't you know that?"

"I love my husband," Katy said emphatically. "And he loves me."

"Love!" Pablo muttered disdainfully. "What could a heathen Indian possibly know about love?"

Katy's anger flared as she heard her husband referred to as a savage and a heathen. It did not matter that she had once referred to Iron Wing in exactly the same terms. Now she knew him to be one of the sweetest, kindest men on earth.

Jerking out of Pablo's arms, Katy raised her hand and slapped him soundly across the face. "How dare you!" she hissed. "Don't you ever say such a thing about my husband again!"

Pivoting on her heel to leave the dance floor, Katy almost ran into Iron Wing, who had come soundlessly up behind her.

Iron Wing's black eyes were ablaze with anger as he glared at Pablo Alvarado. "What did you say to my wife?" he demanded.

Pablo drew himself up to his full height as he glared back at Iron Wing. "I told her she was too good for the likes of you," the Mexican said with a sneer.

"Perhaps," Iron wing replied coldly. "But she *is* my woman, and if you ever touch her again, I will cut out your heart."

355

Katy laid a restraining hand on Iron Wing's arm as she became aware of the silence that had fallen over the ballroom. All eyes were focused on Pablo and Iron Wing, waiting to see what would happen next.

Michael Sommers walked purposefully toward the trio, his face set in hard lines. "Mr. Alvarado, I think it would be best for all concerned if you would say good night."

Pablo's face flushed with anger and embarrassment as the host invited him to leave. Head high, back straight as a ramrod, he stalked out of the room.

"Thank you, Michael," Katy said in a tight voice.

"Glad to be of help, Katy Marie," Sommers replied, giving her arm an affectionate squeeze. "Iron Wing, would you mind if I danced with my stepdaughter?"

"No."

Iron Wing watched Michael Sommers guide Katy around the floor as the music began again. Too angry and tense to remain indoors, he left the house and walked around the yard, his whole being urging him to follow Alvarado and kill him. But he was a civilized man now, Iron Wing mused bitterly, and civilized people did not behave like savages.

Pausing, he looked back toward the house. He could see Katy dancing with Sommers. How beautiful she was! Just looking at her made his heart swell with love. Michael bent to whisper something in Katy's ear, and she smiled prettily at him. It was good to see her laughing and smiling, Iron Wing mused. Good to know she was happy. She deserved to be happy and carefree after all she had been through. She had suffered much, first with his people, and then at the hands of El Lobo and Frank Herrera. She belonged here, in her own land, among her own people.

Seeing her in her childhood home, at ease among the white man's wealth and comfort, he realized what an effort it must have been for her to adjust to life with the Cheyenne. The fact that she had managed to embrace his way of life so wholeheartedly amazed him anew. She belonged here, surrounded by her family and friends. But he did not belong, and he never would.

With a sigh, he walked toward the stable. He would never belong in the white man's world. He would never feel at ease in the white man's clothes that hampered his movements. He despised the stiff white collars that threatened to squeeze the breath from his body. And the white man's shoes that he had agreed to wear tonight to please Katy were as cruel and painful a torture as any ever devised by the Indians.

Inside the stable, he stripped off his coat, cravat, shirt, pants and shoes, and then, clad only in his breechcloth, he swung onto the back of a fine chestnut mare and rode away from the hacienda. Urging the mare into a lope, he cleared his mind of everything but the exhilaration of riding through the night with the wind stinging his face.

He let the horse run until she slowed and stopped of her own accord. By then, they were far into the hills that rose to the south of the Alvarez rancho. Dismounting, Iron Wing dropped down on his haunches and stared out into the darkness. His nostrils filled with the scent of damp grass and earth and sage, reminding him of home, of Cheyenne lodges rising against the sacred hills, of milling pony herds and shaggy hump-backed buffalo. He thought of Many Eagles Flying, and wondered if the old chief were still alive. He thought of Tall Buffalo and Yellow Flower. Were they still alive?

The Sioux and the Cheyenne were mentioned often in the newspapers since the death of Yellow Hair Custer. People in the east were crying out for the extermination of the red man, declaring the West would not be a fit place for decent people to live until the last Indian was wiped from the face of the earth. The Army was in full agreement. Bent on revenge for the Custer massacre at Little Big Horn, they were pushing the tribes with a vengeance.

Iron Wing wondered if his tribe had been wiped out, or if they had somehow managed to elude the soldier coats and their big guns mounted on wheels. His blood burned to be with his people, fighting with them for their freedom, but he could not leave Katy and the baby. She was his heart, his soul. To leave her was to die inside . . .

It was near dawn when he swung aboard the chestnut mare and rode back to the hacienda.

The house was quiet as Katy nursed her son. The party had ended hours ago and still there was no sign of Iron Wing. It had been most embarrassing, trying to explain his sudden disappearance to their guests.

She finished nursing John, changed his diaper, and laid him in his bed. When she was certain he was asleep, she went downstairs to see if Iron Wing had returned, but there was still no sign of him anywhere. Knowing she would never be able to sleep until she found her husband, she went outside, her anger at his unexplained absence turning to worry as the minutes ticked by. Where was he? Why had he gone off without a word to anyone?

She was standing on the veranda staring into the distance when he rode into the yard. He was naked save for his clout, his hair windblown.

Katy felt a thrill of desire race down her spine as she stared up at him. How proud and arrogant he looked sitting there with the sun rising behind him. Her heart began to flutter wildly as he walked his horse toward her. He looked savage and formidable as he closed the distance between them.

Katy's eyes lingered on his broad chest and shoulders and she remembered the first time she had seen him in the Cheyenne village and how frightened she had been.

He was beside her now, his face impassive, his black eyes unfathomable. For a moment, they gazed at each other. Then, slowly, Katy lifted her arms. She knew with a sudden intuition where Iron Wing had been and why, knew deep in her heart that he needed her.

Iron Wing smiled as he reached down to lift her to the back of his horse. Then, uttering a low-pitched cry of victory, he drummed his heels into the horse's flanks.

Katy wrapped her arms around his waist and held on tightly as they galloped into the hills. It was a wildly exhilarating feeling, being carried through the night with her face pressed against Iron Wing's bare back. The wind whipped through her hair and stung her cheeks, but she didn't care. Nothing mattered but being alone with the man she loved.

High in the hills, Iron Wing reined the chestnut to an abrupt halt. Dismounting, he lifted Katy from the back of the horse and set her on the ground. His dark eyes burned into hers as he tossed his breechcloth aside to stand naked before her. The sun turned his skin to flame and Katy feld her insides melt with desire as his hand reached out to draw her close. His eyes never left her face as he slowly unfastened the bodice of her gown and pulled it down around her hips. Her chemise went the way of her dress, her pantalets also, and then she was naked before him.

The grass was soft as he laid her down, his hands like fire as they played over her quivering flesh. There was no tenderness in him now, no gentle wooing. He was a warrior and she was his woman, and he claimed her fiercely, savagely, his mouth branding her flesh as his, his whispered words enforcing the possession of his hands upon her body as she willingly surrendered to his strength.

Katy thrilled at his touch, reveling in his power over her, in the way his hands fired her passion. She could feel his whole body quivering as he held back his own release until she had reached hers, and then there was a warm flood of satisfaction and pleasure as his manhood spilled into her.

Sated and content, they fell asleep in each other's arms.

Mike and Sarah were standing on the veranda, their faces lined with worry when Katy and Iron Wing rode up to the house.

"Looks like we did a lot of worrying for nothing," Mike remarked, grinning.

Sarah nodded curtly. It took but one look at Katy's rumpled gown and flushed cheeks to know what had kept her out all night.

Dismounting, Iron Wing helped Katy to the ground. His arm went around her waist possessively as he faced Mike's knowing grin and Sarah's disapproval.

"I'm sorry if we worried you," Katy said in a small voice.

"It's all right," Mike replied, still grinning broadly. "But the next time you two get the urge to . . . uh, see the hills in the moonlight, you might leave a note."

"Yes," Iron Wing said. "Next time."

Sarah bit back the angry words that rose to her lips as Iron Wing took Katy by the hand and led her into the house. It was none of her business if Katy wanted to cavort in the hills with her husband like a common trollop.

Sarah looked at Mike. He was still grinning foolishly, and it riled her that he found it all so amusing.

"It's scandalous," Sarah said stiffly. "Going off into the hills like a couple of animals."

"You think so?" Mike said, drawing her into his arms. "I was thinking it might be kind of romantic."

"You're not serious!"

"Tonight, maybe," Mike proposed, kissing her ear. "About midnight?"

Sarah looked shocked. Pleased, but shocked. "Are you sure you aren't part Indian yourself?"

"There's a little of the savage in all of us," Mike said, winking at her. "Be ready at midnight."

Inside the house, Katy and Iron Wing smiled at each other.

"Imagine my mother having a midnight rendezvous," Katy exclaimed. "My, how things have changed!"

# 24

Several days after the party, Katy left John with his grandmother and rode out on the range. It was a beautiful spring day, balmy and clear, and she urged her dainty gray Arab mare into a lope. She laughed aloud as the wind brushed her cheeks and played in her hair.

After the long months of confinement in Miguel Herrera's fortress, and then months of pregnancy and limited activity, it felt divine to be riding across the grassland with no cares and no worries. She loved Iron Wing. She loved her mother, was fond of Michael Sommers, adored her son.

Topping a rise, Katy drew her horse to a halt, felt her heart beat a little faster as she spied Iron Wing in the shallow valley below. He was chasing a cow and calf, and Katy watched with pride as man and horse worked together. Iron Wing rode flawlessly, moving as though he were a part of the horse. He had removed his shirt, and his long black hair flowed down his back. He almost looked like a warrior again, and she felt her heart thrill with excitement as her eyes lovingly went over the powerful muscles rippling in his arms and legs and back. His skin was sheened with a fine layer of sweat, his dark eyes intent upon the fleeing calf.

Katy grinned as he cut the calf from the milling herd, marveling that he had so quickly learned to rope and tie cattle. Effortlessly, he vaulted from his horse, threw and tied the calf. Moments later, its hip carrying the Alvarez brand, the calf jumped to its feet and ran, bawling loudly, to its mother.

Katy was still grinning when she rode down the hill. "Hi, cowboy," she called to her husband. "Working hard?"

Iron Wing shrugged. "Not too hard. Is something wrong?"

"No. I just thought I'd ride out and say hello." Katy waved to the three cowhands squatting beside the fire. Until now, she had not even noticed them, or the other two cowhands riding through the herd, so absorbed had she been in watching her husband.

The vacqueros touched their hats respectfully, then reheated the branding iron as another wrangler cut a calf from the herd.

Katy looked up at Iron Wing, a smile playing over her lips. "Can I talk you into taking me for a swim in the lake?"

"You must know by now that you could talk me into anything." Iron Wing muttered dryly.

"Good. Race you to the lake," Katy shouted, and drummed her heels into her mare's flanks.

With a loud cry, Iron Wing vaulted into the saddle and gave chase, but his cow pony, while agile and fleet of foot, was no match for Katy's desert-bred Arab.

She was waiting for him at the lake, a broad grin on her face, as he drew rein beside her.

"You would have made a fine warrior," Iron Wing mused, dismounting. Placing his hands around her trim waist, he lifted her from the saddle and placed her on the ground.

"Would you have liked me better if I were a warrior?" Katy teased, wantonly pressing herself against the length of his body.

Iron Wing ran his hands seductively over her hips and buttocks. "What do you think?"

Katy uttered a little squeal of pleasure as Iron Wing bent and kissed her neck, his hands grinding her hips against his.

"Do you still want to swim, Ka-ty?" he asked huskily.

"Later," she murmured breathlessly. "Later . . ."

Sarah smiled at her husband as Katy and Iron Wing rode by the house on their way to the barn.

"She looks happy, doesn't she?" Michael remarked.

"Yes," Sarah agreed. "Much as I hate to admit it, I think Katy has made a fine match. I doubt Pablo Alvarado, or even Wellingham, would have been as good for her."

"You've been very good for me," Mike said, squeezing Sarah's hand. "I've never been happier in my life."

"Nor I," Sarah murmured, smiling. She gazed fondly at the infant sleeping in her lap. At last, she had everything she had ever wanted. Her relationship with Katy was everything it should be, she had a darling grandson, a kind and loving husband. The ranch was prospering.

"Do you think Iron Wing is happy here?" Mike asked.

Sarah glanced over at the barn. She could see Iron Wing unsaddling the horses while Katy looked on. They were talking and smiling, apparently content.

"Yes, he seems happy," Sarah said. "Don't you think so?"

Mike shook his head slowly. "No."

"Has he said anything?"

"No, it's just a gut feeling."

A cold chill washed over Sarah as she watched Iron Wing and Katy rub down their horses. If Iron Wing decided to go back to his own people, Katy would go with him. Sarah glanced down at the child in her lap, gently smoothed his dark hair. She could not bear to lose him. He was so precious, so very dear to her heart. She longed to see him grow to manhood, to watch him learn to walk and talk and ride. She wanted to share his birthdays and see his face light up at Christmas. Impulsively, she picked him up and hugged him close to her breast.

Michael Sommers chewed on his lower lip as he watched Sarah and the baby. He knew what she was thinking, and he could have kicked himself for worrying her, perhaps needlessly.

"I could be wrong," Mike said. "I've been wrong before."

"I don't know how I'd bear it if Katy left home again," Sarah said, her voice edged with pain. "Not now, when we've only just really found each other."

"Let's cross that bridge when we come to it," Sommers suggested, wishing he had kept his big mouth shut.

Sarah nodded, but it was a thought that was never out of her mind from that day on. She made a conscious effort to include Iron Wing in everything they did. She instructed Juanita to serve his favorite foods more often. She asked his advice about ranch affairs, asked him to be in charge of the remuda.

One evening, after dinner, she asked him when his birthday was, and when he said he didn't know, only that it was in the early summer, she picked the date of June first and planned a small surprise party for him.

And Iron Wing was surprised beyond words the night he entered the dining room and saw it decorated with colored streamers and a large handpainted sign that read "HAPPY BIRTHDAY, IRON WING." There were three gaily wrapped packages beside his dinner plate.

"They're for you," Sarah said, smiling at the astonished expression on his usually impassive face. "Tonight we're celebrating your birthday. It's an American custom."

"But I have nothing to give you in return," Iron Wing protested.

"It isn't necessary," Katy said. "This isn't a giveaway feast. It's your birthday. How old are you, anyway?"

"I am twenty-seven summers." He looked at Katy, a bemused smile on his face. "How old are you?"

"A woman never tells," Katy said, shaking her head.

"Surely a husband has a right to know."

"I suppose so. I'm twenty-two."

"When is your . . . birthday?"

"It's past," Katy said, her good mood shattered.

Iron Wing's eyes searched hers, and he knew intuitively that her birthday must have occurred during her stay with Miguel. Or perhaps it had been when they were fleeing across the desert toward her home. Somehow, he would make it up to her.

Mike cleared his throat. "Uh, Iron Wing, why don't you open your presents?"

"Yes," Katy said, forcing a smile. "Open them."

Nodding, Iron Wing unwrapped the packages. There was a blue checked shirt from Sarah, a finely crafted knife from Mike, a pair of soft moccasins from Katy.

"I made them myself," Katy said. "Are they all right?"

"Perfect," he declared, touched by her thoughtfulness. His old moccasins were just about worn out, and Katy knew how much he disliked boots.

"Thank you," Iron Wing said, touched by their gifts and warm wishes. "Thank you all."

Juanita served his favorite dinner that night, and then Katy, Sarah and Mike sang Happy Birthday, while Juanita lit the candles on the cake.

Iron Wing felt a little embarrassed by all the fuss, but he dutifully blew out the candles.

"What did you wish for?" Katy asked.

"Wish for?" Iron Wing said.

"You're supposed to make a wish," Mike explained. "But don't tell what it is, or it won't come true."

Sitting across the table, Sarah prayed fervently that Iron Wing's wish would not come true, for she knew in her heart that he had wished to be home with his own people.

Iron Wing went into town the next day. He had been touched by the gifts he had received, but he felt guilty that he had given nothing in return. So now he shopped, buying a black lace mantilla for Katy's mother to wear to church, a box of fine cigars for Sommers. For Katy, he chose a delicate gold heart on a fine chain, a pair of pearl-drop earrings, and a wide gold wedding band. He hoped she would be pleased with the gifts and that, somehow, they would make up for the birthday she had missed. She must never feel cheated of anything because of him.

There was another birthday cake on the dinner table. Katy looked at her mother, her expression one of bafflement.

"Is it Mike's birthday?" Katy asked. "I know it isn't yours."

"No," Sarah answered, shaking her head.

"It's your birthday, Ka-ty," Iron Wing said. "Tonight we are having all of your favorite foods." Turning, he picked up a parcel from the sideboard. "Sit, all of you," he said. "Sarah, this is for you. Michael, this is yours. And, Ka-ty, these are for you."

Katy blinked back her tears as she opened the gifts. The heart was lovely, the gold chain exquisite, the earrings worthy of a duchess. But the gold band was her undoing. "Oh, Iron Wing," she breathed, touched to the depths of her heart. "It's beautiful. Will you put it on my finger?"

He nodded solemnly. Taking her hand in his, he slid the wedding ring on her finger.

"Now a kiss," Katy said.

Sarah felt the tears start as she watched Iron Wing bend down and give Katy a heart-felt kiss. How could she have ever thought her son-in-law incapable of love? His feelings for Katy were clear in his eyes, in the way he thought always of her happiness.

For Katy, it was the best birthday she'd ever had. And later that night, when Iron Wing took her in his arms, her joy was complete.

# 25

One Saturday morning, Katy woke to find herself alone in bed. Rising quickly, she checked on John. He was sleeping peacefully on his stomach, his little legs bunched underneath him, his fist jammed into his mouth. She paused a moment to place a kiss on his cheek. How fast he was growing!

Smiling, she went to her closet, pulled out a dark blue skirt and a white blouse. Dressing, she hurried downstairs to find Iron Wing. She expected to find him in the kitchen having coffee, but he wasn't there. Frowning, she checked the parlor and the den and when she couldn't find him anywhere in the house, she went outside, shading her eyes against the early morning sun. It was unlike him to leave without telling her where he was going, and she grew more and more worried as she left the front yard and walked rapidly toward the barn. She knew she was behaving foolishly. After all, he was a grown man, and quite able to take care of himself.

Katy came to an abrupt halt as she neared one of the breaking pens. Relief erupted in a long sigh as she saw Iron Wing leading a tall blue roan into the corral. Recognizing the animal, she felt her relief turn to apprehension. The horse was a wild stud, caught off the range only a few days ago. All efforts to break the horse had failed; three wranglers had been injured, one had been killed. Ordinarily, such a rank stallion would have been gelded or disposed of, but the blue roan was an exceptional animal. His conformation was close to perfect, and Michael hoped to breed him to some of the ranch mares.

Katy watched with awe as Iron Wing swung agilely into the saddle. A prayer rose in her heart as the big blue horse began bucking wildly.

Iron Wing grinned as the stallion bucked and pitched, now sunfishing, now swapping ends, now jumping straight up and landing with jarring impact on all four feet. Several times the horse reached around, big yellow teeth bared as it tried to sink its teeth into Iron Wing's leg.

A minute passed; two, five. Katy wrung her hands together as she watched Iron Wing. The horse bucked without tiring, its fury mounting as it failed to dislodge the man clinging stubbornly to its back.

Iron Wing was sweating profusely as he fought the stallion. And yet, for all the struggle, the battle was invigorating, filling him with a sense of exhilaration he had not felt in months. As a warrior, he had been needed, important to the survival of his people. His bow had brought down the enemies of the Cheyenne, had provided food and clothing for those who could not provide for themselves. Men had sought his advice, boys had imitated him. He had been respected and admired. Here, living as a white man, he was of little worth. His knowledge of the wild was unimportant. There were no enemies threatening the survival of the ranch or its inhabitants. Food and clothing were readily available.

Now, as he fought the wild stallion to see who would be the master, he felt vitally alive again. It was good to pit his strength against the strength of the horse, good to feel his blood flowing hot in his veins.

Another five minutes passed, and at last the big horse began to show signs of tiring. Its sides were heaving mightily, yellow lather covered its sleek hide, foam dripped from its mouth. Abruptly, the horse reared straight up on its hind legs and pitched over backwards. Katy held her breath as Iron Wing threw himself out of the saddle, rolling sideways to avoid being crushed under the heavy stock saddle and a thousand pounds of irate horseflesh.

Man and beast sprang to their feet, facing each other warily. Slowly, Iron Wing walked toward the horse. Right hand outstretched, he talked softly to the stud. He was reaching for the dangling reins when the stallion let out a scream of rage and lashed out with its front feet. One unshod hoof caught Iron Wing in the leg just below his knee.

Iron Wing gasped with pain. Then, with a mighty cry of his own, he grabbed a handful of the stallion's mane and vaulted into the saddle. As soon as the horse felt Iron Wing's weight on its back, it began bucking wildly again, squealing with rage and pain as Iron Wing lashed its flanks with the ends of the reins. When the horse started to rear, Iron Wing was ready. Raising his fist, he brought it down hard between the stud's ears.

Katy grinned as the horse let out a grunt and dropped its forefeet to the ground. Serves you right, she mused, and then frowned as she noticed the ribbon of blood staining Iron Wing's pant leg.

Some twenty-five minutes after the battle began, the horse gave up. A last, half-hearted buck and then it stood still, its front legs spraddled, its head hanging in defeat. Yellow lather dripped from its heaving sides, gathering in dirty puddles on the ground.

With a grin of triumph, Iron Wing dismounted. Patting the horse on the neck, he pulled off the heavy saddle. Using the saddle blanket, he began to rub down the stallion.

"You were wonderful!" Katy exclaimed as she climbed up on the top rail of the corral and sat down. "Just wonderful."

Iron Wing smiled at her, pleased by her words of praise. "I think he will make a good horse after all," he said, scratching the roan's ears. "He is a fighter."

"So are you."

"Not any more," Iron Wing murmured, and there was such a note of unhappiness in his voice that Katy winced.

"You're bleeding," she said, pointing at his leg.

Iron Wing glanced down at the blood and shrugged unconcerned. "I did not notice."

"Come up to the house and I'll bandage it for you."

"I am all right."

"Iron Wing, you can't just stand there and bleed all over the place," Katy scolded.

"I am all right, Ka-ty," he said sharply. "Go

back to the house. I will come when I am ready."

Katy looked at him reproachfully, then jumped to the ground and walked briskly back to the house, brushing at her tears as she went. What had she said, to make him growl at her like that? She only wanted to help.

John was awake when she reached her room. Lifting him, she kissed his downy cheek, smiled as he grabbed a handful of her hair. She hummed softly as she changed his diaper, then sat on the bed to nurse him, but her heart was heavy. She and Iron Wing had rarely spoken crossly to each other. Their trials and heartaches had always been caused by others, and they had found comfort and solace in the love they shared. But lately, Iron Wing had seemed withdrawn and alone.

When the baby had taken his fill, she put him back to bed, then went to the window and looked down at the corral where Iron Wing was cooling out the stud. There were any number of hired hands to care for the horse, she thought irritably. There was no reason for him to do it. He was limping now, she saw, his pant leg was soaked with blood. But still he walked, determinedly leading the horse around and around the corral until the animal was cool enough to be put away without danger of colicking. Lord, what a stubborn man, she thought, shaking her head in disgust. And how she loved him.

She was waiting for Iron Wing when he entered the house. "Can I take care of your leg now?" she asked quietly.

Iron Wing nodded. Hobbling into the

kitchen, he eased down onto one of the chairs and closed his eyes. His whole leg throbbed with pain.

"For goodness sakes, what's going on in here?" Sarah gasped moments later when she stepped into the kitchen.

"Iron Wing broke the blue roan," Katy explained.

"Looks more like the roan broke him," Michael observed, coming up behind his wife. "Is his leg broke?"

"No," Katy said. Using a knife, she slit Iron Wing's pant leg up the seam, exposing the wound. Blood trickled from an ugly gash where the stallion's hoof had gouged the skin. The area just below his knee was a hideous shade of purple, the leg swollen to almost twice its normal size.

With a look of concern on her face, Sarah put some water on the stove to heat. Taking a rag from a cupboard, she handed it to Katy. "It's clean," she said. "You can use it to stop the bleeding."

Katy nodded. Taking the cloth from her mother, she pressed it over the gash in Iron Wing's leg. He winced involuntarily as she touched his leg.

Sommers left the room, returning a moment later with a bottle of Kentucky bourbon. "Here," he said, handing the bottle to Iron Wing. "I think this might help ease the pain."

Iron Wing grinned wryly as he uncorked the bottle. "Don't you know it is against the law to give firewater to Indians?" he said before taking a long swallow. The amber liquid burned a fiery path to the pit of his stomach, then suffused him with a warm glow that did indeed cause the pain to recede a little.

Sommers grinned knowingly. "I thought that would help," he said, chuckling.

Iron Wing grinned crookedly. He took another drink as Sarah and Katy worked over his leg, wiping the blood away with a rag soaked in hot water, then applying cold cloths to reduce the swelling.

"I don't think that cut will require stitching," Sarah remarked. "But he'd best stay off his feet for a day or two. That's a nasty bruise."

With Michael's help, they managed to get Iron Wing up the stairs. He was slightly drunk by then, and offered no resistance as Sommers and Katy put him to bed. He was asleep almost instantly.

Katy turned troubled eyes on Sommers. "I don't understand him any more," she said. "Why did he have to ride that mustang? What was he trying to prove?"

"I don't know, Katy," Mike answered kindly. He placed a hand on her shoulder and gave it an affectionate squeeze. "I don't claim to know much about Indians, but I do know that Indian men set a high price on their pride and their manhood. In the wild, a man knows he's important. His life is dedicated to protecting his people, to fighting their enemies and providing food and shelter. Perhaps Iron Wing doesn't feel like he's contributing anything here," Sommers shrugged. "Hell, Katy, I don't know. Maybe he was just trying to prove he was stronger and smarter than the horse."

Standing on tiptoe, Katy kissed Sommers on the cheek. "My mother was smart to marry you."

"Thanks, kid. Be patient with Iron Wing, Katy. If there's one thing I do know, it's that he loves you very much."

"I know. And I love him."

"Then I guess everything will work out," Sommers said. "Come on, let's go get some breakfast. I think he'll be asleep for quite some time."

Iron Wing refused to stay in bed the next day. After breakfast, he limped down to the corral and saddled the blue roan, then rode the animal out of the yard and into the hills.

Katy was on pins and needles waiting for him to return. When he had been gone for over two hours, she began to imagine everything that could have gone wrong. The horse had thrown Iron Wing and trampled him to death. The horse had bolted and run off a cliff, killing them both. A snake had spooked the stallion, Iron Wing had been thrown and bitten and was even now slowly dying as the deadly poison coursed through his veins.

She nursed John, then rocked him for an hour, singing softly to him until he fell asleep. But her mind was in turmoil. Where was Iron Wing?

Just after lunch, she heard a horse approaching, and she ran out onto the front porch expecting to see Iron Wing showing off. Instead, she saw Pablo Alvarado.

"Pablo, what are you doing here?" she

asked bluntly, too worried about Iron Wing's whereabouts to be polite.

"I have come to apologize for my scandalous behavior at the party," Pablo said, dismounting. Tossing his horse's reins over the hitchrack, he walked up the stairs. Removing his hat, he asked, "Will you forgive me?"

"Yes, of course," Katy said, willing to let bygones be bygones. She would never approve of what he had done or said, but they were friends, and there was no point in holding a grudge.

"Will you come in?" Katy asked. "I know my mother would like to see you."

"Perhaps some other time."

"Very well," Katy said, smiling. "I'm glad we're friends again."

"So am I, Katy mia. *Adios.*"

"*Adios.*"

When Iron Wing finally came home, Katy ran into his arms, all thought of Pablo Alvarado's visit forgotten.

Iron Wing looked at Katy, a bemused expression on his face as she held him tight. "Did you miss me so much, Ka-ty?"

"Of course, I missed you, you big dope. Don't ever worry me like that again."

"Worry?" he echoed, genuinely puzzled. "Why were you worried?"

"Because you were gone so long on that awful horse. I was sure you had been hurt or killed."

"He is not an awful horse, Ka-ty. He would have made a fine war horse. He is fast and strong and fearless."

Katy sighed, exasperated. Didn't he understand how she worried about him, how much she depended on his love? Didn't he know she would die without him?

"How is my son?" Iron Wing asked, going to the baby's bed. He grinned to see the child was awake. Lifting the boy in his arms, he swung him high in the air. John laughed happily, waving his arms and legs as his father swung him up and down, shrieking with delight when Iron Wing tossed him in the air.

"Soon you will ride the blue," Iron Wing told the boy. "He will carry you like the wind across the plains."

"Don't you ever put my child on that demon," Katy warned.

"Do not listen to her," Iron Wing whispered in his son's ear. "She is only a woman. She knows nothing of the ways of warriors."

"Only a woman, am I?" Katy said in mock anger. "Ha! I know all about the ways of warriors. One warrior, anyway."

"Do you?" Iron Wing asked. His eyes caressed her face, then moved suggestively down her body, lingering a moment on her breasts.

"Oh, yes," Katy murmured, all thought of Pablo Alvarado forgotten as she swayed provocatively toward her husband. "I know all about you. I know exactly what you're thinking right now."

"Do you?" Iron Wing asked huskily.

Katy laughed as she glanced at the growing bulge in Iron Wing's trousers. "Yes, indeed." With great deliberation, she began to unfasten the tiny buttons on the bodice of her dress.

Iron Wing swallowed hard as inch after inch of Katy's creamy white flesh was exposed to his gaze. "Your mother is a witch," he murmured as he laid John back in his bed. "A witch who has me completely in her power."

Katy smiled, her eyes smoking like blue fire as she stepped out of her dress and let it fall about her ankles. Tilting her head to one side, she slowly began to unfasten the ribbon at the neck of her chemise.

With a groan, Iron Wing caught her in his arms and carried her to their bed. Impatiently, he removed her chemise and petticoats, loudly cursing at the extraordinary amount of clothing white women were forced to wear. That done, he removed the pins from Katy's hair, so that it fell in a black swirl around her face and shoulders.

"Witch," he moaned, and made love to her, stroking, caressing, as if he could never get enough of her.

Reveling in his touch, Katy put all her fears from her mind. Iron Wing loved her, and as long as he loved her, everything would be all right.

In the next few weeks, Pablo Alvarado stopped frequently at the Alvarez ranch, ostensibly on matters of business. Usually he happened to drop in just at dinnertime. Naturally, Sarah invited him to dine with them. It would have been impolite to turn him away, especially since he had humbly apologized to the whole family for his conduct at the party.

Pablo never said or did anything out of

line. He treated Katy with the utmost respect, complimented her on a becoming gown, admired John. He was equally polite to Mike and Sarah, but the tension between Alvarado and Iron Wing remained unchanged. The two men were careful to stay clear of each other, wary of saying the wrong thing. Wary of making Katy angry.

As the days went by, however, Pablo grew more and more bold. He brought Katy flowers. His compliments came more freely and grew more personal. He found numerous excuses to touch her hand, her hair.

Katy saw nothing wrong in Pablo's attention. They had been friends all her life and if Pablo was a little flowery in his speech, well, that was just he way he was. The way he had always been.

Iron Wing put up with Pablo Alvarado as long as he could, careful to keep his temper in check because he knew Katy regarded the man as a good friend, almost one of the family. But one day in Mesa Blanca things came to a head.

Katy and Iron Wing had been shopping and were about to head for home when Alvarado entered the store. Pablo was impeccably dressed as always. This day he wore a pair of tight black pants, a red shirt, and a short charro jacket stitched with fine silver thread. A black sombrero shaded his face.

Seeing Katy, Pablo removed his hat and bowed. Then, taking her hand, he brought it to his lips. "Sweet," he murmured, his dark brown eyes lingering on Katy's face. "Sweeter than the finest Mexican wine."

Jealousy flamed through Iron Wing as

Alvarado smiled at Katy. The kind words, the kiss that had lasted longer than was necessary, that smile that seemed to hint at something intimate between Alvarado and Katy, it was too much.

"Unhand my wife," Iron Wing said through clenched teeth.

Pablo Alvarado looked down his nose at Iron Wing, as if seeing him for the first time and not caring for what he saw. "I beg your pardon?"

"I said unhand my wife," Iron Wing repeated, speaking each word slowly and distinctly.

"Don't be such a bore," Pablo chided with a condescending smile. "If you're going to live with civilized people, you must learn to behave like one."

"I have watched the way you look at Ka-ty," Iron Wing said in a tone as hard as flint. "I have heard the hunger in your voice when you speak to her. I have seen the way your hand lingers on hers when you meet, the way you undress her with your eyes. I tell you now, it is enough. If you ever touch her again, I will kill you."

Katy had been astonished by Iron Wing's words. Now, hearing a gasp from behind her, she was embarrassed to realize that others in the store had witnessed the scene between Iron Wing and Pablo. Turning slightly, Katy saw Daphne Rogers standing across the aisle. The girl looked horrified. A short distance away, Jake Simmons and Dave Trotter, two of the Alvarado cowhands, were lounging against a counter looking amused.

"Iron Wing, let's go," Katy urged, taking

his arm. "Please, let's not cause a scene."

Iron Wing's eyes bored into Alvarado's. "Remember what I said," he warned. Taking Katy's arm, he led her out of the store.

The next day, after Iron Wing had left the house, Katy rode to the Alvarado hacienda. Dismounting, she ran up the stone steps and knocked on the door.

"Katy," Pablo said when he saw her. "How good of you to come by. Come in, come in."

He held the door for her, politely took her arm and led her into the parlor, even though she knew the way.

Closing the parlor door, Pablo moved to take Katy in his arms. "Katy, beloved, I knew you would come to me one day."

Katy frowned as she pushed his arms away. "Pablo, we have to talk. You've got to stop coming to the house. Iron Wing is very jealous, and I'm afraid of what he might do. I think it would be best if you stay away."

"You don't mean it?"

"I do mean it. I love Iron Wing, and I won't let you or anyone else come between us."

"I'm sorry, *amada mia,* but I cannot believe you are serious about that Indian. Why don't you divorce him and marry me? I know we would be happy together. It was always your mother's wish that we marry."

Katy stamped her foot angrily. "Haven't you listened to what I've been saying?" she demanded. "I love Iron Wing. I don't love you. I never did."

"Then I will make you love me," Pablo said firmly. Grabbing her, he began to kiss her, his mouth hot on hers.

Katy struggled in his arms, but she was no

match for his strength. He was murmuring love words to her, promising to make her forget Iron Wing, to make her love him. His tongue probed her lips, but she kept her mouth tightly shut, refusing to kiss him back.

There was a light knock on the door. "Pablo?" called Jose Alvarado. "Are you in there?"

Muttering an oath, Pablo released Katy. "*Si*, papa. What is it you want?"

The door opened and the old man stepped into the parlor. "A matter of business," he began. "Don Ortega . . ." His voice trailed off when he saw Katy. Her hair was tangled, her clothing mussed, and she was breathing heavily.

Jose Alvarado glanced at his son, his eyes narrowing suspiciously.

"I hope I am not disturbing you," the old man remarked.

"No," Katy said quickly. "I was just leaving." She walked to the door, paused to look at Alvarado. "Remember what I said." Before Pablo could reply, she smiled fondly at Jose Alvarado and bid him good day.

Pablo Alvarado glared at his father, irritated by his untimely appearance.

"What is going on?" Jose demanded. "Have you been bothering Katy again?"

"I am not bothering her," Pablo snapped. "I am going to marry her."

Jose Alvarado stared at his son in disbelief. "Are you crazy? From all I have heard, Katy Marie is in love with her husband."

"I will make her love me!"

Jose Alvarado shook his head, his eyes filled with disgust. "Where is your honor? No man worthy of the name interferes between a man and his wife. What right do you have to try and ruin Katy's marriage? There are many girls in Mesa Blanca who would gladly be your wife. Why don't you marry one of them?"

"They are nothing."

"Nothing! What about Angelina Fuentes?"

"Angelina." Pablo spat her name from his mouth. "She looks like a cow next to Katy Marie."

"What about Carlotte Sanchez, and Gloria Gonzales, and Carolyn Weber? Are they all cows, too?"

"I love Katy. I will marry Katy."

"I am wasting my time trying to talk to you," Jose Alvarado said, annoyed. "I tell you now, as your father, leave Katy Marie alone. She is not for you."

Pablo's eyes burned as he watched his father stride out of the room and slam the door. "I will have her," he said under his breath. "I swear it on my mother's grave."

For the next few days, Pablo watched the Alvarez hacienda. Slowly, a pattern of activity emerged. Daily, Iron Wing rode the blue stud into the hills. Always, he left the ranch just after breakfast. Always, he rode alone, and did not return until shortly before noon.

Pablo nodded with satisfaction. It would be a simple thing to ambush the Indian. Then, with Iron Wing out of the way, he would court Katy Marie. He had no doubt he would win her love. No woman had ever been able to resist him once he set out to win her.

He struck the next day. High in the hills, he waited, hidden behind a boulder that gave him a clear view of the area below. Right on time, Iron Wing rode into sight.

Pablo was smiling as he pulled the trigger. The bullet knocked the Indian out of the saddle. The stallion, wild-eyed, turned tail and ran down the hill. Cursing, Pablo fired after the animal, but the bullet went wide, slamming into the hillside.

Pablo frowned as he jacked another round into the breech of the rifle. His original plan had been to get rid of both Iron Wing and the horse. He would call on Katy, offering his sympathy because Iron Wing had obviously left her and returned to his own people. Eventually, she would realize the Indian was never coming back, and she would realize it was Pablo she truly loved. They would be married and live happily ever after. He supposed he would have to take the child, too, but, in time, they could send the brat off to school somewhere and then he would have Katy all to himself . . .

But there was still the Indian to be reckoned with. One more shot, to make sure he was dead. When the stud returned home, riders would come in search of the missing Indian. He would tell Katy that her husband had tried to kill him, and that he had fired in self-defense. It was actually better this way, Pablo mused. People in town had heard the Indian threaten his life.

Iron Wing did not move, did not breathe, as he heard his attacker making his way down the hill. Through slitted eyes, he saw Pablo

Alvarado coming toward him. The man was smiling as he sighted down the barrel of his rifle.

"So long, you bastard," Pablo sneered, and then grunted with surprise as a hand reached out and jerked him off his feet.

With a cry, Iron Wing rolled nimbly to his feet. Grabbing the rifle from Pablo's hands, he smashed the heavy rosewood stock into the back of Alvarado's head. There was a sickening thud as the man's head split open.

Breathing heavily, Iron Wing stared at Pablo Alvarado's inert form. With an oath, he dropped the rifle. He had killed a white man. The thought filled him with exultation and dread. What would Katy think when she learned he had killed her old friend?

A sticky warmth dripped onto his cheek, reminding him he had been hit, and he lifted a hand to his head. The bullet had barely grazed his temple, but the wound was bleeding.

He was wrapping his kerchief around his forehead when a trio of riders rode up mounted on horses wearing the Alvarado brand. Iron Wing looked at each face. Two of the men he recognized. They had been in Mesa Blanca the day he threatened to kill Pablo Alvarado.

Dave Trotter, foreman of the Alvarado ranch, quickly reacted to the scene before him. "Hands up, Injun," he growled, drawing his gun. "Jake, Pete, cover him while I check on the boss."

Slowly, Iron Wing raised his hands over his head while Trotter dismounted and knelt beside Alvarado's body.

"He's dead," Trotter announced curtly.

"Let's kill the redskin," Jake said, cocking his pistol.

"Ease off, Jake," Dave Trotter ordered brusquely. "Throw me your rope. We'll tie him up and haul him into town. Pete, you find Pablo's horse and bring the body home."

Iron Wing had stood passive while the white men made their plans. Now, as Trotter moved behind him to tie his hands, he pivoted on his heel, drove his fist into the man's face, and made a run for it.

Pete Cox let loose a rebel yell as he touched his spurs to his horse's flanks and gave chase. Lifting his lariat from the pommel of his saddle, he shook out a loop, sent it sailing through the air to close over Iron Wing's neck. Expertly, he took up the slack and jerked Iron Wing off his feet.

With a grunt, Iron Wing fell over backwards as the rope pulled him off balance. Lights flashed before his eyes as his head hit the ground, hard.

Pete Cox was grinning as he pulled his horse to a halt and vaulted from the saddle. As Iron Wing started to stand up, Cox lashed out, kicking Iron Wing in the side. Iron Wing hit his head a second time as he fell back. There were no lights this time, no stars, only a deep black void.

When he came to, he was in the Mesa Blanca jail.

Katy stared blankly at Sheriff Porter Smithfield. " . . . looks like your husband killed Pablo Alvarado in cold blood," the sheriff was saying. "I've got him locked up in town. There'll be a trial just as soon as Judge Braxton Howard arrives." The sheriff tipped his hat to Katy, shook hands with Michael Sommers. "Sorry I had to be the one to bring you the bad news," Porter said, scratching his ear. "Good night, folks."

"Good night, Sheriff," Mike said, seeing the lawman to the front door. "Thanks for coming."

Smithfield nodded. "Sometimes this job ain't all it's cracked up to be."

Mike shrugged, wishing the man would leave.

"Yeah," Smithfield muttered. "I've got to go out to the Alvarado place now. Dave and a couple of the boys are the ones who found the body. I'll have to take their statements, but it sounds like an open and shut case to me. I hear the Injun threatened Pablo publicly a few weeks back."

"Is that right?" Sommers asked innocently.

Smithfield nodded. "Yeah. Well, once a savage, always a savage. Too bad about Pablo, though, he was a hell of a nice guy."

"Yes. Well, good night, sheriff," Mike said firmly, and shut the door.

Katy was still sitting on the sofa, her hands folded in her lap, her eyes staring at the floor, when Michael returned to the parlor. "It's got to be a mistake, Katy," Mike said. "I can't believe Iron Wing would kill him in cold blood."

"They'll hang him," Katy said dully. "He'll never get a fair trial, and they'll hang him."

"Katy . . ."

"You know it's true!" Katy cried in

390

despair. "He's an Indian. No one will believe he's innocent. No one."

Mike Sommers paced the floor, his brow lined with worry. Katy was right. What white man would believe Iron Wing was innocent? Damn. He wished Sarah would get home from the Randall place. He needed her. Katy needed her.

"Mike."

Sommers stopped pacing. One look at Katy's face and he hurried to take her in his arms. Great sobs wracked her slender frame as she buried her face in his shoulder and began to cry.

"Go on, honey, let it all out," Mike said soothingly. "Maybe you'll feel better."

"It's all my fault," Katy babbled. "I should never have gone to see Pablo last week. I thought I could make him understand that I love Iron Wing, but he refused to listen. He said I should divorce Iron Wing and marry *him*. And now Iron Wing has killed him. But how did Iron Wing find out?" Katy lifted tormented eyes to Mike's face. "Iron Wing has always been so jealous. I knew he'd kill Pablo if he thought there was anything between us, and now he has." Fresh tears filled her eyes.

"Calm down, Katy Marie," Mike said, patting her on the back. "I'm going to get Juanita to look after John, and then you and I are going into town. I want to hear what Iron Wing has to say about all this."

Iron Wing paced the narrow jail cell like a caged tiger, his moccasined feet making little noise on the raw wood plank floor. Now and then he paused to look out the barred window that gave him a clear view of the town's main street. There were a dozen men milling about in front of the nearest saloon, all talking loudly about a lynching before the night was out. One man had a rope over his shoulder.

Near the jailhouse, three deputies stood in the street, rifles cradled in their arms. A fourth deputy sat in the sheriff's office, keeping watch until Smithfield returned.

With a last look at the crowd, Iron Wing began pacing again. He had seen men hang. It was not a pleasant way to die, with your feet kicking in the air and your eyes bulging from their sockets. He shuddered violently. It was no way for a Cheyenne warrior to meet death. A warrior should die in battle, killing his enemies.

He felt a wave of hopelessness wash over him as more and more men joined those gathered in the street. Sooner or later, those men would rush the jail and string him up. He would never see Katy or his son again, never return to the sacred hills.

There was a sudden commotion in the street as Porter Smithfield rode up and ordered the crowd to disperse. Amid considerable grumbling, the mob cleared the street. But they only went as far as the saloon.

Thirty minutes later, Katy and Sommers swept into the jail.

Iron Wing's eyes devoured Katy, wanting to memorize every detail of her face so he could carry her image into the afterlife.

Katy hurried toward Iron Wing, her hands

reaching through the bars so she could touch him.

"You've got just fifteen minutes," Smithfield said, closing the door that divided the cellblock from his office.

"We don't have much time," Sommers said. "What the hell happened?"

"Alvarado ambushed me in the hills. When he came to make sure I was dead, I killed him."

"That's it?" Mike asked irritably. "That's all you've got to say?"

Iron Wing shrugged. "What differrence does it make what happened? No one will believe me."

"I believe you," Katy said softly.

"But they will not listen to you," Iron Wing muttered bitterly. "They will see only that a white man is dead, and I am alive."

"Damn, that crowd out there looks nasty," Mike said, jerking his head toward the street where the mob had gathered once again.

"Mike, take Katy out of here. I do not want her to get hurt."

"Yeah, you're right," Sommers said. "Those men sound pretty liquored up. Anything's liable to happen."

"I won't go," Katy protested, locking her arms around Iron Wing's waist, though the bars made such a thing difficult.

"You must think of our son," Iron Wing said, loosening her grasp.

"Iron Wing, please don't send me away."

For a moment, Iron Wing looked at her tenderly. "Go, Ka-ty," he said thickly. "I am not afraid."

"Kiss me good-bye."

With a faint smile, he drew her close to the bars. "I love you," he said as his mouth came down on hers and his arm squeezed her tight. "Go now."

There was a loud crash as the jailhouse door was forced open. Mike cursed under his breath. Smithfield had taken his gun. Unarmed, he was no match for a crowd of drunken men.

"Get her out of here!" Iron Wing shouted, his fear for Katy's safety making his voice ragged.

"I'll take care of her and the baby," Sommers promised. "Come on, Katy. Damn it!" He cursed as she bit his hand, whirling out of his grasp.

"I'm not going!"

"Don't be a fool," Mike said harshly. "Think of John."

Indecision overwhelmed Katy. She could hear the men arguing with the sheriff in the next room, demanding that Smithfield surrender the prisoner. There was a loud crash, an oath, and then a loud pounding on the door.

With a sob, Katy pressed her face to the cell door, felt her tears start as Iron Wing gave her a hasty kiss. "Take care of our son," he said, wiping the tears from her eyes.

Katy nodded, unable to speak.

A gunshot tore the lock from the door and the mob rushed into the cellblock, guns drawn. One man had a rope. Another had the key to Iron Wing's cell.

Michael pulled Katy close to him, drawing

her into his arms as he eased back into a corner, while all hell broke loose.

There was no fear on Iron Wing's face, only contempt as three men entered his cell, their guns aimed in his direction.

"Come on, Injun," drawled a man in a black leather vest and black whipcord pants. "We're gonna have us a little party, and you're the guest of honor."

"Yeah," another man said with a grin. "A necktie party!"

When Iron Wing refused to move, the man in the black vest drove the butt of his rifle into Iron Wing's belly. Iron Wing doubled in half, his hands clutching his stomach. A second man brought his fist down on the back of Iron Wing's neck, dropping him to the floor, while the third man quickly hand-cuffed the Indian's hands behind his back.

"Listen here," Mike said, starting forward. "You've no right to . . ."

"No right to what?" sneered the man in the vest as he swung his rifle around to cover Sommers.

"Lynching is against the law," Mike went on doggedly. "Every man is entitled to a fair trial."

"We're gonna try him," the man in the vest declared insolently. "And then we're gonna hang him. You wanna try and stop us?"

Mike glared at the man, itching to make a grab for the rifle aimed at his guts, but he had Katy to think of. He could not start something that might get her hurt or killed. Sarah would never forgive him.

"Well?" the man in the vest said disdainfully.

Clenching his fists, Mike shook his head.

"I didn't think you had the guts," the man jeered. "Come on, boys, get him outside."

Katy turned pleading eyes on Mike as Iron Wing was dragged out of the cell and thrust onto the back of a slat-sided gray horse.

"Do something!" Katy cried frantically. "You can't let them hang him. Please!"

"I'll try," Sommers said. Running out of the cellblock, he scooped up a rifle from the rack in the sheriff's office and headed down the street, wondering if Smithfield would survive the nasty blow to the side of his head.

Katy ran after Mike, then stopped in horror as she saw the noose around Iron Wing's neck.

She stared at the rope, and it seemed as if everything happened in slow motion.

Mike was running down the street, but he was going to be too late. Already, one of the men standing nearby was raising his hand to slap the gray horse on the rump. When the horse bolted, Iron Wing would be left swinging in the air . . .

A sudden gunshot cracked across the noisy street, slicing through the commotion like a knife through butter.

All eyes turned toward the north end of the street to where Jose Alvarado sat atop a snowy white stallion.

"Cut him down!" Alvarado said. His voice carried loud and clear in the stillness.

"Cut him down!" someone hollered. "He killed your son."

"No," Jose Alvarado said sadly. "My son killed himself."

"Now, listen, Don Alvarado," Jake Simmons said. "We were there."

"I know you all mean well," Alvarado said, his eyes moving over the crowd. "But you do not know the full story. I know that man did not kill my son in cold blood. If anything, it was self-defense. Now cut him down, and go home where you belong. There has been enough bloodshed."

Chastened, the men standing beside Iron Wing cut his hands free. In moments, the street was empty save for Iron Wing, Katy and Sommers.

Katy ran to Iron Wing and threw herself into his arms, covering his face with kisses and tears.

"Let's go home," Mike said. "Your mother will never believe any of this."

Strangely, Iron Wing never questioned why Pablo Alvarado had tried to kill him. Katy suspected he had a pretty good idea, but they never spoke of it.

The day after the attempted lynching, Katy received a letter from Jose Alvarado.

"My dear Katy," the letter read, "Please forgive my son for the near-tragedy of last night. Pablo was obsessed with the idea of having you for his wife. Last night, as I went through his drawers, I found a wedding dress with your name on it, as well as a large trousseau. Apparently he could not believe that you would prefer your husband to himself. I am sure Pablo believed that if your husband were out of the way, he could win your love. I do not like to think that my son would have killed your husband in cold blood, and yet I am sure in my heart that such was his intention. I am equally certain that your husband killed Pablo in self-defense. I am truly sorry that my family has caused you such pain. Your humble servant, Jose Alvarado."

Poor man, Katy thought as she folded the letter and put it away. How hard it must have been for him to write to her, with his eldest son not even buried yet, his good name tarnished.

She clung to Iron Wing that night. She had almost lost him. Thank God that Jose Alvarado's sense of honor was stronger than any need for vengeance.

Their lovemaking that night was both tender and violent, gentle and frenzied. Because she had almost lost him, Katy poured out her whole heart and soul, giving her love with both hands, wanting him to know how much she needed him, wanted him, loved him. She dug her fingernails into his flesh, reveling in the muscles that bunched beneath her hand, reassuring herself that he was still hers, to touch, to take. Twining her legs around his waist, she pulled him closer, deeper, seemingly unable to get enough of him. She purred with delight as he drove into her, his manhood filling her, making her complete.

Iron Wing understood Katy's need to possess and be possessed, for the same primal craving spurred him on, urging him to prove his mastery. He buried his face in the silky mass of her hair, breathing in its fresh sweet scent, drowning in its blackness. His hands moved over her willing flesh, branding every inch of his. He sought her lips, his mouth claiming hers in a kiss that sent fingers of fire darting to every part of her body.

They made love all through the night, their passion a celebration of life, of renewal, until, at last, they slept, sated and content, locked in each other's arms.

# 26 FALL
## 1877

When her son was seven months old, Katy realized there was something very wrong between herself and Iron Wing. Though he treated her as tenderly and lovingly as ever, he often seemed withdrawn and far away from her. He spent long hours on the range, ostensibly searching for stray cattle or mending fences. Some nights he did not come home at all, but bedded down under the stars, alone. He had never been one to make idle chatter and now he became even more quiet and subdued. Only when he played with John did his eyes shine with the joy of living.

More and more Iron Wing excused himself from the parties and sociables that Katy so dearly enjoyed, preferring to spend his time outside, away from the noise and the laughter and the music.

That fall, he began going away for several days at a stretch. Ostensibly, he was hunting, and he always came home with a deer or some rabbits or a wild turkey, but Katy knew that, in reality, he was seeking escape from the ranch and civilization. Alone in the hills, he could pretend, if only for a little while, that he was a warrior again.

It was late one night, after a birthday party for one of Katy's friends, that Katy found

Iron Wing sitting on the veranda, his eyes dark and brooding as he stared into the distance. Katy knew then that what she had secretly feared all along was true: Iron Wing was homesick for his old life, homesick for the rolling Montana prairies, for the sight of the sacred black hills.

Sitting down beside him, her hand resting on his thigh, she let her thoughts go back to the days she had spent with the Cheyenne. Once she had accepted her true feelings for Iron Wing and admitted she loved him, her life with the Indians had been good. True, the work had been hard, the days long, the luxuries few, but there had been a feeling of being a part of the land, a feeling of accomplishment and pride in the work of her hands. And there had been the land itself, the rolling hills, the lush valleys, the endless miles of grass. Iron Wing was a part of that land. The mountains, the rich black earth, the song of the eagle and the hawk were in his blood.

Her heart went out to him then, and with a little cry of sympathy, she crawled into his lap and buried her face in his shoulder. How foolish she had been! You could catch a wild animal, tame it, and love it, but it was never truly happy again, no matter how big the cage. Wild things were meant to live wild. And Iron Wing had never been happy living in a house, surrounded by solid walls, burdened with alien traditions and the trappings of civilization. That he had put up with such nonsense at all told her more than words how much he loved her.

"You're not happy here, are you?" Katy asked, though she did not need to hear the words to know what his answer would be.

"No," Iron Wing replied glumly. "But you are."

"This is my home," Katy murmured. "I belong here."

"Yes."

"Are you . . . you aren't going to leave, are you?"

"I think so," Iron Wing answered after a long pause. "I cannot live like a white man, Ka-ty," he said in a tortured voice. "I thought I could, for you, but I cannot. I feel like I am dying inside."

Katy went cold all over as she realized what he was saying, and what it meant. She could beg him to stay, and perhaps he would, because he loved her. But he would never be happy. He needed to be free as only an Indian is free.

He had not asked her to go with him, and that made Katy smile faintly. No doubt he thought she could only be happy amid the luxury and ease of her mother's house. And she was happy here, Katy thought, but then, she could be happy anywhere as long as Iron Wing was beside her. He was her home, her land, and she would gladly follow him through fire and flood just to be near him.

"Well," Katy said briskly, "when do we leave?"

Iron Wing looked at her in disbelief, and then a smile lit his face. Throwing back his head, he gave a mighty shout and then he grabbed her in his arms and swung her high in the air.

"Ka-ty," he murmured, his voice brimming

with emotion. "Do you realize what you are doing? You would leave all this to be with me?"

"All this and more." Much more, she thought, just to have him look at her like that, as if she were the most wonderful woman in the world.

"We will wait until spring, when the grass is new." Iron Wing looked past Katy to the house. He could see Sarah and Mike sitting in the parlor, reading. It was a cozy scene: the fireplace, the couple sitting together, the expensive furniture and pictures and carpets.

Iron Wing took Katy's face in his hands and looked deep into her eyes. "I will understand if you change your mind. I can never give you the things you are leaving behind."

"I won't change my mind. You've given me much more than I'm leaving behind. So much more." A sound from inside the house drew Katy's attention, and she looked in the window to see her mother and Mike tussling on the sofa like a couple of kids. It would be hard, telling her mother they were leaving.

"Let's not tell anyone we're going," Katy said. "Not for a while. Christmas is coming, and I don't want to spoil our holiday."

"What is Christmas?"

"It's a time of celebration," Katy explained, grinning.

"What do you celebrate?"

"The birth of Jesus."

"Jesus." Iron Wing nodded as he remembered the stories the missionary lady had told him of the man, Jesus, and how he was the son of the white man's god, sent to earth to save the white eyes from their sins, and how they had killed him.

"When is this Christmas?"

"Next month. It's a lovely time of the year."

And it was a special holiday that year. Knowing it would be the last Christmas she would enjoy at home, Katy was determined to make it perfect. She shopped for just the right gift for her mother and Mike, and finally decided that the best thing she could give them would be a portrait of Iron Wing, John, and herself. Iron Wing balked at sitting so long to have his picture painted, but he did it to please Katy. The painting, when it was finished, perfectly captured Katy's delicate beauty, John's delightful personality, and Iron Wing's strength of character.

Sarah and Mike were thrilled with the portrait, declaring it was the best present they could have had.

Katy bought Iron Wing a set of buckskins so he would have something to wear when they left for the Dakotas. Sarah experienced a sense of foreboding when Iron Wing unwrapped the heavy buckskin shirt and pants, but she put the feeling from her.

Iron Wing gave Katy a set of wooden combs for her hair, and she treasured them because she knew he had made them with his own hands.

There were numerous gifts for John—toys and rattles and clothes. There was a new Winchester rifle for Iron Wing, a gift from Sarah and Mike. There was a bottle of perfume for Katy, and a new dress, also from Sarah and Mike.

That night, as the family sat before the fireplace, Sarah declared it was the best Christmas she had ever known.

"I agree," Mike said, lifting his glass. "Let's drink a toast. May all our Christmases be as happy as this one."

"Here, here," Sarah said.

Katy smiled as she touched her glass to her mother's, but inside she felt terribly guilty knowing that at this time next year she would be far from her mother's home. She put the thought from her, not wanting anything to spoil the joy of the moment.

Iron Wing caught the look in Katy's eye and he reached out to squeeze her arm. It would be hard for her to leave Mesa Blanca. Would she be able to ride away without looking back when the time came?

Late that night, when everyone was asleep, Iron Wing left the house and wandered aimlessly around the yard. The air was cold, but it felt good after the constant warmth of the house. The sky was black, splashed with stars, the night quiet. He felt a quick excitement in the pit of his stomach as he stared out into the darkness beyond the ranch. Soon, he mused, soon he would go home, back to the plains, back to the hills and valleys where he had been born. It would be good to see Indian faces again, good to see the Sacred Hills, to sleep in a hide-covered lodge beneath a curly buffalo robe.

He glanced down at his clothing and grimaced with distaste. It would be good to wear buckskins again, to be free of collars and cuffs and the other trappings of the white man.

He thought of his son and thought how

exciting it would be to teach the boy to ride and hunt and fight. To teach him the ways of the People, to sing the old songs and tell the old stories . . .

When Katy woke the next morning, she was alone in the room. A quick panic seized her heart, but then she forced herself to relax. It was not yet spring; and even if it was, Iron Wing would not leave without her.

Rising, she pulled on her robe and went in search of her husband.

She found him sitting in the shadow of a tree. His clothes were rumpled, as if he had slept in them.

"What are you doing out here?" Katy asked, sitting down beside him on the ground.

"I spent the night out here," Iron Wing admitted somewhat sheepishly. "Sometimes the walls of the house close in on me and I feel like I must get out or die."

Katy nodded. She had hoped that Iron Wing might grow to like living in Mesa Blanca, but she knew now it was a hope founded on air.

Iron Wing gazed into the distance toward home. "You do not have to go with me, Ka-ty," he said quietly. "I will understand if you want to stay here. I will come to visit you and the little one as often as I can."

"I want to go with you," Katy said. "Please believe me."

Iron Wing smiled at her, pleased by her words, and Katy thought the comforts of civilization a small price to pay for the pleasure of her husband's smile.

* * *

It was on a day late in March that one of the vaqueros rode up to the hacienda with an Apache warrior in tow. The Indian had been wounded while trying to steal one of the Alvarez cows. Hands tied behind his back, he glared at the man who had captured him, then turned his slit-eyed stare toward Mike Sommers as Sommers stepped out on the veranda.

"What's going on, Rafael?" Mike asked.

"Caught him trying to steal a cow. You want I should string him up?"

"No," Mike said, conscious of Iron Wing standing behind him. "Lock him up in the tack room. I'll decide what to do with him later."

Sarah was not pleased to learn of the attempted theft. "He should be punished," she said sternly. "He should be made an example of. We can't let the Indians think we're easy pickings."

"We can spare one cow," Katy said. "We have hundreds."

"That's not the point," Sarah retorted. "We haven't had any trouble with the Indians for some years, not since we . . ." She broke off abruptly, her cheeks flushing guiltily as she felt Iron Wing's eyes on her face.

"Since what, mama?"

"Since Montoya caught one of the Apache bucks making off with one of our cows," Sommers said flatly. "Montoya hung the warrior and left the body as a warning to others." Mike met Iron Wing's accusing stare. "We haven't had any trouble with the Apaches since."

407

"Will you hang this Apache, too?" Iron Wing asked.

"Yes," Mike answered, his gaze unwavering. "The Apaches know the penalty if they get caught on Alvarez land. It's the only thing that's kept us safe from attack. They know we have guns, and men who aren't afraid to use them. They know our punishment is swift and final."

"You must do what you think is right," Iron Wing said. "It is not for me to judge."

The sound of a door closing woke Katy. Sitting up in bed, she listened for footsteps. Hearing none, she knew it must be Iron Wing, for he moved soundlessly. Slipping out of bed, she drew on her robe and went downstairs. The front door was open, and she padded softly across the parlor and out onto the veranda. Iron Wing was a dark shadow moving across the yard.

"I know where you're going," she mused to herself, and tiptoed down the stairs after her husband.

She reached the tack room as Iron Wing was putting the key in the lock.

"I know a girl who was whipped for doing that very thing," Katy said, coming up behind Iron Wing.

He whirled around, startled by her presence. "Ka-ty!"

"What are you doing?" she asked. It was a foolish question, but one she could not resist.

"I am going to set the Indian free," he admitted sheepishly. "If you wish to whip me for it, the penalty is still ten lashes."

"If you'll wait a few minutes, I'll get him some food and a horse."

Moved beyond words, Iron Wing nodded. His eyes gleamed with love and admiration as he watched her walk back to the house.

She returned ten minutes later with a parcel of food. Handing it to Iron Wing, she went to the corral and caught up a fine buckskin gelding.

"You can turn him loose now," Katy said. "I'm going back to bed."

Before she reached the house, she heard the quick tattoo of pounding hooves as the Apache rode out of the yard toward the hills.

"Ka-ty?"

She stopped, waiting for him to catch up to her.

"You are quite a woman," Iron Wing said, taking her in his arms.

"Am I?" she teased, snuggling against him.

"How did you know I would set him free?"

"Because it's what I would have done."

"And I whipped you for it," Iron Wing said bitterly. The memory filled him with pain. Looking back, he wondered how he could ever have done it. Now, he would die before he let anyone, including himself, lay a hand on her. "No wonder you hated me."

"I don't think I ever hated you," Katy said, kissing his cheek. "Anyway, it doesn't matter now."

"It matters to me. I am sorry I hurt you."

"I know," Katy said, touched by the remorse in his eyes.

"Forgive me?"

"There's nothing to forgive." She smiled up

at him, her blue eyes shining with love and mischief. "I'm your woman, remember? You can do with me whatever you wish."

"And do you know what I wish?" he asked, smiling down at her.

"Oh, yes, I know," Katy said, and taking his hand, she led him back to the house and the privacy of their room.

They were at breakfast the following morning when Pedro Montoya entered the dining room, his hat in his hand, a worried expression on his weathered face.

"Pedro, what is it?" Sarah asked.

"The Apache, senora. He is gone."

"Gone!" Sommers exclaimed.

"Si."

"How did he get out of the tack room? The door was locked, his hands and feet were bound behind his back."

Montoya shrugged. "Someone unlocked the door."

Sarah and Mike looked at each other; then, as one, they turned to look at Iron Wing.

"I turned him loose," Iron Wing admitted in answer to the unspoken question in their eyes.

"Why would you do such a thing?" Sarah demanded.

"I could not stand by and watch him hanged," Iron Wing said levelly. Too well, he remembered the rope that had once circled his own neck, the rough rasp of the hemp, the heavy knot under his jaw, the fear that turned his mouth to dust. "It is a bad way for an Indian to die."

"He should have thought of that before he

tried to steal one of our cows," Sommers remarked.

"He has a wife and two little ones and no food in his lodge," Iron Wing explained. "What would you have done in his place?"

"Hell, I suppose I'd steal, too, if my family was hungry," Mike allowed.

"The Apaches are more than hungry. They are starving to death. There is no food on the reservation. Their children are dying."

Katy thought of her own child. How could she bear it if he were hungry, dying, and no one cared? "We have plenty of cattle," she said. "Why don't we send some to the Indians?"

Mike shook his head. "No. We can't interfere with the reservation Indians."

"There are Indians living off the reservation," Iron Wing remarked. "We could take the cattle to them. They will see that some of the meat finds its way to the reservation."

"Yes, we could do that," Mike agreed, warming to the idea. "What do you think, Sarah?"

"I think we're asking for trouble."

"Maybe, maybe not. Montoya, have the men round up fifty head of our best cattle. Iron Wing, will you go with us?"

"Yes, I will go."

"I'm going, too," Katy said, jumping to her feet.

"No," Iron Wing said curtly. "You must stay here, with John."

"Mother can watch him, can't you, Mama?"

"Don't get me involved in your family squabbles," Sarah said, rising from the table.

"You and Iron Wing decide what you're going to do, and then let me know. I'll be in my office."

"Why can't I go?" Katy demanded. "I can ride. And we won't be gone long."

"I think he's right, Katy," Sommers said. "It might be best if you stay home."

Katy looked up at Iron Wing, her eyes wide, her lower lip quivering just a little. "Please let me go. I don't want to stay here without you, not even for a day."

Iron Wing looked over Katy's head to where Mike stood.

"Don't look at me for help," Sommers said, shaking his head. "She's your woman. Your problem."

"I cannot tell her no when she looks at me like that," Iron Wing muttered helplessly.

"I was afraid of that," Mike said. "I'll go tell Sarah that Katy is coming with us. We'll leave in an hour."


Driving a herd of cattle was dusty work, but Katy found it thrilling to be on the trail with Iron Wing and Mike. They rode ahead of the herd where the dust wasn't so bad, leaving Montoya and four vaqueros to ride flank and drag. The day was cold and cloudy, the air brisk. It would take the better part of the day to reach the Apache village. They would drop off the herd, spend the night on the trail, and return home by midafternoon.

It had been a long time since Katy had spent so many hours in the saddle, but she dared not complain of being tired. She had wanted to come, and she was here. Still, she was glad when Mike called for a rest.

Dismounting, they ate a quick meal of cold biscuits and beans washed down with water. It was not the most appetizing food in the world, but she ate it without complaint.

"How do you think the Indians will react when they see us?" Mike asked when they were in the saddle again.

Iron Wing shrugged. "The Apache are a proud warrior people. They do not care for charity. But I think they will be glad to see us."

"I only hope they honor our white flag," Mike muttered dryly. "I'd hate to get killed trying to do a good deed."

It was late afternoon when they reached the Apache village. Katy was appalled at what she saw. The Apache wickiups were crude, the camp was quiet. No dogs barked as they rode into the village, no children played in front of the Indian lodges. A handful of warriors dressed in cheap cotton shirts and ragged leggings came to meet them. The men were terribly thin, their eyes dull, their faces flat.

"What do you want here?" one of the warriors asked in sign language. He held a rifle in the crook of his arm.

"We have brought you food," Iron Wing answered, also in sign language. "Your brother, Crooked Leg, told me of your need for meat. My wife's people have many fat cattle. We have brought you some of them as a gift of friendship. We ask only that you send meat to the reservation so that Crooked Leg and his people may have food in their lodges."

"We do not want the white man's charity,"

the Apache said haughtily, but his eyes belied his words. Fifty head of cattle would feed his people for a long time.

"It is not charity," Iron Wing said. "I am Crooked Leg's friend. I cannot take the cattle to the reservation. I ask that you do it for me. In the spring, when the hunting is good, perhaps you will kill more meat then you need. Perhaps you will bring me some venison and a deer hide, as a gift from one friend to another."

"Perhaps," the warrior said. "Stay, eat with us."

Iron Wing dismounted and motioned for Katy and Mike to do the same.

"I am called Yellow Deer," the warrior said.

"I am Iron Wing. This is my wife, and my father-in-law, Michael Sommers."

Yellow Deer nodded his head in greeting.

Iron Wing put his arm around Katy's shoulders. He knew she did not want to stay, but to refuse would be an insult.

The Apaches killed one of the cows on the spot. Katy watched as the women emerged from their wickiups to skin the carcass. A hindquarter was skewered and hung over a low flame.

The meat was barely cooked when the Apaches tore into it. They ate ravenously, the juice running out of their mouths and down their chins.

Knowing it would be impolite to refuse, Katy forced herself to eat a slice of the blood-red meat. She slid a glance at Mike and saw that he, too, was having trouble swallowing the hunk of meat that had been handed to him. Only Iron Wing asked for more.

The arrival of so much meat was a cause for celebration. When everyone in the village had eaten their fill, they began to dance. Almost, Katy thought, it was like being back in the Dakotas with the Cheyenne.

She gazed at the Indians around her, careful not to stare at anyone too long. For the most part, the Indian men wore cotton shirts, buckskin leggings, and knee-high moccasins. The women were dressed in brightly colored blouses and calico skirts. There was little resemblance between the Apache and the Cheyenne. The Apache were short of stature, their faces broad and flat. The Cheyenne were a much more handsome people, Katy thought, glancing at Iron Wing. He was tall and lean, his features finely chiseled.

During a lull in the festivities, Yellow Deer hunkered down on his heels beside Iron Wing.

"You will stay the night," the Apache said, clapping Iron Wing on the shoulder in a friendly gesture. "My lodge will be yours. I will share my brother's wickiup."

"You are very kind," Iron Wing said. "We are grateful for your hospitality."

"I don't want to stay here overnight," Katy whispered as Yellow Deer led them to his wickiup later that night.

"We will stay," Iron Wing said firmly. "Do not be afraid. I will keep watch while you sleep."

The wickiup was a round, brush-covered

dwelling with a domed roof. It was roomy inside, though neither Iron Wing or Mike could stand upright, not even in the center.

"Well, we might as well make ourselves comfortable," Mike said, stretching out on a pile of blankets. "If you get tired, wake me up."

Iron Wing nodded, but he knew he would not sleep this night.

With a sigh of resignation, Katy settled down across the way from Mike, certain she would never be able to sleep. Why had she come here? These were the same Indians who had killed her father, who had killed Robert. The same Indians who had attacked the stage coach carrying her to the convent. Closing her eyes, she tried to sleep, but instead she saw images of the Apaches as they gulped down chunks of nearly raw beef. She saw the children, scrawny and listless. The women, thin and without hope. The men, dull-eyed, yet still proud, still warriors. What if they attacked them while they slept? These were not reservation Indians, but wild Apaches. Once they had been the most feared tribe in the Southwest. Their atrocities far surpassed those of any other tribe . . . Opening her eyes, she saw Iron Wing sitting beside the entrance to the wickiup and her fears dissolved. He would protect her.

Feeling Katy's gaze, Iron Wing turned to face her. "Go to sleep," he said quietly. "There is nothing to be afraid of."

Obediently, Katy closed her eyes again. Moments later, she was asleep.

They left early the next morning. Katy was

glad to be leaving. The village, the people, she found it all depressing. And yet, some of the listlessness seemed to have been lifted from the Indians. Perhaps, with food enough to last, they would rouse themselves from their lethargy. Perhaps the children would laugh again.

As they rode out of the village, Montoya and the Alvarez vaqueros jogged up behind them. Montoya and his men had spent the night with the herd.

"Everything all right?" Mike asked, reining up beside Montoya.

"Si. Already, the Indians have taken half the herd to the reservation."

Sommers nodded. The remainder of the cattle were grazing on the sparse grass behind the village, guarded by several young braves.

"I'm glad we were able to help," Katy said.

"Yeah," Mike drawled. "I feel pretty good about it myself. Maybe we can look into furnishing beef for the reservation from now on. It's close to the ranch. We'd know if the cattle were getting to the Indians."

"That's a wonderful idea!" Katy said enthusiastically.

"I'll discuss it with your mother when we get home," Mike promised. "She probably won't like the idea at first, but I think she'll come around."

Pedro Montoya snorted derisively. You could not trust Apaches. Feed them, let them get strong again, and they would soon be on the warpath again.

Iron Wing remained quiet on the long ride

417

back to the Alvarez ranch. How were his people faring, he wondered. Were they hungry, like the Apache? Dying slowly of starvation. Would he find Tall Buffalo in rags, his eyes dulled with hunger and defeat? Did the Cheyenne children cry for food?

He thought bleakly of the Apache village. There was no life in the people. Once the Apache had been a proud warrior race. Now they were beaten. Only a handful of warriors still lived wild and free in the old way. Geronimo was the most notorious, and he was raiding in Mexico.

Iron Wing glanced at Katy. In a few weeks they would leave her mother's house and go back to the Dakotas, back to his people. He offered a silent prayer to Man Above that all would be well when they arrived.

Spring came, and, reluctantly, Katy told her mother that they were going back to the Dakotas. It was one of the hardest things she had ever done.

Sarah was not surprised. Deep down, she had known this day was coming. But it was hard to accept, hard to face the fact that she might never see Katy or John again. Even Iron Wing would be missed, Sarah thought with surprise. He had become a part of her life, and she knew she would miss his presence in her home.

Later that day, Katy went out to the family cemetery which was located on a grassy knoll a few miles west of the house.

Dismounting, Katy knelt beside her father's grave, her head bowed as grief washed over her. The tears came freely, tears for her father's untimely death, tears for Robert, for the life she was about to give up for the man she loved. She would miss the security of her childhood home, she would miss her mother and the close relationship they now shared. She would miss the creature comforts of civilization: the silly little things, like a glass of warm milk on a cold night, and scented soap to bathe with.

But her place was with Iron Wing and she could not be happy unless he was happy. She had always felt sorry for the wild creatures that were captured and forced to live in captivity. And while Iron Wing was not a prisoner, she knew he felt trapped just the same, knew he longed for his homeland. And she loved him too much to keep him from the life he longed for.

Their leave-taking was sad and filled with tears. Sarah wept openly as she hugged John to her breast, but she knew why Katy was leaving, and she understood.

"You will come to visit us once in a while, won't you?" Sarah asked.

"Of course," Katy said, hugging her mother. "And I'll write every chance I get."

"Don't let John forget about me," Mike said, brushing a tear from his eye.

"I won't," Katy promised.

Iron Wing smiled faintly as he took John from Sarah's arms. And then they were gone.

Hand in hand, Sarah and Mike watched the trio ride out of sight.

"Godspeed," Sarah whispered, and then dissolved in tears against her husband's shoulder.

# 27 SUMMER
*1880*

Sarah Alvarez sighed as she put the newspaper down. So much bad news, she thought
wearily. Gazing at the distant mountains, she
wondered how Katy and Iron Wing and John
were doing. Daily, the papers carried stories
of the happenings in the plains of Dakota and
Montana. Always, there were vivid accounts
of battles between scattered bands of hostile
Indians and the Army, lurid tales of death
and disease and bloodshed, of Indians slain
or forced onto the reservation. Where was
Katy? Was she happy, living in the wilds of
Dakota with Iron Wing and John, or were
they living in squalor on some godforsaken
Indian reservation? There were so many
stories of dishonest Indian agents, men who
sold the beef meant for the Indians and
pocketed the money, leaving the Indians to
starve.

Mike had gone to the Army and negotiated
a beef contract just as he had promised he
would. Pedro Montoya insisted it would lead
to disaster, but the Apaches hadn't caused
any trouble. Quite the contrary. Yellow Deer
came to the ranch several times a year, bringing a deer, an elk, a robe, a basket or some
pottery.

But she was not worried about Yellow

Deer and his people. They were being looked after. She was worried about Katy. And John. He would be over three years old now, walking and talking. Did he have enough to eat? Did he remember her at all?

She did not worry about Iron Wing. He was strong and self-sufficient, able to take care of himself. She only hoped he was able to take care of Katy and John.

She had received only one letter from Katy in the past two years. It had been mailed from Fort Lincoln. In it, Katy said only that they were all well and hoped to find Iron Wing's people soon. The rest of the letter had been about John. He was learning to speak both English and Cheyenne, and had his own pony.

Sarah had read and reread the letter until it virtually fell apart in her hands.

Nightly, she prayed for their good health, for some miracle that would bring them all safely home.

Katy smiled fondly at her husband and son, riding double on a big-bay gelding. Iron Wing looked every inch the warrior, even though his buckskin shirt was ragged, his clout smeared with mud, his leggings torn. John, dressed much the same as his father, was a handsome little boy with tawny skin, large brown eyes and straight black hair. Daily, he seemed to grow more like his father in both looks and mannerisms.

Katy glanced down at her own clothes in dismay. Her deerskin dress was torn and stained, her moccasins worn through. She hated to go home looking the way she did, hated for her mother to think Iron Wing hadn't been able to provide for them. More than once he had risked his life so that they might have food and shelter. No man could have done more.

Iron Wing reached out to touch her arm. "Are you tired?" he asked.

"A little."

"Do you want to stop for awhile?"

"No, we're so close. Let's go on."

Iron Wing nodded, his hand lifting to tousle the curly black hair of the baby cradled in Katy's arms. The child stretched and yawned, then drifted back to sleep. She was a pretty little thing, only a few weeks old.

"It won't be much longer," he said.

"I know," Katy replied. "We're fine."

"How about you, son?" Iron Wing asked over his shoulder.

"Fine," John said, though he wanted very much to curl up in his father's arms and go to sleep. They had been traveling since before dawn, and now it was almost dark. But warriors did not complain. What could not be changed must be endured.

Riding on, Iron Wing let his thoughts drift back in time. They had reached the Dakotas late in the summer of ' 78. For months, they had searched for his people, but to no avail. It was as if they had vanished from the face of the earth without a trace. And then, one day in late fall, they had come across a handful of Cheyenne heading for the reservation at Pine Ridge. Yes, an old warrior said, they knew of the tribe of Little Eagles Flying. They had been wiped out the winter before. Refusing to surrender to the soldiers, they had fought to the last man. There were no survivors.

Upon hearing the news, Iron Wing had ridden high into the Black Hills to mourn, leaving Katy and John below. He had slashed his flesh, cut his hair, rent his clothes. And wept for the loss of his people—for Tall Buffalo and Yellow Flower, for Bull Calf and Sun Dreamer, for Quiet Water. For all those who had died at Sand Creek and in the valley of the Washita . . .

When his period of mourning had passed, they had sought shelter with a small band of Sioux hiding out in the Big Horn Mountains, but the Army had routed them and herded them onto a reservation. It was the worst hell Iron Wing had ever known. Alone, he could have endured it. Alone, he would have joined with the renegade warriors hiding out in the badlands. But he could not drag Katy and John into the hills to live like hunted beasts.

Through it all, Katy had never once complained, never begged to go home, never lamented the life she had left behind to be with him. She had stoically endured cold and hunger and heartache. She had nursed the sick, mourned the dying, comforted those who grieved, kept his own spirits from sinking into a mire of depression. Sometimes they had gone for days without food, giving what little they had to John, but Katy had never given up hope. Tomorrow would be better, she said optimistically. But it never was. And when he could no longer bear to see his wife and son in rags, slowly starving to death while they waited for rations that never came, he packed their few belongings and they left the reservation in the dead of night.

Things had been a little better after that. He killed a Crow warrior with his bare hands and took the man's horse, weapons, and clothing. Mounted now, and armed, he felt his flagging spirits rise. A deer provided meat, the hide made a dress for Katy, a coat and pants for John. A bear, found hibernating in a cave, provided them with a warm robe and a change of diet. The cave made a cozy place to wait out the last winter storm.

They were still holed up in the cave when Katy went into labor. He would never forget the trust shining in her eyes as she depended on him to deliver their child. It had been an awe-inspiring experience, watching the tiny, red-faced girl child enter the world. Luckily, Katy's labor had been easier this time, and the child had been born with a minimum of pain and no complications. Katy had named the child Hope.

And now they were topping the last rise. Below lay the Alvarez hacienda, looking much the same as it had when they left over two years ago.

Katy shaded her eyes against the setting sun as they crested the ridge. With a cry of jubilation, she urged her horse down the hill, shouting, "Mama! Mama!" as her horse raced into the yard.

Sarah looked up, her hand going to her heart, as she saw Katy Marie come flying down the road, her long black hair streaming behind her like a banner, her smile as wide as the Missouri River at flood tide.

Jumping to her feet, Sarah shrieked Katy's name as she ran down the veranda stairs. Reining her horse to a dirt-scattering halt, Katy jumped to the ground and the two women hugged each other tight, laughing and crying at the same time.

Standing back a little, Sarah blinked in surprise as she saw the baby bundled in Katy's arms. "Who's this?" she asked, peering at the baby, who was crying lustily.

"This is Hope. Oh, Mama, I missed you so!"

"And I missed you!" Sarah cried, and they embraced again, the baby sandwiched between them.

"What the hell's going on?" Michael Sommers demanded, bursting out onto the veranda. "Katy!" he exclaimed, and ran down the stairs, throwing his arms around Sarah and Katy and the baby, who was still wailing at the top of her lungs.

Iron Wing smiled faintly as he rode up to the happy group. Dismounting, he lifted John from the saddle.

"There you are!" Sarah cried, and swept the startled boy into her arms.

"It's all right, son," Iron Wing assured the boy. "This is your grandmother. She is just glad to see you again."

"Gramma," John said, smiling up at her. John's mother had told him all about his grandparents, about how grandpa had been in the Army, about how grandma ran a big ranch all by herself until she married grandpa. He knew they had a big house, and that he had been born there. Grandma was pretty, John thought as he put his arms around her neck, just like mama. And she smelled good, too, like flowers in the spring.

Fresh tears of joy coursed down Sarah's cheeks as John's arms went around her neck. How he had grown, and how she had missed him!     .

Iron Wing and Michael Sommers shook hands solemnly. Then, muttering, "I'm afraid a handshake just won't do it," Mike threw his arms around Iron Wing and gave him a bear hug. Iron Wing looked a little embarrassed by the unexpected show of affection, but he did not pull away.

"How long can you stay?" Sarah asked. "We've missed you all so much."

"As long as you want us," Katy said, trying to soothe Hope, who was still crying loudly.

Sarah looked at Mike, and then the two of them looked at Iron Wing. He looked tired, Sarah thought sympathetically, and there was a deep sadness lurking in the back of his eyes. And yet, for all that, she could sense the strength and power within him and she knew she had been foolish to worry about Katy so long as she had Iron Wing to protect her.

"The life I knew is gone," Iron Wing explained in a voice edged with pain. "My people are gone. You are all the family that Katy has." He paused, his dark eyes moving slowly from Mike's face to Sarah's. "All the family I have. I would like my children to grow up here, in the midst of those who will love them for what they are, if it is all right with the two of you."

Mike Sommers swallowed hard, touched by Iron Wing's words. He was not a man given to tears, but he felt his eyes burn and he blinked rapidly, not wanting to appear unmanly before Iron Wing.

Sarah did not try to hold back her tears as she murmured, "Oh, Iron Wing, son, welcome home."

"I am glad to be here," Iron Wing said sincerely. "We are all glad to be here."

For a moment, the four adults stood together, aglow with the joy of being together again. Then Iron Wing looked at Katy. It had been a long time since they had been alone, just the two of them, a long time since they had made love. Now they had all the time in the world, and he did not want to waste a single minute.

Katy blushed to the roots of her hair as she recognized the gleam in her husband's eye, and her heart began to thud rapidly in her breast.

Sarah and Mike did not miss the look that passed between Katy and Iron Wing, and they exchanged knowing grins. Without saying a word, Mike took John from Sarah, and Sarah took the baby from Katy.

"Run along, you two," Sarah said. "We'll look after the children."

"Yeah," Mike chimed in, punching Iron Wing on the arm. "That's what grandparents are for, you know."

Iron Wing was grinning broadly as he scooped Katy into his arms and carried her up the stairs into the house. Behind him, he could hear Mike talking to John, promising to take the boy hunting and fishing, promising him he could have his pick of the horses on the ranch. He could hear Sarah crooning softly to the baby, telling the little girl how pretty she was.

"Are you sure you can be happy here?" Katy asked as Iron Wing carried her down the hall to their bedroom.

"Yes. I was wrong to take you away from here," Iron Wing said, opening the door to their room. "Wrong to try and go back to my old way of life. You are my people, Ka-ty. My life. Wherever you are, that is home."

They were the sweetest words she had ever heard, Katy thought happily. And then there was no more time for thinking because Iron Wing was kissing her, his mouth searing hers in a way that made her toes curl with pleasure, blotting everything from her mind but the love they shared and the joy that would be theirs in the years to come.

# MIDNIGHT FIRE

## MADELINE BAKER

**"Lovers of Indian Romance have a special place on their bookshelves for Madeline Baker!"**
*—Romantic Times*

A half-breed who has no use for a frightened girl fleeing an unwanted wedding, Morgan thinks he wants only the money Carolyn Chandler offers him to guide her across the plains, but halfway between Galveston and Ogallala, where the burning prairie meets the endless night sky, he makes her his woman. There in the vast wilderness, Morgan swears to change his life path, to fulfill the challenge of his vision quest—anything to keep Carolyn's love.

_4056-5                                   $5.99 US/$6.99 CAN